Secret
Pleasure

## ALSO BY LORA LEIGH

LORA LEIGH

Secret
Pleasure

CLOSE COVER BEFORE STRIKING

ST. MARTIN'S GRIFFIN

NEW YORK

SECRET PLEASURE. Copyright © 2015 by Lora Leigh. All rights reserved. Printed in the United States of America. For information, address St. Martin's Press, 175 Fifth Avenue, New York, N.Y. 10010.

www.stmartins.com

The Library of Congress Cataloging-in-Publication Data is available upon request.

ISBN 978-0-312-57625-7 (trade paperback)
ISBN 978-1-250-03267-6 (e-book)

St. Martin's Griffin books may be purchased for educational, business, or promotional use. For information on bulk purchases, please contact the Macmillan Corporate and Premium Sales Department at 1-800-221-7945, extension 5442, or write to specialmarkets@macmillan.com.

First Edition: August 2015

10 9 8 7 6 5 4 3 2 1

The truest pleasure
Love

There's the secret in all of us.
The pleasure we dream of, the one we
fantasize about, the one we strive for.

In the truest form, in its most simplistic
form, we strive not for pleasure, though,
but for love.

With love, all things are possible and
filled with depth, with a meaning only
our souls understand.

With love, we're bonded, linked,
we're a part of something far more
cosmic and everlasting than we can
find the words to express.

With love we're complete.

With the truest love, no words or
vows are needed.

With the deepest of those bonds hearts
merge, become one, and touch, no
matter the distance that parts them.

Part
One

The Colliers' Winter Ball was considered one of the most exciting events of the winter season. It was always held a few weeks before Christmas, and the Colliers' gifts to their guests were always the guests themselves. No one ever knew the guest list or the number attending. What one could count on, though, was a broad selection of not just the political and social elite but also those of the entertainment industry.

Landra Collier was known for her wide selection of interests and friends, and it was rumored there were very few immune to her charm. Or to her invitations.

Margot Hampstead, wife to the newly elected Senator Davis Allen Hampstead, was one of the few, her daughter, Alyssa, thought. Margot's unexpected acceptance at the last minute had surprised not just her husband but her daughter as well. Alyssa hadn't begged her mother to accept the invitation. She'd been certain it wasn't accepted when she'd seen it in her mother's wastebasket. The regret she'd felt had been impossible to hide. And Margot hadn't been happy with her. Weeks later, when she'd told Alyssa to begin preparations to attend the event, Alyssa had been so excited she'd actually hugged her mother before racing upstairs to her room to do just that.

Slipping through a set of French doors leading from the huge oval ballroom to the gardens, Alyssa felt the night's excitement building. Rumored to hold exquisite works of holiday art tucked within grottos and sheltered arbors, the gardens were one of the main reasons she'd wanted so desperately to attend.

Alyssa had waited all year to attend this one event. She was eighteen, no longer excluded from the Colliers' parties, and she had already picked out the ball gown she was determined to wear, just in case her mother decided to attend.

The long cashmere gown was such a pale, pale blue that in certain lights it could be mistaken for white. Alyssa hoped few would catch a glimpse of her within the heavy snow that had begun falling over the softly lit mystery of the enchanting wonderland Landra was said to have created this year.

The heated brick walk instantly melted the fluff while all around it several inches of the snow glistened on the ground and clung to the bare branches and evergreens that spread out from the path.

Stepping cautiously along the damp walk, Alyssa made her way as quickly as possible into the shadowed garden, determined to find as many of the sheltered treasures as possible. She'd waited years to see the gardens. And they were just as beautiful, just as mysterious and enchanting, as she'd heard they were.

An ice castle nearly eight feet tall was the first treasure to be found. The soft white lights tucked in the sculptured firs to each side of it reflected off the ice and the shadowed forms of a Christmas tree and presents lightly colored at one window.

An ice door was partially open, and before it stood four ice carolers in front of the ice couple standing at the door, their faces lifted in joy.

It was so beautiful. The workmanship that had gone into it was so precise and detailed, the artistry in no doubt. It was said Landra's nephews and her son did many of the carvings each year, though the nephews' names were never revealed. And Landra had a lot of nephews, Alyssa had heard.

Continuing along the brick path, she found an ice angel next to a bed of straw, and on it lay a beautiful carved babe. Farther along the path blocks of ice carved to resembled gaily wrapped presents sat beneath a fir tree along with an ice-carved teddy bear. There were marble figures of children preparing to open presents, a large metal unicorn with a big red bow tied at the base of his horn.

A large wooden Santa painted in all his red and white finery knelt before a gas fire beneath a sheltered arbor where he lifted presents from his sack. A reindeer waited at his side.

Moving deeper into the grotto, Alyssa took a much narrower path that led away from the main walk. The path itself wasn't as well lit, but a flicker of light along a dark curve filled with thick evergreens drew her attention. The hidden, the mysterious, the rumors and scandalous whispers of some of the more erotic artwork pulled Alyssa into the darker areas.

She found out why. Wide-eyed and curious despite her astonishment, Alyssa found a sculpture that held her spellbound, certain her imagination was playing tricks on her as she saw two male forms embracing a female, her long hair flowing around them.

It was an incredibly sensual piece of ice art, or a rather strange form due to a bit of melting. Alyssa couldn't be completely certain. But it made her heart beat faster at the perceived vision before she drew away and continued deeper into the gardens.

All around her heavy flakes of snow fell gathering higher alongside the path. It held to branches and fir trees, piled atop glittering lights, and gave them a fractured, otherworldly look. The fantasyland atmosphere began to soften and ease a tension she hadn't known she'd possessed until she felt it dissipate.

She wanted to become a part of the magic and erotic sensuality unfolding around her forever. She wanted to find a way to hold it just as it was, never allow it to melt. Never allow it to be taken from sight.

Lifting her face to the falling fluff, eyes closing, she inhaled the cold air, feeling it settle along her bare shoulders where the cashmere dress draped away from the curves.

She belonged here, she thought dreamily. Amid the rich treasure trove of lovingly carved ice and fantasy dreams. Here, where sensual art could be found tucked in the most unlikely of places, deep within the snow-filled night and the fantasies she dared not reveal were being brought to life inside her.

It was that damned carving of the two males with their female lover, she thought with a dreamy smile. How secure would that feel? How completely surrounded with sensuality and eroticism it would have to be. And she would never know, she told herself in amusement as she found another of the sensual poses. One of a reclining female, resting on her elbows, head tipped back, her back arched to lift her breasts closer to the male at one side of her, while the one kissing her cupped one breast as though offering it to his partner.

Wow. Alyssa was going to begin sweating soon. She was amazed the ice wasn't melting from the sensuality of the carving itself.

Landra's nephews had placed the explicit art pieces in an area certain not to be walked through as often. She might have thought there was nothing farther along the way if the snow hadn't picked up a shimmer of light farther ahead.

As she moved quietly along the path a faint shiver caught her, the chill of the snow reaching past her fascination. Interspersed among the carvings here and there were the arbors with their gas fireplaces and enclosed padded seats. That was what she needed to find; otherwise she'd have to return to the ballroom or risk turning into a block of ice herself.

Rounding a bend in the brick walkway, she sighted one of the enclosed shelters and hurried toward it. The sound of whispers took a moment to register, though. Not until she was at the entrance of the arbor did she come to a stop, certain she wasn't seeing what she was seeing.

Just as she tried to step back, the female pressed between the two tall males gave an outraged gasp.

"How dare you!" she exclaimed.

"Because you asked?" Dark, amused laughter spilled into the night along with the faint foreign accent.

"You obviously misunderstood." The false outrage was familiar, Alyssa thought, peeking around the evergreen branches that grew slightly over the walk.

Ah yes. Millicent Raye. She should have recognized the other woman's voice instantly. Recently divorced and looking for her next wealthy meal ticket, the socialite was known for her promiscuity as well as her displays of innocence.

The divorcée rushed from the shelter without attempting to see who had glimpsed her in the rather scandalous position. Alyssa had no doubt the other woman hadn't seen enough of her to know who she was. Millicent was too concerned with the innocent act and escaping the fact that she had been caught.

"You can come out now." The Texas accent was a lazy, amused drawl.

"I wasn't hiding." Alyssa stepped from the cover of the branches. "I was merely giving you a chance to escape as well before I borrow the warmth of that fire." She nodded to the gas flames flickering over fake logs behind them.

"Escape? From an elf?" the darker of the two, the Texan, questioned her curiously, the sound of his voice like a whisper of velvet. "Where are the rest of your kind, little thing?"

"Ha-ha. Aren't I so very amused," she stated, stepping slowly toward them and into the arbor. Some days it just sucked being short. Even in heels, she still didn't gain the height she was trying for. Her delicate build and short stature did very little to convince anyone that she wasn't a pushover.

She'd put up with these two for a moment, though, she decided, amused by them. They were interesting. She liked interesting people. Her mother called it her reckless streak, the habit her daughter had of finding the very people a parent didn't want their child involved with, such as the southern belle with an affinity for knives.

With a rather teasing grin she pushed between them, then stepped to the fire before facing them again.

They were rather handsome as well, she thought. Both about six two or so. The Texan with his pitch-black hair and deep blue eyes, his features chiseled with a rough-hewn appearance and infused with arrogance. The other, with the Spanish accent, had surprisingly dark blond hair that lay long against the back of his tuxedo collar, black eyes, with tempered aristocratic features. There was nothing soft about either man. They were tall, muscular, and far too masculine.

"That isn't an elf, Cousin." The faintly foreign accent stroked over her senses like a verbal caress. It was damned freaky how much her entire body seemed to like their voices. "She's not quite tall enough, I don't believe. Perhaps a wingless fairy of some sort?"

Alyssa gave them a forgiving smile. "You should try for more originality, gentlemen. The elf and fairy jokes were boring by age ten. Would you like to try again?"

++++

She was completely enchanting.

Shane Connor was mesmerized and he fully admitted it. For the first time since he'd realized how exceptional females were, there was one he simply couldn't imagine taking his eyes from or allowing out of his life.

The night had begun as a simple drop from the lovely divorcée, a particularly adept agent with a talent for acquiring information others couldn't. The flash drive with all the information a particular Middle Eastern diplomat carried on his laptop now rested safely in Shane's pocket where Milly had deposited it as she was pressed between them.

"On second thought," he drawled to his cousin, wondering if he sounded as shell-shocked as he felt. "Perhaps not an elf or wingless fairy, 'Bastian. I believe we may have within our sights the sweetest of all fairy creatures. A rare, mesmerizing siren. One that comes out to play in the snow rather than the seas."

Damn, he was getting as good at the poetic descriptions as his cousin.

"Can we keep her?" Sebastian's voice was low and filled with a dark, pulsing hunger Shane could feel invading his own body. "Hurry, grab her. We'll hide her in our pocket and slip out with her."

"Goofy." She laughed, believing Sebastian's demand to be a joke.

Damn, there was nothing more Shane wanted to do than run away with her right now. The urge was so damned strange he made himself ignore it. Kidnapping came with penalties, he'd heard. His bosses, not to mention his family, wouldn't like that.

"Sadly," she answered for him, her gaze sparkling with the laughter still lingering on her lips. "No. I fear the dark queen would have far too much to say about that one." There was a hint of regret in her tone, though. As though she were as fascinated as they were.

"We'll slay her," Sebastian promised instantly, but Shane was watching her eyes, and he had a feeling she wasn't talking about some imagined fantasy figure.

"Unfortunately, I'm still rather fond of her." The impish little thing gave them a rueful smile. "Too bad it was here you found me. Perhaps, in another lifetime where the rules of this land no longer exist." She gave a little shrug.

Where the rules of her world didn't exist, Shane thought as denial raged through him. Yet the thought of letting her go before he knew her, before he could claim her, clear to her soul, had his entire body tight with denial.

"These rules don't exist in every land," Sebastian assured her then, stepping closer until he could lean against the post supporting the arbor, less than a foot from her. "We could find a land where the rules don't apply, little siren."

She flicked him a sideways glance and a small, knowing smile. "Ah, dark knight," she said softly. "The rules I live by apply in every land, I'm afraid."

There was true regret in her soft gray eyes. Sebastian could see her curiosity as well as a hint of the sensuality that ran through her. Innocence marked her as well. Such innocence that even in the knowledge of the sexuality they'd turn loose in her, she appeared as pure and without artifice as the snow falling around them, insulating them.

She was . . . a treasure. The gown she wore lay like a caress from breast to hip before flowing down and away from her delicate frame. The color was indescribable. It wasn't white, nor was it blue or gray. It shifted between the palest of those colors, though, as she moved and the light of the flames flickered behind her.

He wanted to touch her. Taste her.

His hands actually tingled at the thought of touching the silken flesh rising above the gown. And what lay beneath . . . He wanted nothing more than to taste, stroke, possess. She was a siren indeed, and her mysterious song was entrancing him . . .

And she was young, he realized. Eighteen perhaps, no younger. But definitely no more than twenty, and he'd wager his trust fund she had no more than one, perhaps two lovers.

"Rules were made to be broken," Shane assured her. "And here in this fantasy, they can be hidden." He stepped closer as well, moving to stand within inches of her, their warmth now surrounding her.

"As the lovely Ms. Raye was hidden?" she asked, but her breathing was faster, her voice filled with curiosity. And wariness.

"We were unaware Millicent wanted to be hidden," Sebastian assured her. They enclosed her, their larger bodies blocking the doorway. "I dare you. Just a kiss. See if you can choose which of us you'd prefer."

Alyssa felt a heavy lassitude settling over her senses as she looked up at the goof. He wasn't so goofy now, though. He was dark, sensual, and she was dying to have them both kiss her.

It was positively indecent. Her mother would ship her off to a convent to make certain she never did anything so scandalous again. But she would know . . .

And a part of her knew, these men would probably find her.

"One kiss?" It was hard to breathe.

"Two," the dark cowboy whispered from behind her. "One for him, one for me."

"Just a kiss?" She had to be certain. "On the lips only."

The wicked chuckle behind her was filled with sensual knowledge. "An intelligent siren. She'll steal our hearts if we're not careful."

Black eyes stared into hers; mystery, secrets, wicked, carnal delights gleamed in the dark expanse. "Perhaps she's already stolen mine," he murmured, his lips lowering to hers.

She was a virgin, not a robot. Alyssa knew what sex was. Many of the young women she socialized with had been having sex for years. Many, with men far older than they. What they'd described as the perfect kiss had no resemblance to this.

This was dangerous. It should be outlawed.

Her arms wrapped around his neck as he eased her to him, lifting her from her feet and holding her secure as his lips slanted over hers and his tongue forged past them taste hers.

Hot forays past her lips, little licks, tempting, teasing thrusts into her mouth as he dissolved her common sense with no more than the kiss he was taking.

Behind her, her Cowboy brushed his cheek lightly against her bare shoulder, nipped, flicked his tongue teasingly against her flesh. Those kisses roved from her neck to her shoulders, along her back, just beneath her nape, to the other side.

Pleasure was whipping through her senses, heat suffusing her flesh as a heightened sensitivity began building through her body. Every cell she possessed seemed to be demanding this touch.

This kiss. Everywhere.

Dazed, unbidden moans falling from her lips, she tried to follow as he eased back.

Lifting her heavy lashes, Alyssa stared up at him, shocked, her virginal senses pierced to the core.

"My turn."

Alyssa shuddered, suddenly not certain of the bargain she'd made. But her Cowboy didn't give her a chance to object. His lips were more demanding but no less gentle. Holding her to him as her Spanish jokester slid one hand from her thigh to her rear, cupped the flesh of her buttock and breathed a kiss against her spine; her Cowboy kissed her with dark, heady hunger.

The pleasure built, whipped through her, around her, spiraling through her senses and leaving her weak, unresisting to whatever they demanded. To whatever they desired.

As that knowledge whispered through her, the kiss was broken and she found herself back on her feet, swaying as powerful hands steadied her and two strangers stared down at her with a carnal hunger she'd never imagined possible.

"Siren, you should go." His accent thicker than before, the one behind her pressed his forehead to her shoulder. "Before we do something all of us might regret jumping into too quickly."

Her common sense snapped back into place.

Wrong place, wrong time, wrong . . . something.

God, she hoped they didn't expect her to choose one of them from those kisses alone, because it wasn't happening.

Easing from him, her knees weak, lips tingling, she stared back at them, and she wished things were different.

"Perhaps, one day," she murmured. "But not tonight. As much as I wish lives and rules were different. Besides, knowing the divorcée's reputation, she'll no doubt be awaiting you once you retire tonight."

She didn't like the thought of that. Sebastian watched her lashes fall over her incredibly soft gaze to hide the flash of jealousy, but it was there.

"Or perhaps we'll be awaiting you in your room," he suggested.

"Not tonight." She shook her head and stepped from them.

Reaching the entrance to the arbor, she looked back, gave them a long, regretful glance before turning and drifting away as though she were no more than the fantasy they had accused her of being.

She disappeared amid the fall of snow and twinkling lights, the color of her gown hiding her amid the white blanket covering the gardens.

"I believe my heart may be broken," Shane murmured. "The rejection is devastating."

"Rejection? I don't accept rejection, Shane. Not from her." Moving from the arbor, Sebastian stepped into the snow, moving to follow her.

Shane shook his head. Sebastian was rarely a volatile person, but that young woman had somehow managed to reach inside them into a hunger they hadn't known they were capable of, he guessed.

"She's young, 'Bastian," he commented, sliding his hands into the pockets of his tuxedo slacks as he caught up with his cousin. "Perhaps too young."

"I'll find out." Sebastian shrugged. "I'm betting not. Hell, Shane, have you ever wanted to taste a woman's flesh as badly as you wanted to taste hers?" The edge of frustration in his voice was as telling as the brisk pace he was setting to catch up with her.

"You'll frighten her, 'Bastian," he cautioned. "She's too young, too innocent."

"And far too curious," Sebastian muttered. "You saw it as well as I. Young and innocent, yes. Frightened? Hell no, she wasn't. There wasn't an ounce of fear in her."

As they passed the entrance to the gardens they watched her slip into the ballroom, turning to cast a final glance toward them. There was no fear of the meeting in the garden being revealed, no fear of drawing the ire of the dark queen. But as the light reflected fully on Alyssa's face Shane reached out and drew his cousin to a halt.

"I know who she is," he drawled quietly, satisfaction filling him as he stared at the brightly lit ballroom and the guests milling about.

"Who?" Sebastian's tension was a tangible thing.

Hell, she had both of them off balance, almost uncertain of themselves. A rather odd feeling, Shane admitted.

"The dark queen is her mother. There's only one person in that damned ballroom that such a title applies to—"

"Fuck. She's Margot Hampstead's daughter." Sebastian's tone was a hard grumble. "Alyssa."

"And shall I tell you what Landra was discussing with Cousin Jeb earlier?" Shane grinned.

Landra often discussed property decisions with her son, since her husband's death the year before.

"Come on, Shane, get to it," Sebastian demanded impatiently.

"Our little siren is indeed eighteen as of this past fall. In May she'll be heading to Barcelona for three months, and Landra offered the Hampsteads use of her seaside apartment for their daughter," he informed his cousin.

"Barcelona." Irritation filled Sebastian's voice now. "And you think I'll be able to wait until May?"

"She'll be there for three months. Come on, 'Bastian, it's going to take us that long to finish the job we've taken. If we wait, we'll have the summer with her. Let's get this finished and then we'll meet her there," Shane assured him.

Like Sebastian, Shane found the thought of waiting was hell, though.

"We'll be waiting for her," Sebastian growled. "And if we don't leave quickly, Shane, all bets are off. It's all I can do to stay the hell away from her now."

Shane well understood how he felt.

"We're losing it." He chuckled as he clapped Sebastian on the back. "Come on, let's go break into Landra's private bar and get a nice, strong drink. We're overworked, Cousin. Otherwise, a woman wouldn't have our dicks in a twist like this."

Shrugging his shoulders, Sebastian turned and followed his cousin along a narrower part of the walk that led around the ballroom to a private entrance into the rear of the main house.

Staying away from the ballroom was imperative. Staying the hell away from one innocent little siren was without question. Whether exhaustion, stress, too many drinks, or too much excess, she'd suddenly began to embody every fantasy they'd ever had individually, or combined, of a woman. And that was very dangerous.

Right now, it was too damned dangerous.

He didn't want to leave her. For some reason, one Sebastian couldn't make sense of, he didn't want to leave the United States without her. He wanted to slip her away, kidnap her pretty ass, and take her with them now.

Hell, what had she done to him?

"I think a little distance at the moment would be a good thing," Shane suggested. "Perhaps we should meet the divorcée in her room and expend a bit of the lust driving us both crazy." He blew out a hard breath then. "Fuck that. I can wait."

There was a complete lack of desire for any other woman

now. There was only Alyssa. Far too delicate, too innocent, and hiding a vein of sensuality that would burn them alive once it was ignited, Sebastian sensed.

"I say we head to Spain in the morning then." If he waited, Sebastian knew there would be no staying away from her.

Even now, he wanted nothing more than to stride into the ballroom and sweep her into his arms. He wouldn't stop to dance, though. He'd carry her from the mansion and rush her straight to the limo, where he'd order the driver to take them to the airport and the private plane awaiting them.

"I feel mesmerized, Shane," he admitted with a rueful smile and a hard shake of his head. "Perhaps 'siren' isn't far from the truth."

"You're not by yourself, Cousin," Shane admitted, his tone far too serious. "You are not by yourself."

Five months? Waiting was going to be hell.

2

FIVE MONTHS LATER
BARCELONA. SPAIN

The sea and the sun, a breeze as soft and sensual as a lover's caress as the waves slid like silk over her skin. The warmth of the sun, the splash of the water, and the touch of a cooling breeze were more than just invigorating; it was like a magical touch of fantasy.

It was so different from home or the Riviera her mother preferred, or the Bahamas. The difference was one Alyssa couldn't put her finger on, couldn't describe, but how she wished she could.

Wading through the surf, she waved to a couple who called out to her. They lived in the apartment building Alyssa was staying in. The night before, when she'd arrived, the young man had helped her carry her luggage up. A bit later his girlfriend, Marissa, had walked with her to show her the market and shopping district.

Alyssa had expected Giana "Gia" Bennett, the daughter of one of her mother's friends, to have already arrived. Landra had kept the summer rental across from Alyssa for the other girl. She and Gia had known each other for ages. They weren't close, but Alyssa liked her.

"Alyssa, be certain to come down to the water tonight," Roberto Santiago, her downstairs neighbor's brother, called out. "The wine is free, the music is hot, and we will dance."

Oh, she didn't think so. She'd met Roberto the night before and she hadn't been impressed by him in the least. She intended to be there for the music, though.

Throwing him a smile, she gave a quick shake of her head before laughing at his pout. Turning her gaze back to the beach, she came to a stop before ever fully stepping from the surf. A wave caught her just behind her knees, nearly throwing her off balance.

Not that she wasn't already off balance.

At the waves' farthermost edge they stood, like twin gods, one dark haired, one lighter. Shirtless, shoeless, dressed only in loose white pants, the cuffs rolled above their ankles, arms crossed over their chests.

Tall, leanly muscled, natural muscle. The kind that made a woman want to watch the sweat roll off their flesh as they did whatever manual labor had built their exceptional physiques. Then run hell-for-leather because they were guaranteed heartbreakers.

There was no escaping that risk if a woman made the mistake of spending even a small amount of time being charmed by their arrogant sensuality.

Her Goof and her Cowboy, she'd named them. Her fantasy. The men she'd dreamed about and ached for every night for the past five months.

And they'd found her.

She'd somehow known they would. Some part of her far-too-romantic heart had watched for them since the moment she'd met them that first night.

As the next wave hit harder behind her knees she drew in a deep breath, her heart racing, excitement rising inside her no matter her attempts to force it back. Moving to them, she gave them a knowing look, aware they were taking in every inch of pale flesh she was revealing in the incredibly brief two-piece bathing suit she wore.

When she drew abreast of them the lighter-haired sex god lowered his glasses just enough to peer at her over the top of the frame. "Hello, little siren. We've missed you."

Oh, she just bet they had.

"What, Milly suddenly developed a few morals?" she asked pityingly. "How sad for you." She almost laughed at the darker one's mock glare. "So, what brings you to Barcelona?"

The sensual smile and sexual heat in Blondie's black eyes sent a heat wave crashing over her. "We heard a siren was spotted in this very location," he informed her, his expression failing at serious as his eyes twinkled with a gleam of laughter. "We couldn't resist coming out to see this phenomenon ourselves."

"Goof," she accused him with a little spurt of laughter, "someone played a horrid trick on you. You should discuss it with them, because I haven't seen a single siren in the area all day."

Pushing her damp hair back from her face as the breeze pushed it playfully over her shoulder, she moved quickly around them and headed to the beach chair she'd secured into the sand earlier.

"If she doesn't stop running from us we may have to spank her," the faint Spanish accent sounded behind her.

Tossing her head, Alyssa turned, walking backward as she flashed them a teasing grin. "I never allow men whose names I don't know to spank me. It's completely against my personal code of ethics, you understand."

Turning quickly, she closed the distance to the chair, snagged the thin, long shirt she'd worn over the bikini earlier, and shrugged it on.

She felt naked in front of them, her pale skin too sensitive beneath the looks she knew she was getting despite the dark glasses they wore.

"Allow us to rectify that." Smooth, mesmerizing, his dark voice was like heady wine. "I am Sebastian De Loren." Laying his hand against the middle of his chest, he gave her a slight bow. "And this ugly little man is my cousin Shane Connor."

Ugly little man?

Shane scowled at him for a moment before shaking his head and turning the power of that little hint of a grin on her. "We only let him out of the facility every other week. Next week, I'll have you to myself."

Alyssa forced back what she knew would be a far too girlish giggle.

"Alyssa." She inclined her head regally. "And I ask again, why are you here?"

She had a feeling she knew and the thought of them coming there for—

"Why, for you, siren." That South Texas accent was just as potent as the Spanish one was. "Didn't you believe Sebastian a moment ago? The moment we heard you'd be in Barcelona we rushed to make certain our schedules were clear for the summer to allow us to devote our time to you."

Her heart was racing so fast it restricted her breathing for a moment. Men like this should simply be outlawed rather than running around loose and playing havoc with a woman's self-control.

She tilted her head to the side. "And you found out I'd be here, how?"

"We have our ways, sweets." Sebastian smiled down at her. "Did you think we wouldn't do all we could to join you in this land where others' rules need not apply?"

Where they could be with her, together. She finished the sentence for him as her breath caught in her lungs and her knees weakened in response to the rougher sound of his voice.

"I see," she said softly, regretfully. "And how I wish I had the experience to play the games the two of you are so obviously very good at. Since I don't, though, perhaps you should find another toy to play with."

And she had no doubt that was all they would see her as. Another toy. She might not have sought to find out who they were, wanting to keep the fantasy as it was, but she wasn't so innocent that she believed such experienced men would want more than a summer fling.

Gathering her towel and collapsing the chair, she pulled it from the sand and turned to head for the apartment. Before she realized what he was about, Shane had snagged the chair from her hand and Sebastian stared down at her woefully.

"Now, siren," he chided her gently, "we came all this way simply to observe the phenomenon that is you. The least you could do is give us a kind word or two before sending us on our way."

"I thought that was what I just did," she pointed out, hiding her smile.

The chill she'd felt at the thought of walking away eased beneath the warmth in his gaze.

"Come on, darlin'." Shane began walking slowly toward the apartment building just above the beach. "We brought wine, and Sebastian's mother sent homemade tamales. They're not to be missed."

She gave Sebastian a narrow-eyed look. "Just came to see me, huh?"

He shrugged. "We are here, are we not? Why else would we come to such a crowded little beach when our family's property holds several that are quite private?" He glanced around before giving her a considering look. "You could sunbathe nude on them if you wish."

"Incorrigible," she accused him before turning and rushing to catch up with Shane.

If she wasn't very damned careful these two were going to steal her heart before the night was out. She was turning out to be way too easy. And they were just the sort her mother had warned her about. The ones Margot had promised to have her institutionalized over if she dared bring one home.

She had a feeling Margot hadn't been joking, either.

She had a feeling denying them was going to be far harder than her mother assured her it would be.

One winter night, for just a few minutes, the powerful effect they had on her had followed her into her dreams and her fantasies.

She had dreamed of them, wondered about them; now here they were. But just because she was fascinated with them and the forbidden pleasures they represented didn't mean she had to be a pushover. Nor did it mean she was willing to become involved with what was guaranteed to result in a broken heart. She had a hard enough time dealing with Margot. She didn't need more aggravation in her life. Not at a time when her struggle against her mother's plans for her would take on a whole new meaning once she returned home after the summer. Alyssa had no intention of remaining in D.C. and playing the good little political daughter. She had her own life, her own dreams. And they didn't include marrying for her father's dream of the Oval Office, rather than her own dream of love, a home filled with children's laughter and the quiet contentment she hadn't known in so long.

"I imagine the two of you wouldn't consider going away for just a few years," she sighed. "We could pick this up somewhere after my twenty-fourth birthday."

She imagined that would give her a few years away from Margot and time to figure out who she was and what she wanted. So far, she simply wasn't certain.

"She's cute, isn't she?" Sebastian asked his cousin. "A bit unrealistic at moments, but really quite cute."

"And you're far too arrogant and superior," she informed him as they crossed the remaining distance to the back of the apartment building. "And how do you know where I'm staying?"

"Sweets, it's been five months," Sebastian reminded her. "And you're playing in my backyard so to speak. I knew where you'd be staying months before you arrived."

"Oh, what a small world we live in after all," she muttered, throwing him a glare. "I didn't come to Spain for romance. Or sex," she informed him. "Peace was more my aim."

"We can be peaceful, darlin'," Shane promised her, starting up the steps that led to the second-floor balcony outside her apartment. "I promise. You'll get all kinds of peace."

She wasn't going to get any peace at all. But she couldn't deny the fact that excitement was churning through her at a rate she'd never known before meeting them. All her senses were heightened, her flesh sensitive, needs she was completely unfamiliar with before them amping inside her.

Reckless. Her mother had warned her not to give into her penchant for recklessness and she'd promised she wouldn't. She just wanted a quiet, relaxing vacation. She'd promised. And that would be so very boring.

She knew she was too innocent for them. Yet they were fun. Exciting. They offered the forbidden and made her feel alive. They terrified her. For a few brief moments in a hidden grotto the world had been so much brighter and so many things were possible, even fantasies. But when she'd forced herself to return to the ball, she'd found the world as she'd left it and she'd realized the brilliance, the excitement and mystery she'd tasted just a moment of, had become a hunger she ached for.

And she couldn't have that. Her world had no place for fairy tales or dreams. There was no place in it for love until she could find her way out of D.C.

Moving up the steps between them, she could only blink as Shane drew a key from the pocket of his pants and unlocked the French doors.

"And you got that where?" she demanded, one hand moving to prop on a hip as she stared between Shane and Sebastian with a glare, certain she appeared furious rather than simply exasperated.

"We're rather talented that way." He was laughing at her. Behind those sunglasses, she could practically feel the amusement she knew was gleaming there.

"You're rather far too arrogant and confident." She almost wished she were more like Millicent, able to accept their blatant sexuality without her emotions becoming added to the volatile mix of wicked eroticism and superior male certainty.

The problem was, she couldn't seem to make herself be seriously angry with them. Their antics were far too charming, dangerously so, and they were totally forbidden, which she feared made them all the more attractive.

As if they needed anything to make them more appealing.

"Come on, siren." Sebastian was laughing at her again. "Invite us in. We just want to get to you know you."

"Far more intimately than may be good for my peace of mind," she muttered.

"Or ours," Shane assured her as she stepped into the luxurious apartment behind them.

The Collier apartment lacked nothing. Every modern convenience had been added along with many comforts she wouldn't have thought to include herself.

Placing the beach chair to the side of the stone entryway, Shane stared around the cool, spacious residence with an indefinable expression.

"The apartment belongs to a friend of my parents. . . ."

"Landra Collier." Shane nodded. "My parents know her as well. Though she's never offered us use of her apartment."

"Your reputation has probably already reached her," she assured him as she moved into the kitchen. "She seems to be a very down-to-earth person. I rather doubt she'd approve of some of the games you'd become involved in."

She wasn't judging them. She was the one finding amusement with them, now.

Opening the fridge, she pulled free the sweet tea she'd made that morning before collecting three glasses from the cabinet.

"My hand itches," Sebastian muttered.

"I know the feeling," his cousin agreed.

Removing his sunglasses, Shane turned those deep blue eyes on her, his sense of fun clearly reflected in them.

"Be nice now," she cautioned them as she filled the glasses with ice. "I make iced tea that would bring shame to the finest southern belle. It would be a terrible thing if I decided not to share."

Sebastian's brow lifted as he brought one hand to scratch at his chest thoughtfully. "What if I don't like tea?"

"Then Shane can have your share." She shrugged. "A South Texas native? I bet his momma weaned him on sweet tea."

"No truer words were ever spoken," Shane agreed with her.

Handing out the glasses, she stood at the side of the counter separating the kitchen from the informal eating area and entryway.

"I kind of had plans tonight," she told them as they found seats at the glass and metal table across from her. "Shall we make plans for you to begin your seduction next week maybe?"

They looked at each other. Sebastian lowered his head and shook it slowly.

"Love her heart," Shane murmured. "She's got no clue."

"She's actually rather good with clues." Alyssa frowned back at them. "And I'm getting a clue that you two are about to seriously irritate me."

"Irritate you?" Shane leaned back in his seat, stretched his legs out, and crossed his arms over his chest again. "Is that why those hard little nipples of yours are teasing the hell out of me? Or that vein jumping at your neck from the force of your racing heart?"

A flush rushed from her breasts to her hairline.

"It's time for the two of you to go." Straightening from the counter, she watched them warily now.

They'd just passed exasperation, and charm could only take a man so far.

"Excuse me?" Shane seemed a bit surprised by her announcement and not completely certain why she'd made it.

"There's a difference between charm and offensive vulgarity Mr. Conner and you're crossing. I might enjoy the little word games, and the friendly flirting, but I'm no toy, nor am I some trollop you picked up off the streets. And I won't be spoken to as though I am. The two of you can leave now." Alyssa had been raised to understand her worth, not just as a person, but as a woman. She was reckless, yes, and she loved to flirt and laugh and enjoyed the experiences of getting to know a wide variety of people. But she'd be damned if she'd let some over-confident male speak to her as though the interest and growing sensual curiosity was something to be ashamed of.

"Well, thank you, Cousin." Sebastian grimaced as he leaned his elbows on the table and growled at Shane, "You just had to go and offend her, didn't you?"

Shane didn't take his eyes off her, though. And as aroused as she was, as curious as she was, she didn't break his stare. She gave it right back to him, certain if she didn't do it now, then the respect she knew she deserved would never be gained.

"She's not as offended as she is frightened," Shane informed him. "She might be right, though, she's far too innocent for us, Sebastian."

Rising from his chair, he finished his tea, tipping the empty glass in her direction before setting it on the table and heading for the door.

Sebastian grinned and winked at her. "Bye, Cousin. I'll tell you all about candy kisses when I get back tonight. Or in the morning."

Alyssa had to roll her eyes to keep from laughing at both of them. Again. Damn them. They were completely impossible.

Shane paused at the door, a thoughtful look on his face as she watched him in anticipation, wondering what these two would use to poke at each other with next time. They seemed to enjoy goading each other as much as they enjoyed goading her.

"We could spank him," Alyssa suggested to Shane with an arch of her brow willing to forgive as long as he didn't forget. "I don't think he'd protest nearly as strenuously as I would."

"The hell I wouldn't." Sebastian's black eyes sparkled with a hint of blue as he leaned back in his chair, watching her with heated anticipation. "Protesting won't help you, sweets. You're determined to get that spanking sooner rather than later."

She probably should be real scared, but she wasn't. There was something about them that assured a woman that they'd never hurt her in any way but the emotional. The broken heart heading her way would suck, though.

"Your partner's leaving, though," she pointed out, unable to keep from teasing back. "You'll have a hard time doing it alone."

His crack of laughter had her sliding a look at Shane's back.

"Wonderful view," he complimented her with all apparent innocence. "Were you expecting me to leave, sweets? Shame on you."

"Shame on the two of you," she accused them lightly before steeling herself to assert her own control. "So tell me, do you actually intend to leave so I can shower and maybe take a nap? There's a party on the beach tonight I really wanted to attend."

Parties of the beach variety were strictly forbidden. Here Alyssa intended to experience all she could before returning to the states and the battle to separate herself from her parents' political lives.

"What sort of party?" The question was asked quite casually, but there was nothing casual in Sebastian's suddenly flat gaze.

"A beach party," she said softly. "You know, music, bonfire, laughing, dancing? Fun?"

"Come, Sebastian, we'll collect the tamales Aunt Tabby made her and bring them to her, then see what we can find to entertain ourselves tonight." Shane gave all appearances of being jovial and easygoing, but it was his eyes that gave him away. Alyssa had learned at Margot's knee to always pay attention to the eyes.

Lifting her chin, she stared back at both of the men. "I'm no toy the two of you can decide should be placed on a shelf until you want to play, either. If that was what you had in mind when you followed me here, then it's best you don't come back."

Oh, but she was a fiery little thing.

Shane had to hide the grin and look away from her for a moment. She was a slick one, this little siren they had become far too fascinated with. She didn't just hear the tone of voice and take in the expression. She was very careful to pay attention to their eyes as well. Not that he didn't know how to lie with his eyes, but he and Sebastian both knew that for whatever reason, Alyssa was different. For that reason alone they'd made the decision not to lie to her.

"Playing with you wasn't our intent." Sebastian rose slowly to his feet; the casual move didn't have her backing down, but Shane saw the flicker of wariness in her gaze. "At least, not tonight. We thought we'd at least ease you into the debauchery first."

"Ha-ha." The mock laugh was indication that his humor in this case was most likely not appreciated.

"No worries, love," Shane assured her. "Perhaps your memories of us weren't as fond as ours of you. A winter siren is a rare and wonderful sight. Rather like unicorns." He winked teasingly. "We looked forward to seeing you again. Nothing more, I promise."

It was normally Sebastian soothing a female's anger at them, not Shane. Hell, he was usually the one causing the anger.

"I didn't say that." She shifted a bit nervously, the hem of the shirt riding a bit to reveal the extremely low band of the bikini and a flash of creamy, barely sun-kissed flesh.

Hell, the beachwear they'd chosen before leaving the De Loren hacienda wasn't nearly enough to hide the full erection he was going to be sporting if he kept sneaking peeks.

Lifting his gaze to her face again, he had to grin at the little glare she directed his way.

"I won't apologize for looking," he teased her. "You're far too pretty a sight to pretend otherwise."

The little roll of her eyes assured him the compliment wasn't taken seriously.

"We'll find other amusements tonight," Sebastian spoke up then, the tone of his voice causing Shane to glance at him warningly.

It was rare for Sebastian to become out of sorts over a woman if she'd made other plans. Though, to be honest, Alyssa wasn't just another woman.

Her lips thinned for a moment. After she glanced toward the ceiling as though debating something far too seriously, it took her only seconds to direct those soft gray eyes at them once more.

"You're aware I'm only eighteen, right?" The question was a bit defensive. "And not exactly experienced. I had the impression the two of you much preferred women with a bit more sexual expertise than I possess."

Sebastian was riding a line he found discomforting, especially after that little declaration. His cock was hardening despite his best efforts to keep it from doing so. The thought of touching her, seeing her wonder with each new pleasure, was like an aphrodisiac. Instantly he was hungrier for her, the sexual need rising with such strength he was wary of it himself.

Son of a bitch. She was right; she was too young for them, too inexperienced. And it was the same thing he'd been telling himself for five months. Still, she was under his skin in a way he couldn't seem to help.

"We just want to get to know you, Alyssa," he told her, shoving his hands into his pockets as he stood staring back at her. "We didn't intend to frighten you. Perhaps in this enchantment you've cast over us we've neglected to consider the fact that perhaps the fascination doesn't go both ways."

He knew better, just as Shane did. She was so aroused it was all she could do to make herself stand still. Her nipples were like little pebbles beneath that shirt and bikini top, a light, telltale flush tinted her flesh, and the slight additional fullness to her lips assured him she was more than just interested.

They were experienced enough to know the signs, while her inexperience ensured she couldn't hide them.

"I didn't say I wasn't attracted." A frown flirted with her brow as she fought the wariness of her response to them. "I'm not willing to be steamrolled out of the holiday I came here to enjoy, though. I didn't come looking for a summer romance or a broken heart. And that's exactly what will happen if I'm not very, very careful."

"Then be careful, love." Pulling his hands from his pockets, he moved to her, bent his head, and brushed a kiss against her forehead. "We'll return. And if you need us . . ."

Her cell phone lay on the counter. Picking it up, he keyed in both his and Shane's numbers.

"Or if you get lonely," he suggested as flirtatiously as such overwhelming hunger allowed, "you've only to call us."

Staring back at him, Alyssa drew her lower lip between her teeth and worried it uncertainly as he turned and joined his cousin at the French doors. As she watched them leave, it was all she could do not to call them back.

A frustrated groan spilled from her lips before she moved to the doors to lock them, only to find them locked. Damn it, she'd forgotten to make him give her the key.

Stalking to her bedroom, she stripped the shirt and bikini off before pulling on the loose white sundress she wore around the house. This situation was going to make her crazy, she decided. Having those two here was going to ruin all her plans for the summer.

Okay, the plans were boring to begin with, but she wouldn't

leave Spain with more baggage than she arrived with if she stuck to her plan. And now that plan was burned to cinders, the ashes scattered. Because if they came back, and she had a feeling they would, then she wouldn't be able to continue resisting them.

She actually expected them to show up before she left for the beach party. As she showered and dressed in the long, tan chiffon skirt and white cami-tank, she listened for them. Securing a leather bracelet around her ankle, she then pushed her feet into a pair of leather sandals and left the apartment.

As darkness settled around the beach the soft strains of Spanish love songs could be heard from the small band set up not far from the apartment building.

Alyssa stared out over the beach and the small crowd gathered around the bonfire. There were quite a few partygoers milling around, chatting, laughing. There was no sign of Shane and Sebastian, though. And Alyssa admitted her excitement at the thought of attending the party had waned.

If it hadn't been for her fears, for her certainty that there wasn't a chance in hell of handling them, then she could have been with them tonight.

"Alyssa, coming down?" Gia Bennett, the daughter of one of Davis Hampstead's backers, waved up at her. "The band's warming up and the wine's going fast."

Taller than Alyssa, though most people were, lanky in a tomboyish way, with dark brown hair and hazel eyes, Gia could have been a model. Instead, she'd told Alyssa, when she returned home she intended to apply for an apprenticeship program with the FBI.

She'd make a hell of an agent too.

Moving down the wide steps, sandals in hand, Alyssa met the other woman at the bottom of the stairs.

"Dish, girl, what were De Loren and his cousin doing waiting for you at the beach?" Gia asked with teasing inquisitiveness. "I bet every woman there was watching them as they waited for you."

"You know them?" she asked.

"I know *of* them," Gia stressed. "What do you know about them?"

"I met them at the Collier party in December," she admitted. "Why?"

"I'd keep those cute asses a secret if they were visiting me." Gia turned and headed into the sand, glancing back as Alyssa followed her. "A real close kind of secret, if you get my drift." Her warning wasn't lost on Alyssa. "One you might get away with, but both of the De Loren get coming to call? Honey, you're playing hardball there. You know they share their lovers, right?"

"I rather got that idea in December when I came upon them in the garden with one of the guests. She wasn't happy at the thought of being caught, either." Millicent had watched her closely after Alyssa returned to the party, obviously worried.

"Just watch your heart, girlfriend," Gia warned. "I'm not so worried about tales reaching D.C. What happens in Vegas stays in Vegas? Well, what happens in Barcelona didn't happen, ya know?"

Yeah, she pretty much got that idea.

"Sebastian and Shane are pretty rough around the edges. The women love them. But they never stick with one for more than a few nights. Don't go pinning dreams on them, girlfriend."

"I understand," Alyssa assured her with a confidence she didn't feel.

Thankfully, Gia dropped the subject as they neared the crowd. Collecting a glass of wine, Alyssa moved to the outskirts of the slowly growing throng, the number increasing as the night wore on and the wine loosened inhibitions. The beach party was becoming a bit wilder than she'd expected. So much so that she found herself retreating farther into the shadows as the night wore on.

No doubt she would have not been hiding in the dark had Shane and Sebastian been there. Of course, if they had been there, she'd be having more fun either way.

A little more than an hour or two into the party Alyssa began slipping away. Things were becoming just a little too wild to suit her. The flagrant sexual exhibitionism already beginning was enough to make her uncomfortable. Damn, sometimes being that good girl virgin could be a hell of a drawback.

"Hey, leaving?" The swarthy Mediterranean suddenly blocking her way as she began to step onto the sidewalk from the beach had her heart jumping in her throat.

Where the hell had he come from?

"Excuse me, my friends are waiting—"

"What friends?" He snickered, staying in the shadows but continuing to keep her from passing as she tried to get to her apartment. "Baby, there's no one here but me and you."

"You're wrong." She was normally quite good at bluffing. "And you don't want to make them angry. Trust me."

"Stuck-up bitch." Grabbing her arm, he jerked her to him, despite her instinctive attempt to jerk back. "Too good for me, are you?"

As the words left his lips she found herself suddenly free.

"Actually, she is." The icy threat in Shane's voice sent a chill down her spine. "Now, do you want us to prove to you how much better she is than the likes of you?"

"You're giving him an option?" If Shane's voice was lethal, then Sebastian's was pure, black vengeance.

Before Alyssa could fully comprehend everything that was going on Sebastian had one hand wrapped around the thick neck of the younger man and he was slowly wilting, trying to claw at Sebastian's hands, fighting for air.

"Stop. Stop this now." Rushing for Sebastian, she gripped his arm, glaring up at him "I won't have it."

The man dropped, gasping, freed from a grip guaranteed to choke the life from him.

Scrambling while spewing curses, he scuttled back, made it to his feet, and raced around the apartment building. Not that Alyssa had a chance to make certain he left. In the next breath she was thrown over Sebastian's shoulder as he walked rather calmly up the steps.

"What are you doing?" Bracing her arms against his lower back, she struggled to lift herself enough to gain some leverage to break his hold. "Let me go!"

A swift little slap to her rear had her freezing in outrage a second before he stepped into the apartment, bent, and deposited her on her feet.

"How dare you!" Shaking, glaring up at him, she adjusted the snug top she felt like stomping her feet in anger.

"How dare I?" His head lowered, eyes as black as coal and glittering with fury suddenly only inches from hers. "Let me tell you how I dare, Alyssa. I dare because that son of a cocksucker thought he could put his damned hands on you. That he could take what you most likely would refuse to allow him to touch. That is how I dare. And if he makes the attempt again, don't even bother demanding I let him go. You won't have time. I'll break his fucking neck."

Shock exploded through her. This wasn't the goof he pretended to be. He was stone cold. Hard. Vengeful.

Alyssa stepped back from him slowly.

"'Bastian, easy," Shane murmured, coming to stand next to Alyssa. "She's scared enough."

"Easy, my ass." Straightening, he shot Shane a fulminating glare. "She could influence me to many things, Shane. God knows I'm so fucking enchanted with her I let that bastard go before I realized I was obeying her," he snarled, obviously quite put out. "But some things are better understood from the beginning. I'll kill anyone stupid enough to attempt to hurt her. And God help them if they actually succeed."

Alyssa stared up at him with wide eyes.

All this fury for her? Because someone had frightened her in the dark? Okay, so maybe he'd terrified her. But all this protectiveness, even as arrogant and irritating as it was, was something so new, such an alien concept to her, that she could only stare up at Sebastian, fascinated and confused.

"Why?" she asked.

Sebastian stilled, a brooding frown crossing his face as he pushed his fingers restlessly through his hair.

"Why what?" He finally shook his head as though he didn't understand the question.

"Why would you kill someone for hurting me? You don't know me—"

"Well, by God let me show you why."

He lifted her to him. His head lowered, but when his lips came over hers there was no violence, no fury, expended into the kiss.

The results were devastating all the same.

Senses spinning, focused entirely upon the kiss, her lips parting beneath his and a moan escaping her throat, she knew she'd never be the same.

Firm, calculatingly masterful, and filled with a dark, rich hunger she could never have expected as he kissed her, Shane's lips brushed over her shoulder, against the side of her neck. As he tenderly gathered her hair from her shoulder and held it out of his way, his teeth suddenly raked against nerve endings in her neck that shattered her concepts of pleasure.

Her cry came with the jolt of fiery, shocking sensation racing from her neck to between her thighs. Sebastian's kiss became hungrier, steadily building each erotic sensation until she could barely breathe, until she was shaking, shuddering.

This was pleasure? Fiery bolts of sensation that threatened to obliterate reality? The need for something closer, something she'd never had before and had no idea how to ask for.

"Easy, Alyssa. Shhh, just this kiss," Shane promised. "Nothing more. Nothing taken. When you want to be released you'll be free."

Did she want to be released?

What did she want?

Her fingers dug into the material of the shirt covering Sebastian's shoulders, fisting into it as she tried and failed to still the erratic storm she sensed gathering inside her. Needs and hungers never known before. Sensations she had no idea how to ease, which only gathered and grew until she was suddenly struggling against them, desperate to be free.

Just that quickly, they released her.

She wasn't left to try to stand alone, though. Sebastian did no more than release her lips and allow her to rest her weight on her own feet as she leaned against him for support.

What had they done to her?

Shane stood behind her, his forehead resting against her outside shoulder, his body so tense, so wired, she was terrified to move.

"That's why," Shane said then. "That's why he'll kill, why I'll kill, if anyone tries to harm you. Because the pleasure you're so confused by you've obviously never felt before. Because it's ours. We brought it to life—"

"And now, it's ours," Sebastian finished for him. "We may not deserve it, but I promise you this: we claim it."

He didn't say she belonged to him. She would have fought that immediately. Instead, he said he was claiming her response to them. That was okay, she decided hazily. That would work. Because Shane was right: they had brought it to life.

"Let's just hope you figure out what to do with it," she stated unsteadily as she moved away from them. "Excuse me, I think I need to go have my nervous breakdown. I'll be back in a few days, 'kay?" Lifting one finger rather facetiously, she turned and all but raced to the bedroom.

She needed just a few years to figure out what the hell was wrong with her body and how to control that storm she'd felt rising inside her. The flesh between her thighs was swollen, so slick and wet she had no idea how to handle it. She'd never been that wet.

She'd never felt what she was feeling now. The overwhelming need to demand his kisses and his touch in places other than her lips.

Along with it was the sudden, fierce demand for the right to claim them as well.

Yep, it was nervous breakdown time.

3

## WEEK ONE

Seduction was a fluid thing.

It was never the same from one woman to the next. Some women, even those experienced in the sexual tastes he and Shane practiced in, were still sometimes hesitant. Being with two men with sexual appetites such as theirs could be a bit discomfiting. In more ways than one.

Seducing Alyssa was pure pleasure, though. Her innocence and unknowing sensuality hinted that her lovers could have been no older than she was herself. Groping, inexperienced boys who had no clue how to ignite the hunger Alyssa was capable of, or how to satisfy it.

Arriving at her apartment, Shane was fully looking forward to giving her the gifts he and Sebastian had purchased for her that morning. The erotic toys were sure to stimulate and build her need if she chose to use them while the cousins weren't there. They fully intended to convince her to allow them to use the toys on her themselves, though.

"Dinner's almost ready," she assured them as they stepped through the French doors. "I'm not much of a cook, though, so I hope you're not expecting anything fancy."

"We told you, sweets, anything was fine," Sebastian assured her as Shane slipped into the living room and laid the bag he carried in one of the wide chairs facing away from the kitchen. Turning, he leaned against the back of it, watching as she moved about the large kitchen preparing the meal.

She wore another of the ankle-length chiffon skirts that flowed around her legs and emphasized the feminine fragility of her small form. This one was white, the same as the racer-back cami she wore with it. The shirt wasn't snug; instead it whispered over the curves of her breasts and midriff, leaving the tiniest hint of skin to flash between the low-rise band of the skirt and the hem of the shirt.

Sun-kissed blond hair, now lighter than it had been when she arrived, was piled haphazardly on her head and secured with a wide clip. Wisps escaped and framed her inquisitive features and made Shane want to force Sebastian to paint her right at that moment, as she looked now.

Glancing at his cousin, Shane had a feeling he wasn't going to have to harass him to paint her. He was watching her with a studied intensity normally reserved for the nature-scapes he could become lost in.

"It's almost ready," she promised them, the intriguing scents of the meal teasing his senses.

"It smells delicious," he assured her. "Is there anything we can do?"

The table was set, bread sliced and layered into a basket. Fresh butter rested in the crock she'd purchased it in from the farmer they'd taken her to the day before for his fresh milk and exceptional cheeses.

The wine sat next to it, uncorked and breathing, along with a platter of fresh vegetables that had been seared before baking.

"Walnut-encrusted chicken and baby tomatoes," she announced, opening the oven door and bending to reach inside.

The view was striking. Shane could feel his entire body tightening at the sight of her curved little rear perfectly outlined by the skirt.

He was about to start sweating despite the comfortable temperature of the apartment.

The meal was perfect. The chicken, baked with walnuts, baby tomatoes, and the fresh cheeses she'd bought from the farmer, a surprising delicate flavor. She was a much better cook than she gave herself credit for.

After the meal Sebastian and Shane urged her to finish her wine as they cleaned the kitchen for her, aware of her amusement as they bickered back and forth.

"You two sound like brothers," she accused them.

Sebastian grimaced at the charge. "I'm nothing like my brother. Lucien's the eldest. He's five years older but far too serious and quiet. He's rarely accused of being anything like me."

"Or you like him?" she guessed as he shot her a little wink.

"I am quite proud to admit I'm nothing like him," he assured her, though his fondness for his brother went deep.

"And you, Shane?" she asked.

"Like 'Bastian, Murphy's around five years and some odd months older than I," he admitted. "He looks more like Sebastian, while I resemble Lucien more, I guess. The resemblance ends there." He chuckled. "Murphy loves the ranch, lives and breathes for those damned cows he's always talking about."

"The two of you are very fond of your brothers, though," she guessed. "That's good. Families should be close."

"Oh, we're close to our families," Sebastian assured her teasingly. "So much so that they often ship us out of the country just to find a little peace."

She laughed at that.

"Brothers or sisters in your family?" Sebastian folded the dish towel he'd used to dry the pans and laid it on the counter as he and Shane watched her.

"Only child," she admitted, propping her chin in her hand, her expression a bit whimsical. "An older brother would have been really nice, but Margot declared I was more trouble than three toddlers and stopped with me."

Ah, already he liked her mother even less than he had before, Shane thought.

"I can't believe you were any trouble at all." Sebastian tipped his head to the side. "I would guess you were a quiet child."

"And you guessed wrong." Delight filled the little laugh in her voice. "Especially whenever my friend Summer was allowed to spend time in D.C. with us. She was a hoyden. And always getting me into trouble." She pouted. But her eyes told a far different story. Filled with the irrepressible spark of a prankster and a child who found wonder in the world.

God, he wanted to paint her. Just as she was now, her expression both innocent woman-child and emerging sensualist. With her elbow propped on the table, her chin resting in her hand as the softness in her gaze hinted at the secrets behind the soft curve of her lips.

"Not Summer Bartlett?" Mock horror filled Shane's voice as Sebastian grimaced and shot Alyssa a surprised look.

Surely not.

"So you know her?" Delight filled Alyssa's voice now. "Isn't she wonderful? She's always causing trouble. Margot never knows quite what to do with her or what to say whenever Summer flashes her one of those little-girl looks and assures her that she deserves all the *credit,* mind you, for whatever catastrophe we caused together. It's the only time I can't convince her that I was behind the disaster myself."

"She should be burned at the stake," Shane muttered, and Sebastian well agreed with him.

"The world would lose so much laughter if you did that." A hint of seriousness stroked over the amusement. "I would be very bored, Shane."

"Honey, I promise, we'll keep boredom at bay." Moving toward her, his expression hinting at the hunger raging beneath the surface, he gave her a slow, sensual smile. "We bought you some presents, just for those times when we might not be here. Would you like to see them?"

Alyssa swallowed tightly. Presents? She had a feeling it wasn't some charming little keepsake.

"Will I know what to do with it?" she asked almost fearfully. She had no doubt it had better come with instructions as well as batteries.

The fact that she could just look at them, no matter how bland their expressions, and often guess what they were up to was scary. Barely a week into the sort of relationship, as she called it, and sometimes it felt as though she'd known them far, far longer.

"Well, if you don't, we'll help you learn," Shane assured her, his expression at once teasing and as hungry as any starving wolf.

She turned to Sebastian. "Is he serious?"

Why had she bothered to ask him? The look on his face was pretty much identical.

She was going to blush. Alyssa could feel it coming. She would start stuttering and they'd get that dazed expression they always got when that happened, which only made her feel more self-conscious.

Breathing out heavily, she stared at the two men. How could hungry wolves get those flashes of male Christmas anticipation at the same time? These two had their moments of incredible contradictions. And frightening sexual intensity.

"Okay, let's get it over with," she told them. "What kind of completely inappropriate presents did the two of you bring me?"

The edible panties she'd hidden hours after they'd left several nights before. The day before, they'd actually brought her edible body oils. She'd not said a word. She took the box to the bedroom and shoved it into an empty drawer.

Shane retrieved the dark gray bag from the chair and approached her with such sexual anticipation she could feel the blush already coming on.

"Sure you don't want to just open it for me?" she suggested.

His grin was positively devilish. "No, but I really think you should let us help you try it out."

She accepted the bag cautiously.

"The two of you are going to have to stop this," she sighed. "Before I die of overexposure to lust."

"That's possible?" Sebastian's completely false look of shock had her shaking her head in exasperation.

Well, hell, she might as well be a good sport about it. She'd learned that fine art when Summer hit sixteen and decided they were dinosaurs for still being virgins and they should just take care of things themselves. She'd even bought the tools required to do so and left Alyssa howling in laughter.

Steeling herself, she glanced in the bag, then reached inside cautiously.

"I promise it doesn't bite." Sebastian was about a breath away from dying of laughter.

The ass.

"Says who?" She had to make herself pull the first item free.

Lifting it from the bag, she stared at it for long minutes. She turned it sideways, upside down, then right side up, and tilted her head as her lips pursed thoughtfully.

"Baby, it's not rocket science," Shane assured her as Sebastian snickered, coughed, and tried frantically not to laugh.

She looked up at Shane. "You know," she said doubtfully, "I really can't imagine you or Goofy over there actually allowing me to use this on you."

For a moment Shane's expression completely cleared.

The butt plug wasn't overly large, at first. It started out kind of narrow actually. The base was a far different story.

"Alyssa, it's not for me," Shane assured her.

She turned to Sebastian, or Goofy. He was dying to completely collapse with laughter. She looked from the toy to him.

"I don't see Goofy taking it, either." She looked up at him with complete seriousness. "Who's it for?"

Sebastian was choking again. If he kept that up she'd hit him on the back. With a chair.

"It's for you." He was glaring at her then.

"Well then." Laying it aside, she turned back to the bag. "What else do we have here?"

She should have kept her mouth shut. One of these days she'd learn.

The black box was too damned big for jewelry, that was for sure. Setting it on the table, she opened it slowly.

She felt the blush move from her toes to her hairline. Before she could catch herself, her eyes widened. Slamming the lid closed, she pushed it and the other toy back into the bag before folding the top over, scared the second item would actually escape and cause some damage.

She cleared her throat.

"Well then . . ." She couldn't find anything else to say.

"All you can say is 'well then'?" Shane was watching her as though he couldn't believe her reaction.

Sitting back in her chair, she regarded both men for a long, thoughtful moment.

Goofy had his forehead against the counter, his shoulders giving a jerk every few seconds.

"Shane? Sebastian?" She even used a totally reasonable tone of voice.

Sebastian lifted his head, his eyes practically watering.

"Uh-huh?" Shane asked, a bit cautious now.

"What part of 'virgin' have the two of you had trouble understanding? Or is it my English? Accent too thick to penetrate or something?" She did not have much of a D.C. accent and she knew it.

Sebastian stumbled. Which was amazing really, because he hadn't moved from behind the kitchen counter. His expression cleared of every emotion but complete confusion.

Shane just blinked.

"You need to repeat that," he finally cleared his throat enough to croak the demand.

Alyssa frowned back at both of them. "I don't stutter, Cowboy," she reminded him. "Do you really want me to use either of those items? Those would not fit, not with a ton of oil or whatever the hell it is you use with them. Now, I understand a few erotic toys, I really do," she assured them seriously. "But come on, get me something I can at least lie about and say I use. Right?"

Shane just blinked again.

Sebastian wasn't laughing anymore at least. He was staring at her. Like she was an alien that had materialized in front of him.

"You two are impossible." She rolled her eyes before standing, grabbing the bag, and walking past them. "I'll put them with the rest of the toys." She paused and glanced back. "Mind you, I love presents. But the next time you get in a buying mood, I think I might deserve something a bit more traditional for putting up with your weird-assed sense of humor." Turning back, she carried her "gifts" to the bedroom, found an empty drawer, and pushed them all the way to the back before closing it.

Lord help her. She needed another glass of wine.

Returning to the kitchen, she found both of them still where she'd left them. They looked a bit disconcerted perhaps.

"Did I offend you?" She hadn't considered that. Maybe they thought the present was a good one. What the hell did she know? She'd never had a steady date, let alone a lover. She didn't dare introduce a guy she was interested in to Margot. It would be a disaster.

"Uh, no." Shane shook his head frowning before glancing at Sebastian. "We need to go, though." He still had that confused look on his face.

"What did I do?" Crossing her arms over her breasts, she glared at both of them. "Come on, spit it out. Did I miss something?"

"No. No." Shane rubbed at the back of his neck, still frowning. "We just need to go now."

A hard shake of his head and he just left.

Sebastian followed, though he shot her a quizzical look through the glass door as he closed it behind him.

She obviously had missed something.

Shrugging, she filled her wineglass before plopping back into the chair she'd vacated moments before. She had a feeling she was going to end up drinking a lot of wine this summer.

+ + + +

Shane managed to drive halfway to the De Loren property before Sebastian actually spoke.

"I told you to get one smaller than we were," he reminded his cousin with a glower. "What did you do? Buy one that looked like a baseball bat or something?"

Shane was in shock. He knew he was. He frowned at the road as he drove, wondering if there was some way he'd misunderstood her. Surely he had.

"Shane?" Sebastian snapped.

"Huh?" he answered a bit absently. "Hey, 'Bastian?"

"What? How did you fuck that up?"

"Did she say she was a virgin?" Shane asked. "I had to have heard her wrong. I did, right?" He had to be sure.

Sebastian went dead silent for a full moment. "You heard that too?" There was an edge of disbelief in his cousin's voice. "I thought I misheard."

"Fuck!" The word exploded from their lips at the same time.

"I thought our sisters were the only virgins left in the world," Sebastian finally ventured.

Shane shook his head. "We heard wrong."

"How big was the fucking dildo, Shane?" Sebastian snapped then. "What did you buy?"

Shane wiped his hand down his face. "Well, that's the thing," he sighed. "It's actually probably much smaller than we are." He glanced at Sebastian. "I don't think we heard wrong, 'Bastian."

Sebastian didn't speak. He stared straight ahead, just as Shane did.

Hell, a virgin.

He was so damned hard his dick was like iron, blood rushing through his body in excitement while pure shock held him a bit mesmerized, Shane thought.

A complete innocent.

Hell, they'd known she was inexperienced. Very inexperienced. But by eighteen, most young women had at least had one sexual encounter that included penetration. That, neither of them had expected. The fact that no other man, young, mature or otherwise, had taken her, was blowing their minds.

They were in some real fucking trouble here. The never-let-her-go kind of trouble that was sure to cause a nuclear meltdown in both D.C. and Barcelona.

And he didn't give a damn.

A virgin. Their virgin. Sweet, innocent, and completely theirs.

Now he just had to figure out what to do about the virginity thing.

"Trouble," Sebastian murmured. "Real fucking trouble this time."

And they were going to love every minute of it.

## WEEK TWO

As the second week of Alyssa's vacation rolled in, Sebastian kept his questions about toys or virgins firmly quiet as he and Shane made all attempts to put a lock on their self-control and continued their slow seduction of Alyssa.

Arriving at her apartment several days after the episode with the toys, armed with sweet treats, fruits, and coffee, they let themselves in.

More often than not she was still asleep when they showed up early. Waking her was becoming a greater test in self-control each time. And they were becoming weaker by the day.

Depositing the sweets and fruits on the table, Shane turned back and locked the kitchen door before pausing.

His gaze swept over the kitchen, eyes narrowed as he surveyed the floor-to-ceiling windows next to the doors. They were easily eight feet tall and they were clean. So clean they almost shimmered without the various fingerprints and bits of salt and sand that sometimes clung to them.

Inside and out.

The kitchen table was closer to the windows, and on the wide deck . . .

"Son of a bitch." He could feel every muscle in his body tightening in impending danger.

Sebastian stepped over; years of being raised together, working as couriers for the CIA between Spain and the United States, had given each of them a sixth sense for the other when it came to danger.

Shane felt the tension that suddenly surrounded Sebastian as he saw the problem.

"She's five five at the most, if she wears those silly built-up sneakers she likes so well," he suddenly growled. "And she's climbing."

"We're six two," Shane murmured. "These windows are easily eight feet tall." Turning, he moved to the table with its rough stone top and surveyed it carefully. "She stood on a chair, 'Bastian. She put the fucking chair on a table, then stood on it."

Visions of what could have happened to her began racing through his head. A fall to the floor, covered in stones matching that of the table, would have killed her. One crack of her head and it would have been over.

He found his insides shaking.

Together he and Sebastian stalked to the bedroom, worry, hell-fucking fear—riding them as they pushed inside the large, dim master suite to find Alyssa sprawled on her stomach, blankets kicked back, the boy shorts and snug T-shirt she wore doing little to dampen the lusts storming inside them now.

"At least she's fucking breathing," Sebastian pushed the words between clenched teeth.

Five five at the tallest, Shane thought. And she was climbing to clean windows clearly out of her reach.

Standing still, assuring himself she was fine, he watched as Sebastian eased closer, bent, and narrowed his gaze on her leg. When he looked up at Shane, his lips were thin, his eyes narrowed in anger.

Moving to where Shane stood, he inhaled hard. There, just below her knee on the side of her leg, a bruise the size of his fist. Black as pitch, the bruising deep and obviously serious.

Turning from the sight of it, Shane swiped his fingers through his hair, clenched his teeth, and held back his possessive, protective instincts. For the moment.

Just for the moment.

Turning back to the bed, he almost grinned at the sight of

Sebastian on the floor next to the bed, his wrists resting on his upraised knees as he glared at the ceiling, cursing silently, though his lips were forming the words perfectly.

That was Sebastian. Playful as a fucking kid, even when he was pissed off.

"Spanking her ass. I'm telling you, Shane. Spanking it. Fucking it. She's going to kill herself." Then he was cursing in Spanish. Shane could only shake his head. When Sebastian began cursing in Spanish they had a problem. He'd never known his cousin to slip to this extreme over a woman before, though. Not that he blamed him; it was just unexpected.

Blowing out a hard breath, Shane watched as Alyssa's legs shifted on the bed and she slowly rolled over, stretching out before him, the slender delicacy of her body holding him spellbound.

How the hell did she manage to do that to him?

His mouth went dry; his cock went from iron hard to painfully stiff. Have mercy. When Sebastian had called her a siren, he'd known what he was about.

One hand rested on her stomach, the other over her head, and when he made himself focus on her face he watched as her lashes drifted open drowsily.

"Morning," she whispered, her lashes drifting over her eyes again.

His gaze moved to her breasts, watching them rise and fall, her tight little engorged nipples trying to poke through the cloth. "It's too early to get up," she breathed sleepily.

"If you don't we're getting in that bed with you, darlin'," he assured her.

If they got in that bed with her, he doubted they'd get out of it for a very long time.

"'Kay." Her lips curled with a hint of feminine satisfaction as Sebastian pulled himself from the floor to stare down at her.

Shane toed the casual leather slippers from his feet. He didn't dare undress. Damn, he wanted to feel her naked skin against his own. But, the loss of self-control would be instantaneous.

"Alyssa darlin'," he drawled, stretching out beside her, wanting her so bad he could barely stand it. "What were you doing last night after we left?"

Sebastian eased into place on the other side of her.

A frown flitted across her brow. "Was I s'posed to do somethin'?" A little stretch and shift had his breath catch and raging hunger building.

"Perhaps there was something you shouldn't have been doing," he suggested, watching as Sebastian lifted the hem of her shirt just enough to lower his head and brush his lips over her stomach.

Bastard. He had even less self-control evidently.

"Hmm, feels good," she mumbled, lifting closer to his touch.

"Answer, siren." Shane wasn't about to let her off the hook this easily. "What did you do that you shouldn't have?"

"Shh," she urged him. "Not yet."

She stretched again, arching against Sebastian's lips as they continued to brush over the silken flesh of her stomach.

"I could make him stop until you answer me," he suggested gently. "Want me to do that, baby?"

A little pout pulled at her lips.

"Alyssa," he added a warning note to his voice.

"They didn't fit anyway," she muttered. "Told you they wouldn't."

Sebastian's head jerked up, his expression tightening, turning savage with need. Shane felt his own control beginning to slip. The bruise was forgotten for the moment in light of that little statement.

"Say that again," Sebastian groaned. "One more time."

A breathy little sigh left her lips. She peeked up at Shane with a little glare as a flush washed from her breasts to her hairline.

"I said they didn't fit. You were playing a prank on me." Ire sparkled in her eyes. "And you woke me, Shane. That was a really nice dream I was having."

He couldn't breathe. The thought of her stretched out in the bed, trying to use the intimate toys, as she thought of them, had every cell in his body burning to take her.

"It wasn't a prank," he told her, his voice rough.

"You're lying to me." The accusation held no doubt whatsoever.

"God help me." He drew in a hard breath. "No, no joke. Actually, I bought smaller than our own. I had no idea . . ." He cleared his throat. "I knew you were innocent; I didn't know you were a virgin."

They bought smaller than their own?

Alyssa licked her lips nervously. "Smaller?"

"Sorry, baby." He wanted to grin, but he was too busy trying to breathe.

"Well then, that's too bad." The disappointment in her gaze was sincere. "They wouldn't fit. There's no way. . . ." A moan slipped past her lips as Sebastian lifted her top over her hardened nipples.

"Take the shirt off," Shane demanded, the sight of those little nipples destroying him with the need to taste them.

"There's no way you'll fit," she protested breathlessly, though she took the top off.

Swollen, firm, the satin flesh of her breasts was so damned pretty, those tight nipples making his mouth water to suck them. Just for a minute.

He needed to touch her, needed to taste her.

Sebastian wasn't waiting. His head lowered, his lips claiming an engorged peak. Shane gave up. The battle was lost and his hunger for her took over.

"Oh my—" Alyssa lost her breath.

She lost her mind.

Before she could curl her fingers into their hair they each caught a wrist and secured it above her head, never once easing the incredible sensations surrounding her nipples and intoxicating her senses.

Nothing should feel this good.

Nothing should be this destructive to a woman's senses, to her ability to think.

The sensitive tips were surrounded by such intense pleasure she had no idea how to handle it. Sensation upon sensation whipped through her, heat building beneath her skin and racing to the more tender flesh between her thighs.

As she arched to them, incredible pleasure tearing through her with fierce crashing waves had her crying out, though whether in protest or in a plea for more she wasn't certain.

"Oh God. What are you doing to me?" She arched again, the feel of their teeth raking the sensitive tips; then their mouths suckling her once again, firmer, more heatedly, held her spellbound by the storm rising through her. Their tongues licked, lashed at the tips, as their fingers stroked over her stomach, her spread thighs.

She hadn't expected this. The slashing arcs of electric heat were dizzying. They whipped through her in maddening waves of demand that she had no idea how to ease.

It was too much.

The whipping storm of pleasure and gathering tension would destroy her . . . change her.

Struggling against the sensations, Alyssa tried to dampen them. She tried to protest, to beg one of them to stop, to ease. The tightening of the heat in her belly was stealing her breath, the sensations centering there, burning outward.

A male groan of incredible pleasure vibrated at her nipple as broad calloused fingers slipped beneath the band of her panties.

Alyssa parted her thighs farther, her hips arching. Yes, she needed this, needed touch there where the painful pleasure was gathering in a spiraling storm.

Then it was there. A hard male palm rasped over the swollen bud of her clit—

"No. . . . No. . . ." The whipping storm gathered, tightened. Then shattered.

Sensation spiraled outward, exploded with such force it stole her breath and drew her body tight. It encompassed the clenched inner flesh of her vagina, to her torturously swollen clit, and every sense was held suspended by the ecstatic force.

She was lost. There was no escaping the lashing inferno of exploding sensation. It pulsed through her, each surge blending, burning, and throwing her higher into a realm of pure ecstasy.

There was no stopping it.

There was no controlling it.

There was only the whipping, terrified flight she had no idea how to control or ease.

There was a certainty, though, that somehow she had lost part of herself.

+⟡+⟡+

She was going to kill them and Sebastian knew it.

Sitting on top of the wood picnic table his aunt Landra was so fond of, he stared at the beach below. The lazy roll of the waves, the sun worshipers as they took up nearly every available space along the beach.

Alyssa was a bit uncomfortable among the crowd, he'd noticed. She went out when the sand wasn't as crowded and came in as it began to fill. She would enjoy the private beach he and Shane preferred that the De Loren property bordered. She could lie beneath the heat of the sun without the bikini she wore, brief though it was. The rays of the sun could kiss all her flesh, giving it that lovely lightly golden hue that made her appear a sun goddess.

Their siren. And she was killing them. She would kill them. It couldn't be healthy sporting a hard-on that never seemed to soften.

To be so fascinated by a woman, a virgin. An instinct no man should feel warned them that she wasn't quite ready for their possession.

He'd never felt something so sure and so powerful before rise up inside him. Sebastian looked at his cousin and saw the confusion and wonder on his face that he was sure was stamped on his. Alyssa was indeed a siren. Beautiful. Magical. She was stealing their hearts. If they weren't very careful, she'd mark their souls as well.

The door opened behind him and he swore the scent of her wrapped around him. Feminine, so soft and sweet, as intoxicating as the most potent wine.

"'Bastian?" She said his name softly, uncertainly.

Turning to her, Sebastian couldn't help reaching out his hand and, when she took it, drawing her to him. Pulling her to sit between his spread thighs, he propped his chin at her shoulder, his gaze returning to the beach.

"I'm sorry." The regret in her voice should never be there, he decided.

"If you're sorry for climbing on these damned tables and nearly falling, then I think I should tell you, the next time it happens, I'm paddling your ass," he informed her. "If you're talking about the moments you allowed us to give you such pleasure, then I will definitely paddle your ass. Never apologize for that, Alyssa."

She swallowed tightly.

"Well, I was perfectly safe—"

"Should I give you that paddling now?" he asked.

"Well, perhaps we should wait awhile on that," she sighed. "I have a feeling it would be far too enjoyable, and I'm not certain I'm ready for that quite yet."

"Then perhaps you had better keep your feet off tables; otherwise, I promise you, you will refrain from climbing once I've finished explaining the hazards of it," he grunted.

Turning just enough to give him a little moue of mock retribution, she smiled a moment later.

"So fierce." She wrinkled her nose enchantingly. "I'll give your warning due consideration should I ever want to clean the windows again."

He was definitely going to end up spanking her. But not today. He simply didn't have the self-control.

"I'd give it more than consideration if I were you," he pointed out. "Now, did Shane mention dinner while he was giving you his own warning about the windows?"

"His bribe, you mean?" She laughed.

"His bribe?" He had obviously lost his mind.

"If I promised to never climb again then he'd give me his share of his ranch in Texas." She laughed at the thought. "What the hell would I do with a share in it? I told him; when he could give the whole thing I'd think about it."

Oh hell, there went his own share in the damned place.

"Siren," he murmured, shaking his head. "What are we going to do with you?"

Turning back, she leaned into his chest, her head resting on his shoulder.

"Just hold me, Sebastian," she whispered, and he swore he heard a note of sadness in her voice. "Right here, right now, just hold me."

Holding her was easy; he had a feeling letting her go was going to be rather more difficult.


## WEEK THREE

There were few things Alyssa enjoyed more than a day at the spa, until now.

Making her way back to the apartment from the spa Gia had

told her about the week before, Alyssa grinned at the thought. Once she would have lingered for hours at the spa. A massage, highlights in her hair, facial, the complete wax, a manicure and pedicure. It could take most of the day for a full treatment. Today, she'd limited herself to the wax, manicure, and pedicure. The rest could wait, she decided.

She had exactly an hour before Shane and Sebastian were due to pick her up and take her to the private beach they'd told her about. Sun and sand, Shane and Sebastian, and no one to see her sunbathing nude but the men who were consuming more and more of her thoughts. Not to mention making it impossible to remember there was no way they would fit if they took her fully. Well, perhaps it wasn't that she didn't remember so much as she was becoming desperate for the possession herself.

They were dangerous to her common sense, she decided as she neared her borrowed apartment.

Sitting on the wide stone stoop smoking a cigarette, Gregory, the neighbor directly below her, lounged on the step. He was twenty-one and living with his girlfriend, a university student from Madrid who was currently vacationing in Barcelona as well.

"Hello, Alyssa," he greeted her, his heavily accented tone open and friendly as he disposed of the cigarette and rose to his feet.

Clad in low, loose jeans and a sleeveless T-shirt and with bare feet, he smiled at her brightly.

"Hello, Gregory." She smiled, pausing before stepping up to make her way down the narrow walk to the back of the building and the steps leading to the deck. "Is Marissa returning today?"

His girlfriend had gone home for a few days to attend her brother's birthday party.

"Thankfully, any moment now." Anticipation filled his dark brown eyes. "I thought to meet her. I expect every time she goes home that her poppa will lock her in the cellar and refuse to let her return to me."

Gregory might be smiling, but there was just a hint of serious uncertainty in his voice.

"She's crazy about you, Gregory," she assured him, tucking her hands into the pockets of her shorts. "She would never let her father lock her up anywhere to keep her from you."

"Eh, fathers, you don't know how they are here." Lifting his hands at his sides to emphasis the claim, he gave a brief little roll of his eyes. "And Marissa's poppa, he is crazy."

Alyssa laughed at the declaration. "Gregory, every girl's poppa that loves her is crazy when it comes to her leaving the nest. That never changes, either."

Gregory grimaced at the sound of Sebastian's car purring to the curve and parking.

"Ah, your friends have arrived," Gregory announced. "Which one is yours?"

She gave him an innocent look. "They're both friends."

Gregory blinked back at her, a knowing light in his dark eyes.

"Ah, I see," he murmured.

As Shane and Sebastian stepped to the sidewalk she turned to them with a smile. "Hi there. I'd like you to meet my neighbor . . ."

Shane's expression was so hard she paused for a second. Just a second. "Shane, Sebastian, this is Gregory—"

"I'm in a hurry Alyssa," Shane announced, gripping her arm and pulling her up the stoop. "Let's get your things."

Behind her, she heard Sebastian greet the young man, his voice a bit amused. Evidently he wasn't surprised by his cousin's behavior.

"Excuse me!" She jerked her arm from Shane's grip, obviously catching him by surprise, because he actually let her go.

"You heard me. . . ."

The pain that struck at her chest surprised her. They had the power to hurt her now. A power only one person in her life had ever used in the same way, and she swore she'd never tolerate it from anyone else.

"I think the two of you should leave." She could feel the tears gathering behind her eyes, the sense of loss tearing her apart.

She'd started the day so happy, so confident, only to now see a side of Shane she knew she could never bear to see again.

Shane stiffened; behind him she heard Sebastian mutter a curse.

"Come on, sweets, you know what a bear Shane can be." Sebastian deserved an A for effort.

Keeping her gaze locked with Shane's as he slowly drew the dark sunglasses off, she glimpsed a wild, primitive flash of some emotion she didn't want to define.

"What did you say?" he asked her softly.

"I didn't stutter, Cowboy. Leave. Until you can learn some manners I don't want to see you again."

"Come on, Alyssa," Sebastian protested behind him, obviously shocked. "I was polite. Gregory, tell her I was polite."

Gregory said nothing.

"Gregory!" Sebastian snapped. "Tell her I was polite, dammit."

"Well, he was polite." Gregory didn't seem the least bit intimidated.

"Doesn't matter," she informed him scathingly, still staring at Shane. "Evidently you forgot to remind your cousin that I'm no man's property, even his. Nor am I a child to be dragged away as though I've broken some rule. I have no desire to speak to either of you for a while." She could feel the tears building in her eyes now, threatening to fall. "Maybe not at all."

Before they could stop her, Alyssa ran down the narrow walk, her heart breaking.

How could he have treated her like that? To embarrass her in front of her neighbor, to attempt to make it appear she were some possession no one else could speak to?

The tears were falling before she made it to the landing, the sound of Sebastian calling her name as he moved quickly up the walk, making her add speed to her retreat.

Slamming the door closed behind her, Alyssa threw the inner latch home once she locked the doors. Twenty keys wouldn't get them in now. The shades came down and she retreated to her bedroom, where the sobs finally broke free.

"Damn you!" she cried, throwing the small bag she'd carried on her wrist from the spa. "You don't own me. No one owns me."

Sebastian heard the tear-filled declaration as it drifted through the open bedroom window. The sound of her quiet sobs following it broke his heart and infuriated him.

Not that he didn't understand Shane. Hell, he'd hated seeing Alyssa smile at another man, a man closer to her age, one who lived just below her. Gregory was a charming little bastard, and they knew it. All the girls had loved him before he'd moved from the quiet little town close to the De Loren lands.

Still, even Sebastian knew better than to embarrass their siren in such a way. Her sweet song could lead them to paradise, but he'd also sensed that if they hurt her, treated her unfairly in any way, then she'd make damned sure that sweet voice lashed at them like the sharpest whip.

Sliding the key from his pocket, he attempted to open the door. It unlocked, but the inner bolt had been slid in place, ensuring the key would do him little good.

He was going to kill Shane.

Turning and moving quickly down the stairs, then the narrow walk, he met his cousin at the other side before lifting his lip in an insulting snarl.

"You are a fucking moron, Cousin," he bit out. "She secured the door. There's no getting in."

Shane's expression went blank, his blue eyes darkening.

"She'll open the fucker for me," he decided.

"And I will call the police if you try to force her to do so," Gregory threatened, though he was smart enough to move back from Shane as his girlfriend, Marissa, glared at both of them.

Dammit to hell. They knew both of them, and neither Shane nor Sebastian cared for Gregory. The little bastard was always getting into everyone's business.

"And I will call Lucien," Marissa threw the ultimate threat at them. "He would be greatly displeased, Shane Connor, to know his cousin had so insulted such a young woman. She is not yet twenty and that the two of you play your games with her is bad enough. But to treat her so is uncalled for." She turned to Gregory. "Never try such a thing with me or I will call Poppa immediately."

Fuck.

Marissa had overheard the confrontation, moving to Gregory as Alyssa had spat her rage at Shane. And Marissa would indeed call Lucien if she felt it was warranted.

"Don't worry, Marissa," Sebastian assured her, the snap in his tone drawing her gaze. "It's going to be hard for Shane to ever speak again after I push his teeth down his throat."

"That little shit flirts with every woman he sees. . . ." Shane threw his hand toward Gregory furiously.

"Not anymore he doesn't," Marissa came to her boyfriend's aid as the boy in question smirked at Shane. "Not since vowing to love me he doesn't flirt with others. Alyssa is our neighbor, Shane." Her curvy body vibrating with anger, she clenched her fists and glared at Shane. "It is not flirting to be nice. To say hello or to be introduced to friends. You are the little shit, not my Gregory." She linked her arm with the boy and tugged at it demandingly. "Come, Gregory, I too cannot bear to speak to him. I will check on her later and agree with her when she calls him the ass he is."

As Marissa pulled him away Gregory threw Shane one last smug-assed grin that just irritated the fuck out of Sebastian as well.

Shane stood silent, his expression implacable as he stared back at the walk Alyssa had disappeared down.

"She is crying," Sebastian stated, fury vibrating in his low voice.

"She will not let us comfort her, and I cannot blame her. If you cannot trust her to be a woman, to smile and grow in who she is, then you cannot be trusted with any part of her."

Shane turned to him, brooding fury building in his expression.

"I won't leave her crying," he bit out.

"But you will!" Sebastian snapped, all but throwing the keys to the car at him. "Leave now. Perhaps, without your ignorance to remind her of how she's been hurt, she will at least allow me to ease her tears. Leave now."

"Go to hell, Cousin!" Shane snapped. "I'll sit on that fucking porch until she does come out. Then I'll fix it."

Sebastian followed him as he stalked to the back of the apartment. It looked like it would be a very, very long day. Because even Sebastian had gotten to know Alyssa well enough to know she was not opening that door.

But he went to the back of the apartment and onto the porch, where Shane took a place on one end of the long picnic table and Sebastian sat on the other.

When his cousin stood to move to the door he stood as well.

"Touch that door and I'll throw you over the fucking rail," he bit out. "Let her calm down first. Then we'll attempt to see if she'll forgive you enough to at least speak with me."

Shane sat back down slowly, not because he was in the least worried about how much such a fall would hurt. No doubt it had more to do with the fact that he wasn't pissed enough yet to push Sebastian.

They sat there silently, for more than an hour before Marissa stomped up the steps to face them once again.

"She's gone." Her arms crossed over her breasts as she faced them, contempt shining in her eyes. "She stopped only long enough to tell Gregory and me she had a girlfriend in Madrid and would be there for a while. I came to tell you because I don't like you lurking out here. She did not mention telling you anything."

Sebastian rose to his feet when Marissa turned and left the way she had come.

"She's been climbing again," Shane said, almost too soft to hear. "She would have had to climb from the window."

"Find your own fucking way home," Sebastian bit out. "I don't even want you in my car now."

Shane sat where he was as Sebastian left. When he heard the car roar away, he sighed heavily and stared out at the ocean.

He would have apologized to the little turd, he thought heavily, if she'd given him a chance.

Now it appeared she wouldn't even give him a chance to beg for her forgiveness.

He frowned.

He'd never begged a woman for anything. Nothing. Shane Connor did not beg.

But he would have begged Alyssa, he realized. On his knees, his hands lifted in supplication, if she'd given him a chance. Now he was going to have to call Aunt Landra for advice. And that wasn't going to be pleasant at all. She'd already warned him and Sebastian about hurting Alyssa and about the hell she'd rain down on them. And Aunt Landra could rain hell with no more than a look.

Fuck. Sebastian was right. He was a fucking moron.

4

It took two days in Madrid with Summer to realize she had most likely overreacted to Shane's bad manners. Not that he'd been right to act such a way, she defended herself. He hadn't. Still, the panic that flooded her at the time had sent all her emotions into a tailspin.

And it was all her mother's fault. Margot was such a strong, controlling person, especially where her daughter was concerned, that Alyssa often lived in a state of caution, knowing her mother could act with such rudeness at any given moment. It was one of the reasons she was still a virgin, Alyssa had often thought. She was too terrified of her mother humiliating her in such a way, so she'd rarely dated any one young man for more than a few weeks, a month at the most.

Friends were in the same category. Only Summer had remained a steady presence in her life. They had been fast friends from age five, their first year together in school. And though Summer's family wasn't liked by Margot, still Summer herself had somehow managed to endear herself to Alyssa's mother. So much so that when Summer had needed help the year she'd turned sixteen it had been Margot who had moved quickly to ensure Alyssa's friend had that help.

Now, though Alyssa counted the other woman as her best friend, she didn't tell Summer about Shane and Sebastian. She didn't dare.

Far too often in past years she'd suspected her friend was too close to Margot, and she couldn't risk her mother learning of a relationship Margot would be certain to move quickly to end.

Instead, Alyssa used the time away from the two men to put them, as well as the relationship itself, in perspective.

It would have been sufficient, she thought, to leave the situation in Sebastian's hands in this case. The two men had a way of balancing each other, of each countering the other's less than appreciable traits.

She wouldn't tolerate having it happen again, but the situation should have been dealt with differently. The differences she should have used she wasn't quite certain, she thought in amusement as she slipped into her apartment, via the window above an iron trellis that supported a lush assortment of blooms.

She came to a stop when she moved into her bedroom, tears filling her eyes at the sight of an envelope taped to the mirror. Her name was written on it, Shane's scrawled handwriting bold and as forceful as he was himself.

Moving to it, she removed it from the glass and pulled the card inside free. As she did, a gold chain with three gems fell to the cherry top of the chest of drawers. Lifting it, she saw the sapphire, her birthstone, suspended between two beautiful diamonds.

*The necklace isn't a gift, siren, it's a promise. We're bound to you, and nothing matters more than ensuring you're a part of us. I'm sorry. I behaved like an animal, fearing the presence of another man you gave your smiles to. I forgot, your smiles aren't gifts, they're a part of you and a part of the warmth that radiates from you. I swear it won't happen again. Shane.*

*P.S. I'll break his legs if it does. Sebastian.*

Holding the necklace, Alyssa closed her fingers around it before turning to find her phone. At that same moment, it rang, her neighbor Marissa's number showing in the caller ID.

"Hello?"

"Please, Alyssa," Marissa all but moaned. "These two assholes have just about moved in with us. They're killing my sex life and making Gregory insane. Please God have mercy on me and let them talk to you."

"How long have they been there?" Alyssa asked, surprised.

"How long have you been gone?" Marissa all but growled. "They even watched you climb back to that window like some damn cat burglar, and I swear they went white when you slipped halfway up. . . . Alyssa, for the love of God . . ." She was whimpering now. "Please."

As Marissa begged, Alyssa walked through the apartment into the kitchen and slid the bolt lock free before releasing the door's main lock.

"Tell them the back door's unlocked," she sighed. "They can come up."

"I owe you my firstborn child," Marissa sighed. "I think I want to kill them."

"Keep the child," Alyssa assured her. "Thank you for watching them for me. I appreciate it."

"They're like two-year-olds," Marissa informed her caustically. "Check in with me later. After you shoot them. I'll help you hide the bodies."

"I'll be sure to," Alyssa promised. "Good-bye, Marissa."

The call disconnected as the door opened and Shane and Sebastian stepped inside the kitchen. They looked haggard. As miserable Alyssa she felt.

They stopped just inside the door, their gazes heavy, watching her silently but moving no closer to her. She would have to make the first move. She could see that in their expressions.

Stepping over to them, the necklace still held loosely in one hand, she drew in a deep breath. "I was angry, but you hurt me, Shane," she said painfully. "And you made me afraid that would be the means you tried to control me in the future, and I couldn't bear that."

"Alyssa," he whispered her name, his voice rough.

"Let me finish." She shook her head before drawing in another deep breath. "I overreacted, though, and I know that." She turned her attention to Sebastian then. "I should have left that ignorance to be dealt with by ' 'Bastian, just as you often deal with his rougher edges. I should have trusted both of you." Tears filled her eyes again before she blinked them back. "I won't make the same mistake in the future, I promise."

Lifting her hand, she held the necklace out to them. "And if you want me to wear your promise, then you have to put it on; otherwise it doesn't count."

They stepped to her. Shane took the chain, but she was surprised when they each took one side of it and latched it together.

"Our heart bound by yours," Shane whispered as he pressed his lips to her shoulder.

"Your heart bound by ours." Sebastian's lips moved to the point where her neck and shoulder met. "And I promise you, he'll never be that stupid again. Just as I promise you, you run from us again and I'll find you, Alyssa. The next time, I will not let you run. And when I catch up with you . . ."

"You'll spank me?" Looking over her shoulder, she met the dark, brooding gaze he directed to her with a small smile.

"Lock you in a basement and chain you to a bed," he threatened.

"Barefoot and pregnant," Shane growled. "Then she can't run near as fast."

Her heart tripped at the thought of having a child at some point. Who the father was she wouldn't care. As long as it was one of them.

Sebastian's gaze seemed to darken further, though, a heavy sensuality moving over his face.

"You'd have to find a way to fit first." The spurt of amusement was unstoppable. "I have a feeling I may yet die a virgin."

"Oh, baby." Shane turned her to him, one hand at the back of her neck, tipping her head back. "That so is not going to happen."

His head lowered then, his lips fitting to hers as he kissed her with such instant carnal demand that she swore her toes were curling against her sandals. Regret, hunger, need. She could feel it all suffusing her. Hers, theirs. A combination of heady desires that had her weakening against them as the knowledge that she was falling in love with them became clear.

She wasn't just falling in love, she thought as pleasure swamped her. They were becoming a part of her, and that was even more frightening, because when she was gone she could have sworn she didn't just feel her pain, but theirs as well.

And that was just crazy.

Breaking the kiss just as abruptly as he began it, Shane pulled Alyssa to him, holding her to his chest as his eyes closed, the overwhelming relief he felt barely containable. He'd suffered while she'd been gone, certain he'd lost her. Certain she would never forgive him.

They knew things she hadn't told them; their aunt had made certain of it. How Alyssa's mother had used humiliation and guilt to control her daughter as she grew up and the subtle ways Alyssa had been drawing from everyone her mother influenced. She'd made friends Margot Hampstead had no idea she'd made. Powerful, older friends willing to step in if she needed them to. Friends who could exert pressure on Margot that Alyssa couldn't.

She hadn't been doing it because she was weak, but to break away from the controlling manipulations her mother practiced. Landra had seen what few people had. Alyssa was ensuring there was no one her mother could use against her when she broke with her family to live her own life.

The quiet strength and courage their siren possessed went far deeper than anyone knew.

"I haven't slept," she finally admitted, her voice quiet, tired.

"I think I've gotten too used to the two of you getting me to sleep."

Lying with her, surrounding her with their warmth, and getting her used to their presence in bed with her. Since the morning her response to them had thrown her so off balance, they'd been attempting a more subtle seduction. Alyssa was more frightened than she was uncertain of her response to them.

"We haven't slept well, either, love," he said, his eyes opening to meet his cousin's.

The warning in them was clear. Alyssa wouldn't be hurt again because of the cousins' possessiveness. She would never be humiliated by another instinctive attempt to warn another male from her. Sebastian had made that clear. If she was hurt again he'd make certain Shane was kept away from her until he could learn to control the unruly impulse.

"Come on, baby, let's get you to sleep then," he whispered.

Instead of walking to the bedroom with her, he picked her up in his arms, the soft fabric of the light tan skirt flowing around her as she looped her arms around his neck and tucked her head against his shoulder.

None of them had slept, it seemed. Shane had spent the nights merely napping, waking at every sound to see if she had returned home. Sebastian had slept little better. Marissa and Gregory had threatened to call Sebastian's brother, Lucien, more than once.

Carrying his precious siren to the bed as Sebastian pulled the sheet and thin quilt back from the bed, Shane swore he'd never let himself forget what he'd nearly destroyed. She was too important. Her presence in their lives was too important. Losing her might well destroy not just his own soul but Sebastian's as well.

## 5

They were killing her.

Lying on the bed between them, Alyssa stared up at the ceiling, her body torturing her, need burning inside her despite the incredible rush of pleasure Shane and Sebastian had thrown her into hours before.

She was more aroused now than she had been, the clenching demand in her sex causing the sensitive flesh to spill more and more of the slick essence from inside her vagina.

She needed them, not just their lips, wicked tongues, and caressing hands. She needed them fully.

She wasn't stupid: after her initial shock had passed she'd gone to the Internet for information she could never ask anyone to supply. What she found there assured her that even the more than normal length and girth Shane and Sebastian had could be accepted without more than an initial flash of pain.

She didn't doubt their patience in preparing her. She knew they'd give her more pleasure than she'd even imagined. Maybe it was just the fear of the unknown, she thought as frustration whipped through her.

She was too inexperienced; she knew that. Most young women she knew had been having sex for years, proud of the experience they were acquiring. Alyssa had never believed that having one lover after another was something she'd find any pride in. Her dreams, on the one hand, hadn't been hugely ambitious when it came to men. Her emotional desires had always seemed out of reach, though. Someone to love her, totally, completely. A man who would wrap her in warmth and pleasure. And now, she had two.

A surge of sensation clenched in her belly at the thought. Two men who wanted her simultaneously, who wanted to take her at one time.

They'd touched her many times now as they wanted to take her. With lips and tongues, with gentle fingers and a need that whipped around them until Alyssa swore she could feel not just her hunger but theirs as well.

Her breath caught at another wave of demand spreading from her lower stomach to her vagina, her swollen clit. She could feel the thick layer of slick juices dampening her panties, more spilling to the swollen folds and encasing her clit.

She needed their touch. She needed them.

A shiver raced through her and it had nothing to do with a chill that might be in the air. Her body was so flushed, so hot, she couldn't bear it. The demands torturing her had her breathing harder, fighting to hold back a moan of restlessness.

Were they asleep? They were quiet, lying still on each side of her. She could slip her fingers into her panties. It wouldn't take but seconds to find relief, she was certain.

Turning her head, she gazed for a moment at Shane. He lay on his side, just as Sebastian did, facing her. His eyes were closed, his lips parted just slightly. Turning to Sebastian, she saw the same image.

She just needed a few moments, she assured herself as she slid her hand from where it rested against her stomach and eased her fingers beneath the band of her lacy panties.

She was so wet. The juices gathered along the folds of her sex covered her clit with such a heavy layer that the slide of her fingers over the sensitive bundle of nerves wasn't enough. Her fingers weren't calloused as theirs were; the rasp of rougher flesh was needed.

Biting her lip, her eyes drifting closed, she let her fingers circle the hard bud, press against it.

The pleasure sent a surge of adrenaline tearing through her, hitching her breath as she tried desperately to find a trigger to throw her into release.

And why she was doing this rather than just waking Shane and Sebastian she couldn't explain. The need for satisfaction was growing by the second, though, and her own attempt to fix it sure as hell wasn't working.

"'Lyssa . . ." Sebastian's hand was suddenly pressing against her fingers, holding them still, his voice gently chastising. "You had only turn to one of us, baby."

Tears gathered beneath her eyes. "It's not enough anymore." She felt as though she were strangling on the admission. "Nothing's enough anymore."

It wasn't. Not matter how they touched her, no matter the strength of her orgasm, it simply wasn't enough.

"We'll fix it," he promised her, easing her fingers from beneath her panties as Shane moved beside her.

Shocking her, he brought her fingers to his lips and one by one covered them with his lips, his mouth, his tongue, tasting the heavy layer of her desire.

"'Bastian." She could barely breathe, the sight of his pleasure in taking her taste rushing through her with a wave of destructive need.

"Everything's good, siren," he said, his voice low as Shane eased closer against her.

Her head swung around, her gaze meeting his before dropping

to the hardened length of his erection as it pressed against her thigh. The low light of the moon spilling through the windows behind the bed did nothing to shadow the huge wedge of flesh throbbing against her.

"Ah, siren, your expression." Amusement tinged Shane's voice as he lifted her chin and let his lips whisper over hers. "I swear, it will fit, baby. I promise."

There was no way, but she was on fire, burning from the inside out with the need to try.

A whimper fell from her lips as they parted for him, the hungry male force spilling to his kiss as it rocked her senses. The pleasure from such a simple act shouldn't be so strong, nor should it send such harsh, clenching demands racing through her and spilling more of the wet heat from her vagina.

As he kissed her, Shane eased her to her back, one hand sliding between her thighs to pull the one nearest him farther open. Sebastian parted the other and braced them open with the width of his broad shoulders.

She cried into the kiss, her hands clenched on Shane's shoulders as Sebastian's lips lowered, his tongue sliding through the narrow slit revealed by the swollen folds of flesh.

Jerking at the contact, pleasure lancing through her, Alyssa lifted her knees, pressing her heels into the bed and arching her hips closer.

Now. She needed it now.

A second later his tongue speared into the clenched entrance, pushed into the narrow passage, and a sharp, demanding cry fell from her lips as she turned her head, breaking the kiss Shane had deepened to a carnal melding of lips and tongues.

"It's not enough!" she cried out, her back arching. "I told you, it wasn't enough."

That wasn't what she needed. It was good, so good. His tongue thrust inside her, parting the tense tissue.

His hands clenched in the rounded curves of her rear, parting them, a finger rubbing against the tiny entrance there, spreading the slick moisture spilling from her vagina.

Gasping, moaning, she pressed down; the prickle of sensation as the tip of his finger pierced the small opening sent waves of desperation tearing through her.

Opening her eyes, she stared up at Shane as he watched her, his eyes so blue, sexual need burning in them.

"It's not enough," she whispered, her hips rolling beneath Sebastian's penetration of her rear as his tongue lashed at her sex, curled around her clit, and sucked it into his mouth.

Broken breaths, strangled moans, escaped her. She arched into each decadent caress of his lips, his tongue, his finger pressing inside the forbidden entrance lower.

"'Bastian." Shane's voice was strangled, his muscles raging with tension as he lifted his upper body, waiting until Sebastian's head lifted. "Fuck her. Now."

Alyssa jerked, crying out as the explicit demand sent a power punch of sensation racing to her vagina. Juices spilled, rushing to slicken and prepare her, his head lowered again to catch the rush of her response.

"'Bastian!" she cried out when he seemed to become lost in catching each taste of her again. "Please. Now." He didn't let up, his tongue rimming her entrance as her hips lifted to him again. "Fuck me. Now. . . ."

He came to his knees so quickly she was shocked. His fingers wrapping around the base of his cock as his expression tightened, his gaze moving to Shane.

Whatever he saw there convinced him to move closer as Shane lifted her knee, spreading her thighs farther as he brought it back, allowing him to watch.

Alyssa watched the broad shaft with its dark, engorged crest as Sebastian released it. He slid his hands beneath her rear and lifted her closer until the thick, blunt head of his cock eased into position.

She was shaking, Alyssa realized. Anticipation was racing through her, spilling more of the slick warmth from her sex.

"Watch, baby," Shane whispered at her side. "See how he'll fit."

It wasn't possible. . . .

He pressed against the opening, flaring it open, parting her flesh as the sense of stretching heat began to build, became a flame as he worked the head in and out of her with slow rocking movements.

Shane caught her hands as she reached for Sebastian, holding them above her head.

"Watch, baby," he crooned, his voice tight. "Look how your pretty pussy parts for him." She shuddered in reaction to his words, to the sight of Sebastian's cock head disappearing inside her again.

Just the crown, nothing more. And she needed more.

"Please," she whimpered, watching, anticipation tightening her as he sank inside again.

She tightened on the small penetration. As the wide crest entered her a wave of sensation tightened her vagina and stole her breath.

Sebastian stilled, his hands bunching in the cheeks of her rear where they lifted her to meet his thrust. "It's not enough. Shane, please, fuck me—"

"'Bastian, no," Shane suddenly growled.

Too late. A broken groan left Sebastian's lips before his hips jerked, pushing his cock deeper, spearing past the hymen that tore at the first thrust.

He pulled back quickly, ignoring Shane's curses now, and pushed inside her again, again; each sharp increment he added as he pushed inside her only amped the level of sensation inside her. Three hard thrusts and Alyssa felt each burning stretch of untried flesh, of muscles unused to the intrusion, protesting even as more of her juices spilled and her body attempted to ease his way.

"Fuck!" 'Bastian groaned as he pushed in to the hilt, the fiery intrusion dragging a sharp cry from her lips. Her hips arched into him, the sharp sensation against her clit as his body met it melting her further. "Fuck. Shane, she's too fucking tight."

Perspiration gleamed on 'Bastian's shoulders, the side of his face, as he stared at the point where his body was now a part of hers.

So much a part of her. Painful pleasure was lancing her, demanding, intoxicating.

She rolled her hips against him.

"God, 'Lyssa, stay still," he groaned.

"I can't." She could barely breathe, let alone speak.

Dizzy from the sensations, she jerked her gaze to where Shane rose to his knees as though to leave the bed.

He couldn't leave. She wouldn't let him. Reaching out, her fingers tried to wrap around the base of his cock. Curling around it, the touch brought him to a stop. Clenching her fingers on him, she lifted her head just enough to catch the pre-cum glistening at the head against her tongue.

Before she could draw back, the throbbing crest pressed between her lips, following her as her head lowered more comfortably, her lips tightening around it, sucking it. He filled her mouth, the engorged crown throbbing in demand as she tightened her lips around it.

"Ah hell," Shane groaned.

He couldn't bear it. Fuck, he was dying. Her mouth tightened on his dick with hungry need, making his gaze unfocused, his need ravaging his self-control.

Sebastian was moving, thrusting inside her as her mouth destroyed Shane.

"Fuck her," he gritted out, dying inside her mouth. "Hurry, Sebastian. . . ."

Make her come. Throw her into orgasm before he couldn't take it anymore.

Pulling her lips from his cock, Alyssa gave him no more than a moment's respite.

"Both of you," she demanded, her voice filled with a pinnacle of arousal that he had to close his eyes to deny. "Please, Shane. Both of you."

"Alyssa." His eyes opened to see Sebastian easing from her, her juices clinging to his cock, her body looking far too small, too fragile, for one of their cocks pushing inside her, let alone both.

"Shut the fuck up, Shane," Sebastian growled. "She's too far gone. We pushed her too far."

Pushed her too far. Played with her sweet body without taking her, without giving her what she needed sooner.

Lying back as Shane watched, Sebastian drew her over her his body, easing her above him, spreading her thighs over his hips and pulling her down.

Her head tipped back, a long-drawn-out wail leaving her lips as he rocked her, holding her hips and easing her into a rhythm that would only make her pussy tighter, her grip hotter around his cock.

Once he impaled her fully Shane was already behind her, the tube of lubrication Sebastian handed him smeared over his fingers. Watching as his cousin parted the pretty globes of her ass, Shane pressed his fingers to the rear opening.

As he watched her response shiver through her body, her cries spilling to the room with a touch to her anus stole more of his common sense. After taking her first with one finger, penetrating and easing the tiny entrance, he then took her with two.

"Ah fuck," Sebastian snarled as Shane watched two fingers fucking her, scissoring apart inside her, preparing her for his cock, for the penetration that would be far wider. "She's so tight I'm dying. So fucking tight . . ."

Easing his fingers free, Shane moved behind her, his hands actually shaking as he gripped his cock and pressed it against the narrow entrance.

And watched.

Sebastian had flipped the low light next to the bed on allowing them to see her response to their touch. Shane watched as her flesh flared open with the pressure against it, parting, flowering over the slow invasion as he pushed closer, rocking against her to penetrate the hot depths of her rear.

Slowly, so fucking tight he was dying from the pleasure surrounding each inch of his dick as her body eased and began accepting him.

Shane watched. Watched his iron-hard erection part her, stretch her. Her inner flesh contracted, drawing him deeper, deeper, until he passed the ultra-tight ring of muscle and sank inside her ass with a guttural moan of exquisite pleasure.

Alyssa's cry below him of both pleasure and pain speared inside him, rocking him to the core with the sharp whip of ecstasy threatening to burn him alive. She was trembling between them, her flesh milking his cock continually, threatening to draw free the explosion building in his balls and a release he suspected would destroy the man he was and leave only the man who lived for this woman.

Suspended between agony and ecstasy, Alyssa felt Shane and Sebastian pause. Held between them, her cheek resting against Sebastian's shoulder, her fingers digging into his hard biceps, she felt each thick, throbbing shaft inside her. She was stretched to the point that so much as a hair's thickness more would have sent the point she was riding between the ultimate pain and the ultimate pleasure too far into the realm of agony.

Poised as she was on that border, her body hummed with the sensations, demanding more, demanding they move, that they push her instead into that realm of rapture waiting ahead.

The first shift came from Shane. As he groaned, the smallest thrust had the whirlwind gathering inside her again.

"I'm dying," he whispered behind her, his hands clenching her hips as he drew back, just a little, then sank inside her again. "Sweet baby. That's it. Tighten on my dick just like that, baby."

She jerked in his grip, her hips shifting, more sensation dragging a cry from her lips.

"That's it, sweets," Sebastian groaned. "Let more of those juices fall. So fucking wet," he bit off. "So slick and ready. Can I fuck you now, baby?"

He moved.

Shane sank inside her as Sebastian drew nearly free before working the length inside her again. "Ah fuck. Tight. I won't last long, siren."

As he sank fully inside her Shane eased back. A second later he was pushing inside her again, the lashing sensations flaying her senses and causing more of her juices to spill.

Slowly, working in, out, they began moving. Each thrust and retreat sent dizzying waves of pleasure rushing through her, crashing through her senses and pushing her higher into the vortex gathering with more strength than ever before.

"Not enough," she panted, barely able to think, to talk. "Faster . . . please . . ."

"Easy, love," Shane groaned, desperate to hold back, to ensure this act was an unrelenting pleasure rather than pain.

"No." She ground her forehead against Sebastian's chest. "Fuck me. Fuck me harder. God, please . . ."

As though she'd lit a match to gasoline, the response was instant.

Control shattered, fracturing his determined efforts immediately.

Harder.

Faster.

They moved inside her, fucking her with smooth, practiced thrusts that kept her flying higher, stretched her and burned, and lit a fuse she had no idea existed inside her senses.

She felt the waves gathering. Fear began to coil at the edge of the pleasure, the arcs of so much sensation gathering, tightening.

"I have you, baby," Sebastian groaned, his arms holding her, steadying her as she felt them racing through the same storm she was within. "I have you, siren. Let go. Just let go; I swear I'll hold you right here."

As though she needed no more than that, Alyssa let herself fly. Emotion, pleasure and rapture, ecstasy and sweet, pleasure-pain intensity, began whipping around her. Their thrusts increased, moving inside her, triggering each level of sensation

Spasms tore through her body. Ecstasy ruptured her mind, her heart, shot to her very spirit, and gathered in intensity before exploding again. She could feel her lovers, their final thrusts harder, their cocks swelling further in that second before her world dissolved.

Heat exploded in the depths of her vagina, in her rear, pulses of fiery blasts as their semen filled her. Each explosive release added to the ecstasy whipping through her. She felt so much, too much, but through it all, a pleasure as violent as any storm she'd heard of nature producing, an inferno sweeping through her, laying waste to any preconceived notions of what this release should be. And through it, Shane and Sebastian centered her. Anchored. She felt those anchors; the hearts and souls of the men who had taken her there holding her between them. She couldn't become lost in the merging. There was no way to become lost.

They held her.

Eased her.

Spilling their own pleasure inside her, taking hers as they flew into the storm with her, still they held her.

Possessed her.

Loved her.

They bound her to them even as she felt them becoming bound.

In a world where love had become a commodity, they found the treasure it was meant to be in each other.

One the loss of which would destroy them all, forever.

✦✦✦

With each week, each touch, each wildly explosive possession of her lithe body and incredible sensuality, each day spent laughing with her, testing her wit and often finding themselves bested by innocent gray eyes and a surprisingly sharp little mind, Shane and Sebastian felt their world balancing in a way it never had before.

She balanced them.

Just as she balanced their lives. Alyssa refused to spend every waking moment with them. Through the week, she demanded they leave her from morning until late afternoon. She needed to breathe without them a few hours a day, she informed them. Sebastian knew the decision for what it was, though. As young as she was, Alyssa needed a measure of independence, time to do the things women did without feeling as though she were abandoning them.

At first, they hadn't thought much of that decision. It seemed, though, she was far wiser than they in enforcing it though. Because it forced them to find something to do with their time that didn't include spy games, parties, or hangovers.

The effect wasn't seen just by themselves, either, or felt just by their hearts. The maturity and lessening of quick tempers were immediately recognized by friends and family they saw during those hours. Their refusal to take further courier assignments from the agency they'd worked for for nearly three years was a surprise to the agents overseeing them. Their interest in De Loren business affairs that their grandfather had been pushing them to take was quietly noticed by their grandfather, Fernando De Loren, as well as Sebastian's parents and brother, Lucien.

As summer deepened Shane and Sebastian more or less moved into the apartment with Alyssa. Through the week they helped

Sebastian's brother with the prized horses he bred as well as several business interests they owned in Barcelona. The rest of the time Shane and Sebastian spent with Alyssa.

Quiet evenings were spent talking, learning each other's dreams for the future, their hopes and fears.

Alyssa hadn't dreamed of college and a career, they learned. She dreamed of loving and being loved, of a house full of laughing children, and a life rich and filled with caring for them, as well as Shane and Sebastian.

She didn't vow her love every day, but neither did they. The words weren't spoken, but neither Shane nor Sebastian was in doubt as to who would father those babies.

In Alyssa they found a contentment they hadn't known was possible. A peace that filled them, and laughter in the smallest things.

In Shane and Sebastian Alyssa found her freedom. Secure in the knowledge she wasn't alone or unprotected, she found the balance she had been searching for to be able to look to the future and know the dreams she'd had could survive Margot's machinations and too-strong personality.

She loved her mother. It was Margot who had taught her that loving someone didn't mean the words had to be said with each breath, just felt with each beat of the heart. She was harsh, uncompromising, but what no one ever saw in Margot Hampstead was her complete dedication to her husband and child.

That dedication wasn't always kind, but Alyssa had never doubted it, just as she never doubted her mother's love.

What she did doubt was Margot's ability to ever fully let Alyssa go. Neither of her parents had other family now that their parents were gone. They had no brothers, sisters, or nieces and nephews. They had Alyssa. And she hoped that one day her children would give her parents more to focus on than just their daughter. Enough to focus on that having two sons-in-law wouldn't be impossible to accept.

As the second month of her vacation rolled by, Alyssa didn't worry about promises, she didn't worry about what would come next, because she had no intention of leaving Barcelona alone. If she left at all.

Shane and Sebastian had already made their plans. The purchase of the two-story apartment building in Alexandria, Virginia, had been made. Their agreement that Sebastian would take the position of her lover to her friends and family while Shane stepped back from the limelight until her father's political career was realized. They would ensure Margot's cooperation by bringing in contributors to the Hampstead political campaign who would more or less ensure Davis Allen Hampstead's political dreams were brought to fruition.

Quietly the cousins made their plans, saying little to anyone, even Alyssa. As though their hearts were so much a part of each other that they had no fears of the future together, they found themselves simply enjoying the happiness that filled them.

A happiness they should have realized could never come so easily. Their friends saw it, Lucien De Loren watched it with somber knowledge, and their grandfather, Fernando, waited for the fall he knew was coming.

Such love, such complete inner peace in one person, never came without first paying a hefty price. The world simply didn't work that way. The greater the love, the deeper the love, the higher the price demanded in compensation.

And, Fernando knew, the price his grandsons and their lover paid would be exceptionally high. What he hadn't expected was the price the rest of the family would pay.

## 6

Shane and Sebastian entered the De Loren hacienda with its gracefully arched doorways and centuries-old elegance before dawn that morning. For decades De Lorens had resided within its walls, their wealth and carefully invested fortunes overseen with an eye to each future generation and the changes of the world's financial landscape.

They had weathered wars, upheavals, rebellions, and personal losses that would have destroyed other families. The De Loren patriarchs had always believed in preparation, though. In both personal and private defenses as well as political strengths.

The summons the cousins had received before dawn had brought them from Alyssa's bed for the early-morning meeting as suspicion tightened inside them with each mile covered. They knew, the closer they came, that somehow Alyssa lay at the center of this meeting.

Moving through the large, expansive rooms to the back of the hacienda, Sebastian knocked at the heavy wood door of his grandfather's office firmly, his shoulders tight with tension.

"Enter," the old man's voice called out, as arrogant as ever, but now with a hint of anger as well.

As he glanced at his cousin Sebastian's lips tightened at the certainty that this meeting would bring nothing good. Shane's knowledge was reflected in the deep blue of his eyes, in the implacable expression he too carried.

Opening the door, Sebastian stepped inside, almost pausing at the sight of his father, Alberto, his brother, Lucien, and Shane's brother, Murphy.

"Gang's all here," Shane muttered behind him, his voice low enough that only Sebastian heard him.

"Hmm." Sebastian could only imagine what awaited them.

"Sit." Fernando waved his hand to the two red leather chairs in front of the desk that sat prominently in front of the high, wide windows overlooking the rich green pastures that spread out from the hacienda.

Fernando De Loren was in his eighties, not that he was willing to give in to age. His black hair was silver now, his dark brown gaze eagle sharp, and his mind just as calculating as it had ever been. That mind often gave Sebastian and his cousin pause.

"It's early, Grandfather," Sebastian stated as he and Shane took their seats. "Let's get this over with."

"Early?" Fernando's silver brows nearly lifted to his hairline. "No more than a few months before you were still partying at the time you were texted. Or making your rounds about the globe in your quest for your next adventure. Now it's early?"

The mocking surprise Sebastian decided to let slide.

"Nevertheless, now it's early," he stated. "What couldn't wait until we arrived tomorrow to help Lucien with the new colts?"

Lucien's horse-breeding enterprise was a highly profitable venture for the De Loren family.

"This is what could not wait." The large manila envelopes were tossed to them, his grandfather's anger glittering momentarily in his brown eyes. "Be certain to read the letter included, if you don't mind."

Opening the envelope and pulling the contents free, Sebastian felt everything inside him explode in rage. A rage he kept carefully contained, silent, as he stared at the eight-by-ten photos.

They were taken from inside the apartment Landra had given Alyssa for the summer. Explicit, damning photos of the three of them. In each, Alyssa featured prominently between the cousins. Naked, her expression tight with sensuality and such love for them that even now he felt humbled by it. Humbled and filled with a murderous rage that anyone would invade their privacy in such a vile way.

"What is the meaning of this?" Lifting his gaze to his grandfather, he could feel the violent fury gathering in him.

"Read the letter, Sebastian," his father demanded, his compassion in no doubt. "It explains everything."

Pulling the single sheet of paper from below the photos, he read it. He had to reread it to be certain he'd read correctly.

*It would be a shame if these pictures of the eighteen-year-old senator's daughter were sent to various porn sites that would undoubtedly pay a generous sum for them. It is understood that the De Loren political interests would be adversely affected once the men with her are identified.*

*All association with the girl will cease immediately. She will return to the United States, in no doubt that the grandsons of Fernando De Loren have been doing no more than enjoying a summer romance. Should they, at any time, be found or suspected to be involved or attempting to become involved with Alyssa Hampstead again, then the pictures enclosed will be sent to the above-mentioned sites.*

*A payment will be made, monthly, to the overseas account listed on the back, in the amount stated. Should a payment be late, the pictures will be sent to those sites.*

*At no time will either Shane Connor or Sebastian De Loren be seen in her company. Should it be learned the authorities were contacted or any investigation into the demand be made, then the pictures will be sent.*

*Decide for yourself if allowing such to happen is in your political best interests.*

Sebastian could feel the world crashing around him, destroying him. The implications of the letter as well as the pictures couldn't be ignored, nor could the danger to Alyssa.

It would destroy her, her family, and everything she knew. The cyberworld and journalists far and wide would spread the news of her humiliation with such a public announcement of it there would be no doubt she'd be destroyed.

With her shy innocence it would break her before she ever had a chance to realize what was happening around her. It would break all of them. What it would do to all three families would be catastrophic.

"The family will ensure the payments are made as demanded until the blackmailer is identified," Sebastian's father, Alberto, stated as Shane tried to assimilate the hell he could feel his life becoming. "Landra has volunteered to make the first payments, with your parents, Shane, making the second, I and Sebastian's mother, then your other aunts, to Fernando, while we quietly attempt to learn who this is."

"The demands will be followed precisely," Shane's grandfather stated with no room for argument. "The sum we will pay to protect this woman who is nothing to us. No blood to us—"

"She's something to us," Shane stated, fighting to hold back his fury. "She's everything to us."

"Then you forgot, Grandson, how easily such a weakness can be used against you." Fernando slapped the table furiously. "You share your women, and I have warned you repeatedly of the impact of such a thing. I have warned you how easy it will be for others to use this against you or the lover your hearts grew fond of. And you refused to heed my warnings, did you not? Now, this threatens not just her father's political aspirations, but the political connections of this family as well. Do the two of you forget our financial stability is directly tied to our ability to export the products we ship to the U.S.? Exports that took us decades to implement? Do you think we will hold on to the favor we've acquired with U.S. politicians in recent years should her father's rise to the White House be destroyed?"

"We'll return immediately and explain—"

"You will not." Outrage filled Fernando's voice. "Read the letter again, Grandson. Does it say you will return and explain anything? It says from the hour the sun has risen the demand is in effect. Why do you think you were called here at such an early hour?"

Shane could feel the rage building, burning, and could find no outlet to release it.

"I had two of my own people waiting when you left," Lucien said then, "women with the training and experience to enter the apartment and gather all your belongings, as well as pictures or items that could be used to prove your association with her, once she slept. A letter will be left informing her the summer is over and she's to return to her home. Once we've neutralized this threat and we have the negatives and copies in hand, then you can decide if you will attempt to explain this to her."

"I can't do that." Shane lifted his head before Sebastian could protest. "I won't do that to her. We can get to her without anyone seeing—"

"There are cameras in the bloody apartment, Shane, or didn't you catch on to that fact?" his brother, Murphy, snapped with furious outrage. "For God's sake, you can't go anywhere near her. Her plane leaves tomorrow. You will stay the hell away from her. If you care for her as you claim, then you will not risk what the release of those pictures would do to her."

"This will destroy her." Sebastian came from his seat, denial racing through him, erupting with such force that he felt it exploding through him. "You don't know what this will do to her!"

"And what will those pictures do to her if they're released?" Lucien argued. "Think of that, Sebastian. What will happen then?

Your belongings have already been collected. Everything. The letter has been left on the chest in the bedroom. Let her go for now. It's the kindest thing you can do."

"And what do you know of kindness, Sebastian?" he sneered back at the other man. "You care for nothing and no one outside those fucking horses and the wealth you and Fernando watch with such painstaking care. Do not lecture me on kindness."

Lucien stared back at him for long moments in silence, his arms crossed over his chest, the black shirt he wore straining over his biceps as he obviously fought to restrain his own anger.

"Sebastian, you are my brother, and I do this for love of you, not that woman who is the center of this strife. I could cast her to this person who is so determined to drain this family because of your love for her. Because of you and Shane, because you are important to us, we will attempt to stop this threat. But we can do nothing without your cooperation."

Without their cooperation. Without their willingness to stay away from her. Without their ability to stand back as they felt her pain ripping their souls apart.

"She's eighteen years old. She has no idea the depth of the men dedicating themselves to her. . . . ," Murphy began.

"You are fucking ignorant when it comes to that woman," Shane informed him, the disgust and fury in his tone unmistakable. "You have no idea, Murphy, what this will do to her." He stared back at his brother, agony racing through him. "You have no idea the pain doing this will bring her. Or how deeply we'll feel it."

"De Loren males do not love; they become soul bound," Fernando said softly, heavily.

Swinging to him, Shane saw the knowledge and the incredible regret on his grandfather's face.

Regret? Shane's soul was fucking ripping in half and all they could do was regret it. God help him. This would destroy her. It would destroy them.

"If all my wealth would change this decision you must make, then I would give it gladly," Fernando swore, and the truth of that statement was in his eyes. "I cannot fix this. For three days we have fought to find a way and there is none. Give me a solution, Shane," he said kindly. "And I will do whatever it takes."

"Shoot us now," Sebastian whispered. "Kill us quickly, Grandfather, for that will be far preferable to the long, slow death that awaits us now."

"Sebastian, wait," his father protested as he threw the chair back with such force it fell to the floor.

Stalking to the open bar at one side of the library, he grabbed one of the bottles of liquor—he didn't care what it was—then grabbed another for his cousin. Sober, there was no way they could deal with the hell they knew was about to descend upon them. No other way to numb themselves to the overwhelming pain and loneliness facing them.

All their plans were exploding around them, destroying everything they had been, every dream they hadn't realized they'd had until Alyssa. It was stealing their souls and they had no way of fighting it.

For the first time in their lives, they were truly and completely helpless.

✦✦✦✦

Alyssa awoke the second time that morning, some sense of rage racing through her with swift, certain agony. It was there, then gone, leaving only the certainty that something was wrong.

Reaching for her cell phone next to the bed, she quickly hit the contact list for Shane's or Sebastian's number, to call and make certain they were all right. Their contact listing wasn't there. Moving to the message icon, she pulled it up. She would just text them. But they were gone from there as well along with all the loving, sometimes silly little messages they had sent her.

It was all gone.

Jumping from the bed, she all but ran to the bathroom where she'd left the test she'd taken that morning, certain one of them would find it when they returned. There, on the counter where she'd left it, was a folded piece of paper instead, the strong scrawl of her name on it identifiable. Only Shane or Sebastian used such a defined way of writing.

She moved to it carefully, her hands shaking, her chest tightening with each breath as she picked it up and opened the letter.

*The summer's over. Hope you have a nice flight home.*

Have a nice flight home?

She wasn't aware of the cry that slipped past her lips, so filled with agony, with the explosion of pain that stole her breath, her strength.

Hope you have a nice flight home?

"No. . . ." She read the words again, half-formed sobs on every breath now. "Shane? Sebastian? Don't do this to me. . . . No. Don't do this to me. . . ."

It was overwhelming. Stealing her breath and her senses as well as her strength as she sank to the marble floor, sobs tearing from her as she fought the reality of it.

"I'll wake up," she sobbed, clutching the letter to her chest. "I'll wake up. Oh God, please let me wake up."

She was dying inside. Alyssa could feel it, Like a slow wave of destruction. She was dying inside and there was nothing she could do to stop it. It raced through her heart, ripping it apart piece by piece before striking at her very soul.

"Don't do this to me," she sobbed, leaning her head against the tile wall as the force of the destruction left nothing but ragged, gaping wounds through her senses. "Don't do this to us." Her hand pressed to her stomach, to the child the test had revealed existed inside her. "Please. Please. Don't do this to us. . . ."

The summer was over, the note had stated.

The summer wasn't the only thing dying.

⊹⊹⊹⊹⊹

Lucien's men were waiting for them. As the explosion of agony reverberated inside them the bottles of liquor, only half-empty, were tossed aside as Shane and Sebastian raced from the sitting room they'd retreated to.

Lucien and Murphy stood silently as the dozen men blocked the door, catching their brothers when they would have run to the woman Fernando informed them would reach out to them.

Soul bound, their grandfather called it.

When the other half of their souls called out to them, they would have no choice but to run to her, to ease her pain, to destroy all three of them when the terms of the blackmail weren't heeded.

Rage erupted from the two younger men. Such black, violent fury that to hold them back Lucien's men were finally forced to knock them out. Twelve men, and the fury that met them would have overwhelmed them if the younger men had remained conscious.

"They would kill us to get to her." The manager of the estate turned to Lucien to excuse the choice he'd made and ordered his men to carry through. "You knew there would be no other way to stop them."

Lucien merely nodded and watched as his brother and cousin were lifted gently by several of the men and taken back to the room. Shane was placed on the couch in the sitting room, Sebastian placed in the bed.

Behind him, Lucien could hear his mother sobbing, her heart breaking at the choice they were forced to make to protect not just the girl but Shane and Sebastian as well.

"They will never forgive us!" his mother cried as his father held her from going to her son. "Never, Alberto. He will never forgive what we have done to him. Never."

Their mother knew her sons well, Lucien thought heavily. He had no doubt if Shane and Sebastian completely lost that woman then there would be no forgiveness for any of them.

"I managed to purchase a ticket on her flight," Murphy informed him, his voice edged with grief. "Shane will return home as well, I'm certain. They will not be able to remain in each other's company and stay away from her as well."

Lucien nodded silently before rubbing at the back of his neck.

Fernando had warned them; he just hadn't believed the old man. Yet his grandfather had known that the moment Alyssa Hampstead realized her lovers weren't returning her pain would call them back to her.

"Landra has Jed working to trace the overseas account number," Murphy continued. "Hopefully, we will resolve this soon."

Lucien knew better. His contacts from the CIA had been working on the cameras for over twenty-four hours. They'd managed to get into the remote configurations but still hadn't managed to trace where the digital content was going. Whoever was behind the blackmail knew their electronics. No doubt, the safeguards on the overseas account would be just as difficult to trace once the funds began moving.

The problem was, the funds hadn't yet begun moving. Until they had, they didn't have a hope in hell.

"I'll send Shane home on the De Loren plane," he promised. "Have you heard from your contact in D.C.?"

"Everything in the Hampstead residence is quiet." Murphy shrugged. "To my knowledge, they know nothing of the pictures. If they did, every agency the federal government possesses would be called in."

Lucien sighed heavily. At least the blackmailer had kept his word and not sent the pictures to Alyssa's parents. Perhaps she would escape this with only the pain of losing the men she loved. They did for their brothers, Shane reminded himself. He only prayed it didn't break all of them finally and emotionally before it ended.

If they were lucky, if there was any mercy for Shane and Sebastian, then this threat would soon be over.

Hampstead Residence
Alexandria, Virginia
United States

The envelope, when it arrived, had seemed so unassuming. Margot opened it at her husband's desk while he went over e-mail. After she pulled the pages inside free, it took long moments before she could actually believe what she was looking at. That the lurid, pornographic images actually included her daughter.

Her child.

Had it been pictures of merely one lover, perhaps Margot's heart wouldn't have stopped beating for a moment. Maybe the all-consuming rage that filled her could have been held back.

"Margot?" Davis asked, concerned, moments later.

How had he known the shock racing through her? The pain and fear that sliced through a lifetime of icy control.

She stared at the pictures, shock, outrage, fury racing through her at the sight of her daughter, her child. Alyssa was no more than a child, only eighteen and so very sheltered. Who would do this to her?

Two men. Two men with her child? Taking her as though she were some whore to be used without concern or care?

She was shaking. She could feel her hands shaking, her fingers curling in fury as Davis took one of the pictures.

"Oh my God!" He threw the only one he had taken. Threw it from him as though the paper itself were evil. "What the fuck is this?"

Margot stared at the letter accompanying it, handed it to him, then stared down at the second picture. Not at what those vile creatures were doing to her child, but at her child's expression. And if Margot were the sort to weep, she would have wept for Alyssa.

Love.

Love transformed Alyssa's features, softened them further, and emphasized the innocence and pleasure that filled her face and eyes.

She couldn't look at the others.

The pictures were no more than proof; the letter said it all.

*Having been informed of this degrading affair by the two young men involved, it is my greatest regret to include these pictures as proof of your daughter's attempts to coerce my grandsons into a relationship they find both distasteful and humiliating. It is their wish that Miss Hampstead have no further contact with them. She is not to call them, seek them out, or approach them if circumstances should find them in the same place at the same time. Should she do so, the enclosed pictures will be released to all media in America and Europe and Internet sites pertaining to such matters. I would hope you would ask your daughter, in light of these intentions, to ensure she does not cling to the hope they wish to have any further contact with her. Such perversions and degrading carnal activities they have found abhorrent, and though they would be greatly distressed to see their own identities revealed along with hers, they are still determined that all pictures will be released should she not follow their wishes. You may contact me at the below number as their chosen emissary in this matter.*

"I knew not to allow this trip," Margot whispered, taking the blame herself because she had known better. She remembered clearly the many times she'd attempted to convince Alyssa to vacation in the states for her first trip alone.

But Summer was in Madrid and the Bennett girl was in the

apartment building with Alyssa. Each time Margot had talked to Giana's parents they had mentioned how Alyssa and Gia were having such a wonderful time together.

Each time Margot had spoken to Alyssa, though, she'd sensed something more than what her daughter was telling her. She'd be regaled with tales of all the tourist sites, how crowded the beaches were, how wonderful Landra Collier's apartment was. Friends she'd made, the beauty of the city. Everything but a potential summer lover, let alone two lovers.

Two lovers. Not young men, either. These were men, nearly mature, clearly ages more experienced than her child.

"My God!" Davis repeated, reading the letter again before looking up at Margot. "Alyssa would never initiate such a relationship."

No, Alyssa would not. Margot might not know the two men involved, but she would before much longer.

"She's due home in several hours." Rage was vibrating through her. "I'll know what happened and I'll know who they are before the morning's over."

To even suggest that Alyssa would initiate such a thing was preposterous. She doubted her daughter knew what a ménage was, let alone how to begin such an affair. But she would make damned certain her daughter understood that there would never be any contact with them again. Even better, once Margo learned their identities she'd make certain they felt her wrath.

+ + + +

The flight from Spain was uneventful. She hadn't slept on the flight. Each time she closed her eyes she'd seen Shane and Sebastian the day they'd given her the necklace with the sapphire hanging between two beautiful diamonds. She hadn't taken it off since they'd given it to her and made the promise that they were bound to her.

They had broken that bond. Everything had been taken. All their possessions, their numbers from her phone and the text messages, and somehow, they'd taken the chain with its three gems from around her neck. In stealing the necklace, in stealing every memory she had of them, they had broken the promises they'd made.

Stepping into the house as her father's butler took care of getting her luggage from the car, she moved to his office, where he'd directed her.

She just wanted to go to bed and go to sleep. She felt ravaged inside, broken in so many pieces that she had no idea how to deal with life now.

Knocking on the office door, she stepped inside a second later and knew the day wasn't quite over. As much as she wished she could block out the world, she would first have to deal with Margot.

"You asked to see me when I returned?" Stepping to her father's desk, she stood before him, determined to get through whatever awaited her now.

Silence greeted her. For some reason her parents' faces lost their expressions of fury. They simply stared back at her now as though uncertain what to say to her.

Margot sighed heavily. "Oh, Alyssa, what have you let them do to you?"

Alyssa didn't think she'd ever heard such a tone of pain and regret in her mother's voice, but that observation was quickly overshadowed by the implication of what she'd said.

Her gaze locked with her mother's pale one, and in it Alyssa saw a bitter anger that would have terrified her before she left for Spain.

"How did you find out?" She stood before them, unashamed. She wasn't ashamed, just so very, very tired and broken inside.

Margot moved stiffly. Lifting the envelope from the desk as Alyssa watched her father jerk from his chair and pace to the other side of the office. Accepting it, she opened the envelope and pulled the contents free.

She'd already been ravaged. Everything inside her was already broken, her heart and soul devastated by Shane and Sebastian's betrayal. Only to face yet another blow.

She did so stoically. She looked at each picture, wanting to see, to know the brutal truth of the lengths they were willing to go to in distancing themselves from her. When she read the note that accompanied the pictures, she sat down abruptly in the chair behind her.

The strength in her knees abandoned her. The tears she swore she would hold back for the baby's sake she lost temporary control of. Her breath hitched as they spilled from her eyes. Silent tears— the sobs had been silenced in Spain—several hitting the letter before she finished it.

"Well then," she whispered, and tucked the letter back into the envelope with the pictures. "I guess I didn't see that coming."

She carefully folded the flap before rising to her feet and facing her parents.

"They had no reason to worry," she assured her parents. "Neither do you. There will be no attempt to contact them."

It was all she could do to stand before them. Why had Shane and Sebastian done this to her? What point was there in sending her parents such horrible photos or such threats?

"Alyssa, what possessed you?" Margot's voice was rough, the barely banked fury resonating in it. "Where was your common sense?"

Where was her common sense?

She shook her head wearily. "I'm so sorry, Mother," she whispered painfully. "Sorrier than you could ever know. But I have no excuses—"

"I didn't ask for a fucking excuse, girl!" Margot snapped, her voice rising as she leaned forward, her hands braced on the desk. "I asked what happened to your common sense?"

What had happened to it? What had happened to her heart and soul?

"I don't know," she admitted softly. "I just don't know. . . ."

Turning from her parents, she moved slowly to the office door once again and left her parents standing, watching her, as she left the room. It took everything she had to walk through the house and climb the stairs to her bedroom. Every ounce of strength she possessed just to get to that last sanctuary she had to hide.

Closing the door behind her, she made it to the bed, crawled in fully clothed, and pulled the comforter around her.

Margot, being Margot, of course had to follow her. God, her mother was like a bulldog with a bone.

Entering the bedroom, she stood at Alyssa's bed for long moments before pulling the chair that sat next to the nightstand closer and sitting down heavily.

"Alyssa . . ."

"I won't discuss it." She couldn't discuss it. She couldn't let herself speak of it; she couldn't let herself remove the shield she'd placed around the memories long enough to make sense of anything right now.

"What did they do to you?" The faint horror in her mother's tone did nothing to cover the rage. "What did you let them do to you, Alyssa?"

She had let them cut her heart and soul from her body. She'd left both in Spain, searching endlessly, sobbing out in agony at the destruction the cousins had left in their wake.

"I'll be okay," she promised, her hand lying on her stomach beneath the comforter, the child resting there her only certainty that she hadn't imagined the months she'd spent in their arms. "I'm just so tired. I just need to sleep. Please, just let me sleep." And she hoped when she awoke she'd learn it was all just a very, very bad dream.

She'd awaken in their arms, their warmth surrounding her, their promise still suspended from a chain about her neck. Everything would be okay. It was just a very bad dream.

". . . just a very bad dream."

Margot heard the faint words as shock resounded through her entire system. The chill that swept over her shook her to the core and enraged her at the same time.

This wasn't her daughter. She looked like her, but she wasn't the girl who had left for Spain three months before. And she wasn't the daughter who had feared her mother's wrath. There was no fear left in Alyssa. There was nothing left inside her. Not fear, not the dreams that always had filled her eyes, or the emotions she always had allowed to get the better of her.

Bleak, ravaged pain was all she'd seen in her daughter's eyes.

And in that moment Margot knew a regret that sliced open her heart. This gentle, sensitive soul she'd never believed she knew how to love, had actually been the one person she truly loved, clear to her soul.

## 7

EIGHTEEN WEEKS LATER

The pain was like nothing she had ever known in her life. It brought her from a deep sleep, from dreams of Barcelona, of the summer sun and Shane's and Sebastian's touch. Whispered promises, their voices gentle, filled with passion. From the dreams that wrapped around her and gave her what little comfort could be found in the knowledge of betrayal to the agonizing, brutal waves of pain tearing through her stomach.

"No. God. Please!" she cried out, dragging herself from the bed as she looked down, the deep, dark stain of blood covering the cotton shorts she wore and running down her legs in rivulets.

"Momma!" Lurching for the door, the agonizing pain intensifying, Alyssa stumbled into the hall, sobs tearing from her chest as the pain and the realization of this final loss swept through her. "Oh God! Momma!"

She had made it along the landing to the stairs, her parents' suite just ahead when she collapsed, the next wave like a brutal punch to her abdomen, ripping through her with a force that sent her stumbling to the floor.

Clutching her stomach, Alyssa prayed. Whispered, desperate prayers even as she felt that life she'd gone to such lengths to protect ease from her.

She could hear her mother screaming, issuing orders with a desperation that barely registered as Alyssa felt herself being eased from the floor.

*I have you, baby.* The whisper barely registered, the male voice comforting as pain resonated through every particle of her body.

"Shane. Shane, help me," she sobbed. "Please help me."

*It's okay, Alyssa. I have you. . . .*

"Find Sebastian," she begged, staring up at him, her vision blurred, unable to see those beloved features. "Sebastian!"

She was screaming their names, the pain ripping through her, knowledge tearing her mind apart even as she felt as though her body were being torn apart.

She was losing their baby. The baby she'd fought to protect, whom she had married to protect. She couldn't lose her last link to them. She couldn't lose all she had left.

"Please . . ." Darkness edged her vision, moved swiftly through her, stealing her strength, her ability to understand the agony tearing at her.

But she felt them. For the first time in so long they were there, whispering through what was left of her soul.

"I love you!" she cried, sobbing in desperation, reaching out for them with everything inside her. "Please, please don't take him. Please. . . ."

But she felt him leaving her. Felt the baby she'd wanted more than anything in the world leaving her, just as his fathers had left her. Easing away and taking the last of the girl she had been, ripping away the last of her dreams.

"Shane, please . . . ," she whispered as consciousness eased from her. "Please don't take him . . . please. . . ."

Margot felt the tears falling from her own eyes as Davis' bodyguard, an Army medic, worked to save Alyssa as the physician rushed into the bedroom.

Stepping from the room, her hand covering her lips, silent sobs shaking her body, Margot fought the overwhelming rage, fought to keep the vow she'd made to her daughter. That she would never, for any reason, attempt to hurt the men who had fathered that baby. The men Alyssa still loved with what little was left of her ragged heart.

How long she stood there she didn't know. She couldn't stop crying, couldn't contain her own pain. When the doctor stepped from the bedroom, his expression was heavy with grief.

"She miscarried," he sighed heavily as Margot closed her eyes and felt Davis wrap his arms around her, drawing her to him. "She was about eighteen weeks along, Margot." His voice thickened. "The baby . . ." He cleared his throat. "The nurse is cleaning him up. I'm sure Alyssa will need closure. I'd like to perform a few tests, though."

"What happened?" It was all she could do to speak, to ask the question she knew her daughter would ask.

"I don't know." Dr. Brennan shook his head, his kindly eyes filled with distress. "I just don't know, Margot."

Margot's fingers clenched in Davis' shirt, a ragged cry escaping her lips.

"Margot, don't let her ignore this loss," Dr. Brennan advised her heavily. "Though to be honest, I don't know if we'll ever have Alyssa as she was, back."

Alyssa's physician had cared for her since she was a baby. He knew her, had seen her through childhood illnesses and a young woman's development. The girl he'd seen at the end of summer wasn't the same girl who had come to him before she left.

"How long before you'll know what happened?" Davis asked, and in his voice Margot heard the grief and the love he'd already extended to his grandson.

"A few days, no more," the doctor promised. "Just a few days."

A few days.

Alyssa was nearly five months along. Margot had felt her

daughter's child move as Alyssa held her hand to the slight mound of her stomach, felt its strength. And she'd seen hope in her daughter's eyes that hadn't been there the day she returned from Spain.

And now, that life they had been so looking forward to, was gone.

Alyssa wouldn't have the child she so desperately needed to hold the pain at bay. Margot wouldn't have the grandchild she'd found herself loving as she'd felt it moving beneath her palm.

Alyssa had screamed for the bastards who had given her that child, Margot thought. Screamed, begged them not to take her baby. To help her. And there was nothing Margot could do to make them pay she thought as she pulled from Davis and moved into her daughter's bedroom, to the grandchild she would never know, the child whose loss might be the final one that stole her child as well.

God help her, how would Alyssa bear this?

## SPAIN

The howl of enraged fury brought Lucien and Alberto racing through the house to the front room where Sebastian had been earlier.

Like the howls of an animal, demented from pain, the sound echoed through the halls again as he heard his mother cry Sebastian's name from upstairs.

Running to the front room, they found him standing; how he was standing, as drunk as he was, Lucien didn't know.

"Sebastian." Alberto gripped his shoulders, jerking him around before pulling back from his son in shock as Sebastian swung out at him with a powerful fist.

Sebastian went to his knees, his lips pulled back from his teeth as his head tipped back and another of those enraged howls of complete agony tore from his lips.

"Sebastian." Tabitha was racing for him, ignoring her husband as he tried to stop her, going to her knees in front of her younger son and gripping his face in desperate hands. "Sebastian. What is wrong? Tell me, now! Sebastian!"

Making it to his feet, he stumbled from her and fell into a table, his arm swiping out and throwing the lamp, the antique picture frames, to the floor.

"I'll never forgive you!" Turning on them, his eyes so black they were like the pits of hell, burning with rage. "Never." Going to his knees again, he stayed there, shaking his head, his breathing ragged. "Alyssa . . . ," her name whispered from his lips. "Siren—"

Toppling to the floor, he passed out, the weeks of drinking, of raging, catching up with him until there was no fight left within him.

Slowly, Tabitha crawled to her son, her arms going around him, her sobs destroying Lucien.

"Find out what happened to the girl," his father ordered, his voice heavy with fear. "Now, Lucien. Find out what happened to her."

Across the room Tabitha held her unconscious son to her, sobbing, whispering his name, crying the tears Sebastian couldn't shed for the woman he couldn't have.

## TEXAS

Trying to find Shane was an exercise in futility in most cases, Murphy knew, but when his brother had torn from the house, screaming the girl's name, his mother had sent Murphy to stop him. As drunk as the younger Connor was, breaking the terms of the blackmail could be easily done.

The sound of his voice when he'd slammed from the house, the broken, hollow rage, had been terrifying. The fact that he was actually able to start the Viper parked in the driveway and race from the house sent horror racing through Murphy.

The months-long drunk Shane and Sebastian had been on to keep themselves from Alyssa had appeared to be working but it couldn't continue. Until she stopped dying inside, Shane had explained, his voice slurred, when Murphy had raged at him. Just until he couldn't feel her dying inside.

Murphy's Viper sat waiting, parked next to where Shane's had sat. Jumping in it, he raced after his brother, certain he'd never catch up with him. When he did, the sight of the vehicle lying on its top, tires spinning, filled him with such gut-wrenching fear he swore he felt his strength bleeding from his body.

Until he saw his brother crawling from the wreckage. Stumbling to his feet, he was screaming something, and kicked the car only to fall to his knees when his booted foot connected with it.

Sliding to a stop, Murphy jumped from the car and raced to his brother, the sight of the blood on his face, his torn shirt, spurring him to ensure the damage wasn't life threatening.

"Shane, damn it, stand the fuck down," he snarled.

"I'm not one of your fucking soldiers." Shane rounded on him, animalistic rage pulling his expression into a snarl and roughening his voice with deadly fury. "Get her back!"

He was suddenly in Murphy's face, his fingers fisted in the shirt Murphy wore as he stared at his brother in shock.

"What?"

"Get her back!" Shane screamed, the grief on his face a terrible thing for Murphy to see. "Damn all of you. Damn you." He sank to his knees, staring at his hands, shaking his head slowly. "Damn all of you. Just get her back."

He couldn't feel her anymore. Her screams had echoed in his head, begging him to help her, only to be silenced just as quickly. And with the silence came the complete absence of her. That fragile connection Sebastian had called her siren song was just gone. Her song completely silent.

And he couldn't bear it. How was he supposed to live without that?

When he'd learned she'd married he'd nearly killed the bastard who had married her. He still wanted to kill . . . her husband and whoever had dared to separate him and Sebastian from her. Whoever had dared.

Lifting his head, he focused blearily on his brother.

"I'll kill him," he snarled. "Whoever did this. I'll kill him."

"Find him and I'll help you." Kneeling in front of him, Murphy placed his hand on his brother's shoulder, the vow all he had to give the baby brother he so treasured. "Find him, Shane, and I swear to you, I'll help you."

## 8

She slipped into the house, using skills she'd learned over the summer in Madrid. And she was quite proud of what she'd learned as well. She managed to sneak right into the senator's house without tripping alarms or alerting security. Just as her trainers had taught her to do.

God, she just loved the CIA. They rocked.

What didn't rock was the past months of unreturned calls and messages she'd sent to her only and best friend, Alyssa. Summer owed Alyssa and her parents more than her life. But to Alyssa she owed a debt that could never be repaid. One she'd sworn she would at least pay the interest on by ensuring her friend's protection.

They'd lost touch after Alyssa's visit to Madrid, though. It was partly her own fault, Summer knew. Her training had been hell. The limited amount of time she had to put into it without alerting her brothers to her new vocation had required more hours in the day than she'd had.

When she'd pulled her head out of her ass a month ago to realize Alyssa hadn't called, texted, or attempted to get hold of her in any way, she'd begun calling. To no avail. Then she'd begun texting. When Alyssa hadn't answered the texts Summer had come straight to D.C., once she'd landed in the States again.

She'd learned immediately that Alyssa had married.

Married. Without letting her best friend know? Oh, the girl was going to pay for that one. Summer was supposed to be her maid of honor, no matter what.

Moving quietly through the house and up the servants' stairs to the second floor, she paused at the doorway that led to the long open hall where the family suites were located. As she tilted her head, the sound of sobs barely drifting from the master suite caused Summer's heart to clench with dread.

That was Margot crying. The woman titled the Ice Bitch because of her supposed lack of emotion? Crying?

Of course Summer knew the title was undeserved, but still, Margot never had cried. Not in all the years Summer had known her.

Senator Hampstead was out of town, which meant Alyssa's mother should be alone. She'd better be alone anyway.

Moving to the door, Summer frowned. It was partially open, as though Margot was expecting someone, or listening for someone. Stepping inside, she paused, staring at Margot as suspicion began to rise inside her.

"Tears?" she asked softly as Margot moved quickly to her feet, attempting to dry her soaked face. "What did you do to Alyssa? She hasn't answered my calls or texts, so you must be involved. What the fuck did you do to her, Margot?"

The woman was a robot, Summer sometimes thought. Oh, Margot loved Alyssa, but she simply had no idea how to be a mother, even after all these years.

Or did she?

Grief twisted Margot's face.

"What's happened to Alyssa?" The demand came as ice began to fill Summer's veins. The deep southern accent she'd been trying to smooth slipped free as did the rein she kept on her temper.

Alyssa was the only person in the world she totally trusted. If she was hurt . . .

"Oh, Summer," Margot whispered, her breath hitching. "If only Alyssa had your courage."

If she had what? Alyssa had immeasurably more courage than any of them. She put up with Margot's ice, Summer's antics, and still loved them all.

"This isn't courage, Margot," Summer assured her, the heavy drawl accompanied by a hard smile. "It's straight up fuckin' don't give a shit. Alyssa's the one with courage, because she dares to love you, you mean old hag. I'd have sliced your skinny neck by now. So why don't you tell me what you did to Alyssa before I go find out for myself."

"It wasn't me." Margot's choked voice and tears caused fear to tighten Summer's chest. "I've hurt her in the past, Summer; I know that. But she's not hurt this time, she's dead inside, and I would never do that to her. I would never do that to my baby . . ."

Summer didn't make another demand or wait for an explanation. Turning, she moved quickly from Margot's room and rushed to Alyssa's. What had happened to her? She was fine in Madrid. . . .

She'd been quiet, though, very thoughtful. She'd ignored several calls and texts, and when Summer had asked about them Alyssa had just said she'd wanted to spend time with her. Summer had assumed it was Margot.

Stepping into Alyssa's suite, she moved quickly through the sitting area and entered the bedroom before coming to a hard stop.

God, it was three in the morning and Alyssa was awake?

"Aly?" she whispered, moving closer as Alyssa's gray eyes moved to her.

She could barely hold back the shock that filled her. This wasn't her friend. Where was the laughter, the amazement that Summer was there? Where was the life?

"Darlin'," she said softly, kneeling next to Alyssa's bed and staring at her with rising fear. "What did you let happen to you?"

There was no laughter in Alyssa's eyes. They were dull, the gray color so still and dark.

"I'm fine, Summer," she said, her voice even and with little inflection. "You didn't have to come here."

She didn't have to come there?

"Alyssa, do you want me to go completely postal here, darlin'?" she asked, the fear building inside her. "Tell me what happened to you, sweetie. And do it now, or you know how I can get."

Alyssa looked so tired, so blank, as though she really didn't care how Summer could get.

"I finally loved," Alyssa stated as though she'd done no more than awakened that day. "I loved too deep and I lost too much." Slicing agony flashed in her eyes as she focused on Summer. "I lost my baby, Summer. I lost my last hope."

Her baby?

"Harvey's baby?" How had that happened? She'd only married the bastard a few months before.

"Not Harvey's," Alyssa assured her.

"Whose?" Summer demanded.

"Go home, Summer," Alyssa whispered, her eyes closing as though she were going to sleep. "I promise you, I'm fine."

"You're not fine," Summer protested. "What happened to you, Alyssa? You have to tell me."

But Alyssa wasn't talking. She lay there, eyes closed, her breathing light, her eyes so shadowed they looked bruised.

"Summer," Margot said her name softly.

Turning to her, seeing the motion Alyssa's mother made for her to follow her, Summer moved quickly to her feet and into the hall. Closing the door softly behind her, she faced Margot, her fists clenched, fear for Alyssa raging through her.

"Whose baby?" she snapped.

And those tears fell from light green eyes that had once been icy, cold. They weren't cold anymore.

Keeping her voice low, Margot told her what had happened. From the arrival of the pictures to the loss of the baby Alyssa had carried. A baby she'd been forced to bury before she'd ever heard his first cry or seen him open his eyes. A little boy with black hair tipped in blond. "A headful of it," Margot sobbed at the mention of it.

"Who?" Summer asked again. "Who did this to her?"

Margot shook her head. "She made me swear, Summer. I swore I wouldn't tell you. I swore I wouldn't allow them to be harmed. Then she slipped and married Harvey Stanhope to make certain no one else suspected who the child belonged to."

Summer stepped closer, her eyes narrowing. "Who?"

Margot should know the lengths she'd go to in protecting Alyssa.

"She has the pictures hidden in her bedroom," Margot revealed. "Probably in that fucking hole in her closet that she called a wish box when she was a child. Look there first."

Summer looked there.

As she drew the pictures free her eyes widened in shock.

They had done this to Alyssa? Shane Connor and Sebastian De Loren? But that made no sense.

The pictures didn't lie, though. Alyssa's face was suffused in pleasure and love, and their faces, their expressions, were cut in the same emotions. What Summer saw in their eyes wasn't the cold calculation of the men that Margot had seen. These were men who had loved.

Replacing the pictures, she sat back on her heels, her eyes narrowed. She'd overheard something at the De La Cruz home she'd stayed in. Something about the two CIA couriers and a loss that had destroyed them.

What the hell was going on?

What had they done to her friend to steal the life, the love that had shone so bright in clear eyes that were now dull and all but dead? What had they done, and how did she find a way to kill them for it?

## 9

## SIX YEARS LATER

Stepping into the house she had moved into with Harvey Stanhope five years before, Alyssa stared around the pristine, far too opulent D.C. home his father had purchased for them.

How ecstatic Marion Stanhope had been when she and Harvey had married. Certain his son was turning over a new leaf, as his father called it, and giving up his depravities. The judgmental bastard. He'd been furious when he'd learned his son was gay. So furious he'd beaten Harvey to the point that when he showed up on the Hampstead doorstep he'd nearly been dead.

He had been her friend at one time. He and Summer had been the only friends she'd really had when she was younger. Summer had remained, but Harvey had followed his own pursuits until she'd returned from Barcelona.

He'd begged her to marry him even before he'd learned of the baby. Begged her to give him just a few years of peace from the beatings to enable him to find a way to make it stop. Against her mother's arguments, she'd married him.

For her baby. To ensure Shane and Sebastian knew she had no intentions of asking them for anything. That she would raise her child without them.

That was six years ago. It seemed a lifetime ago. They'd been each other's shields, so Alyssa had allowed the marriage to stand. The platonic relationship had given them both a chance to recover in some ways. Except something had changed.

It had been slow. A subtle contempt she'd felt at odd times. An anger that had begun building in the past years. And she'd had enough of it. She'd had enough of a lot of things, though. The political machinations, her sterile life, the dreams that haunted her until she thought they'd drive her insane.

Taking the staircase to the second floor, she entered her private suite and, collecting fresh clothing, entered the bathroom. Her return from England had left her exhausted but unwilling to remain in the house with Harvey. Before leaving he'd been a little erratic. Just enough to begin worrying her. Just enough to make her start looking into certain things. Things like her personal checking and savings and the huge amount taken out in the last month. The money was hers. Her income for the past years working as her parent's social director and he'd forged her signature to her checks and stolen it. The bastard. She'd been saving for a reason, and it wasn't so Harvey could steal it all.

She'd called her father on her way home and told him she'd be returning later that night. She just needed to pack a bag and wash the stench of the flight from her body.

Once the divorce was final she intended to leave for Pennsylvania and the house her grandparents had left her next to a gorgeous mountain lake. The house she'd once dreamed of living in with a husband, a houseful of children.

That dream was forever dead. After six years she'd accepted the fact that something vital inside her was dead as well. Shane and Sebastian had so destroyed her that once she'd lost the baby there had been nothing left for another man. No desire left for more children.

She, who had dreamed of a house filled with children, would die childless. How ironic was that?

And there was no way to revive those dreams. She'd tried. God knew she had, but she'd failed. Just as she'd failed at so many other dreams she'd had before that summer in Barcelona. Before she'd given every part of herself to two men. She should have seen the writing on the wall there, she thought painfully. Two men willing to share her? As Summer said once, where was the love?

Not that Alyssa had ever made herself fully believe that there had been no love. She'd tried. It wasn't as though there wasn't enough proof. There was. But believing it . . . if she believed it, she wouldn't still dream of them or awake with the feel of their arms and their warmth surrounding her.

She wouldn't still lie in silence and try to reach out to them as she once had, just to imagine she could feel their warmth.

Finishing her shower and dressing in a pair of jeans with a soft cotton shirt, she laced the sneakers she'd chosen to wear before entering the attached closet and packing a small leather bag. Just enough clothes for a few days. Anything else and she risked Harvey learning that she wasn't coming back.

Harvey was up to something and it wasn't just stealing her money.

She didn't know what or what it involved, but whatever it was, it hadn't been working out for him. He'd been confrontational and insulting when she called the night before, and she didn't expect it would be any different now that she was home. She refused to stay and listen to his ranting when the bottom fell out of whatever plans he had this time, which was no doubt his problem.

Stepping from the bedroom, she paused at the sight of her husband waiting for her.

She hadn't expected this, she admitted. She'd been certain he wasn't home when she arrived.

"Hello," she greeted him as though everything were fine and moved to her dresser. "I need to go to my parents' for a few days.

Dad has a Senate briefing he has to have completed before Monday. I should be back that evening."

Not if she could help it.

Placing her makeup in the bag along with the small box of jewelry she kept in her dresser, she turned to face Harvey once again.

"Is everything okay?" she asked, as though everything were perfectly normal with her.

Trepidation was beginning to build inside her, though, the certainty that Harvey was far more dangerous than she'd suspected.

"Not really." He stood at the bottom of her bed, his hazel eyes narrowed and glittering with malice.

That look had the first feeling of fear that she'd ever felt in his presence rising inside her.

"Is your father bothering you again?" Gripping the bag, she left the bedroom, desperate to get out of the house now. She should have never returned to the house, but he was supposed to be gone this weekend. He'd told her he wouldn't be there before she left, that he had business to take care of out of the country.

And he followed her. Moving behind her from the bedroom, he followed her to the stairs and moved quickly to catch up with her.

Reaching the landing, Alyssa headed for the front door only to have him push her roughly to the side, throwing her against the wall as he blocked the exit.

"What the hell is your problem?" Straightening, Alyssa slid her hand into the pocket of the light jacket she wore and hit the emergency button her father's chief of staff had programmed on her phone. "Get away from the door, Harvey."

The sneer that contorted his face wasn't in the least complimentary to his looks. Though in the past years the once almost pretty features had taken a turn for the worse anyway. Whatever he'd been involved in hadn't been healthy. Nor had it been sane, evidently.

"Like hell!" he snapped. "Tell me, Wife, why do you think I

married your bitch ass, anyway? Do you really think I needed you to protect me from dear old Dad? Do you really think Marion Stanhope would lay a hand on his only heir? Gay or not? He didn't beat me that weekend. I did that to myself. I knew that pathetically soft heart of yours would feel sorry for me."

Well, didn't that just figure? She hadn't expected it, but she wasn't really surprised at this point. She should have suspected it, actually.

Panic was beginning to set in now. She could hear someone yelling at her from the phone in her pocket, knew she'd connected with either her father or his chief, Raeg. Someone would be there soon, she assured herself. Once she hit the panic button her father and Raeg would be rushing to the house.

"I don't care why you married me, Harvey," she informed him calmly, despite the fact that she felt anything but calm. "It didn't matter to me then and it doesn't matter to me now."

"Because poor little Alyssa's heart was already broken." He seemed to take mocking delight in that. Not that she'd ever told him it had been broken.

"You don't know what you're talking about," she assured him. "Now get away from the door and let me leave. We'll discuss this at another time."

They would discuss it never. She'd be damned if she'd ever allow him to so much as be in the same room with her.

The smile that curled his lips was far too confident. Far too knowing.

"You mean I don't know about Shane Connor and Sebastian De Loren?" he asked softly, the malice in his gaze growing brighter. "But I do know about them, Alyssa. I know about how you fucked both of them. Do you know how long I've waited to throw that in your goody-two-shoes face? That I know you were dumped by the De Loren get? That you left Barcelona with a baby and a broken heart?" He laughed at that. "Poor little Alyssa. It was too bad about the kid. I could have said it was mine. How I would have loved that."

As he crowed over whatever triumph he felt he had over her, Alyssa slid her hand from the pocket of her jacket, the phone gripped in it to allow everything he said to be heard by Raeg. She was certain it was Raeg. His voice had a particular timbre when he was pissed.

"Let me leave, Harvey," she repeated, despite the pain she felt at the accusations. Not because he wanted to hurt her. Because remembering had the power to hurt her that much more. "You don't want to try to make me stay."

"Oh, Alyssa," he sighed; the smile on his face terrified her. "I can't do that. I'm sorry, bitch, but you're not going anywhere."

She turned her hand, showing him the phone. "Dad will be here soon, Harvey," she warned him. "And Raeg. Do you really want to have to deal with them? You don't want to."

His eyes narrowed on her, fury flushing his face.

"I was so close to not even needing you anymore," he informed her, his voice lowering, as though that would save him.

"Harvey, just let me leave—"

"Let you leave? You fucking whore," he snarled. "I put up with six years of marriage to you, letting you sleep in that cold little bed of yours, listening to you whimper and whine at night for your lost lovers. For what? What did I gain from it?"

What the hell was he supposed to gain from it anyway?

"I didn't promise you anything." Dropping the overnight bag, she backed into the living room. "You begged me to marry you, not the other way around."

"You coldhearted little cunt," he hissed. "If I had time I'd spread you out and fuck you like a real man instead of one that needs his cousin's help. But then you don't know what being fucked by one man feels like, do you?"

Just a few more minutes, she told herself as he advanced on her. Just a few more minutes.

"Why are you doing this?" she cried out. "You know Dad will kill you. If you lay a hand on me, he'll kill you."

"He'll be too busy grieving for you." He was on her before she could evade him.

As he jerked her to him with one hand the other moved in a wide arc. A second later, Alyssa stiffened, a cry falling from her lips as she felt overwhelming agony pierce her side, ripping through flesh and burying deep.

Shocked, she stared up at him, the betrayal so shocking she didn't know what to say, what to do.

"I tried to help you, Harvey," she whispered, the feel of the knife lodged between her ribs agonizing. "Why? I tried to help you."

"Because I didn't need your help, you fucking little bitch," he snarled. "I never needed it. And now, all you can offer me is the life insurance policy I put on you. I'm not here, remember? Looks like you surprised a thief instead."

And was he so insane that he didn't know Raeg would record every word caught on the line? This was Raeg's job. Security. Anything that would affect his boss. And the panic mode on her phone wasn't just answered by Raeg or her father, but it automatically recorded everything.

"You won't get a penny," she promised, fighting to breathe as he released her.

The strength left her immediately.

Sinking to the floor, Alyssa lay there, her fingers holding to the phone so tight that when Harvey tried to pry it from her, he cursed her. As he straightened, his foot landed in her arm before he turned and left, slamming the door behind him.

Alyssa lay there, feeling her blood ease from where the knife had penetrated her flesh. It hurt. It hurt so bad. It was so unexpected.

She'd never imagined Harvey could become so angry. And she didn't understand why he was so angry.

Breathing was so hard. The slight sound of dampness with each breath wasn't a good thing, she knew. Just as she knew she was dying. Just as she'd felt her baby's life bleed from her, she could feel her own bleeding away as well.

She'd hurt worse in her life, though. This pain wasn't nearly as bad as the pain she'd felt when she'd lost her little boy. But she was just as cold, just as terrified. And just as out of it as she had been then, because she swore she felt Shane and Sebastian there with her. Their warmth, their rage spilling into her.

They were there, their promise no longer broken. Bound to her, as she was bound to them. Their souls reaching out to touch.

She smiled at the fanciful thought. Perhaps delusions were common before death. Because they were inside her senses so clear. So clear she could hear Sebastian's voice.

*'Lyssa?* Sleepy and a bit confused.

"I love you, Goofy," she whispered, needing the warmth, needing the comfort. "Don't let me die alone, Sebastian. Don't leave me alone."

Rage exploded through her. Warmth surrounded her and fury rushed over her senses like a wave, striking at her, fueling her own.

*Don't you leave me, siren. You will not leave me.*

Why did she feel that? What was it about death that made a person long for the one thing she knew wasn't real? Because his voice wasn't really there. Their warmth wasn't really wrapping around her, shielding her, demanding she live.

"I'm cold," she whispered, as she heard her father screaming, heard Raeg barking commands and her doctor's steady voice. "So cold. . . ."

How had Dr. Brennan gotten there?

"You promised to keep me warm . . . ," she whispered. "You promised. . . ."

+-+-+-+

Sebastian came awake with a suddenness he'd only experienced once in his life before.

This time, the difference wasn't the excruciating physical and mental pain he'd sworn Alyssa was feeling.

This time, it was her death.

*I'm cold. . . . You promised to keep me warm. . . . You promised. . . .*

They had made so many promises to her, only to have to break each one.

Shane wasn't the only one who had felt that connection snap back into place, felt her, the bond so fragile, almost non-existent now.

As he jerked his boots on he was aware of the light switching on in the sitting room and knew Shane was hurriedly dressing as well.

They had to hurry. God help him, they had to get to her.

"I'm calling the pilot!" Shane yelled out, panic edging his tone, his certainty that they were losing Alyssa.

Sebastian ran through the connecting door. "Call him on the way."

They'd been certain she was safe.

Gregory Santiago, the neighbor who had once lived beneath Alyssa in Barcelona, had been killed in the raid on his apartment where they'd found the original videos he'd taken while Alyssa was at Landra's apartment six years before.

He'd finally moved to transfer the blackmail payments that had been made over the years by the De Loren family. Their CIA contacts had instantly traced the transfer, pinpointed Santiago, then with Shane and Sebastian rushed his Barcelona apartment.

The cousins hadn't trusted him six years before, but Sebastian had never suspected he was involved with the blackmail. They should have, he knew. Not many people had known they were more or less living with Alyssa there. Gregory had known, though. He'd known, just as he'd known their reputations.

All the videos and digital files had been recovered, even the one addressed to a U.S. gossip rag, and left with his lawyer in Madrid.

The operation had finished the day before. Would fate be so cruel as to take her from them now?

Running from the house, Shane shouted directions to the pilot as well as the flight plan. He had twenty minutes to get prepared to take off.

They were racing for the airport, that fragile, so very fragile connection they felt to Alyssa dimming by the second.

"Don't you die on me, siren!" Sebastian screamed as he pushed the little sports car as fast as it would travel on the winding roads. "Don't you fucking die on me. We're coming, baby. We're coming. . . ."

As fast as they could get to her. God, why hadn't they left the day before? Why had they allowed their brothers to convince them to wait, to sleep first so they could go with them? They should have left for her immediately.

They'd failed her again. And God help them, they might have failed her one time too many.

✦✦✦

Ice formed in Margot's veins. It chilled rage and froze out fury. It left only the steely determination and cold, hard vengeance cementing inside her.

"Why didn't you call nine-one-one?" she demanded as Davis and Dr. Brennan rushed through the foyer, following Raeg, and Davis' bodyguard, Crane, as they carried Alyssa to the downstairs guest room rather than up the stairs to her room.

The gurney they used was no more than a flat slat with hand-holds, and blood dripped from it, running from her daughter's body in a long, slow rivulet.

"Davis." She grabbed his arm imperatively as he went to pass her. "She needs a hospital."

"Margot, let him be," the doctor demanded, passing them as Margot held her husband's gaze. "We can deal with this."

"Why?" She ignored the doctor. "Why isn't she in the hospital?"

"Because we don't know what the hell is going on!" he snapped, pulling her with him as he rushed for the guest room Alyssa had been taken to. "Summer called just before Alyssa's panic call came through. She's on her way home from Spain and told Raeg to make certain Alyssa was safe. That's why Brennan was with us. I'd already called him. The only reason she's alive is because we were already on our way there."

Standing in the doorway, Margot stared in at the rushed efforts being made to save Alyssa's life. Raeg and Crane had placed Alyssa on the narrow bed and were hastily cutting her clothes from her.

The hilt of a knife extended from Alyssa's side. It looked so big, so lethal, the blade buried completely inside her small body.

The doctor's wife was unpacking the totes she and the nurse had carried ahead of Raeg and Crane. The RN attaching an IV to Alyssa's arm, her expression grim as Mrs. Brennan placed several monitors on the bedside table, and attaching electrodes. They moved quickly, the monitors beeping, IV attached, and the doctor striding from the connecting bathroom, his sterilized, gloved hands held up as another nurse strode behind him, her own hands covered with sterilized gloves.

"Who did this?" Margot asked her husband, fighting to remain calm.

She had to stay calm. She had to make someone pay for this.

"Harvey." It was Raeg who answered her as the doctor motioned them away from Alyssa. "We heard everything after she hit the panic button on her phone. And he knew about Barcelona. He knew too much about it."

Focusing on her daughter, Margot made herself watch as the

doctor removed the blade, the size of it causing her breath to catch. How Brennan managed to do everything required to stabilize the pierced lung, take care of the wound to her side, and keep Alyssa alive she had no idea.

Margot paced the hall, the ice freezing to the depths of her mother's soul as she listened to the doctor and nurse talking to each other. Dr. Brennan barked out orders to both his nurse and his wife, while monitors beeped too fast and beeped too slow.

"You will not die, Alyssa Paige," Margot muttered, determined that her daughter sense the determination pouring from her. "You will not."

Margot watched the clock at the end of the hall as time passed. First one hour, then two. Just before the third hour struck, the door opened and the doctor stepped out, his expression somber.

"She's alive," he told them. "And trust me, Margot." He focused completely on her. "There's nothing that can't be done better here than I can do at a hospital. But it's not good."

He went through the complications. The collapsed lung, the amount of blood lost, and, most especially, Alyssa's lack of determination to live.

"If her will to live hasn't strengthened in the past six years, and I'm not convinced it has, then there's no way we can keep her from giving up."

Margot heard every word the doctor said, and what he didn't say as well. Alyssa didn't live. She drifted through life as though waiting for a reason to give up and join the child she'd lost.

"The hell she will." Stalking into the bedroom, Margot paused beside Alyssa's bed.

She was too pale, her breathing too shallow. The doctor was right: Alyssa could easily drift away from them now.

"Alyssa Paige, I've watched you suffer for six years and I've had enough of this fight I've waged to keep you alive. Do you understand me, girl?" She didn't speak gently. Her voice was hard, the voice she had used before her daughter had returned broken inside.

"Did you hear me, Alyssa Paige?" she yelled, causing the nurse to flinch at the sound of her voice. "Buck your ass up, girl. I have six of the meanest, best-trained Special Forces soldiers ready to head out the second I give the order. They will suffer, Alyssa. If you die, then I swear to you, they will suffer."

It was a vow she'd made to herself six years before. Shane Connor and Sebastian De Loren would suffer.

But Harvey Stanhope would suffer first.

Alyssa's lashes fluttered, an almost silent moan leaving her lips.

"Die on me. Leave me to face this alone," Margot informed her daughter furiously, "and I will no longer have a reason to allow them to live."

Her daughter moaned again. The sound was faint and filled with such pain.

"Understand me, Alyssa," Margot snarled, "as you have never understood anything. Die, and before they take their last breath, they'll suffer a hundred times more than you have before I'll allow them to slip away."

Straightening, Margot turned to her husband. The moment Alyssa was no longer in danger Davis would go after Harvey. She would beat him to it.

"Notify me immediately if she begins to worsen," she told him.

"So you can bully her?" Raeg snapped, his expression filled with contempt as he watched her.

"Whatever it takes," Davis answered for her. "Whatever it takes to keep her alive."

Margot nodded sharply and left the room. What she had to do

next would require all the deceit she'd learned to practice over the years. All the lies she'd learned to tell.

She was going to convince Harvey to come to her.

Then she was going to ensure the little bastard could never hurt her daughter again.

## 10

**FOUR DAYS LATER**

What happened?

Why was she in her parents' downstairs guest room? It made no sense. And why was Margot sitting next to her bed, texting? Margot hated texting.

She hated texting worse than she hated e-mail. She could be convinced to do e-mail, but Alyssa had never known her to text.

"Momma?" It slipped. She rarely called her mother Momma. She remembered doing it six years before, but until now she hadn't done so again.

Margot lifted her head, the smile that curled her lips so hard and cold that for a moment she thought her mother was angry with her.

"I love you, Alyssa," Margot said then.

"I know." Sadness sank inside her; the confrontational relationship she and her mother had was as much her fault as Margot's. She knew that. "I always knew."

God, she was so tired. She just want to sleep, to drift away on the warm currents she could feel reaching out to her. She was always so cold. Margot couldn't understand that; neither could

Summer. Alyssa was always so cold except when she slept. When dreams of Shane and Sebastian wrapped around her and warmed her.

"I'm so tired, Momma," she tried to explain, but it was so hard to focus. "Please just let me go."

"Will you be back, Alyssa?"

She wanted to lie to her mother, but lying to her was something Alyssa was always loath to do. Margot never lied to her. She was always honest, even when it hurt.

Alyssa forced her eyes open, forced herself to stare back at her mother. "Let me go," she whispered.

She'd heard her mother's voice, even in her dreams, demanding she live or Shane and Sebastian would be hurt. Why should she care? Why did their suffering bother her? Why did she dream that they already suffered so deeply?

"Well then," Margot's voice hitched. "Sebastian and Shane just arrived in town and they called your cell. I've been texting for you, sweetie."

Texting for her? Trepidation shot through Alyssa then. Why would her mother text Shane and Sebastian for her?

"No. . . ." They weren't there; they didn't want her. They were afraid she would be a nuisance.

"Oh yes." Satisfaction filled Margot's voice then. "When you take your last breath I'll direct those sons of bitches straight to the men awaiting my order. They're here for you, you know? Can you believe they came for you after betraying you so cruelly? Do you think I'll have any mercy on them, Alyssa? I swear to you, I will not."

Came for her? Was she a pet, some toy they thought they could play with, toss aside, then come back for? She'd be damned if they would.

Life flared in Alyssa's eyes in ways it hadn't since she'd returned from Barcelona. Then anger. Margot wanted to shout in victory, but the realization of what she was about to do was too heart-rending.

"Good then. I'll just text them back. As you of course. Ask them to give me a few days to think," she said, returning to the messages she'd been exchanging with Sebastian. "We'll not discuss this again."

"I'll win the next argument," Alyssa promised her, though she was already drifting off back to sleep.

"When you wake, Alyssa, I put something in your wish box," Margot said softly. "Find it." Brushing back the heavy strands of her daughter's hair, she whispered a kiss against her brow. "I love you, girl. I always loved you so very much."

Sitting back, she read the text reply to the request for a few days.

*Do you think we'll accept that? You should know better!*

Oh, how arrogant, she thought, rather pleased by the reply, though she wasn't certain why.

*Go to hell* [she texted in reply].
*Where the fuck do you think we've been? We live there, dammit.*

Poor babies, she thought caustically. Didn't she just feel so sorry for them?

*Alyssa, ignoring us is not a good idea! You know it's not! Alyssa, damn you, answer me!*

She placed the phone next to Alyssa's hand.
"Good-bye, girl," she whispered.

Picking up her purse, she left the room. She had a date with Harvey, and she would be taking him straight to hell.

Summer would have to care for Alyssa now.

## MARGOT'S FUNERAL
## FIVE DAYS LATER

Margot Hampstead's funeral was attended by damned near every politician Senator Hampstead knew and their family. They might not have liked Margot, but many had respected her. Most had feared her, but they had known they could depend upon her to keep her word.

Sitting in the limo that had joined the procession to the grave site, Shane and Sebastian watched for Alyssa. Whoever stood next to the senator resembled Alyssa enough, considering she was hiding behind a black veil. She was the same height and build, but it wasn't Alyssa.

Just as whoever was texting from Alyssa's phone wasn't her, either. At first they hadn't been so certain; now there was no doubt.

Sebastian glanced at the latest texts on the phone.

*Go back to Spain. U R not wanted here!*

Not at any time on any text had Alyssa ever used text spelling. It was typical spelling all the way without a single typo.

*Liar, answer my fucking call.*
  *Suck my dick!*

And she damned sure knew better than to write anything so explicit.

Alyssa wasn't crass, she wasn't explicit, unless encouraged by him or Shane and only then during the height of arousal. She was a lady. Soft, sweet, but with a steel spine.

He turned the phone to Shane.

His cousin read it, reread it; then his lips flattened in anger.

"That's not Alyssa," he stated, certain now.

"And the woman at Margot Hampstead's grave site isn't Alyssa, either." He nodded to the mourners. "She resembles her in height and build close enough; I'll give her that. But the way she stands is too self-conscious. She's scared of being revealed as an imposter. And the senator's not comfortable in the least with the way she's tucking herself against his chest."

That one was almost amusing, Sebastian thought, before turning his gaze back to Shane. "Have you located her phone yet?"

His cousin turned a surprised look on him. "Finished that hours ago. I have a lock on it and it hasn't left one particular room downstairs, along the back of the house. We'll go in tonight."

Sebastian nodded silently. No doubt they'd find their texter there. There was no way Alyssa would turn her phone over to someone else to text for her, and they knew it. And tonight, by God, he'd find out how someone was managing to do it.

The sudden, overwhelming feeling of Alyssa's death the night they'd left had been followed by another hours later. That connection to her that they'd never understood had gone all but silent about four months after she returned home. No matter how they reached for her, they only found her in their dreams.

They'd stayed away from her, following the demands in the blackmail letter implicitly. Their families had ensured it. Otherwise, they would have never been able to resist that first, agonizing loss they'd felt. The hell they'd endured for the past six years had nearly driven them past the brink of sanity. The aching loneliness and broken dreams had driven sharpened spikes of loss through their souls.

The need to see her now, to touch her, took all the self-control he could muster to resist. She was so close, waiting for him, needing him.

She was cold. All the way to the soul cold that had fear building inside him. He could only imagine what such a deep, dark chill could be. The kind where there was no warmth at all, nothing to comfort the body or the spirit.

It wasn't death, but so close to it, he feared, that she might never find her way back.

## 11

Security had definitely been beefed up at the house, Shane noticed as he and Sebastian slipped onto the grounds and made their way patiently to the small patio at the back of the senator's D.C. mansion.

The senator had doubled the security guards and added canine reinforcement, and though the guards were good, they weren't military or Special Forces trained. They were civilian and not nearly as diligent as their better-trained, highly intuitive military counterparts.

Slipping through the break in the guards' perimeter checks, they made it across the grounds, using shadows to cover their approach until they made it to the tree-shaded patio at the back of the two-story mansion.

The first set of French doors led to a hall lined with offices used by the senator's staff. Farther along the precisely placed flagstone walk was another set of doors, all but hidden behind another, much smaller, tree-lined patio. There a small suite had been left intact, though the shades at the doors and windows blocked any attempt to see inside.

Using an ultra-thin camera connected to telescopic cable he worked between the panels of the window, Shane was able to glimpse the part of the suite they'd be slipping into. It was clear, though it was impossible to glimpse what waited behind the ornate room divider that hid the other half of the room.

Waiting to be certain there was no movement, he gave Sebastian the go-ahead to disable the alarm and move into the room as he kept watch.

Nothing moved. Even as the door opened and Shane slipped in, no more than a shadow along the side of the wall, and indicated Sebastian could proceed in.

Sebastian's first sight of Alyssa as she lay unconscious in the narrow bed, tucked against the wall away from the doors and window, nearly brought him to his knees. Fear congealed in his belly, had his heart racing, and tightened his throat with so much emotion he felt swamped by it.

He moved across the room, uncaring if anyone waited in the darkened bathroom or entered by the door leading to the hall. Nothing mattered but Alyssa and getting to her as quickly as possible.

Reaching out, almost terrified to touch her, he let his fingers stroke down her arm, his breath catching as a sound similar to an animal's whimper left his throat.

"She's so cold, Shane," he said softly, his gaze moving over her still, silent face. "She hates being cold."

She would often chill at night for some reason, unless one of them cuddled her against his body. Now she wasn't just chilled; she was cold. So cold and so still that he feared she'd never waken.

Kneeling next to the bed, he could only stare at her, count each breath, and fight back the rage threatening to engulf him.

Behind him, Shane sat heavily in the chair that had been pulled close to the bed. The cousins had both suffered the past six years, one just as deeply as the other. The first six months they had spent so drunk they barely remembered anything but the day they'd felt her pain striking inside them like stabbing blows.

For weeks Lucien and Murphy had kept the hands at the hacienda on alert. Many of them hadn't escaped unscathed during the bitter, violent fights that ensued when Shane and Sebastian had fought to leave, to get to Alyssa. To ease that black, agonizing pain that had reached out to them.

"Look at you, siren," he whispered raggedly, lifting her hand to lay his cheek in her palm, holding her lax fingers to his flesh. "I bet you were climbing again." He knew better. "You were, weren't you? Didn't I warn you? We're going to talk about that spanking, baby."

God, what he wouldn't do to hear her call him Goofy, to see her smile, perhaps hear her laughter?

Behind him, Shane rose, collected the doctor's metal file at the bottom of the bed, and returned to the chair.

"You're going to have to wake up, siren," Sebastian whispered. "It's been so long since I've seen those pretty eyes. Since you've given me that little scowl you used so often on me."

She had called him incorrigible so many times, but the love in her voice had assured him she'd found joy in the antics he'd pulled just to hear her laughter.

He'd loved her laughter.

"Come on now, you know how Shane gets when you won't speak to us." His voice thickened painfully. "He gets impossible to deal with, starts threatening me."

It was actually the other way around.

There was no response, though. Not even the slightest movement of her fingers against his cheek. She was completely still, far too cool, as though death had already stolen her from them.

"What did we do to you, siren?" With his free hand he reached out and brushed her hair back from her cheek, his fingers following the line of her delicate ear.

"She was stabbed. Three days before her mother's death."

Shane's announcement, delivered with a growl of rage, had Sebastian freezing. "Right side. The blade pierced her lung, significant blood loss. The lung was stabilized, blood transfusion. They nearly lost her hours later but managed to revive her."

Sebastian couldn't breathe. Horror raced through him.

"The night we headed here, fuck me they had to revive her twice, 'Bastian."

That made no sense. The lung was stabilized, blood transfused. The wound shouldn't have caused her to slip away from them once, let alone twice.

"Exhaustion." Shane's voice was lower, so thick that his Texas accent almost slurred the word. "Anemia. The overriding concern is the infection that developed, though." The file clattered to the floor. "It isn't good, 'Bastian. She's not fighting to live."

Sebastian swallowed tightly, his gaze locked on Alyssa's face as fear surged through him.

"The hell she's going to give up," he snarled, his hand cupping the side of her face as he pressed her fingers closer to his cheek. "You can't give up, siren. Not now. We fixed it, baby. We fixed everything. You're safe now."

A heartbeat later he and Shane were both moving as the French doors pushed open. Positioning themselves protectively between Alyssa's still form and the small, black-clad, armed young woman who entered the room. Sebastian kept his gaze on the amused expression and brilliant violet eyes staring back at them.

"Well now, are we havin' a party?" The southern accent was heavy with anger, those violet eyes snapping dangerously. "Little late, aren't you?" she queried with a lift of graceful midnight brows. "Like by maybe six years?"

Shane watched her carefully, recognizing the accent, the way she held the weapon, and her unique eyes. Summer Bartlett was well known to both of them as was her connection to Alyssa and her family.

"Stand down, Belle." Shane ordered firmly.

Belle. The CIA asset had trained in Spain for several years.

Once they'd even worked with her for a very brief time. They had known she was Alyssa's friend, but she'd never mentioned it, and they had forced themselves not to.

Belle smiled, a hard turn of her lips that wasn't encouraging.

"Do you know how hard it was to keep from killin' the two of you in Italy?" she asked with savage amusement. "Several times, it would have been so easy."

"Stand down, Belle," Shane repeated the order.

She rolled her eyes in disgust. "Darlin', this aint a Company assignment," she assured them. "This is personal." Her voice hardened. "That's the most important person in my world layin' in that bed. And I've watched her grieve like a widow for six years. I think it's high time she has a real reason for all that grief. Maybe if she buries you, she'll get over you."

The bloodthirst in that little hellion's gaze was a bit concerning. And she had just enough training that it wouldn't be easy to take her down. Unless they killed her; that would be easy. But if Alyssa knew her, then their little siren might not speak to them when she woke. For a while anyway.

"Or will she follow us?" Sebastian asked softly. "If she takes her last breath, you won't have to worry about killing us, Belle. We'll follow her. There would be no saving us. Can you be certain she wouldn't do the same?"

He struck a nerve. Belle's gaze flickered with concern, with pain. If Alyssa was that important to her, then how important was she to Alyssa?

"I really want ta cap your asses, ya know," she sighed, though a hint of tears filled her voice. "And that wouldn't be nearly enough to pay you back for what you've done to her." She blinked back the tears, her lips tightening as they trembled with the threat of those tears falling. "You destroyed everythin' she was. Every dream. Every part of her exceptional soul. You should burn in hell."

They should burn in hell? Fuck, that was all they knew. Hell.

"We do. Daily," Shane was the one to assure her.

There could be no hell greater than feeling Alyssa's siren's song calling out to them, filled with so much pain, with such overwhelming need that the only way to deal with it was to drown their senses in booze. And even then, she was there. Whispering to them, her tears burning their souls.

This woman had no idea how closely they were tied to their siren.

Belle, Summer Bartlett, the petite Georgia native with the seductive drawl and perfect aim. She'd been like a shadow in Italy, one of the best covert agents in training Shane had seen. Until now, he hadn't even known Belle possessed emotions, let alone tears.

But those were tears she was fighting now.

"I hate y'all, you know that, right?" she whispered.

"If you're going to kill us, then do it," Sebastian ordered her, his voice harsh as he turned back to Alyssa.

Sitting next to her, his back to the weapon Belle wielded, Sebastian stretched out beside Alyssa slowly and tried to wrap himself around her. She was too fucking cold. Too unresponsive.

"Damn, you have a good friend there, siren," he whispered at her ear as he tried to surround her with his warmth. "She's going to put a bullet in our asses. You going to let her do that? I thought only you were going to shoot us if you got that pissed. Come on, open your eyes and I'll hand you a loaded gun myself. Please, baby, come back to us."

The monitor at her left gave a strong beat, the heart rate indication spiking marginally and remaining stronger.

"There you are, siren," he whispered at her ear again, allowing his lips to brush against the shell gently. "You're with me now, aren't you, Alyssa. This friend of yours is a little bitch, you know. Has that gun leveled at our balls and she's really wanting to pull the trigger. Don't you want to pull that trigger yourself? You going to let her do your job for you?"

The heart rate stayed strong and Sebastian swore, he swore he felt the fingers of her left hand tighten just a bit beneath his hold.

Summer moved tentatively to the bottom of the bed, her eyes on that monitor, the weapon held ready at the side of her leg, though.

"They deserve to die, darlin'," she told her friend softly. "You know they do. Just as we both know there's no way you'd kill them. Ain't you just too soft for somethin' like that? You'd just let them get away with walkin' away from you. I won't."

"I need you, 'Lyssa," Sebastian told her, allowing all the pain, all the grief, of the past six years into his voice. "I swear to you on all I hold dear we didn't leave you willingly. We didn't let you go without dying inside. At least come back to us long enough to punish us yourself if you don't believe me." He laid his head against hers, the shards of his heart gouging straight to his spirit as he held her, tried to warm her. "Don't leave us, siren. We won't survive without you."

"Come on back, girlfriend," Summer drawled. "I'll draw and quarter them and tell ya all about it."

+ + + +

She had been so cold for so long.

As Alyssa felt the tendrils of warmth moving around her, pushing back the black, bleak cold that held her in its grip, she focused on what the warmth could be. Where could it be coming from? She hadn't felt it in so long she wasn't certain what it was.

It seemed like she had been in this place forever. A place where even dreams of Barcelona and the dizzying heat she'd found there couldn't reach her. No dreams. No memories. Nothing but the inability to move from the darkness or to sink deeper into it.

If she let the darkness have her then she knew something terrible would happen. Something she couldn't allow. But she couldn't face leaving it, either. At least here there was no pain, there was no loss. And she couldn't bear losing more. She'd lost so much. . . .

That warmth wrapping around her, barely there, yet encasing

her, was lifting her from the darkness. Despite the struggle to remain where she was, to have the warmth as well as the dark, she knew she couldn't have both.

One or the other.

And it had been so long . . . she cried out, silence meeting the wounded thought. It had been so long since this warmth had been a part of her. . . .

It was them. It was their warmth wrapping around her and pulling her to them.

How long had it been since she'd felt them? Since she'd been able to close her eyes and just feel them?

Don't let it be a dream.

Desperation gouged at the darkness, the warmth easing her closer to the light as the pervading nothingness began to fill with shadows rather than the overwhelming starless midnight. The closer she came to the light, the warmer those tendrils surrounding her became. The closer the whispers trapped in the shadows seemed. Their whispers. Their insistence that she come to them, that she let them in.

That she allow them to remind her of all she had lost.

But she wanted to go to them, to let the warmth touch her just one more time.

Just one more time.

She wanted to stop the light as it began to overtake the darkened landscape she was held within. Just for a moment. Just to be certain if it was a dream or if it was real.

She couldn't face another dream. Couldn't face waking to learn that reality was an ugly, cold place, without laughter or joy.

Without dreams.

The warmth tightened around her, urging her closer to the surface where only pain existed.

"Darlin', these two are startin' to piss me off." Summer didn't sound happy in the least. "Please let me kill them. I'm beggin' ya."

Kill them?

Why was Summer being so cruel as to trick her away from the dark, where she needed to hide?

"Siren . . ." Soft, that hint of Spanish in his voice, some tortured emotion making his voice ragged . . .

'Bastian. His warmth surrounding her. She could feel him against her. She'd never felt him against her as she was pulled from her dreams. She hadn't felt his warmth or the beat of his heart against her shoulder as she did now. Oh God, how she'd missed that. The feel of them surrounding her, warming her, holding her until nothing existed but being wherever they were.

"You can't leave now. I won't let you leave us." His voice was so ragged, so filled with aching need and tortured dreams. Just as hers were. Just as she ached and needed. "We wouldn't survive without you."

She knew that. She knew, in this place where she could feel them, touch what was left of their souls with what was left of hers. But there was so little of hers left now.

Tears filled her eyes. She hadn't cried in years. Those tears had lain trapped inside the shattered remnants of her soul, unable to escape.

One escaped now. She felt it fall from her closed eye as she fought to open her eyes, felt it burn down her cheek.

She knew they wouldn't survive without her. Why did they think she had chosen to remain in the darkness rather than sinking deeper into it and letting go completely? They were bound. She couldn't break that bond, couldn't escape it, no matter how she tried when her conscious mind ruled her.

As she hovered between the soft light surrounding her and reality awaiting her, she felt a cool, longed-for weight settling against her breast, before surrounding her neck.

She knew what it was, knew the promises that had been broken when they had taken it. Promises she'd wanted to die without.

"This was taken from you." Shane's voice penetrated the warmth gently. "Remember the promises that went with it, baby? Our promises?"

Another tear fell, scalding her flesh, forcing her to drag her eyes open despite the pain that lanced her body and the fears that filled her mind.

She had to open her eyes. She had to see them.

Blurry at first, her vision cleared enough that she found herself staring into Sebastian's black eyes. He hadn't been sleeping again, she thought, exhaustion trying to swamp her.

"Siren," he whispered, his eyes damp. "Have you been climbing again? That spanking's coming."

God, how she wanted to smile.

"Goofy." The word was slurred, instinctive.

"Oh God. Alyssa." His head lowered, his lips against her ear. "Don't you leave me. Don't dare leave."

Behind him, Shane stared down at her, his face haggard, his blue eyes so dark. They knew not to go so long without sleep. They became irritable and made her snappish. She didn't like it when they were irritable.

Swallowing to dampen her lips, she breathed out in exasperation, so tired it was all she could do to speak. "Sleep, Cowboy."

Shane's throat tightened, working as though he had difficulty swallowing before he nodded sharply. "When I know you'll wake for us again I'll sleep."

Wasn't that just like them? The hazy thought drifted through her mind.

"Bossy," she sighed weakly. Staying awake was so hard.

"Alyssa. You can't let them just get away with this," Summer drawled, though Alyssa could hear the tears in her voice.

"Never." Her eyes drifted closed. "Never. Just had to know . . ."

Had to know they were there. Had to know the bonds weren't broken.

Oh, they were going to pay. Because as the warmth and heal-ing sleep pulled her back into that place of dreams rather than darkness, there was the fragile thought that she would never re-member a moment of it anyway.

And she'd sworn to herself before she was thrown into the dark-ness that she would break the hold they had on her.

Forever.

That she would definitely remember.

"I hate the two of you for real," Summer muttered.

"Shh." The drugged sound coming from Alyssa shocked Sum-mer and had her eyes filling with tears again.

*Fuckin' bastards!* she mouthed silently.

"She's ours," Shane said softly, his head resting next to hers, his larger body still sheltering her.

"Too bad you didn't remember that six years ago," Summer told them. "Maybe she wouldn't be here now. And it doesn't change the fact that you can't stay."

"The hell we can't—"

"You don't understand. You will not stay with her, De Loren." She spoke slowly, firmly, as though speaking to a child. "Because whatever made her husband decide to kill her had somethin' to do with you, and that's a fact."

"We took care of it. And Stanhope had nothing to do with it," Shane snarled. "It's over."

"That's not what my intel says, Cowboy." She fluttered her lashes at him as though flirting, though the sneer in her voice was any-thing but. "From what I hear, you two have that little mess you made in Spain to clean up, and you're gonna give Alyssa time to regain her strength before she has to deal with you and the obvious destruction you evidently bring to her life."

He couldn't argue that, as much as he wanted to.

"You're in no position to make that demand," Shane pointed out, determined to stay with Alyssa now.

"I'll make a deal with you then." Summer smiled back at them. The curve of her lips would be frightening to some. "You give her time to finish healin' and regain her strength; then I'll contact you and give you a clear path to her once she's done so." Her expression hardened. "Until then, you use the next two years to clear the danger out of your lives and put the agency behind you. Otherwise, me and her daddy will have a little talk. And he really likes me. And the CIA really likes his influence on their fundin' at the moment." She glanced at her nails while the other hand still held the weapon. "Get the danger out of your lives; then you can have your shot. Make a choice and make it now."

"The doctor believes if she begins to recover then she'll be at full strength in eighteen months," Shane pointed out.

"That was his best-case scenario, sugah," she assured them. "Twenty-four months is his actual time line for her. It will take you that long to clear the agency junk out of your life and make damned certain nothing in your past endangers her. Because I promise you if it ever does, you won't have a chance against the hillbillies I send out after you. That's a Georgia promise, assholes. Take it to the bank." She wrinkled her nose in an expression that would have been enchanting if it hadn't gone along with a threat to kill them.

As much as Sebastian hated to admit it, she was right. There was also the follow-up investigation needed to ensure Gregory Santiago hadn't been working with anyone else. There was no evidence he had been, but Sebastian knew it was foolhardy not to make certain.

Looking down at Alyssa, he touched her cheek, then leaned to her and let his lips touch hers.

"Sing for me, siren," he whispered. "Let me feel you again."

Having that part of the bond disappear had nearly broken him. The one they'd shared in Barcelona, a sense, a certainty she was there, waiting for them.

Letting his lips caress hers a moment longer, he moved from the bed, standing between Summer and Shane as he took that place next to her.

Shane hated leaving her. Hated knowing Summer was right, that there was garbage they had to clean up before they could come back to her. At least now that sense of urgency that Alyssa could be taken from them at any moment was gone.

Leaning to her, he kissed her as well. A gentle, lingering touch of his lips to hers before he moved to whisper in her ear.

"Feel me, siren," he whispered. "Feel us. Are you warm now, baby? I promise, you get cold again and we'll be here. And soon, you won't be able to chase us out of your bed. I swear it."

A final kiss to her brow and he stood. Giving her one last worried glance, he turned to Sebastian.

"Let's go," he breathed out, his voice rough. "While I can make myself do it."

They left her room, stepping back into the night and leaving the heart they'd fought to return to for so long.

Summer stepped closer to the bed. She'd be damned, but Alyssa was breathing easier, the monitors showing a small but noticeable improvement. And she knew she hadn't seen Shane or Sebastian wrap Alyssa's fingers around the stones of that necklace, but that was where they were. Shane had to have done it, she told herself. There was no way in hell Alyssa had the strength to do so.

"Girlfriend." Crossing her arms over her breasts, she glared down at the closest friend she had. "You don't even know the bill you're gettin' on this one."

It was going to be a helluva debt, though, because she'd played the best bluff of her life. It was gonna be hell topping this one.

Part
Two

## 12

Two years, three weeks, and six days and oh, about twelve hours, give or take a few. Math was Shane's area of expertise, not his. Sebastian knew it had been too fucking long, though. And his siren had grown only more beautiful.

Two years after Summer's demand that they give Alyssa time to heal, to fight back from the attack and the weakened condition it had left her in, her father's lover and soon-to-be fiancée, Landra Collier was hosting his fifty-fourth birthday party. God love Aunt Landra's heart. His aunt ensured Alyssa had to stay in one place for a few hours tonight anyway. Something she hadn't done at any of the other parties he'd tried to corner her at over the past weeks. She ignored their phone calls, their texts, and refused to see them. And catching her at a party proved impossible.

Sebastian had waited, though. The gifts were presented, the cake was cut, and now everyone was enjoying champagne, dancing, and a jovial atmosphere sure to be the talk of the town come morning. For Sebastian, it was the first chance to approach Alyssa since he and Shane had been forced away from her eight years before.

His siren. God help him, he missed her.

Tonight, she was wearing black rather than the icy, pale, almost white blue she'd worn the first time they'd seen her.

Little sleeves trailed just off her shoulder, gathered, and led to the low-cut back. Her full, beautiful breasts rose above the snug material cupping her like a lover's hand from breast to hip, where it flared out in yards of material. Behind her, the flow of the dress was gathered just slightly above that pretty ass before falling into a train that trailed behind her a good twelve to fourteen inches. In front, the material whispered to the floor, giving just a glimpse of the toes of her matching four-inch heels.

Diamonds and a single sapphire gleamed between the tempting mounds of her breasts and she wore no other jewelry. Not in her hair or in her pretty ears.

Sebastian made a note to have Shane take the rest of the collection from the De Lorens' safe and bring it back with him. Pretty diamond and sapphire drops for her hair and around her wrist. The engagement ring he and Shane had had made and pretty earrings.

The rest of the jewelry carried the same theme. A single sapphire protected by two diamonds. The siren protected by them. By their promise.

Always bound, they'd promised her.

Since the night they'd been forced to leave her with Summer two years before, one of them had always watched over her. She was never left without protection, never allowed to be at risk again.

Watching her move now, the feminine shift of hips and rear, he gave a little sigh. His cock was so damned hard it was like iron trying to bust the zipper of his tuxedo slacks.

Eight years. It had been eight years since he'd allowed himself to face her. At least while she was conscious. Eight years since he'd dared to consider approaching her. For six of those years, to do so would have been meant a punishment she would have never recovered from, one he and Shane would have carried the guilt of. For the past two years Sebastian had simply watched her from afar, the changes in her more unsettling than he wanted to admit.

Those changes in personality and behavior were so striking, it was as though he'd never known her. Never touched her or heard her cries of pleasure. They were changes he knew hadn't occurred without trauma. And now he wondered how he'd managed to stay away from her in the past two years, let alone the full eight. Kept from coming to her, from touching her, loving her, hearing her cries of ecstasy as he and Shane possessed her.

The pleasure they found with her was like nothing they had ever known. It was like being part of a storm, part of ecstasy itself.

She wasn't the same girl they'd lost themselves to in Barcelona, though. The laughing, sensual young woman in those damned frilly skirts and little sleeveless shirts, her feet bare, her long hair tangled around her face, was gone.

Or naked, perspiration glistening across sun-kissed flesh as she stared at them, crying out her pleasure.

No, she wasn't the same woman.

This woman moved with restraint. There was none of the promise of passion, and wild pleasure was nowhere in sight. It was deeply hidden, sensed now rather than felt.

Her thick, heavy fall of ash-blond hair that would have fallen to just below her shoulders. Now it was upswept and pinned into artful disarray. Little curls and precisely pulled strands of the multi-hued strands trailed along her neck and the side of her face. Finely arched brows swept over icy gray eyes. Eyes the color of winter clouds, darkened and filled with an oncoming storm.

Lithe, graceful, enchanting. And untouchable. Restrained, careful, without the passion and love for adventure that had filled her that summer in Spain.

Every look, from her perfectly composed expression, her chilly gaze, and her proud posture spelled untouchable. Unapproachable.

The Ice Princess was merely taking a stroll among her subjects and they dare not attempt to even touch the hem of her gown for fear of retribution. Or of frostbite.

The fanciful thought had a scowl pulling at his brow. Alyssa wasn't icy. She wasn't uncaring or without emotion. The woman he watched now was the same woman they'd warmed two years ago, the same one whose innocence they'd taken, but the heart of that woman was so carefully frozen now that reaching it was only done when she dreamed.

How they did it, how they'd known her pain, her fears, for the past eight years he didn't always understand.

His grandfather called it being soul bound. Some lucky men of the De Loren line knew a love that flowed so deep, so strong, that their souls would meld with their women's. Fernando De Loren had been confused how two of his grandsons had soul-bound the same woman, but he'd been certain the bond was there.

What Sebastian knew was the bond between Alyssa and him was unbroken. Just as the bond she and Shane shared had remained strong, steady.

When she slept.

It was almost amusing how she'd blocked herself from them. It would have been amusing if it didn't piss Sebastian off so damned much.

Forcing his gaze from her, Sebastian let it travel around the room, as he watched the lustful stares that followed her. Every man watching her imagined she belonged to them. How could they help but to lust after her? She was every man's fantasy. A wet dream walking. She sure as hell had his unruly flesh reacting despite the invisible Do Not Touch sign he could feel guarding her virtue.

She might be untouchable, but the male eyes there were definitely enjoying the view, Sebastian thought, as he shot the middle-aged tycoon eyeing her ass as she passed, a glare. The bastard was older than her father. He should be ashamed of himself.

The look on Grandpa's face wasn't one of shame, though. It was pure appreciation and wishful thinking. That was one treasure the graying grandfather of eight would never have a chance to touch. A sweet the bastard would never have a chance to taste.

She did have a fine ass, though. Nicely curved and pert, it bunched and flexed with graceful movements, the toned muscle shifting beneath her dress and drawing the eye without being in the least overt.

Every move she made whispered come-hither, while every look from her cold gray eyes sent the chill of rejection. And she could have had damned near any man in the ballroom and many of the women as well if that was what she wanted.

The cream of Alexandria's social set had turned out for her father's birthday party, thrown by none other than one of the most popular widows among the political elite. Rumored to be occupying the senator's bed after his wife's death two years before, his soon-to-be-announced fiancée, Landra Collier, had thrown a lavish celebration.

Aunt Landra was the queen of parties as far as Sebastian was concerned. Imaginative decorations, always with the utmost taste and style, and a guest list that had the political elite vying for invitations.

Champagne flowed from crystal fountains; a buffet of the choicest tidbits was offered as well as sweets so elaborately decorated they looked more like confections of art. Several box-office stars were in attendance, as well as a couple of *Billboard*'s highest-ranking musicians. Music drifted through the ballroom, seducing those who ventured out to dance and making brave even the most timid of guests. And occasionally those *Billboard* stars stepped to the stage to croon to a rapt, appreciative audience.

The party was also rumored to be a preliminary step to establish backing for a presidential bid for the senator as well. After eight years serving as senator, Davis Allen Hampstead was said to be ready to make his move on the White House. And there were those who believed he had an excellent chance at succeeding.

Though that rumor hadn't been confirmed among Sebastian's sources. And his sources were some of the best, even among this crowd.

"Would you explain why you're watching Ms. Hampstead-Stanhope make her rounds?" Khalid Mustafa questioned him from where he had stepped to Sebastian and leaned against the white marble pillar near the foyer entrance.

Stanhope. Her married name was guaranteed to have him gritting his teeth. Why she'd kept it after the death of her husband he had yet to figure out. Harvey Stanhope had died, along with Alyssa's mother, only days after Shane and Sebastian had rushed to reach Alyssa. The certainty that Alyssa was dying had nearly driven them crazy before they reached the United States.

They had nearly lost her, twice. Her husband's attempt to murder her had nearly succeeded. Margot Hampstead's plan to ensure Alyssa's husband never harmed her again *had* succeeded, though. She'd killed Stanhope, even as she'd ensured her own death, according to Summer.

"I don't consider this your business, Khalid," Sebastian informed him softly, never taking his gaze from Alyssa. "Go play with your wife."

Khalid didn't often need an invitation to get nosy, though, Sebastian had learned, especially when it came to his sense of protectiveness where certain women were concerned.

"It would appear Marty is rather busy at the moment," Khalid sighed. "But I'm fairly certain I have warned you that Ms. Hampstead-Stanhope wasn't a woman I would be pleased to learn you and your cousin were attempting to seduce, though. You're about to make us enemies, De Loren."

Yeah, that one really worried him into the deepest hours of the night.

"I think perhaps I might not have been paying attention then," Sebastian murmured, not in the least interested in dragging his attention from Alyssa to the half-Saudi onetime bastard prince. "I'll try to do better next time."

He probably wouldn't but sometimes it was best to pacify Khalid, just to shut him up.

"Ignoring such warnings isn't considered advisable, Sebastian," he drawled. "It wasn't given casually, as you should know."

Sebastian was getting tired of the warnings too. As far as he was concerned, Khalid could go to hell. Neither Alyssa nor his interest in her was anyone's business but his and Shane's.

"Isn't it getting close to your bedtime, Khalid?" Sebastian asked. "Why don't you hurry along so your pretty wife can tuck you in?"

A tense silence filled the air around them for long moments. Not that Sebastian paid much attention to it.

"Marty will wait for me." Khalid's brooding glare was ignored by Sebastian, his attention remaining on Alyssa as she stopped to chat with none other than Khalid's wife, Marty.

His siren.

She'd shut herself down so completely that the laughter and warmth that had been so much a part of her seemed to have evaporated.

Eight years ago she'd walked through this same ballroom, laughing with friends, Summer Bartlett and Gia Bennett. She'd been young, more innocent than they'd imagined, and so very open. Now she was cool, distant, and mysterious.

Then Sebastian had had no doubt that he and Shane could seduce her. Now he was certain he'd have to kidnap her to get a dance. She ignored his texts, his phone calls, and refused the single written invitation he'd sent her for dinner.

She had his confidence a bit dented for sure.

"She's far too fragile to deal with you and your cousin, Sebastian," Khalid warned him again.

Sebastian's jaw tensed. He heard the tone in the other man's voice, the knowledge that added an edge of pure confidence to the accented tone. There were times Khalid could be a pain in the ass. This was beginning to look like one of those times.

Acquiring information was one of Khalid's more interesting hobbies. Unfortunately, it appeared he'd become far too curious in the time Sebastian had been watching Alyssa. No doubt he would begin investigating why very soon. If he hadn't already put that far too intelligent brain of his to work in a matter that didn't concern him.

"That look of shattered pain in her eyes hadn't been there until she returned from a trip she took after graduating high school. Many attributed it to her mother. They said Margot wasn't kind to the girl, though I'm not one of those who believe it. A few of us deduced a broken heart. What do you think?" Khalid's question almost caught him off guard. And he damned well knew better than to allow Khalid's chatter to slip beneath his defenses. "I'm beginning to believe it was a broken heart myself."

"I think you better go join Marty now," Sebastian snorted as Alyssa moved to continue walking gracefully through the crowded ballroom. "You're giving me a headache."

Not to mention some heavily suspicious looks.

Khalid chuckled at the invitation, though he wasn't quite finished yet, it seemed.

"Alyssa was once part of a rather unique little group. She joined just after her twentieth birthday." Khalid lowered his voice further as he spoke of the Sinclair Men's Club Khalid was a member of and Sebastian had managed for the past two years.

"I know this." He was growing rather irritated with the other man now. Khalid merely stared back at him for long moments before evidently deciding to let that question pass.

"She maneuvered her dismissal from it very well about two years ago, though," Khalid continued. "I was actually rather proud of how she killed two birds with one stone so to speak."

Sebastian restrained the tug of a smile at his lips. He had to agree with Khalid, though he was still rather curious why she had maneuvered her dismissal rather than simply resigning from the club. She'd been married at the time. She'd never had an affair with any of the men; according to club files, she'd simply been a member, accepted under a special-circumstances clause in the Club membership rules.

Hell, she'd married six fucking weeks after she'd left Barcelona and no one knew why. There was so little gossip where she was concerned that it was impossible to figure out what the hell was going on.

"Your chatter is irritating me, Khalid," Sebastian sighed. "And that nose of yours is going to get you into trouble. Stay out of it."

He didn't need Khalid in a troublemaking mood. It didn't happen often, but when it did happen the other man could become a problem.

"Have I mentioned I sometimes get bored when Marty's busy?" Khalid asked curiously, crossing his arms as he settled in against the heavy support. "It's a terrible failing, I must admit."

He got bored when Marty was busy?

Khalid didn't have enough sense to give himself time to get bored. He jumped right into everyone's business without invitation or warning.

"How long has it been since you've touched her, my friend? Since you broke her once tender heart?" Khalid queried then, his voice much lower, more dangerous, than before. "And still you watch her with the hunger of a new lover. Tell me, were you and your cousin the reason she returned from Spain eight years before with all the passion and love for life she held, silenced?"

And his cousin Shane accused him of getting overdescriptive

and poetic? He obviously hadn't been paying attention to Khalid over the years.

"Shut the hell up, Khalid," Sebastian ordered him, still watching her profile as she moved for the wide French doors that led to the gardens.

It was in those gardens that he and Shane had first seen her. They'd been attempting to seduce another CIA courier they had worked with before heading back to Spain.

How they'd managed to miss the beauty who had found them in the farthest corner of the garden that night so long ago they had never figured out. They'd spent several hours in the ballroom, yet they hadn't seen Alyssa until she nearly stepped into a sheltered arbor where they'd stood with another woman.

"Excuse me." He moved to follow Alyssa, stopping when the other man blocked his exit with a subtle move of his body.

"Have I mentioned Alyssa is a friend? One I am quite fond of, actually. This could be a problem for me. Loyalty issues, you know? I'm very protective of the opposite sex in general. Friends even more so."

The warning in his voice could be a prelude to something far more dangerous, Sebastian knew. Not that the danger worried him; he was fairly confident he could at least match the other man in any fight. It was the sheer aggravation of time taken to do so that had resignation drawing a frown to his face.

Sebastian turned his full attention on Khalid then, tension beginning to prepare him to confront anyone daring to keep him from his siren.

"Stay away from her, De Loren," Khalid ordered with dark menace. "Don't make me tell you again."

"Do you really want to deal with me, Mustafa?" Sebastian stared back at him, his determination to get to Alyssa tightening in each muscle of his body. "Because, trust me, tonight's not a good night for that."

"I would deal with you now or whenever I feel the need." Khalid's smile was cold, and Sebastian was certain he thought it was intimidating. "I said she's been through enough. She does not need the pain you and Shane would no doubt bring her, because your hearts are not your own. I've checked into your pasts. Two men rumored to have lost their hearts as well as their souls, years before—"

"Don't get between me and Alyssa, Mustafa." Sebastian barely managed to keep the snarl in his voice from attracting undue attention. "You won't like the consequences. I promise you that."

Pushing past the far too nosy Khalid, he strode through the ballroom, following the woman his soul was still bound to.

He'd waited too damned long for this. The need for her was like a sickness in his gut, destroying him from the inside out.

It was bad enough Summer had made certain she forced the cousins to wait the full two years projected for Alyssa's full recovery and tortured the hell out of them with texts and pictures. She'd been cruel. Pictures of Alyssa in her sexy little gowns, barely there bikinis . . . just the memory of them threatened his control.

They could wait until Alyssa's first public appearance, she'd demanded when he and Shane had put their CIA ties behind them. Alyssa wasn't well enough yet. And each time they'd tried to slip past the woman she'd turned into a damned bulldog blocking their way.

Until two months before.

*Headed out, y'all. Good luck* [Summer had texted them].

The text had come the day after she and Alyssa had left for an undisclosed location for vacation. At the same time Shane had been called away to Barcelona to give the details of Gregory Santiago's death. Again. It seemed there had been some pages missing from his statement.

Sebastian had no doubt Summer was behind that as well.

Now Khalid thought he could stand in his way?

One more time, Sebastian thought, and the other man was going to have to back up those threats that kept spilling from his mocking lips.

Slipping past the French doors, Sebastian stared around the dimly lit gardens, searching for the slight, graceful figure of his dark siren. A satisfied smile curled at his lips when he saw the path Alyssa was taking. Narrower than the others, more dimly lit, and less used. The same path she'd taken eight years before that brought her to him and Shane.

It wasn't winter, but neither was summer in full bloom. It was cool enough to be comfortable, a light breeze playing along the sheltering trees and ornamental shrubs, whispering of far too many years of hunger, too many years of pain, and the woman he was dying to hold once again.

## 13

Alyssa had attended parties at the Collier mansion several times a year after returning from Barcelona. For some reason, she was one of the few guests to receive invitations to every party Landra Collier threw, even before the widow had become Alyssa's father's lover.

The first invitation after her return had been for the second Winter Ball. Though she didn't venture from the ballroom and she hadn't stayed long, still, Alyssa had accepted the invitation.

Just being there had been hell that year.

It was hell now.

A part of her wanted, ached, to run and hide. She wanted to pull the blankets over her head and stay there until she could face the world without the pain that followed her every waking second. Until she could emerge whole. She hadn't been whole for so long that she didn't even remember what it felt like.

She definitely didn't know what being whole felt like whenever she came to the Collier parties. She only drifted through the crowds, feeling Shane and Sebastian with such strength she'd not known if it was agony or comfort she'd felt. And she had no idea why she even cared. They'd torn her soul from her body. They'd taken everything, everything, from her and she'd had so little left to hold on to.

She'd felt them. As though they lingered just behind her, just out of sight, their warmth touching her, she had felt them each time she accepted Landra Collier's invitations to her parties and balls.

It was because this was where she'd met them, she told herself. This was her first memory of them. Because of that, she would always feel them there. But it was the gardens she was drawn to, the gardens she'd always refused to make her way to.

She'd been a mess that first year. Not that she'd improved much with each visit to the Collier mansion. And despite Margot's anger and disapproval, Alyssa had attended every social event Landra Collier sent her an invitation to.

Had she glimpsed either Shane or Sebastian, she would have had no choice but to leave. And no matter the temptation she had never returned to the darkened arbor. The memories were too painful and until tonight, until this particular ball, she'd sworn she could feel them pulling her to that darkened section of the shadowed gardens. Which made so very little sense. Why send her parents those pictures and their demands and still attempt to ambush her in the dark? It had been her silly imagination and hunger for them, she'd told herself. Nothing more.

That sense of being pulled there wasn't present tonight, though. That second sense she'd been convinced she had of them in Barcelona had been no more than a fantasy. A girlish attempt to excuse her need for love, Margot had suggested regretfully. But still there were moments it tortured her.

Moving along the softly lit path she paused for a moment before looking behind her. She almost smiled at the sense of being followed. How paranoid she could be whenever she was here. Always imagining they were so close. Always certain she was being watched.

She was pathetic and weak, just as Harvey had once accused her of being. Too weak to get over whoever broke her heart, he'd sneered. Then somehow, he'd learned of her time in Barcelona and the fact that there had been two lovers rather than one who shared her bed. No one but her parents had known whom she'd shared those months with. She hadn't even told Summer whom she had been with and the other woman was her dearest friend. One of only a few friends, actually.

Once Alyssa stepped cautiously along the path it didn't take her too long to find the hidden, sheltered arbor where she'd first met Shane and Sebastian. How charming they had been. The Spanish goof and the South Texas cowboy. They'd stolen her heart that night, locked it up so tight that no one else could have penetrated it even if they had been willing to face Margot's icy regard to attempt it. Not that any of the young men she'd known had been willing to face Margot. Her mother had been such a strong, forceful personality during her life that nearly everyone walked warily around her.

Coming to a stop outside the arbor, she stared at the stones beneath her feet for long moments. She was terrified to look inside. Knowing it was empty, knowing there was no one there but needing them to be there. Needing a closure that only facing them would ever bring her.

Lifting her head, she made herself peer into the shadowed shelter. And it was empty. Shadows lay thick inside it; the lights used for holiday parties were absent, the shadows thicker, heavier, than they had been years before. Ornamental trees and flowering shrubs surrounded it, increasing the darkness. Still, she had to force herself to step inside and walk to the now cold fireplace where she'd stood that first time.

Turning slightly, she faced the brightly upholstered padded bench that sat along one side. It was wide and appeared incredibly comfortable. Comfortable enough to lie back on, or to lie atop the hard, powerful body of a lover as another moved behind her.

She had to smother the whimper that threatened to escape as the jagged, ever-present pain swelled inside her. It was always waiting to strike. Always there, willing to ambush her at the most inopportune times. To remind her, to overwhelm her with memories she had no business allowing free.

She had to burn the memories out of her mind. She had to find a way to cauterize the wounds in her heart and soul that refused to allow her to heal. She couldn't face them or she risked those pictures being released to the media as well as every porn site in existence.

Pictures of her between her two lovers. Explicit, erotic pictures of them penetrating her. Both of them penetrating her. One beneath her, the other behind her.

As she stood in front of the fireplace, her gaze focused on the brightly colored padded bench in front of her, Alyssa realized she was clenching the sapphire and diamond stones that hung from the gold chain around her neck. She held them like a talisman. As though they were all that held her from the sometimes overwhelming need to let loose the fury raging inside her.

She'd been certain the necklace was taken while she slept that last day in Barcelona when Shane and Sebastian had collected their other belongings. She had grieved for it, missed the weight of it with such desperation that it had been agony at times.

"Why?" The word was torn from the deepest part of her, ragged and filled with grief. Closing her eyes, she felt the bleak fear that she would never be free of one fantasy summer spent amid two men's lies.

"Siren," soft, aching, the whisper eased around her, light as air, as a familiar warmth enfolded her. "Sing for me, siren."

Oh God. It was so real.

Like a dream come to life, Sebastian's whisper at her ear, his warmth against her back.

Eyes closed, she swayed for a heartbeat, her knees weakening as the sensual, erotic needs rushed from the dark, hidden well she'd forced them to so long ago. His presence was so clear that the feel of his strong arms sliding around her, enfolding her, had her fearing she was finally succumbing to madness.

"I feel you, siren," he breathed at her ear. "Your sweet song wrapping around me. Pulling me to you."

Heated male lips brushed her neck, setting fire to every nerve ending in her body. Her breasts swelled, engorged nipples rasping against the snug fit of her gown. Between her thighs the folds there became drenched with need, her clit throbbing, coming to full, aching life. The complete lack of sexual need outside her dreams flared to life, the sensation of touch, of sound, had her fearing she was no longer able to separate fantasy from reality.

"How I've longed to touch you, to taste you again." The brush of air against her neck, the softly accented sound of his voice, took fear to certainty.

"How sweet you taste," Sebastian's voice rumbled at her neck. "What I wouldn't give to lay you down and taste all the sweet cream flowing from your pussy. Are you wet, siren? Are you ready for me to fill you?"

She'd been ready. God help her, she'd been ready for so long.

"I want to lay you down." His teeth rasped along the sensitive tendon of her neck. "Push your gown to your hips and eat all that candy syrup spilling from you. And when you're crying out, shaking from your orgasm, I'll push my cock inside you." His voice thickened. "Feel your tight little pussy milk me. Feel it, so hot and tight, clamping on my dick as you beg me to take you hard. To shove every inch inside you hard and deep."

And she would.

She remembered the striking ecstatic pain of having him or Shane push inside her with those hard thrusts, forcing her inner flesh to stretch with fiery sensations that threatened to throw her immediately into orgasm.

Fighting to breathe, to hold back the whimpers she knew would destroy the fantasy, Alyssa waited in desperate anticipation to see what her imagination would come up with next. Clenching her thighs, Alyssa felt the soaked condition of the thin panties she wore. Her clit was more swollen, more sensitive, than it had ever been.

"Let me have you, siren," he whispered, his fingers tugging the bodice of her gown over her breasts. When they captured the hard points of her nipples, calloused fingertips applied just enough pressure to drag her fully into the fantasy she'd slipped into.

Pleasure and pain erupted in the hard points he was pressing and rolling between his fingers. As the erotic dream fully enfolded her, Alyssa let her head fall back, feeling his shoulder cushion it as little moans of desperate, rising pleasure fell from her lips.

"You love the mix of pleasure and pain, don't you, siren," a whisper, so soft, so destructive. "That's why you loved the feel of both of us at once. The higher your pleasure, the more you craved it. The feel of us pushing inside you, keeping you stretched and filled."

She sank deeper into the fantasy, into the sensations rushing over her. His fingers tugging at her nipples, milking them firmly.

Behind her, his erection pressed against the small of her back, the heat of it sinking through his slacks and past her gown.

"I'll eat your pretty pussy later," he groaned. "Bend over for me, siren. On the bench. Let me fuck you. Let me feel your pussy clenching on my dick until it feels like a vise I'll never be free of."

Releasing her nipples, he pushed her forward, a ghostly pressure against her shoulders until she braced her hands against the padded seat of the bench. Behind her, Sebastian lifted the yards of material before easing one knee to the seat as well and flowing the material of the dress along the side of it.

A second later the fragile lace panties were torn from her. Firm hands parted her thighs further.

The swift penetration of her vagina with the hard press of his tongue had her falling against the padded cushions at the back of the bench. There was no strength left inside her, only the desperate cries falling from her lips as his tongue pushed past the swollen, slick folds of her sex, licked, stroked, causing more of her juices to rush from her and meet his tongue.

"Fuck, so sweet," he snarled, the sound so guttural it was nearly unrecognizable as his.

Then that wicked tongue slid back, licked its way to the forbidden entrance just below it, and rimmed it erotically. His tongue flicked over it, stroking and teasing as he drew the juices spilling from her back to lubricate that entrance with his fingers.

"Oh God!" The prayer tore from her at the swift penetration of her rear by two calloused, forceful fingers.

Pleasure and pain, just as he'd said. Fire and sharp fingers of lightning-infused pleasure striking through her as his fingers penetrated her rear entrance, the tight ring of tissue deeper inside flaring open against the firm thrust.

Pushing his fingers in, filling her, then retreating, he impaled her again, his hand turning, pushing his fingers deeper before withdrawing completely.

"Don't stop." She could barely breathe, barely keep her grip on the back frame of the bench to hold herself in place. She needed more, so much more.

It was the madness finally overtaking her, Alyssa told herself. Too many years without them, too much hunger—

"I can't wait, siren," he groaned, one hand gripping her hip tighter as she felt the engorged head of his cock part the swollen folds of her pussy and begin pushing forward. "I have to have you. Feel you around me, so slick and tight. So hot—"

The storm was beginning to spiral through her senses. Sensation and pleasure, all her senses opening, converging.

A hard thrust shattered what might have been left of reality. The heavy crest buried itself inside her, taking only a small part of her as her inner tissue clamped around it with convulsive ripples of pleasure and pain.

Sebastian paused abruptly, his hands clenching on her hips, groaning as her vagina clenched, rippled in tortured pleasure around the thick, flared crest.

"Don't stop," she whispered, desperate now.

Her fantasies had never made it this far. Never taken her to such an extreme point that she knew her orgasm hovered just within reach.

"I can't stop." A snarl of agonized need, Sebastian's hunger, echoed around her, inside her. One hand gripped her hip with bruising strength as he began moving.

Surging hard, he buried yet more of his throbbing, iron-hard cock inside her, helpless cries falling from her lips as she pushed back into the thrust. The thumb of his other hand tucked between her buttocks, buried itself in her rear entrance and added to the blistering agony-ecstasy sensations. Thrusting hard inside her, he worked his cock with furious strokes. Stretching her, burning her inner flesh with each desperate impalement until he surged in to the hilt with a strangled groan.

Agony. Ecstasy. It all converged as he moved inside her, shafting her with stroke after furious stroke. Each impalement was iron-hard flames parting her with shocking, brilliant sensations of not just excessive pleasure but also heated pain. He rode her with a pace that blurred the borders between the two extremes until they disappeared entirely with the sudden, brilliant explosion of ecstasy.

Her body convulsed, jerking with helpless spasms as her vagina tightened and rippled around the heavy erection buried deep inside her. Both hands gripping her hands now, holding her tight to his body. The width of his cock seemed to expand. Hard, hot jets of semen erupted inside her, flinging her into another violent orgasm.

Even as the second explosion overtook her Alyssa was forced to admit . . .

This wasn't a dream.

Not a fantasy or madness.

This was real.

◆+◆+◆

What had she done?

Oh God, what had she done?

Alyssa could feel the dizzying nausea beginning to build inside her. Panic tightened her chest, making it hard to breathe, hard to swallow, as the realization of her weakness flooded her senses.

Her fingers tightened in the cushion she rested against as Sebastian eased his still-hard cock from inside her with a groan, while she concentrated on just breathing.

When he straightened, she began to ease up herself, but he placed his hand on her back, holding her there. The feel of what she assumed was his handkerchief wiping the slick spill of her release and his semen from between her thighs had her eyes closing as rage seemed to pour through her.

"Sweet, sweet Alyssa," he whispered, drawing back as he helped her to ease her leg from the bench and stand with her back to him. "As sweet and beautiful as my dreams. Hell, more so."

Tugging the material of her gown back over her breasts, she felt them shaking, felt her entire body quivering from the inside out.

"As beautiful as your dreams," she whispered, bitterness burning inside her, roiling in her stomach as she fought to keep from throwing up. "I didn't bother you."

She had to force that statement past her lips, force him to acknowledge that she had not broken the terms of their cruel demands.

Her father would be so angry, so disappointed in her yet again. And humiliated.

She could feel that humiliation beginning to burn inside her already.

"Bother me?" The derisive laugh that sounded behind her had

her cringing. "Baby, you've bothered me every second of my life for eight years."

Alyssa pressed her hands to her stomach, eight years of rage pushing aside humiliation and fear.

"Guilt, Sebastian?" She stared into the darkness, focused there. Turning, facing him, might break her as nothing else had yet.

"Guilt," he agreed. "Regret."

The admission caused her teeth to clench, her lips to pull back with the effort it took not to lose the control she was forcing over her ragged emotions.

She swung around, the rage blistering, searing. "What gives you the right to ambush me like this? To even attempt to come near me?" she sneered. "Need an excuse to punish me more than you already have?"

Her voice was thick as she realized her eyes were growing wet. Tears that had lain trapped inside her for years were now trying to make themselves known.

She would not cry for the cousins again, not after everything they'd taken from her. Not after everything she'd lost because of them.

"Now, siren, let's be nice," he whispered, his expression so drawn, so filled with such false misery, that she hated him for it. Hated him for the bleak pain he could project into his eyes, the lines at the sides of his lips and eyes that indicated he'd known far too many smiles.

Goofy. He'd always smiled, always laughed—

"I hate you!" The vehemence in her tone had shock resonating through Sebastian.

"Alyssa . . ." He moved to reach for her, to be certain he had to be imagining the shudders shaking her small frame.

"What, were you bored?" she sneered, contempt filling her voice, her expression, as her fingers formed fists at her sides. "The game far too unexciting, Sebastian? Did you think I'd willingly give you an excuse to shred me further than you already have?"

"Siren—" His expression tightened, hardening as he watched her in the dim light.

"I'm not your fucking siren!" Alyssa cried, rage contorting her expression, agony racing from her, slapping against his senses with such black, overwhelming pain Sebastian could only stare back at her in shock. "Sirens are fairy tales, Sebastian, just like summer love and promises made to stupid little girls. Well, this stupid little girl finally grew up and realized the difference. Sirens, summer love, empty promises, and happily-ever-afters are right up there with dragons and knights in shining armor. None of which exist. They never existed."

God, how she'd been hurt. The insanity that had forced them from her had taken something so precious, so innocent, and bred such fury in its place. And now, for the first time since he'd held her two years before, he feared it couldn't be fixed.

"Perhaps I never grew up," he said softly. "Let me explain, Alyssa—"

"Explain?" She stared at him as though he'd lost his mind. "What possible explanation could you give?"

"It's not what you believe—"

"Not what I believe?" She jerked back farther, as though his words were a whip slicing into her flesh. "How could it be anything but?"

She was staring at him as though she couldn't believe he was actually there, actually speaking.

"Alyssa, please," he said softly. "Let me explain, siren. I can fix it."

"Fix it?" She stepped back, shaking her head as she watched him in disbelief. "Yes, Sebastian, fix it," she suggested as though she knew he couldn't. "Fix my walking into my parents' home the day

I flew back from Barcelona to face those fucking pictures and your threats."

He froze. Everything inside him froze. Life, the blood in his veins, his very breath.

"Fix it, 'Bastian," she breathed with mocking gentleness. "Fix having someone kill our baby." Her voice broke. "Fix that, you son of a bitch. Bring my baby back to me, Sebastian, and then I might, *might* be able to look at you without hating the fact that you even draw breath. Fix those pictures you sent my parents. Fix stealing every text, every picture of us on my phone. . . . Fix destroying every memory and scarring my soul until just living hurts," she cried with such agony . . . And despair rocked his soul. Their baby . . .

She turned, running from the arbor, running from him. He heard a broken, dry sob and as though on autopilot raced from the arbor to find her struggling to get back to her feet. She'd fallen on the stones. Her gown pooled around her; her hair had fallen from one carefully placed pin along her shoulder.

Gently, Sebastian eased her back to her feet. When she would have jerked from him, he restrained her, the growl that left his chest holding her in place more effectively, though, as he repaired the hair that had fallen.

He was living in a nightmare.

He could see her pale face, her gray eyes dry of tears but the horror and bitter, furious agony trapped inside her filling her gaze instead.

Their baby?

Someone had killed their baby?

"I hate you," she snarled again.

Sebastian shook his head. "I didn't know—"

"Liar!" The agonized accusation was like a slap in the face. "You knew. You knew because I left you that damned test before I left Barcelona. Don't you dare lie to me."

Fists clenched, shattered agony and rage burning in her eyes, she swung away from him. Rather than running from him, this time she moved at a fast walk, another of those horrifying dry sobs slashing at his soul as he watched her go.

Their baby? Someone had killed their baby?

The shock that surged through him as she'd thrown those words at him was like nothing he'd ever known. Rage pounded at the shield encasing him, agony was exploding through what was left of his soul, but the calm that descended over him was unrelenting. It pushed aside emotion. Pain, rage, love, hate, it was all pushed aside as he followed after Alyssa, memories of the past eight years crowding through his mind.

Over four months after she'd returned home he'd awakened from a drunken stupor, her pain sobering him in an instant, her horror reaching out to him, strangling him with the agony he could sense her experiencing. Not just the emotional pain but also physical pain. In Texas, Shane had wrecked the powerful sports car he'd stumbled into, trying to race for her after days of attempting to drink enough liquor to make him pass out.

They'd known . . . But they hadn't known she was pregnant. She said she left the test for them to find. Whoever had stolen their belongings from her would pay for that one. They had wiped the pictures from her phone, erased the texts.

That was okay; Sebastian had them all. They'd be returned soon.

Until then, he would have answers. Answers that only Alyssa could provide.

Because she'd also said he'd sent pictures and threats. That her parents had received them just before she'd returned home. They had abided by the conditions a blackmailer had set out, but Gregory must have hedged his bets, and his blackmail, by doing the same to the Hampstead family.

They wouldn't know it was over, Sebastian thought, and for some reason the CIA hadn't found another overseas account for him. They'd find it, though, he swore as he stepped into the ballroom, tracking Alyssa, stalking her in her attempted escape from him.

There was no escaping him. There was no running; there was no denying the bonds that had linked him and Shane with her for eight agonizing years.

"Sebastian, hold up." Khalid made the mistake of attempting to stop him. The other man's hand gripped his shoulder, his dark eyes filled with concern.

Before the half-Saudi could counter the move Sebastian had pushed him to the other side of a thick, heavy column, his arm slamming into Khalid's throat, pressing in tight as dark eyes just stared back at him, narrowed and assessing.

"One more time," Sebastian said softly. "Stand between me and that woman, one more time, and by all that's holy, Khalid, I will kill you. Do you understand me?"

The rage pounding through him, the violence welling from some primitive, previously unknown source, was like a sickness invading every cell of his brain, his body.

Khalid stared back at him, eyes narrowed, his expression thoughtful now when it should be filled with the awareness of death settling over him.

"Understand me?" he asked again, increasing the pressure.

"For now." Khalid didn't sound as though he were strangling, but Sebastian knew that breathing wouldn't be comfortable.

Releasing Khalid, Sebastian slid around the column and moved to catch up with Alyssa. She wasn't going anywhere. Too much lay between them. Too many questions, too much pain, and far too many fucking secrets.

# 14

She had to get away from there. Alyssa knew she did. She also had to warn her father of her stupidity. What a wonderful present to give him for his birthday, she thought, amazed at how desperate she had been. So desperate she'd allowed herself to believe she was slipping into a fantasy as Sebastian touched her.

How was she supposed to explain this to her father? Explain that she'd allowed one of the men who destroyed her life to not just fuck her like a whore in the garden, but to do so unprotected. And now, no doubt, those pictures would soon be released now that she'd managed to piss him off.

God, how would she survive Sebastian's punishment for daring to call him and Shane on what they had done to her?

The thought of those pictures splashed across the Internet had her swallowing back the bile gathering in her throat. This would destroy her father, and his dreams of the presidency.

What had she done? She could feel the implications of her weakness rushing through her like a wave of dizzying sickness.

"Alyssa, there you are." Courtney Sinclair caught her arm just as Alyssa felt her knees weakening.

"I told you she was heading our way." Marty caught the other arm.

"Smile, sweetie," Courtney muttered, the demand firm despite the softness of her tone. "Let's get you from gossiping eyes."

"I'm fine," Alyssa assured her, though why she was allowing them to drag her along a nearby exit from the ballroom she wasn't certain.

"Of course you are," Courtney assured her. "This is why your eyes are filled with tears and your face ashen. Did you fall? Your dress is torn as well."

It had been her own clumsiness, her desperation to run from Sebastian before she shed the tears she'd kept trapped inside for so long.

The tears and the rage. Fury was unraveling inside her in a dark, heavy wave. And it had no place to crash.

"Let's get you presentable, sweetie," Marty suggested as they drew her to a private room Landra used for impromptu meetings.

"Here we go." Releasing her in front of the comfortable, thickly cushioned sofa, Courtney headed across the room. "You definitely need a drink."

"I think I need a lot of drinks." Glancing down at her dress, she restrained a sigh at the sight of the torn material. It extended from her knees to her ankles, the flowing fabric now showing the layered slip below.

"Alyssa, what happened?" Sitting next to her, Marty touched her arm gently. "Dear, this very much looks like finger marks on your arm. Did someone try to hurt you?"

A sharp, bitter laugh left her lips. "I think it might have been the other way around."

She shook her head at the question in Marty's eyes and made herself ignore the concern.

"Were you defending yourself?" Courtney handed her a shot glass of amber liquid. "Drink. You're white as a ghost."

She drank, quickly. The liquor slid down her throat, heated and bracing as she inhaled sharply at the strength of it. The door to the room pushed open, Landra Collier stepping inside in all her stylish glory.

The pale cream Grecian evening gown was the perfect foil for her black hair, dark eyes, and the sun-loving color of her skin. The hint of Spanish ancestry in her exceptional looks and fiery temper had always caused Alyssa to wonder at her connection to Shane and Sebastian, but she'd never asked.

Now, Landra's expression was creased with worry, her dark brown gaze gleaming with it as she held the skirt of her dress up enough to allow her to step quickly to Alyssa.

"Alyssa, darling, what happened?" Kneeling in front of her, Landra touched the torn dress before her gaze immediately latched on to the faint discoloration along Alyssa's upper arm.

Strangely enough, the bruising had occurred in Sebastian's efforts to steady her as he rode her with the power and strength she'd begged him for.

"I'm fine, Landra," Alyssa told her. "I fell in the gardens. . . ."

"I'm sure you are, dear," Landra agreed solemnly. "I guess I should have the gardens trimmed back a bit. It appears a branch might have poked your neck a bit hard."

The suspicious tone of the older woman's voice caused Alyssa to flush. Sebastian had marked her; that was where the reddened brand had come from.

Covering the mark with her fingers, she stared back at Landra miserably.

"I've done something terrible, Landra," she whispered. "Father will never forgive me."

Landra's dark gaze softened, gentled. "Alyssa, sweetheart, your father would forgive you anything."

"Not this." Her fingers curled into fists where they lay in her lap. "Never this."

The heavy slam of the door had Alyssa and Landra both

surging to their feet as Courtney and Marty moved quickly in front of Alyssa.

"Sebastian?" Courtney questioned him as she remained where she was beside Marty, trying to block his view of Alyssa. "Now is not the time for this. She is in no shape to battle with you."

"Don't, Courtney." There was no doubt of their familiarity, even if Alyssa hadn't already known they were friends. "Leave. Now. All of you get the fuck out of here and let me talk to her."

"It's not going to happen like that, Sebastian." Marty sounded just a bit confrontational.

"Stop this." Alyssa moved away from them, glaring at Sebastian, at Courtney and Marty. "He's not going to beat me, for God's sake. He just wants to see how many of his lies I can stomach."

She didn't need their protection; they should know that. She was perfectly competent in other areas of her life. Everywhere but where Sebastian and his cousin had completely destroyed it.

"Sebastian, this is enough." Landra sounded less than pleased with him now. "You swore you would not upset her. Look at her. The child is shaking like a leaf, disheveled, and obviously upset."

"Disheveled" wasn't a good way to describe it, Alyssa thought with a sigh. And she wasn't disheveled; she was furious. There was a difference. Yet so was he. And he had no right to be angry at all.

"Courtney, if you and Marty will allow us a few moments of privacy," Landra asked of the other two women firmly. "And please inform Davis it may be a few moments before I return. Do not tell him who I am with. That is my prerogative alone."

Courtney all but pouted while Marty gave a little roll of her eyes.

"Unlike Khalid, I know when to butt out," Marty informed Landra. "But don't expect me to cover for something like this again, Landra. I won't do it."

Whatever "this" was, Alyssa thought with bitter amusement.

"Just go." Alyssa lent her own firmly voiced demand. "I don't need protection from him. And there are no weapons present, so he doesn't need protection from me."

"Oh dear," Landra murmured before breathing in deeply and turning to Courtney and Marty. "Go on. I promise I'll handle this."

Landra would handle it. Alyssa had to force back bitter laughter at the thought. No doubt her father would learn everything before the night was out. What did it matter, though? The whole sordid tale would no doubt be revealed far too soon anyway.

Stomping to the bar as the two women left, Sebastian poured himself a whisky, tossed it back, then poured another and repeated the action.

Standing with his back to Alyssa, he seemed to be considering a third before he slowly released the glass and decanter.

"Tell me, Landra." He sounded tortured. "Did you know she lost our baby? That she was pregnant when she returned from Barcelona?"

Landra gasped in shock and seemed to sway as she gripped the back of the chair she was standing next to, her gaze swinging back to Alyssa.

"That was why you were so ill after you returned from Barcelona?" she asked, shocked, paling as she stared at Alyssa with tears in her eyes. "My God, you would have been at least—"

"Nearly five months," she whispered. "I became pregnant the first month I was in Barcelona. I was eighteen weeks pregnant when someone managed to slip a drug into me that aborted my baby. My personal physician became suspicious . . ." She had to breathe, just for a moment as agony lanced her. "The baby was fine during my checkup the week before. He ran tests after . . ." She couldn't go on.

She'd been able to hold her baby, as tiny as he'd been. Touch perfect fingers, thick golden-tipped black hair. She'd felt him move before she'd lost him. Felt his little foot against her palm as it lay on her stomach.

And she wasn't throwing any of this up at Sebastian. Why? Why wasn't she trying to hurt him as she'd been hurt?

Sebastian poured another drink that he finished quickly. A second later the glass shattered from where he'd thrown it to impact on the wall across from him.

"Sebastian," Landra whispered his name, tears filling her eyes as Alyssa watched. She turned then, a tear falling as she stared at Alyssa. "I am so sorry. So sorry."

"Why would Landra know?" Alyssa asked Sebastian rather than commenting on Landra's sympathy. "It's not as though she was part of our lives at the time."

Sebastian's lips thinned, but instead of speaking he pushed his fingers through his hair before his gaze settled on Alyssa again.

"I am Sebastian and Shane's aunt, Alyssa," Landra told her, her voice low. "Sebastian's father is my brother. Shane's mother my sister. Once you returned from Barcelona, I tried to watch out for you, but Margot rather blocked allowing others around for a while."

Yes, her mother had become incredibly protective after Alyssa had lost the baby. Only a few people had known of her pregnancy. Alyssa hadn't gone out in public, the pregnancy wasn't announced, yet someone had found out and managed to poison her child.

"That's why you married Stanhope," Landra said then. "For the child."

Alyssa nodded sharply. "Look, as interesting as all this is," she mocked Sebastian's pretense of grief, "I have a question." She focused on Landra. "Does Dad know you're his aunt?"

Landra at least had the grace to glance away for a moment and shake her head. "The subject hasn't come up," she admitted.

"Then I would say you're unaware of the pictures he and Shane sent my parents? That they accused me of initiating the relationship that they found distasteful. And if I wasn't kept from them, even if we were at the same social event, then those pictures would be sent to every porn site, paper and Internet based." She would have sneered; instead, she watched as Sebastian seemed to pale.

"My God!" Landra lifted her hand to her throat, shock filling her expression. "Alyssa, I know for a fact this is not true. I and my other sisters are all that kept Shane's and Sebastian's families from being bankrupted by the blackmailer that demanded Shane and Sebastian never see you again. Such pictures were used as well. For you, dear, for Shane's and Sebastian's love for you, five families paid a blackmailer for six years, until they were able to learn his identity and end the threat."

That couldn't be true. It wasn't possible.

Dizziness threatened to wash over her before she steadied herself.

"I have to say, you're good," she accused him, forcing the words past numb lips. "A liar to the end. Where's the money you and Shane stole from your family?"

"Sweet mercy, Alyssa," Landra gasped, shocked. "You can't think such a thing." She stared between Alyssa and Sebastian before turning back, her lips trembling. "Alyssa, had they known about the child, nothing could have held them back. I swear that to you."

She couldn't let herself think anything else. She couldn't.

"Keep fucking with me, Alyssa. We'll both regret it—" Something dangerous rumbled in Sebastian's voice.

"You are a liar to the end," she accused him, ignoring that warning, ignoring the trepidation, the suspicions beginning to rise inside her. "And I won't stand here and listen to it."

"Then fucking sit!" The lash of his voice had a flinch jerking her body tight.

Violence throbbed in his voice, tightened his haggard expression. Stalking to her, he caught her arm, holding her in place when she made a move for the door.

"Shane and I did not do that—"

She smacked him. A hard, open-handed blow. The sound

exploded around her. When he turned his gaze back she smacked him again, just as hard. Before she could draw back for another blow he secured her wrists with one hand.

Gently, so gently, he held her immobile, staring into her eyes as she met the black, swirling rage in his eyes.

Releasing her slowly, he lifted the weight of the chain between her breasts, his gaze centered on the gems as her eyes opened.

"Your heart bound by ours," he reminded her. "I swear to you, may God strike me now, neither Shane nor I would ever do something so vile. Especially to you. To the one we pledged ourselves to."

She ripped the chain from her neck, throwing it in his face as she jerked from him. "I struck you for Him."

But she was breaking apart inside because she wanted nothing more than to believe Sebastian.

"You will not run from me again." Swinging her around, he forced her to face him. Refusing to let her escape the bleak suspicion rising inside her.

"I won't listen to your lies—"

"By God, you will hear me," he cursed furiously. "You know we didn't do that to you, Alyssa. You know it."

"I won't hear this—"

"Do you think you suffered alone? We suffered with you, dammit. We felt your pain when you lost our child, and knew no reason for it. Two years ago we felt you die, felt you cry out to us that you were cold. That we had promised to keep you warm."

Shock had her swaying for a moment. How could he have known that? No one was there when she'd whispered those words.

"We suffered a blackmail so vile it nearly destroyed five families to keep those pictures from being released. To protect you we followed a blackmailer's demands to the letter until we fucking killed him six years later. Gregory Santiago, Alyssa. He orchestrated it, he was the only one that could have sent your parents those pictures, and we collected all the negatives, everything he had. And all we could think about was coming for you. Only to feel your death hours before we were to leave Spain and fly here."

"No. . . ." It couldn't be true. It couldn't be.

"We tracked him when he finally tried to transfer that money six years after beginning to collect the monthly payments. Two days before Stanhope stabbed you."

"It's too late!" she screamed, ripping away from his hold once again, all the rage and pain of the past eight years exploding in her head. "It's too late."

"Now who's the liar, Alyssa," he accused her, furious. "Do you believe for one second I'll accept that?"

"You have no other choice—" She couldn't accept anything else. She'd suffered, she'd lost her baby, lost the men it had killed her to be torn from, and only in the past two years had she found a measure of peace.

"Oh, siren, you just watch me show you the choices I have," he bit out, his expression savage, sensual. "And I can prove your words for the lie they are."

"Kiss my ass, Sebastian," she raged.

"Oh, I will," he promised her. "Right before I fuck it."

"My cue to leave, children," Landra announced, making her presence known after Alyssa had forgotten she was even there.

"No, it's my cue to leave," she told the other woman, backing slowly away from Sebastian. "I've had enough."

"We're going to discuss this, Alyssa." But he didn't move to stop her. He glared at her, his eyes so black, bottomless, but filled with so many emotions she simply couldn't face them now.

"We have nothing to discuss." She felt exhausted. "Content yourself with my earlier weakness, Sebastian," she warned him with what she hoped was firm rejection. "There won't be another slip. Thank you for the truth, eight years too late. At least now I know what I died inside for," she told him, the weight of the knowledge dragging at her shoulders. "Too bad you didn't tell me to begin with. Maybe then there would have been some part of me left for you to return to."

She slipped from the room without anyone stopping her. Sebastian hadn't said another word, and that was for the best, she told herself.

Rather than returning to the party to find her father, she left the mansion by the main entrance after calling the chauffeur and giving him her location. She wanted to go home, crawl into bed, and find a way to reconcile the past eight years of her life, eight years of loss and lies, with the reality she was facing now.

The reality that, despite the danger of it, the cousins could have told her the truth. There were any number of ways they could have met with her secretly, at least told her. If they had, the betrayal wouldn't have followed her every waking moment. Fear wouldn't have lain about her like a heavy, wet cape, and the belief that the men she hadn't been able to release had betrayed her wouldn't have destroyed her from the inside out.

They had shaped her life until two years before. Shaped it to the point that she'd nearly died, believing that the bond she couldn't break was on her side alone.

They hadn't trusted her. Not even enough to see her one last time and tell her the truth.

Just as Sebastian had never explained what had happened to the pregnancy test she'd left in the bathroom. The one that hadn't been there when she'd awakened later that morning to find all the cousins' belongings gone. If they hadn't taken everything, then who had?

✦✦✦

Sebastian forced himself not to race after her. Shane was within hours of landing in D.C., and once he learned the truth of the past eight years, then they'd decide the best way to handle her determination to push them out of her life.

"'Bastian, I had no idea . . . ," his aunt whispered.

"I know." He nodded, a sharp, certain movement. "I had to be certain."

A baby. A little boy, Alyssa had said. At five months the child would have been fully developed. Unable to survive outside her body, but growing, moving.

"I guess I understand her mother's abrupt departure from a cold, unfeeling shrew where Alyssa was concerned to one so protective it was sometimes impossible to speak with her without Margot hovering near," Landra said quietly, her gaze filled with sorrow as she stared back at him. "Had I even suspected . . ."

At least someone had tried to protect her, Sebastian thought. They sure as hell hadn't done so.

They'd believed she was safe. Married, and no gossip had been whispered of problems either with the marriage or with Alyssa herself.

They'd failed her, though, in so many ways.

Turning, he made his way back to the bar before staring at the liquor for a long moment. He'd spent those first two years existing in a bottle in one way or the other, to force back the demand that he find a way to see her, one last time. That he explain. That he hold her, let her shed her tears or her rage, whatever she needed to do, before releasing her and continuing to search for the bastard blackmailing them.

Her siren song, he thought painfully. She'd tried—

The door to the small private room opened again.

"Davis." Landra turned to her lover as Sebastian slowly turned to face him.

He knew the moment Senator Davis Allen Hampstead recognized him. Alyssa's father would have made certain he knew the identities of the men who had stolen his daughter's innocence and apparently sent such pictures to him.

The door closed rather hard. The senator's eyes narrowed on him before he turned to his lover. "When did you intend to introduce me to your nephew, Landra?"

Sebastian faced the painful knowledge that his aunt might have lost the man she had come to love so deeply.

"It's not her fault, Hampstead," Sebastian informed him, watching the other man closely.

The senator held his hand out to Landra, though he made no comment either way to Sebastian's claim.

"Davis, you should have told me what happened to Alyssa," she whispered. "Especially if you knew Sebastian was my nephew."

She went to him, taking his hand and allowing him to draw her to his chest. His hard, cold gaze remained on Sebastian, though.

"Summer finally got around to telling me a few things a few weeks ago," he stated. "I've let it ride until I could meet them myself." Anger flashed in his gaze. "Where's your cousin, De Loren?"

Sebastian crossed his arms over his chest and stared back at Alyssa's father silently. Shane's location was no one's business at the moment.

"Davis, they're good boys," Landra protested the air of tension in the room.

"They seduced an eighteen-year-old girl with no experience, and no concept of the pain they could end up causing her," Hampstead retorted. "They were nearly twenty-five years old, Landra. Old enough to know what they were doing. And they had been doing it long enough to know what she would face."

"You believe all we wanted was Alyssa in our bed for a few paltry months?" Sebastian could barely believe her father would accept such a simplistic view of the cousins' relationship with her. "We met her here, Senator, at the Winter Ball Landra threw. We didn't seduce her then, nor did we pursue her until she came to Spain. By the time she arrived we could think of nothing but her. Neither of us could. She belongs to us—"

"No, Sebastian, not anymore she doesn't." Hampstead shook his head wearily. "She might have, until two years ago. Whatever Stanhope did to her changed something inside her. When she woke, Alyssa wasn't the same. There's nothing inside her but anger now. Anger and a determination to never need either of you again."

She might have wanted to be determined, but she still wanted them. With a fiery, feminine heat he'd carried in his dreams for eight years now, she still wanted them.

"We won't accept that." He wouldn't accept it. Ever.

"You waited too long," the senator stated with a brief shake of his head. "Eight years too long is my guess."

"She's still ours." Her response to him in the gardens had proven that. If he hadn't felt her, hadn't lost himself in her for that brief period of time, then he might have believed too much time had passed, too much hurt stood between them. But he had felt her need for him, and he had lost himself in her. "And trust me, Senator, there's not a chance in hell we're going to let her go."

## 15

Alyssa had known once she'd seen Sebastian's reaction and realized the past wasn't as she'd believed that there were going to be problems. Once, she had known them well enough that she had the ability to guess fairly accurately what they would do from one moment to the next in any given situation. And she'd known that she'd have to face Shane next. For that reason, she found herself on pins and needles the day after her father's party, certain he would arrive at any given moment.

As the day progressed far too quietly instead, Alyssa told herself she wasn't in the least disappointed that he didn't show. She hoped that, unlike Sebastian, he was willing to accept the fact that too many years had passed and far too much pain filled the void and the years between them. Bridging that time and the memories that filled them would be impossible now.

As Sunday rolled into Monday and Monday slid silently into Tuesday, she assured herself the faint ache she felt in her chest wasn't because he hadn't shown. Yet Tuesday night she was still in her office, next to the renovated suite she'd been stuck in for months two years before, after Harvey's attack.

Harvey had planned to kill her, she thought painfully, reaching to rub at the scar beneath the blouse she'd pulled from the band of her skirt hours ago. The resulting infection combined with blood loss, anemia, and her weakened system should have killed her.

Without thought her fingers returned to the three gems hanging on the gold chain around her neck. Rising from her desk and stepping to the opened door, she stared into the night beyond the sheltered patio, still worrying the two nearly flawless diamonds and accompanying sapphire.

Summer had never told her where she'd found the necklace. She had frowned, looked at it, and given her one of those wide-eyed little-girl looks and said, "Well, honey, I guess I found it wherever you lost it. I thought it was too pretty not to be worn, though."

She'd never lost it. It had been stolen from her. She had thought Summer had found a way to re-steal it and return it.

Leaning against the side of the open French doors, her head resting against the glass as the summer breeze played over her, she wondered what would have happened if Gregory hadn't stolen eight years of their lives. Had he been behind the death of their son? Of the last link she'd had to the men she loved with everything inside her heart and soul?

Her baby would have lived. Dr. Brennan's tests had revealed a drug in her system at the time known to result in miscarriages. Somehow, she'd been drugged, and there were so many of her father's staff members and employees who worked in the mansion at any given time that there had been no way to determine whom to suspect or the reason behind taking her child from her.

Margot had been certain the order had originated from Shane and Sebastian. She'd been furious, so enraged by Alyssa's loss that for a while Alyssa had feared what her mother would do. A lifetime of her mother's distance had ended that night. In the years that passed Alyssa had gotten to know her in ways she'd never imagined possible.

That loss had stolen a part of Alyssa's soul, though. Taken a part of her so vital, so intrinsic to who and what she was, that there had been no healing from the loss.

The child she had named Shane Sebastian Hampstead—not Stanhope, she would not have allowed their child to carry another man's name—had been stolen from life with such monstrous cruelty that Alyssa still fought to fathom why, to make sense of the reason for it.

She'd never been able to suspect Shane and Sebastian as Margot had, though. And she'd tried to, many times. Now . . . what a mess she'd allowed herself to be drawn into once again. She'd let herself believe a whisper was a fantasy, a touch a dream, and Sebastian's possession of her simply a manifestation of hunger. And she'd known better all along. Even as she let him bend her over that bench and surge into her, she'd known better.

Pressing softly against her abdomen, Alyssa reminded herself that she hadn't been protected and Sebastian hadn't worn a condom. She'd become pregnant that first week that the cousins had taken her, their cocks bare, spilling semen into her as they cried out her name, as lost in the pleasure as she had been.

*"We don't protect you well enough, sweets," Shane had breathed out against her neck, his heartbeat racing beneath her cheek as he finished taking her at the kitchen counter, his cock still filling her, still throbbing after releasing inside her. "If you weren't protected, you'd have already ended up pregnant."*

*"And you and Sebastian would be trying to figure out how to hide from Daddy's wrath." She'd laughed, only half-joking.*

*"Only if you were hiding with us." His voice was strained, his cock immediately iron hard again and moving inside her. "Only if you were hiding with us."*

She would have already been carrying their baby then, tiny, silently, secretly, forming inside her. Her body had defied the medication she'd been taking for birth control and, without any of their knowledge, had created a son.

"I think it's my turn to have what was taken from us, now."

Her eyes flared open. Straightening with a gasp, Alyssa stared into Shane's deep blue eyes. Standing at the entrance created by the house and the evergreen border of narrow, interwoven pines that grew around the patio, he watched her with hooded, brooding eyes.

His statement had her shoulders straightening, her gaze narrowing on him before she turned and walked stiffly back into her office.

"I don't think that's how it works." Turning to confront him, she found herself confronting his wide chest instead.

"I think that's exactly how it's going to work." His voice was so dark, so deep, that the danger inherent in it vibrated through her senses.

"Wrong." Her body was screaming yes, though, and she had no idea how to shut it up. "You need to leave and come back at a more acceptable hour and with a more acceptable way of greeting me. We can talk then."

Alyssa forced herself to meet his eyes; she found herself pressed between the edge of the desk and his advancing body. And her senses were reacting with such strength that she found herself cursing her own awakening sensuality. A sensuality she believed had died a slow, painful death after she'd left Spain.

"Do you really think that's how it's going to work?" he growled, hemming her in between the desk and his body. "After everything I've learned since Saturday night, do you really think that's how this night is going to go?"

The cousins' arrogance had definitely grown in the eight years that had passed.

"After everything you've learned," she murmured, the bitterness seeping into her voice. "How like you and Sebastian to think of it in those terms. How about everything I learned since Saturday, Shane? What about learning that the men I loved beyond anything couldn't even trust me enough to tell me how my entire world was being threatened?" Her voice rose, though she managed, just barely, to keep from screaming. To keep the throttled rage from spilling out and destroying both of them. "You let me think you no longer wanted me." A trembling finger stabbed toward him. "You let me marry to ensure you knew I wouldn't try to claim the child as yours. You let me lose my child alone, and you let me nearly die alone." She was shaking now, just as she had while confronting Sebastian. "Neither of you could trust me enough to tell me why—"

"Because we didn't know!" he snapped, moving closer as Alyssa retreated, desperate to keep the cousins from touching her. "We didn't know about the test you left. We didn't know about the baby, Alyssa. We did not know about the pictures and the threats sent to you. But just as you accuse us for not coming to you, neither did you come to us."

"I was terrified—"

"And you think we weren't?" His expression was like stone; his voice throbbed with anger, with remembered rage. "You were our life. You always have been."

"You sent me away; I didn't send you away." The retort was thick with remembered pain. "No, Shane, you have no right to question why I didn't come to you for anything. You sent me away believing I was a summer fuck and nothing else."

"You knew better!" Now his voice did rise. Not enough to be heard far, but it rose.

"And according to Sebastian you knew when I lost my baby." Fists clenched, she fought to hold on to what little control she had left. What little sanity she had salvaged from the past eight years. "You knew something horrible happened. And you stayed in your drunken stupors until you could bear what you sensed had happened to me. And where were you two years ago?" she sneered. "I nearly died twice and Sebastian said you heard my whisper to you that I was cold?" She had to laugh at that, but there was no amusement left in her. Only the bleak knowledge that they had ignored her every time she needed them. "I screamed for you and Sebastian as I felt our baby die. I screamed for you, Shane. I cried until there were no tears left inside me. And when I felt myself dying two years ago I reached out to you with every fragment left of my soul. Where the hell were you?"

"In this fucking room the night your mother was buried," he snarled, the fury lining his face now a terrible sight, the words silencing her as nothing else could have. "And we've been watching out for you ever since."

"Like hell—"

"How do you think you came by that necklace that was stolen from you the morning my grandfather had two employees slip in and steal our belongings?" he snapped. "We came to you, Alyssa, and that damned viper Summer Bartlett demanded we give you two years to recover before claiming what was ours. Two more fucking years on top of the hell we had already lived through, and we gave it to you rather than see you suffer more."

Alyssa felt herself stumble.

Sometime after the infection that raged through her finally responded to the antibiotics she was given, Summer had asked her if she remembered anything that had happened before she woke.

Alyssa hadn't remembered anything but the darkness and scattered remnants of what she'd believed were dreams.

"We replaced the promises we made to you, Alyssa." His voice was lower now, the bitterness in it thicker, though. "We made certain Gregory couldn't hurt you and we came back to you—"

"And it was too late then, just as it's too late now." Her hands lifted helplessly as she stared back at him.

Shane was so still, so silent, his blue eyes like lasers boring into her as the tension and air of dominance strengthened around him.

"Too late?" he repeated softly. "Do you really think either of us will accept that now?"

"I don't care if you accept it, Shane." Shaking her head, she realized that allowing him to confront her alone might not have been the wisest course of action.

He wouldn't hurt her, but her ability to deny herself once the cousins touched her was already proven to be completely ineffective.

"I really don't care if you accept it; that's how it will be." Unfortunately, the conviction she felt wasn't nearly as deep as she hoped.

The hard, less than amused features shifted, became more sensual and far too hungry.

"Keep telling yourself that. See if you can convince yourself of it while I'm working my cock inside you," he suggested, the low rasp of his voice sending a shiver of remembered pleasure up her spine.

She couldn't do this again. She couldn't risk what she could feel it doing to her, weakening the shields she'd placed around her emotions, around her ability to be hurt.

"And you really think I'm just going to give in to that fantasy as easily as Sebastian managed to fool me with it?" Anger rose inside her again, swift and hot.

"At least you admit to wanting us," he pointed her error out, his smile hard, his eyes filled with lust and rage. "Eight years of that hunger, Alyssa. Six of those years knowing you had married another man, slept with another man. And lost our child while married to another goddamned man!"

The fury slipped free. Shane had never had the same control of his anger or the ability to channel as Sebastian did. It rolled through him now, though the hands that gripped her hips, tilted them, and lifted her until her rear rested on the desk weren't hurtful.

Sexual dominance and determined lust did fill them, though. That leashed, forceful hunger had always made denying him impossible. Not that she'd been able to deny Sebastian's charm, either.

"This isn't the time for this—"

"There's no better time for it," Shane informed her, the guttural sound of his voice slicing through her anger, eight years of pain and need pushed aside as she felt her body refusing to obey the demand that she tear herself from him. That she put enough distance between them to be able to think.

"Shane, this isn't a good idea," she tried to object again.

"Do you know, Alyssa, of every woman I've been with, there has been none that I've hungered to fuck as I've hungered to fuck you. None," he snarled. "That gave me such pleasure as I received while watching your tight little ass open for me, watching it stretch and burn my cock as you whimpered, gasped, and begged for that mix of pleasure and pain that only comes while your lover's taking you so intimately."

Taking her so intimately. And that was what it had been. An intimacy, a trust she'd never known with anyone else but him and Sebastian.

Alyssa fought to breathe as her body clenched, her sex heating and instantly so wet that her response began dampening her panties.

He and Sebastian both had always seemed surprised at how eagerly she came to them, no matter how they took her. That particular act had been like throwing gas on a conflagration.

"You have no right to come here like this—"

"The hell I don't." Gripping her jaw, Shane forced her to stare up at him, forced her to see the emotions burning in his gaze.

Emotions she had fought herself for so long were now reflected in the haggard features staring down at her.

"I knew the moment Sebastian touched you," he whispered, the rage in his eyes softening, sensuality and lust flickering in the brilliancy of the color now. "I felt your pleasure, Alyssa. Just as we would each sense it each time the other took you and we weren't there, in Spain. I sensed the ever-present pain locked in my soul ease, felt you aching, desperate, then felt all that pleasure whipping inside you."

"Shane!" The buttons of her blouse scattered over the floor as he tore the edges apart to reveal the minuscule lace bra she wore, the cups barely covering her engorged nipples.

"Eight years we ached for you." His voice dropped, became thick and rough. "Eight years, Alyssa, and all I could dream of was taking you. Tasting your kiss. Sucking those pretty, sweet nipples until you came. . . ." He cupped one swollen mound gently. "Do you remember the afternoon we took you to the private beach in Sebastian's boat?"

She did. Oh God. . . . "I won't—" She didn't want to remember, but she remembered.

"I sucked those pretty, tight nipples while Sebastian pulled you down where he sat in the cockpit seat?"

Her breath caught, her vagina clenching, knowing Shane caught the response as he watched her carefully. "You were begging him to fuck you hard, to make you burn," he whispered as he leaned closer, easing her to her back on the top of the desk. "Then you begged me."

"Stop. Stop—" She tried to cover his lips, to make the words stop.

"Sebastian was groaning your name as he came inside you," Shane reminded her. "But we were going to take you together, remember? Before you rode his cock into orgasm, he had your sweet rear ready to be fucked. And you were already primed for it."

Her eyes closed, the memory pulling her in, the drugging pleasure and need for the sensations she knew Shane could give her weakening her.

"Don't do this to me," she whispered, her lips brushing against his as he teased her with the threat of his kiss.

"I pulled you to me, turned your back to me, and that pretty hand gripped my cock and placed the head there at the entrance of your tight little ass."

She jerked, the memory of that pleasure, the lashing, burning sensations, destroying her.

"As I pushed inside you, you were crying for me, Alyssa," he reminded her. "Moving against me, taking every increment with such heat I thought I'd die. Backing to me until my dick was buried to the hilt inside you, and begging Sebastian to fuck you again. And he did." His jaw flexed with the strength of the tension rising higher inside him. "While you leaned back to me, my cock stretching you until you were crying out your pleasure, until you screamed with each thrust as Sebastian sank into your sweet pussy again."

Her eyes closed, a cry spilling from her lips at the sudden heat surrounding her nipple. Her knees were pushed back, held in place with his arms, and before she could draw in a shocked breath he'd torn her panties from her hips and two fingers pushed demandingly, dominantly, inside the clenched depths of her sex.

Her orgasm was immediate. Shocking.

It exploded through her senses with a detonation that seared her senses as his lips slammed over hers.

It wasn't a gentle kiss. It wasn't an easy kiss. It was a prelude to the thick, heavy weight of the flared crest of his cock pushing inside her a moment later.

"Alyssa . . . Ah God. Ah, baby . . ."

Tight heat, rippling, clenching, flexed around his cock like a silken vise as it pulled the hard flesh inside; her pussy milked and caressed the engorged head of his dick, then inch by inch the throbbing, sensitized stalk.

Holding back his release would kill him. It would destroy him.

No condom. Sebastian had already spilled his release inside her and Shane was desperate to do the same. She'd known he would be here. She'd known he was coming for her. She'd been standing there waiting for him and he'd known it. Her expression soft, filled with remembered pleasure and aching need.

Taking her easy wasn't an option. As hungry for her as he was, eight years of pent-up, desperate greed was like a crazed instinct now. Get inside her, ride her with the hard, burning thrusts he knew she craved, then spill himself inside the giving depths of her body.

He couldn't push back the animalistic urge. Had she mentioned it, had she, for even a second, questioned the lack of protection, then he would have donned the condom he'd brought. He'd meant to protect her. But he knew what they'd had in Spain was all the sweeter for feeling her inner flesh rippling around his naked cock, clenching it and tugging his release from him with those spasming little ripples in her pussy.

Pushing in hard, deep, he stilled, some broken edge of consideration digging into him with razor sharpness.

"Tell me now," he groaned, one hand gripping the back of her head to tilt it back, watching as her eyes drifted open. "Tell me to protect you now." The words strangled him as he forced them from his lips. "Tell me to protect you, Alyssa, or I swear to God I'm going to come inside you so hard it will burn both of us alive."

Her nails rasped along his belly before her slender fingers gripped his naked hips, her knees clenching at them while the internal muscles of her pussy rippled over his cock with flexing strokes. He couldn't imagine losing the feel of her naked flesh clamped on him, but he would, if that was what she wanted.

Dark stormy gray eyes slitted open, a flush rushing from her breasts to her hairline.

"Then make us burn," she seemed to dare him. "Burn us alive, Shane."

Levering back, spreading her thighs, and holding them in the wide grip of his fingers, Shane watched as he withdrew from her body, the heavy layer of her juices clinging to the broad shaft stretching her, stroking her.

"Look, baby," he crooned, flicking a glance at her to be certain she was indeed watching as all but the engorged crest pulled free of her. "Am I hurting you, Alyssa? Be sure."

He had never understood how he and Sebastian hadn't hurt her.

There had been times in Spain that their hungry lusts had ridden her for hours at a time, exhausting her, leaving her wilted against their bodies as they fought to still the hunger for her.

It had never stilled. It never would still.

"I love watching your pretty pussy take me," he groaned. "To see your clit, so swollen and red, throbbing, begging for that one touch that'll set it off." He looked up at her again. "Stroke your pretty clit, Alyssa. Let me watch. Let me feel you come for me there. Feel your pussy clamp down on me—" A harsh, brutally guttural groan was torn from him as her fingers moved to the little bud.

Graceful, sensual, she stroked the flushed little knot of nerves, her breath catching as her inner muscles tightened further on the stiff erection he pushed inside her again.

Hard. Her juices rushed to meet the impalement as her hips jerked, a cry tearing from her lips.

"Fuck me, Shane." She was barely coherent, her fingers moving on her clit as he began thrusting heavily inside her. "Give me, before I die for it—"

Give me. Those two words. Give me . . .

He gave her. He gave her every hard inch, every thick, furious thrust, as he stared down at her, ached for everything he and Sebastian had lost with her. And when she twisted beneath him, jerking, shuddering, and flying into ecstasy with her second orgasm, Shane let himself give everything to her.

He gave her each fierce ejaculation. Each hard pulse of ecstasy ripping through his senses with such pleasure he felt destroyed by it as the spiraling, stormy release overtook both of them.

+ + + +

Both Sebastian and Shane confused her more than she could say. Curled in the corner of the large sofa that sat to the side in her office, she watched as Shane stared into the night, his back to her, his shoulders tight with tension.

He hadn't said much since insisting on gently drying the spill of both their releases from between her thighs. He and Sebastian had both always been diligent about taking care of her in such a way. Even in Spain, when exhaustion had weighed upon all of them, one or sometimes both of the cousins had gotten from the bed and ensured she was comfortable after the excesses they participated in.

"You can't stay here all night, Shane," she warned him when he didn't appear to be leaving. "I need to get some sleep soon. I have a long day ahead of me tomorrow."

That long day included a meeting in town. Ian Sinclair, the owner of the Sinclair Men's Club she'd once actually had membership in, had called and requested she meet with him. He'd hesitated to give her the reason for the requested meeting, which only made her more curious. She'd actually forgotten about it until that moment, though. Until she'd needed to find a reason for Shane to leave, to give her the last few hours before daylight to figure this out.

Still dressed in the torn blouse—the bra he'd all but ripped from her had been discarded, as were the panties he'd left in shreds—she wanted to undress and crawl into bed, his scent still lingering on her, his touch still imprinted on her flesh.

"I'm not leaving, Alyssa." He turned to her and she saw the tight, grim set of his lips, the muscle that flicked at his jaw.

Leaning against the open door frame, he simply watched her, seemingly relaxed.

There was nothing relaxed about him, though. Alyssa could sense the tension and determined arrogance he wore like an invisible cloak.

"What do you mean, you're not leaving?" There had to be a way to make him see that simply was not going to work. Not now. Not ever—

Her fingers clenched on the edges of her blouse at the "past" part of that thought. Something so dark, so filled with denial, swirled inside her, pulling free long-forgotten dreams of just that. Of at least one of the cousins, either of them, holding her in the dark, sheltering her from the nightmares.

"Exactly what I said." Straightening, he pulled the door closed, secured it, then tilted his head lazily to the side as his gaze continued to hold hers. "Let's go to bed, siren."

She almost rose eagerly to her feet.

The muscles in her legs were actually tightening to do just that.

"No. Absolutely not." She did rise, but not to lead him to her suite next door. "That is unacceptable."

The bleak, tight-lipped smile he gave her assured her he believed otherwise.

"Evidently you mistake me for Sebastian." The lazy drawl in his voice was a warning, and Alyssa knew it. He'd made up his mind, and as far as he was concerned, he wasn't budging.

"I've grown rather used to sleeping alone," she tried to argue. She had always tried to sway him.

"You still think you can convince me to do something I know neither of us want." He shook his head, buttoning his shirt as he moved slowly to her. "Since your bed's so close, darlin', and attached right to your office, it will be no problem at all to hide the fact that you slept with me."

The shirt hung loose across his chest, the broad expanse of bronzed flesh pulling her gaze to the hair-roughened breadth.

She wanted so desperately to let him draw her into the suite, to her bed, beneath the blankets, against the heated power of his body where she wouldn't feel the cold again.

"I can't do this—"

"Of course you can." Bending, he had her in his arms before she could protest, cradling her against that heated chest and moving to the connecting door.

"Shane, I won't let you—"

"Sebastian's on his way," he informed her as he moved into her suite, his voice tight, his complete denial of her objections obvious. "Stop fighting, Alyssa; this is a battle you know you're not going to win."

Staring at the hard, grim profile, she acknowledged that the fight wouldn't make a difference. It would take more than she was willing to give it. It would take a force of nature, several law enforcement battalions no doubt, and the National Guard.

"Bossy," she muttered.

For a second, the briefest second, a memory teased her mind. Summer bitching at her, Shane commanding, and her own muttered "bossy."

Summer was in so much trouble. That southern charm and wide-eyed innocent look would not get her out of trouble this time. She hadn't told Alyssa that Shane and Sebastian had been there after Margot's death. Just as she hadn't told her how Alyssa had reaquired the necklace. Alyssa had actually thought Summer had stolen it somehow. The wretch.

"Whatever it takes." Stepping into the bedroom, he moved through darkness to the bed and laid Alyssa gently on the blankets the maid had turned down earlier.

The maid turned them down every night, pulled them up every day. Alyssa never slept in the bed, despite the months she'd spent searching for it.

Light spilled into the room from the small table lamp and she felt Shane pause. Tension mounted inside her as he stared around the room.

"Did Stanhope ever sleep in this room with you?" His voice was harsh, rasping in his throat.

Alyssa shook her head.

Harvey had never slept in any bed with her. He'd never been a husband in any way but name. She'd insisted on it.

She knew what Shane saw, though. A near replica of the bedroom in Spain. The tile floors and scattered rugs. The iron bed and antique tables next to it. The windows behind the headboard.

It was her only concession to moving back to the Hampstead mansion after her mother's death. The renovations to the bedroom had to be completed quickly. Alyssa didn't sleep there, though. She slept on the couch in the other room and watched the night outside the windows.

"Alyssa," the whispered sound of her name had her throat tightening.

"Leave," she demanded, though her voice lacked any true strength this time.

"Alyssa." His fingers clenched in her hair, pulling her head back.

She couldn't meet his gaze, but that wasn't what he wanted.

He wanted her kiss.

With hungry demands and fierce, arrogant eroticism his lips moved over hers, his tongue stroking forcefully between them to meet hers. It was nothing like any other kiss he or Sebastian had given her. It was nothing like any kiss she'd ever had in her life.

Hot, filled with dominance and sexual intent, it was erotic, spiked with lust and with something more. A something she didn't want to feel, didn't want to know.

When he pulled back, his lips slid to her ear and brushed against it softly. "Let it be another dream, siren," he whispered, the bleak hunger in his voice tightening her chest. "When you wake, we'll be gone and you can tell yourself it never really happened."

## 16

Alyssa would have considered lunch at her favorite restaurant a treat at any other time, she thought as the waiter showed her to the private veranda where Ian Sinclair, owner of the Sinclair Men's Club, his private investigator, Chase Falladay, and one of the higher-ranking members, Khalid Mustafa, were awaiting for her along with Ian's wife, Courtney, and Khalid's wife, Marty, a former FBI agent.

Allowing Ian to help her with her chair, Alyssa looked at each of them as Khalid poured her a glass of wine and placed it in front of her.

"Well then," she said softly, letting her fingers touch the flared base of the glass. "I wasn't really hungry this afternoon, so should we go ahead and get down to the reason for this little meeting?"

Ian grimaced at the question as she noticed Courtney's arm moving as though to place a comforting hand on her husband's leg.

"I knew it wasn't a social call when you asked for the meeting, Ian." Alyssa sat back and watched him closely. "So why not just get to the point so I can finish my errands for the day. Does this have something to do with Saturday night?" Her gaze flicked to Marty and Courtney.

"Not yet," Khalid assured her, and though his dark eyes were friendly and warm, there was a tightness at his lips that assured Alyssa she didn't want to hear whatever it was.

"Discussions concerning Saturday night are off the table," she stated firmly, then turned back to Ian. "Is that why you're here as well?"

"Unfortunately, no," he sighed. "I wish my reason for being here were that simple, Alyssa. It isn't."

She picked up the wine and sipped. On second thought, she went ahead and took a healthy drink. She had a feeling she was going to need it.

"Shall I begin, Ian?" Chase asked then, though his tone of voice wasn't one of a man seeking permission. "Alyssa, as you're aware, the rules concerning the club aren't just those that they agree to for the protection of the club. There's also those the club itself makes for each member for their protection as well."

Alyssa nodded warily. She could feel the trepidation rising inside her now, some warning that this meeting wasn't going to be just about Sebastian and Shane. If it was about them at all.

"Yesterday, a little after daylight, a program was isolated in several computers used by members in the social rooms. The program was created to infiltrate the club's mainframe and isolate all files and information concerning several club members. You were one of those members, as well as a close associate of the other two."

She could feel herself paling.

"As I said, the program's been isolated," he said. "It in no way achieved its programmed parameters. But considering the two members that were also part of those parameters, and in light of other concerns that have been raised, we wanted to alert you to the problem and get as much information as possible. Identifying the member who placed that program is of the utmost importance."

Of course it was. Some of the members who had been a part of Sinclair's Men's Club since before Ian Sinclair was given guardianship of it were more than just of the utmost importance. Hell, even the man her father had stated would be his vice presidential pick if he was to run for the presidency was a member.

"I think I need a real drink," she said, shock resounding through her.

As she covered her face with her hands for a long moment she was only barely aware of Courtney rising from the table. When she lowered them again and inhaled with a slow, even breath, she realized, as much as she wanted it to be, the past wasn't over.

"Alyssa, the club files are completely safe," Ian gave his assurance as well. "This isn't the first time a member has attempted to betray his agreement with the club, and it won't be the last. We have some of the most advanced minds in computer protection working on this. There is no danger to your secrets, nor any other members'. We make certain of it."

"I know that." She nodded, swallowing tightly. She had no doubt the files were safe, if any electronic files even existed. She doubted there were any. "Are you asking if I know who's trying to steal information about me and your other two members?" She lifted a brow with bitter mockery. "Sorry, perhaps you should ask Shane Connor and Sebastian De Loren that question. They may be able to help you far better than I."

"You have no doubt Shane and Sebastian are the other two members," Ian said gently. "Why is that?"

"Really, Ian?" She felt like screaming, raging. When the hell was it going to end? "Shane and Sebastian are the only two members I've had a relationship with. If the members are associated with me, they're the only options."

As she spoke Courtney set a drink in front of her before sitting beside Ian once again.

"Thank you." Nodding to the other woman, she picked up the drink and took a healthy swallow.

It nearly stole her breath.

It had been years since she'd allowed herself the pleasure of the smooth, potent whisky Courtney had brought her. Not since her last night at the club actually. When she had helped Courtney break Ian's famous control and relent to choosing a third to share his lover with. There in the main bar of the club she'd done no more than caress Courtney through her clothes when Ian entered the room. It had been enough to show him his lover was far more adventurous than he'd wanted to consider, though.

It felt like eons ago when in fact it had been only weeks before Harvey had shoved that damned knife in her side.

"Do you have any enemies that you're aware of, Alyssa?" Ian asked her then. "Inside or outside the club?"

"The only enemy I knew I had is dead." Lifting the glass, she finished the drink. "And we'll leave it at that."

"Sebastian didn't exactly appear a friend Saturday night, Alyssa," Khalid pointed out, speaking softly as he lounged back in his chair and ignored his wife's warning look.

Landra had already warned her of the slight confrontation Khalid and Sebastian had been involved in over her. Khalid was intensely protective, but where it came to Shane and Sebastian, his protection wasn't needed. No matter what he believed.

"Don't do this, Khalid," Alyssa asked softly. "Don't destroy the perfectly nice friendship we have. Please."

Silence filled the table. She was aware of Ian, Chase, and Khalid exchanging wary looks while Courtney and Marty simply watched her compassionately.

"Sebastian and Shane are not my enemies—" she'd wanted only to reassure him, but of course, that simply couldn't be enough for him.

"Sebastian didn't appear to be in the friendship category, either," Khalid pointed out as the fingers of one hand played with the butter knife lying next to an empty plate.

Alyssa turned her gaze to Ian. "I'm about one more question away concerning that subject from walking out. Are we clear?"

she warned him, careful to keep her tone as well as her demeanor not just firm but also non-confrontational.

They were all friends, but ignoring her request to let this subject go would result in a definite cooling-down period where those friendships were concerned.

"Enough, Khalid." Ian's voice held an undertone of steel. Khalid wasn't guaranteed to pay attention to it, though.

Khalid's lips thinned for a moment, his fingers lying still next to the cutlery now.

"Should you need a friend," Khalid said then. "I or Marty, or both, would be more than willing to be one."

"You are friends, Khalid," she sighed, so weary she could almost feel the exhaustion pulling her down. "Friends I value. All of you are. But they're . . ." She paused, uncertain how to describe what she wanted to express.

"They're more," Marty offered the explanation gently.

"They're more." So much more, and yet still Alyssa had no idea how to explain even to herself how deep that explanation applied.

"What Khalid meant to say, if you need someone to talk to, someone who values your secrets as we would value your need to talk to someone about them, then we're all here," Marty assured her. "We are your friends, Alyssa, and our concern for you is what spurs Khalid's protectiveness of you. I assure you, it's nothing more."

Her throat was tightening, those damned tears she hadn't been bothered with for so long burning behind her eyes.

She didn't want this. She didn't want the weight of friends, protectiveness that was sometimes more a lie than love was, and the betrayal that threatened to come with it.

They were friends, and she admitted that. But not close friends. She hadn't allowed herself close friends except Summer in such a very long time.

"Thank you for the offer," she told the other woman. "I'll keep that in mind."

She highly doubted she'd take them up on it, though, and the knowledge of that was in Khalid's dark gaze.

"If that's all the business we had to take care of?" She turned to Ian as she slid her chair back and rose from the table. "I need to be going."

"Alyssa." Rising to his feet, Ian caught her hands in his, his touch gentle, without the insistence she expected. "The invitation for lunch was sincere as well," he teased with an air of warmth. "Stay for the meal. No more questions, I promise."

She couldn't bear to eat if her life depended upon it. Her stomach was a mess of nerves, rioting at the very thought of food.

"I really have several errands I must get finished," she assured him, pulling her hands back and hoping she hadn't offended him.

She would deal with it if she must, but she didn't want to offend this man who had been so kind to her over the years.

"I understand then." He nodded. "Perhaps another time?"

"Definitely, another time," she promised.

Clutching the small purse she carried with the fingers of one hand, she nodded to the others before turning and hurrying from the veranda to the exit that led to the private walk rather than through the restaurant as she'd entered.

She wanted to get out of there. She wanted to get her errands finished and return home, where she could make sense of what had happened, make sense of the changes occurring around her, and try to figure out why someone would attempt to steal club files where she was concerned.

Who would want to? She hadn't known Shane and Sebastian were members of the club while she'd been there. If she had, she would have immediately gone to Ian with the pictures and the letter her parents had received before she'd become a member. Once the Judiciary of the club had been apprised they would have immediately ensured that threat was erased. No member had ever gone against the Judiciary. Whoever they were, they were the highest-ranking and most powerful members of the elite men's club and ensured all members were protected if an issue arose.

When it arose. She'd actually never heard of the group being called together while she was there, but she wouldn't have, she imagined.

Pushing the thought back with memories best left alone as well, Alyssa exited the restaurant. Rather than hailing a cab, she turned and headed down the sidewalk. The restaurant was only a few blocks from the caterer whose services she preferred using for luncheons and small dinners held for her father's visiting friends and political allies or visiting dignitaries. With the upcoming luncheon scheduled for one of her father's committees and an arriving overseas political ally, she wanted to make certain the caterer had received the seating charts Alyssa had sent over by her assistant.

The tree-lined sidewalk was shaded by the newly leafed branches, the early-summer sun not yet hot enough to make the walk uncomfortable. It was pleasant. A nice breeze with just a hint of spring's trifling mood swings lingered in the soft brush of air. Just enough to cool the sun's heat, to remind everyone of the previous month's cold.

Normally Alyssa would have enjoyed the walk; normally she would have never allowed her peace to be threatened as she had last night. She'd learned to control her emotions as well as her anger where the past was concerned. She'd had to learn to control them or she would have destroyed herself in the first two years after returning from Madrid.

She'd been weak, Alyssa admitted. Losing the baby as she had, learning she'd somehow been given something to kill the child she was so desperate for, had completed the destruction of all the dreams inside her. She'd never dreamed of a career or making some mark on the world that would outlive her. She'd dreamed of another mark she would make. A family, lots of children. She was an only child, but she wanted a home filled with children, with laughter and warmth. She'd resigned herself to having only the one child after returning from Spain. Once her baby had been born she'd intended to divorce Harvey and move to the property her grandparents had left her in Pennsylvania. She would have filled her home with her son's laughter, loved, and been at peace, she thought.

She would have, if her baby's life hadn't been stolen from her.

She couldn't afford to allow herself to become entangled with Shane and Sebastian again.

She reminded herself how she'd hurt the first time. How horribly her very soul had been wounded. So deeply that even tears wouldn't fall and the knowledge of how alone she was had been like a dagger forever twisting inside her chest.

They weren't going to let her go so easily, though, and Alyssa didn't know if she could ever allow herself to trust in the illusion of love again. Love meant trust and they hadn't trusted her. They had let her believe they hadn't wanted her. They had ignored the pain they swore they had felt coming from her when she had lost their baby. And they hadn't come to her.

When she had needed them the most, they had ignored the knowledge of that need.

And they wanted her to trust in their love? Trust that should anyone else strike out at them, or at her, in such a way again they wouldn't steal that security from her?

She couldn't let herself need them like that. In the past two years she'd finally found a semblance of peace in her life; was she really going to let them destroy it?

Could she keep them from destroying it?

For the first time in years Alyssa had slept in a bed the night before. Sheltered between Shane and Sebastian, warm, secure. When she'd been certain she could never sleep with them surrounding her, she'd slept deeper than she had since returning from Spain.

For once in eight years the total aloneness she had felt had been absent.

But, as she stepped from the curb, she realized she was just as alone now as she had always been. She hadn't found the courage to live again after losing so much. Not really.

At that thought the sound of a woman's terrified screams pulled Alyssa quickly from her musings. Whirling around in shock, she felt horror slam inside her. The black SUV bearing down on her with frightening speed had her freezing for a precious moment.

A hit-and-run? Really? Today of all days?

That astounded thought raced through her as she tried to throw herself out of the path of the oncoming vehicle only to have it swing in her direction once again. The driver was determined to run her down, she realized, feeling herself flying through the air, she was dead.

+ + + + +

Shane curled his body around the delicate fragility of Alyssa's as he took the brunt of the fall, attempting to cushion her from the sudden, bruising tackle he'd made to push her out of the SUV's path.

As he raced for her, he'd taken in every particle of information possible. The make and model of the vehicle, the driver with his dark glasses and dark jacket. There was a sticker on the window, a parking sticker, though the details were blurry.

Shane could hear the shouted orders of the several men following her before his body hit the sidewalk and from his periphery he realized the two men had drawn weapons as tires screamed behind him.

The bastard meant to swerve and come back for her? Son of a bitch, that took balls. A scream of tires and the sound of the racing motor disappearing in the distance assured him Alyssa's would-be murderer was escaping.

"No plates," he heard one of the men shout. "Call Mustafa."

Mustafa? Khalid Mustafa?

Rolling from his back, one hand cushioning Alyssa's head, he laid her back on the pavement, his heart suddenly in his throat as he realized she was unconscious.

"Alyssa? Baby, wake up." His hands raced over her body, searching for wounds, broken bones, whatever could explain her lack of awareness. "God . . ."

Her pulse was present, a bit thready but not alarmingly so. Her heart was beating; there were no gunshot wounds, nothing to explain—. As his hands moved to the back of her head he felt the slightly damp area, pulled back, and saw the blood on his fingers.

His hands shook with fear now.

"She hit her head when she tried to jerk away from you." Marty Mustafa, Khalid's wife, was kneeling next to Alyssa. "You were already rolling with her."

He looked up at Marty, seeing the agent she had once been in her cool, determined features.

"The bodyguard has called the ambulance. They've also called Khalid." She grimaced at that. "He thinks I've gone home." And no doubt Khalid would be there in a matter of moments. The restaurant was less than a block away.

As the thought crossed his mind he glimpsed the three men racing toward them from the other end of the block, one small female protected between them.

Courtney. Damn, he didn't need the coming inquisition.

Turning back to Alyssa, brushing her hair back from her pale face, he focused on her, tried to tell himself she would be okay.

She was breathing.

"The driver was trying to hit her!" Marty snapped. "Dammit, Connor, what the hell are you and Sebastian involved in?"

He ignored her. Just as he ignored Ian and Khalid behind him.

It was Chase Falladay, one of Ian's most trusted employees and friends, who knelt next to Alyssa.

"Get a fucking ambulance here!" Shane snapped.

"Already called," Chase informed him as he checked Alyssa's pupils, her pulse. "Ian put the call in. They should be here quickly."

"What were Khalid's bodyguards doing following her?" Shane snapped. "Not that I'm bitching, mind you."

Chase only snorted at the latter comment.

He wasn't bitching, Shane thought with a surge of complete thankfulness. It had been the bodyguards and the weapons they drew that had saved both him and Alyssa from being struck when the SUV turned and came for her again.

"He said his neck was itching," Chase sighed. "He sent them out behind her when she left the restaurant. Marty followed them. She told Khalid she was taking the limo home."

There was no amusement in Chase's voice.

Any response Shane would have had was forgotten as Alyssa's eyes came open slowly, her gaze connecting immediately with Shane's.

She frowned, her gray eyes dark, resigned.

"I should have guessed," she sighed. "You and 'Bastian are chaos," she whispered miserably. "Complete chaos, Shane."

"I know, baby." Brushing her hair back gently, he kept his gaze trained on her, watching her closely. "Just lie still, honey; the ambulance will be here soon."

He saw the alarm that filled her eyes, her expression.

"No." Struggling to sit up, she slapped at his hands and pushed at Chase's as they tried to convince her to lie still. "Take me home. Now. Call Dad and take me home."

"Alyssa—"

"Chase." She turned her eyes to the investigator. "Get me out of here. You have to. Get me out of here."

"Ms. Hampstead—"

"Do it." Ian stepped up to them, his voice hard as Shane felt a snarl rising to his lips.

"Call Dr. Brennan, Chase; he'll meet us there. I just got off the phone with the senator myself. It's imperative we get her the hell out of here. My car just pulled up. Let's go."

Imperative.

Lifting her quickly, gently, into his arms, Shane moved to the limo and ducked inside, aware that only Ian and Courtney followed. As the vehicle pulled from the curve Shane focused on Ian, anger, fear, racing through him.

"If anything happens to her because of this, Sinclair, I won't be a forgiving man," he promised Ian.

"Shush," Alyssa mumbled, her head resting on his shoulder, shudders of reaction beginning to cause her to tremble in his arms. "Hospital is a last resort only."

"Why?" Frustration ate at him. He could sense too many things she was keeping from him, holding back. Even as he had slept with her slight body shielded between him and Sebastian, both of them had sensed the fact that she was fighting to hold her emotions as far from them as possible.

She didn't answer and he wasn't about to harass her. Yet.

Once he knew she was safe, once he knew her injuries weren't serious, then he'd demand the answers. And by God, he'd get them too.

## 17

Sebastian, Landra, and her son, Jeb, were standing outside Alyssa's suite after Dr. Brennan, his wife, and a fearsome old bat of a nurse ran Shane out. Once he'd placed her on the couch, it seemed they were finished with him.

He wasn't finished, though.

Stepping outside the suite into her office, he faced the others. Ian, Courtney, Khalid, Marty, and Chase were there as well as Jeb and Landra. Alyssa's office, which once seemed rather roomy, was filling up fast.

As Shane stepped from the office to the private, sheltered patio, it was all he could do not to step around the hedges where the scent of tobacco drifted and bum a cigarette from the security guard taking his break.

"Don't even think about it," Sebastian growled as he joined him. "I didn't think you'd ever stop that nasty habit."

"Those weren't cigarettes," he reminded his cousin ruefully. "You should have tried some of it."

Sebastian snorted. "I knew what it was. Just like I knew you were smoking cigarettes on the side. Let me catch you again and I'm telling Alyssa."

Shane turned his gaze to the entrance of the patio. They'd been there two years before when Alyssa had lain so near death. This hadn't been her room at the time, though. Her room had been upstairs according to the information they'd had at the time.

"We didn't protect her well," Shane said softly, the weight of the guilt tightening his chest as he saw the mistakes they'd made. "She's right; we should have come to her."

"We didn't understand the bond we shared then any more than she did, Shane," his cousin reminded him. "Hell, had you ever felt anything like that with anyone else?"

He hadn't. Neither of them had. He knew both their parents had been driven crazy by them after he and Sebastian had met the first time, at five years of age. They'd become inseparable the summer Shane had spent at the hacienda. It was like being reunited with a twin.

Still, it hadn't been the same. What they'd shared with Alyssa was damned confusing to both of them. If one of them took her while the other had been gone, then the other had known the second it began. Like a sixth sense, their Alyssa sense. They'd had no idea how deep it went until the tenth week after she'd left Spain.

They should have known what they were feeling. First her pain, like waves of burning agony rushing through their senses, then an agony that pierced the soul, ripped apart what little was left of it, only to leave them in a void filled with such aloneness that it had been agonizing.

And through it all, every day of every second apart from her, Shane had sworn he could feel her tears, could feel her reaching out for him. The confusion, the hurt, the feelings of betrayal all made sense now, though it had taken years to begin to understand it. And only in the past days were the full ramifications of it making sense.

As he was lost in his thoughts, it took the slam of the office door to shatter them and have him swinging around to meet Senator Hampstead's furious gaze.

Davis Allen was enraged. A scowl marked his expression; his

normally light gray eyes were dark, the color shifting like thunder-clouds building to a storm. The dark blond hair, cut to a conservative length, wasn't as neat as normal, and the moment he saw Sebastian and Shane he looked ready to explode.

"Davis." Moving from the sofa where she'd sat, Landra rushed to her lover, causing him to pause to embrace her as she whispered something at his ear.

Whatever it was, it didn't ease the look of fury, but at least he wasn't glaring specifically at them anymore.

"The doctors are still in with her," Landra told Davis as they began moving the last few feet to where Shane and Sebastian stood at the French doors, just a few feet from the door leading to Alyssa's suite. "She struck her head. I heard Dr. Brennan mention leaving the nurse to make certain she rests for the next forty-eight hours. He's certain she's concussed."

"Don't bet on that," the father snorted doubtfully. "I have yet to know of Alyssa listening to the doctor's advice."

Sebastian turned his gaze back to the other man suspiciously. "She requires medical care often?" he asked carefully.

Alyssa's father spoke as though from much experience with having her treated by the doctor.

"You can shutter that look right now, young man," the senator demanded, obviously less than pleased. "Alyssa's had no more accidents than any other young woman with her reckless tendencies. She climbs ladders in pumps when she knows better without anyone close by in case she falls. If a ladder's not handy she'll climb up on a desk, a chair—"

"A table, or a windowsill," Shane muttered, pushing his fingers through his hair as he shot his cousin an exasperated look. "And here you said she'd stop being so foolish when she got older."

Sebastian shrugged easily.

"When she grew up?" the senator suggested, his voice heavily laced with warning sarcasm. "Is that what you meant?"

"Davis, you promised," Landra reminded him gently.

"Then make them promise not to rub my nose in what they did to my daughter!" he snapped. "I had enough of seeing that child hurt the night I walked into her living room and found her bleeding to death from the knife shoved in her side."

Khalid's muttered, furious curse was low but heard. How the hell any of this was his business Shane couldn't figure out. For some reason, Mustafa was taking an inordinate amount of interest in Alyssa's past. According to Sebastian, his nosiness was only getting worse.

"Davis, now isn't the place," Landra whispered, her gaze flickering to the group Khalid stood with.

Grimacing, the senator reined in his fury. "Ian." He nodded to the other man. "Thank you for helping her. You know how stubborn she can be." He wiped his hand over his face tiredly. "What the hell happened anyway?"

"Someone tried to run her down in the street," Landra said, fingers tightened on Davis' arm, before Ian had a chance to speak. "It was horrible, Davis. It was all caught on one of those cameras Khalid's bodyguard was wearing. The SUV was racing for Alyssa. I'm certain it would have hit her. Then suddenly Shane did this little flying thing." Her hand gave a whirl as she stared at the senator. "And he had his arms around her, throwing both of them clear of the vehicle. Then it turned to attempt to run her down again." Brown eyes wide, her black hair a soft cloud around her face, and her expression animated, Sebastian watched the senator stare down at her as though mesmerized. "Khalid's body guards drew their weapons and the driver sped away instead." She gave a little shudder. "Of course, Alyssa was cursing Shane for carrying her into the house, once they arrived here. And everyone was just rushing in behind him." Her amusement was clear. "The poor thing. She's very upset that anyone witnessed what happened."

Everyone watched her with the same interest they had watched the video the bodyguard had taken when Khalid played it for them. Her son, Jeb, tilted his head thoughtfully, and glanced at the senator. "She's my mother and she makes me feel very old. Do you ever have that problem?"

"Give her time," Davis snorted. "Though I suspect Alyssa will see me in my grave before too much longer. The last time Dr. Brennan was here she'd fallen from the desk in her office while trying to change a lightbulb. My chief of staff was furious, certain she'd broken her leg." He rubbed at his head with both hands for a second. "She only twisted her ankle, bruised her shin, and strained the tendon beneath her knee." He looked slightly confused. "I think the broken leg might have been less complicated and actually kept her out of trouble longer."

"Davis was quite put out with her," Landra stated as the senator rubbed his hand absently over the fingers tucked in the opposite arm. "Two weeks later, his chief of staff, a lovely young man he calls Raeg, found her balancing at the edge of the windowsill in the conference room attempting to clean the ledge over them. The windows are actually taller than her."

"She's going to worry me into a stroke," Davis predicted, glancing at the door to her room once again before glaring back at him and Shane, his expression darkening again with anger. "The two of you should leave—"

"No, sir." They spoke at once.

"Oh dear," Landra whispered, her eyes rounding at the phenomenon. "Davis, shall we discuss this later, when we're not all so upset? Perhaps after we know Alyssa's doing well?"

He wasn't upset, Sebastian thought, staring back at the senator in determination. He simply had no intention of going anywhere, anymore than Shane did.

"You'll destroy her," Davis accused them, his gaze filled with grief. "God help me, I feel like all that child's done is fight to live since she returned from Spain. Because of the two of you."

"Senator, whatever you might think you know about her relationship with us—"

"Relationship?" he growled, his gray eyes, so like his daughter's, darkening dangerously. "An eighteen-year-old child doesn't have a relationship with two twenty-four-year-old men before she's even had her first real date."

From the corners of his eyes Shane glimpsed the dark look Khalid shot him and Sebastian. Just what he needed, that son of a bitch to hear his business and draw his own conclusions.

"The two of you shattered her," he accused them. "And now, the minute you show up in her life again, someone's trying to kill her. You should step away from her now, before there's nothing left of her but a gravestone."

Like hell they would step away from her.

"We took that advice the first time it was given," Shane reminded him with a sneer. "It hasn't worked out well for any of us. I'll be damned if I'll trust it again. This time, we'll face whatever the hell is going on together. We'll stand with her. And she'll stand with us. No one will separate us again."

## 18

Shane and Sebastian were confusion and chaos.

Alyssa had made that claim, albeit laughingly, in Spain. She wasn't laughing forty-eight hours and some odd minutes later when Nurse Lisa Shaw pushed her electronic pad into her purse, gave a cheery wave, and stepped from the sitting room into the office beyond.

Forty-eight hours of that woman watching her with eagle eyes, refusing to let her do more than lie on the couch rather than in the bed. No work, no laptop, no e-pad, no news on the television. Quiet, rest.

She hated just lying around. It gave her far too much time to think and to remember. She'd learned years ago to stay busy. Put one foot in front of the other and push back as many memories as possible.

And she was learning how to do it, she assured herself. She wasn't perfect, but she'd been learning, until Barcelona decided to visit Alexandria.

She was kicking Shane's and Sebastian's asses first chance she had, dammit.

"Thank God she's gone." The door Nurse Shaw had exited through opened again and Alyssa's father slid inside as though he were still sneaking past the prison guard of a nurse. "I'm convinced that woman missed a hell of a career as a dragon trainer."

Dressed in a white shirt, sleeves rolled back, perfectly creased slacks, and his favorite leather shoes, her father took a seat in the chair across from her while giving her one of his quiet smiles and far too perceptive looks.

"Bitching about your best buddy, Father?" she finally accused him, glowering as she flipped the blanket the nurse insisted she keep on her legs. "Shame on you."

His lips tilted in a small grin, his expression becoming playful. "Playing with SUVs in the street, sweetheart? Shame on you, I thought I taught you better."

Swinging her legs to the floor, Alyssa blew out a hard breath. She heard that little undertone in his voice. The one that assured her he wasn't as calm and relaxed as he appeared to be.

"You did teach me better, Dad," she said, shaking her head at the hazy memory of that damned SUV bearing down on her. "It just doesn't stop, does it?"

How many more near misses was she going to survive?

"If you were a cat, I'd start worrying," he admitted before his lips tilted in an ironic grin. "Hell, you passed a cat's lives when you were ten. Between your own reckless nature and those two men, there's not going to be much left of you in another six months or so."

She rolled her eyes at the comment concerning her reckless-ness. She wasn't reckless at all. Things just seemed to happen, that was all.

As for Shane and Sebastian, well, they just kind of seemed to happen as well. At the most inopportune times.

"They do have a way of completely screwing up a plan," she admitted.

"Not to mention your life," he injected, watching her closely.

"I wasn't exactly living, though, was I, Dad," she admitted then.

She felt as though she'd been sleepwalking until the night Sebastian found her in the arbor.

"You were at peace." His expression darkened for a moment before he shook his head and leaned forward to brace his elbows on his knees. "Were you at peace, Alyssa? The last two years you seemed to be."

The concern in her father's expression had guilt tightening in her stomach. Shane and Sebastian weren't going to let her go easily. And she couldn't answer the question of whether she wanted to be let go. Even to herself.

"At peace," she murmured, pushing her hair back behind her shoulder as she stared at the floor. "I was resigned." Looking up at him, she gave him the only answer she had. "Is that the same thing?"

It wouldn't have lasted long, Alyssa knew. She wasn't the resigned sort.

"You're alive now." He grimaced, sitting back in the chair as his brows lowered broodingly. "You haven't been alive for a long time. And I'm terrified that I'll see you dead before it's over with. Something's shadowing those two men and it keeps lashing out at you. One day, you may not be so lucky in your escape."

Rising to her feet, Alyssa walked to the wide bay window with its pillowed window seat on the other side of the sitting room. Her father hadn't questioned a single renovation she wanted for her suite of rooms after she lost the baby. He'd done everything just as she wanted it. For eight years, he'd done everything he could to ensure not just her happiness but also her safety.

"Whatever's shadowing them has always shadowed me anyway," she finally reminded him. "Someone killed my baby, Dad. And I've never been convinced Harvey tried to kill me just because he found out about Shane and Sebastian. We don't know how he found out, or what he was involved in. But the timing in relation to Shane and Sebastian identifying Gregory Santiago as the blackmailer bothers me."

It bothered her a lot.

Gregory had been a bit arrogant, she remembered, and he hadn't appeared to care much for Shane and Sebastian, though he'd never said why. Not that she had asked, either. Most of her time had been spent with her lovers rather than her neighbors. Just as her neighbors did. They were all there for the summer and determined to live their vacations to the fullest.

Alyssa hadn't even known who lived in the apartment beneath Gia. Gregory and Marissa lived beneath her and Gia across from her.

"Do you remember much of what Harvey said that night?" her father asked. "Is it possible he was somehow involved in all this?"

"He said it would have been amusing if the baby had lived. He could have raised their son, and he found that hilarious. But he hadn't known about Shane and Sebastian until recently is the impression I have." Turning back to her father, she met his gaze helplessly. "But hell, what do I know? I thought Harvey had changed in the past few years we were together, but he assured me every reason he gave for needing to marry me was a lie anyway. So maybe he hadn't changed. Maybe that was who he was all along."

He'd been telling her since they were sixteen that his father would have him beaten for being gay. After she returned from Spain he'd confided to her that he had to marry before his father killed him. The last time, weeks before they married, Harvey had shown up with a blackened, swollen eye and fractured wrist. He'd begged Alyssa to marry him. She was pregnant, he'd pointed out desperately. No one knew, but she couldn't hide it forever. He'd give her baby his name; she would get his dad off his ass.

And she'd agreed. Evidently she'd agreed to lies, though.

"Your mother hated him," her father revealed. "She made him believe she was his ally, though. So much so that when he tried to kill you she actually convinced him she was going to help him."

She had helped him all right. She'd killed him. But she'd killed herself as well.

"Mom was the most intuitive, calculating, manipulating person I have ever met in my life." She smiled, remembering how her mother would instruct her after each instance when she'd watched her mother play her political and social games.

"Yes, she was." Fondness still filled Alyssa's father's voice. "She drove me insane every day of the week, but she could maneuver people like no one I knew."

She wouldn't have maneuvered Shane and Sebastian for long, though, Alyssa thought. They would have let Margot think she was doing it, according to how much they wanted to stay on friendly terms with her. But they would have seen through her easily.

She met her father's gaze slowly, saw the knowledge in his eyes, the acceptance and the love that had sheltered her all her life.

"I loved them until it destroyed parts of me that I'll never recover. To survive, I had to shut so many parts of myself down that I'm afraid they're dead as well. Now they're back, the danger is gone, and they want to pick up where we left off." Alyssa shook her head wearily. "And I don't know if there's enough of me left to trust any part of the fantasy they're spinning for me."

"You think it's a lie?" Her father seemed surprised.

"To them?" she asked, then shook her head as she walked back to the couch and sat down heavily. "No, Dad, I don't think they see it as a lie or a fantasy. That's how I see it. It was a fantasy the first time. Who's to say it's anything more than a fantasy now?"

Sitting back, his elbow propped on the arm of the chair, he rubbed at the flesh over his lip as he considered her thoughtfully. "You don't trust them, do you, honey?"

"They should have told me." That regret was like a sickness she couldn't hold back. "All those years, Dad, and I was left to face a betrayal that didn't happen. My soul was ripped from me and they could have stopped some of the pain. And they want me to trust them now. How do I do that?"

They hadn't told her about the blackmail and they hadn't told her that they were trying to protect her. They'd just left, thinking she would be there when they came for her.

"Men do what they think they have to," he sighed heavily, pushing himself from the chair, his expression heavy, if a bit rueful. "Strong men take the weight of the world on their shoulders and never question if it's their responsibility or their right. They take it, because they can't bear the consequences otherwise." Walking to her, he gripped her shoulders before bending his head to kiss the top of her head. "Perhaps they should have told you," he said softly. "But what would you have done if they had? If you had learned of the thousands of dollars per month they were paying to protect you, to keep those pictures from public eyes? To hold forever private the sight of the woman they love amid her pleasure? What would you have done if they had told you, Alyssa?"

"You're defending them?" she asked, amazed that he would do so. After the party he had refused to even discuss their presence in town.

"Defending them?" Stepping back, he shook his graying head slowly. "I'm not defending them, sweetheart. Let's say, I hate what they did to you. Hate them for it. But I like to be honest with myself." Shoving his hands in the pockets of his slacks, her father grimaced tightly. "And honestly, Alyssa, in their position, unaware of what you were suffering, believing they were protecting you from the evil threatening you, I would have done the same damned thing."

He would have done the same thing?

Wonderful.

So she was supposed to just forgive them because her father agreed with the choices they'd made? She didn't think so. They had let some nameless, faceless blackmailer keep them from her for years, but what about the last two?

They were blaming Summer for it.

There was always a reason, always an excuse.

Alyssa didn't want to hear any more excuses. She didn't want to know the cousins' reasons or their excuses. She might not have been happy without them in her life, and she might not have been content. Resignation had sucked, though.

"Alyssa, do you still love them?" her father asked then, tipping her chin up with one finger and staring down at her with all the love and understanding that had seen her through twenty-six years and all his gray hairs, as he told it.

"From the first week I knew them," she whispered. "But I love strawberries too," she sighed. "Until I start swelling up and choking." Her allergy to strawberries could be life threatening. As they'd learned more than once.

For a second, her father's expression was completely blank before his laughter escaped.

"Alyssa, sweetheart, you never fail to remind me why I have so many gray hairs." The amusement could have been offensive, she told herself, but after years of putting him through hell with one scrape or another she imagined he deserved a moment of laughter.

"Well, I'm glad to know I can at least provide you with a moment of amusement, Dad." She shook her head at his laughter. "Don't you have things to do this afternoon? I'm sure I need to go over Candy's notes and see how many files she completely screwed up for me."

Her assistant was still in training, she told herself again. Candy had been in training for over a year now. Her humor and ability to field phone calls while keeping fresh coffee at Alyssa's elbow often made the screwed-up files less of a hassle.

"She guarded your door like a basset hound," her father snorted. "All big sad eyes and silent chastisement until someone actually reached for the doorknob. I thought she was going to bite my hand off before I made it through the door."

Yeah. She was going to believe that one. Just after she started believing in fairy godmothers.

"Try to make it to dinner tonight," he told her firmly as he headed for the door. "Cook has promised one of his premier meals in honor of your survival. It's guaranteed to be a good one."

Alyssa rolled her eyes. "You act like nearly getting run over by some bastard is a monthly occurrence."

Pausing at the door, he turned back, his gaze still sparkling with mirth despite the concern lurking behind it. "Playing with SUVs in the street, falling from trees, or losing your balance while climbing on chairs. The results are actually rather similar, wouldn't you say?"

She glared back at him, but she had to admit, the bruises were pretty much in the same places and her head had taken the brunt of the damage. Just as it usually did.

His expression softened then. "You look like your mother when you get that look. You look remarkably like her anyway. She loved you, Alyssa. She didn't say the words—"

"She showed it in the only ways she knew how," Alyssa finished for him. "I know, Dad."

He breathed out slowly. "We were probably the only two on the face of the earth who saw that part of her. Everyone else saw the ice. Only we saw the fires beneath."

"I know," she said again, and she did.

As the door closed behind her father Alyssa moved back to the large window, wrapping her arms around herself and staring into the sun-splashed day as she tried to make sense of far too many things in her life.

It all came back to Shane and Sebastian, though. Or did it come back to her?

They had been blackmailed to keep pictures from being leaked to porn sites and the media. Pictures that showed her intimate relationship with two men, rather than one.

To ensure Alyssa didn't attempt to contact them, the same pictures were sent to her parents and a far different threat made.

It was all designed to keep her and her lovers apart. And Shane and Sebastian had taken the responsibility of protecting her, as her father said. Without her knowledge of the true danger facing all of them.

Her father asked what she would have done if they had come to her and told her. It was a question she couldn't answer, because they hadn't given her the chance to fight at their sides. Instead, she had existed. Bound to them, a part of her obviously knowing they hadn't considered the summer just a brief sexual escape.

She'd never been able to go on because whatever they'd shared in Barcelona had gone too deep. That connection hadn't died, but the scars it carried still ached with pain.

"Bastards!" she bit out, the frustration she didn't want to deal with rising so sharp inside her that she knew ignoring it would be impossible. "Damn you, I didn't need this. Not now. Probably not ever."

"Talking to yourself again, baby?"

Swinging around, she stared at Sebastian as he stepped past the door her father had left open. Dark, too somber. The playfulness that had been so much a part of him was absent.

Goofy, she'd called him. Because he was always poking fun at something, joking, playing some prank, or making some totally incorrigible comment.

He wasn't goofy anymore and Alyssa realized she hated that.

"I prefer talking to myself." She smiled tightly, crossing her arms over her breasts as she glared back at him. "I actually pay attention, whereas the rest of you ignore good common sense."

"I see." The mocking thoughtfulness only pissed her off. "So what good common sense are the rest of us ignoring? I'm all ears."

He was all ears?

He was a damned pain in the ass and none of the pleasure, she thought in disgust. He and his cousin both.

"Go away, Sebastian. I'm busy."

Go away?

As though he were some peon irritating her royal self? Sweet, deluded little siren. Somewhere in the past eight years she'd evidently concluded that he could be ordered about as though he were the staff.

"Go away?" he repeated the order mockingly. "Siren, you've developed an attitude since being away from us."

The irritated look she shot him caused his jaw to clench, his cock to harden, more. Stiff and throbbing in demand, that portion of his anatomy had always been particularly unruly around her. It was even more so now.

"Go play with Shane for a while and leave me alone," she ordered him, turning her back on him. "I need a shower and I'm in desperate need of some peace and quiet for a change. And lock the damned door on your way out if you don't mind."

Striding across the living area, evidently unaware of the incredible mistake she'd just made, she stepped into her bedroom and closed the door behind her. Then she locked it.

Sebastian's eyes narrowed on the locked door before he stalked to it. Irritation flared through his senses that she would dare to lock a door between them. To speak to him as though she commanded him.

He'd only stepped in to see how she was doing, to perhaps tease her a bit before returning to Landra's, where he and Shane had stayed the past two nights. They'd meant to give Alyssa one more night of rest before continuing their seduction of her.

Testing the doorknob silently, he smiled at its flimsiness.

It wasn't a seduction that was coming now.

It was time for a claiming. Time to show the siren how much more easily mere mortal men were led around by the nose when a sweet song was sung, rather than the angry tune she was singing now.

It was time to show her whom she belonged to, not just who belonged to her.

A quick, firm jerk of his wrist and the lock slipped, allowing the doorknob to move freely. He'd let her shower, let her have her peace and quiet for the moment. Tonight, though, the quiet would be filled with her pleas for release and her peace interrupted by her screams of pleasure.

And when he and Shane finished, she would know all the way to her woman's soul who the alphas were in this particular relationship. One thing was for damned sure: she wasn't one of them.

## 19

As Cook promised, dinner was absolutely fabulous, as the middle-aged chef was a magician when it came to food. Every meal he crafted was wonderful. The difference was how he came from the kitchen and babied her and made certain dessert was just how she liked it.

It was the laughter her father couldn't hold back, Landra's giggles, and her son Jeb's quiet smiles. The black-haired, green-eyed Jeb didn't smile much, and Alyssa was certain she sometimes saw the same kind of shadows in his eyes that lurked in her own when she looked in the mirror.

Cook had been with the family since Alyssa was a teenager. She knew his name was James, knew he could make pancakes so light they nearly floated and that Thanksgiving wouldn't be the same without his turkey. And she would kill for his tiramisu.

He spoiled them like they were his own children and the smallest compliment to his food had smiles wreathing his rough face and pleasure filling his brown eyes.

"Cook, the tiramisu made me want to weep tears of joy," she sighed as he stepped into the dining room, his craggy, often stoic expression suddenly beaming in enjoyment.

"The next time you play with SUVs in the street, no more

tiramisu for a month." He wagged his finger at her as her father turned her head, chuckling. "Your father has ten new gray hairs, he claims."

She turned her gaze on her father, eyes narrowed before giving Cook a gentle, innocent look. "Cook, you know how Daddy tells tales on me," she reminded him with mock sadness. "He's just jealous because you make the tiramisu special for me. You know how vindictive he can get." She wrinkled her nose in her father's direction.

Cook sighed heavily, the laughter in his eyes nearly causing her to spoil the act with an uncontrolled giggle. "Poor Miss Alyssa. He's always told such horrible tales too." Cook nodded. "I'm certain you don't climb on file cabinets or chairs, and certainly you would never attempt to rescue snarling dogs or pull terrified cats from trees, either."

Oh well. She couldn't lie about all of it.

"I'm certain he exaggerated each of those tales." She couldn't stop the grin. "I swear."

Shaking his finger at her, he laughed at her antics before returning to the kitchen.

Within moments steaming coffee and after-dinner mints arrived, signaling the conclusion of another of his tasty meals.

Once she'd enjoyed an after-dinner coffee and listened to her father and Jeb discuss stocks and politics for a half hour she was bored out of her mind and searching desperately for a reason to excuse herself from the table.

"Alyssa, dear, you look so very tired," Landra came to her rescue, causing her to blink and look up at the older woman with an apologetic smile. "It's been a stressful few days for you, hasn't it, dear?"

That was putting things a bit mildly, Alyssa thought with silent amusement.

"I think it's time I head back to my suite," Alyssa admitted, rising from her chair as Jeb moved quickly to help her.

"Jeb, be a dear and see Alyssa to her room," Landra told him firmly. "After two days of enforced rest by Nurse Shaw, her legs must be feeling a bit weak. We wouldn't want her to fall before making it to her room."

Alyssa stared at Landra warily.

"Of course, Mother," Jeb agreed softly, his gaze meeting Alyssa's with a little conspirator's wink.

What the hell was Landra up to?

Was she trying to get her son killed by playing matchmaker? Shane and Sebastian wouldn't stand for it and she should know that. Cousin or no cousin, they would never tolerate another man interfering with their seduction of her. Which was really kind of funny. Shane and Sebastian had no problem sharing her with each other, but Alyssa knew for a fact they'd never willingly let another man touch her.

"It's all good," Jeb murmured as he offered his elbow to her politely and said loud enough for Landra to hear, "Come along, little sister, let's get you safely to your bed."

Yeah, he was related to Shane and Sebastian, there was no doubt. But she took the proffered elbow with a little roll of her eyes.

"You like to live dangerously," she murmured as they left the dining room and headed up the hallway leading to the outer suites.

"Mother likes to shake things up a bit," he agreed with a low chuckle, though his hand remained where it was just beneath her upper arm. "I like to allow her the illusion that she's managing to do so. It keeps her from any real trouble."

He was handsome. His resemblance to Shane was slight; despite Jeb's dark hair, his looks were actually closer to Sebastian's. If Jeb had had lighter hair, she would have figured out they were related before her father began his relationship with Landra.

"It's rarely a good idea where Shane and Sebastian are concerned, to shake anything up," she pointed out. "She should know that. Putting her son in the line of fire could become a problem."

She would really hate to see him hurt.

"They've never been known for their jealousy," he assured her.

"Really?" She glanced up at him in amusement. "Just how well do you know your cousins, Jeb?"

"Well enough to know not to piss them off," he assured her. "We never spent a lot of time around each other, but when we did, it was an interesting visit. I've seen them in a lot of moods, but I've never seen them possessive of a woman."

Briefly she related the incident of them arriving as she talked to Gregory and the resulting confrontation. By the time she and Jeb reached the turn in the hall that led to her suite, he was actually laughing.

"I wouldn't have minded seeing that." He chuckled at the end of the tale. "Shane can be incredibly cutting when he wants to be. But, as I said, 'jealous' wasn't one of the descriptions I've heard applied to him before now."

The door to her suite opened and Shane stood in the doorway, his expression dark, his blue eyes narrowed on Alyssa's hand where it rested on his cousin's arm.

"I guess it's all according to how deeply I've grown attached," Shane drawled. "I can be a very jealous man, when the situation warrants it, Cousin."

Alyssa slid her hand from Jeb's arm, closed her eyes momentarily, then opened them and stared back at Shane. "There's a joke in there, right?" she asked, completely amazed that those words had just slipped past his lips.

"Is there a joke in there, Jeb?" Shane asked, though his gaze stayed on hers; the blue darkening, his expression seemed carved from stone.

"Not that I'm aware of," Jeb assured him, amusement still lingering in his voice. "Should I let Mom know you're here?" There was definitely an air of familial teasing in that question.

"That's up to your discretion," Shane answered, and there was no missing the heavy warning in *his* tone.

"Then I believe I'll be very discreet if you don't care." Jeb snorted at the warning. "Good night, Cousin." Turning, he nodded to Alyssa. "Little sister."

Little sister her ass.

"You and your family are giving me a headache," she announced, pushing past Shane and entering her bedroom.

She was definitely going to have to see about better locks on all her doors. Earlier, Sebastian had somehow managed to slip the lock between her office and her living room. Now the two of them were just making themselves at home in her bedroom. And no one had ever thought to ask if she gave a damn.

It was going to have to stop. They were making her crazy.

Stepping back, Shane lifted a brow and glanced over at Sebastian. His expression was knowing, brooding, as though to remind Shane that she'd become confrontational.

She wasn't just confrontational; she was burning with arousal. The feminine need made the gray of her eyes look stormy, gave the lightest flush to her creamy cheeks. The hunger made her irritable. The sensual, carnal need she refused to name or accept, the possession she was dying for, pushing for, gleamed in the very depths of her eyes.

And tonight, she would have it.

There would be no way to deal with the danger they were facing while this lay between them. While the hungers and the needs driving her, torturing her body and her senses, continued to rise inside her.

It was a rare woman who could match the sensual, overwhelming sex drive of one of the cousins, let alone both of them. And few women would be able to commit to owning both their hearts and sensual hungers. This woman more than owned them, though. She tempted them. She burned within them.

They'd realized that the night of Landra's Winter Ball eight years before. This woman was more than a match for them, for both of them and their erotic needs. Watching her become lost in her pleasure between them, feeling those fires flame brighter, hotter, when both of them touched her together, was like feeding the conflagration with gasoline.

"What are the two of you doing here?" As she turned to confront them, the gray in her eyes shifted, shades of it colliding like storm clouds gathering to rip across the skies.

The soft pale cream skirt flowed around her legs, falling nearly to her ankles, where strappy sandals graced her small feet and made her look incredibly delicate. A cream blouse, designed much like a vest, the buttons beginning low enough to show the tempting rise of her pretty breasts, reminded him how sensitive the peaks of those luscious mounds were.

Jeb had enjoyed the view throughout dinner, no doubt. He'd definitely been enjoying it when Shane opened the door, drawn by their laughter in the hall. Bastard. He could have sworn he'd taught Jeb better as a boy. He might well have to loosen a tooth or two with his fist again if the boy wasn't careful.

"I believe we're here to see you, siren," Sebastian stated, his voice smooth, as though the overriding hunger she was only stoking wasn't ready to burn out of control.

"Well, now you've seen me." Holding her hands out to her sides slightly, she threw them a hard, mocking look. "You can leave now."

Leave now?

Crossing his arms over his chest, he stared back at her with a smile.

He'd waited eight years. They'd never imagined how they would come back into her life; they'd just known they would. They hadn't imagined when they did have her back they'd have this challenge. A challenge that fired their blood as well as their lusts.

"Sweetheart, I think you're well aware that's not happening. Not tonight."

Alyssa was a very intuitive person; they'd always known that. And Shane knew damned good and well she was aware what the night would hold when he'd opened her bedroom door to the sound of her and Jeb's laughter in the hall.

His cousin had stated that his cousins had never been jealous men, and he was right. Until Alyssa, neither he nor Shane had been particularly jealous concerning their women. Protective, yes, but if another man attempted to draw a lover away they didn't fight for her. What would have been the point?

Until Alyssa.

"I can't deal with the two of you tonight." A hard, decisive shake of her head and she turned from them as though she actually expected them to obey the underlying demand to leave.

As Sebastian had related to him earlier, her attitude was one of a princess dismissing a peasant or, rather, one dismissing the stable boy she'd taken as her lover.

"Alyssa," Shane reproved her gently, "do you really think we're leaving so easily? You've indeed forgotten a lot if you've forgotten exactly how untamable and untrainable, we really are."

She turned back to them slowly and shot him a look from the corners of her eyes. What he saw there was all he needed to see. Pure, sensual purpose was reflected there along with sweet innocence and a hint of confused emotional responses.

Alyssa stared between them. From Sebastian's dark, brooding sensuality to Shane's determined lusts they were in some ways so very different yet in others so very alike. And when they were together their eroticism had a way of overwhelming the senses.

"What the two of you have in mind isn't happening, either," she informed them, praying they didn't know just how hard it was to force those words past her lips. "You've both had your little revisit to the past. But I simply can't afford what you'll do to what's left of my heart if this goes any further."

She'd fought too long, too hard, to get herself to a place where she could function without them. She'd given them so much of herself, so much of her heart and soul, that at times she'd hated them for the handicap being without them had given her.

"And you really think that excuse is going to see us out the door, siren?" Sebastian's voice was dark, smooth. It slid over her senses like the softest caress, yet the warning of power lay just beneath the surface.

"It's not an excuse, Sebastian," she assured him, watching him closely. For once, it was Shane who appeared relaxed and amused while Sebastian seemed ready to slip the leash of his control. It was clear neither of them wanted to listen to reason or any sense of logic. "I can't risk destroying myself further. There's just not enough left of me to risk losing any more."

Turning away to escape to the only sanctuary she had left, a shower she didn't need, Alyssa found herself swung around so suddenly she could only gasp.

Sebastian held her to his chest, the look of implacable determination hardening his expression.

"You did not suffer alone, Alyssa." The hard, ruthless snap in his voice was an indication of how thin his control was at the moment.

The loss of that control didn't frighten her, though; it excited her, infuriated her. Just as his statement left her astounded. She hadn't suffered alone? She had been alone. Neither of them had been with her. She had lost everything and had nothing, no one to turn to for comfort, for warmth.

"Didn't I, Sebastian? What do you call six years of not living? Six years of just drifting through life as though the only reason

I existed was to love two men who couldn't be with me and couldn't be honest with me about the reasons why?" Struggling against him, she glared up at his set expression, his dark, tortured gaze. "The two of you made this decision for me."

"To protect you." Dark blond brows furrowed in a brooding frown.

"To protect me? You would have protected me far better if you had come to me and explained what the hell was going on." Pushing her fingers through her hair, she tried to fight the frustration she felt each time she tried to make sense of the past eight years. "I don't understand you," she gritted out, frustration raking at her nerves. "What gives you the right to do this to me, after all these years?"

"The same right you took when you made the choice to wait for us," he pointed out, the dark, latent anger throbbing in his voice. "Think about that, Alyssa. You can hate us for it all you need to, curse us until hell freezes over. But you knew, all these years you knew, we didn't choose to leave you. If you hadn't known that, if your heart hadn't known that, then you would have never waited for us."

"What did I know, Sebastian?" she cried, placing her hand over her heart, over the ache she'd known for as long as she'd been separated from them. "That I was alone? That something held me so locked inside myself that I didn't know how to escape?"

"You didn't want to escape," the whisper came from behind her, from Shane's lips at her ear, his hands settling on her shoulders. "No more than we wanted to escape you."

Those wicked, drugging lips trailed down her neck to her shoulder as his fingers pulled the material of her blouse aside.

"You weren't locked inside yourself, 'Lyssa. We were locked inside you. You were the only solace we could depend on. You were locked inside us. And you placed yourself there willingly when you gave us your heart." His voice, soft, low, had her stilling herself between them, her heart racing as the sensual, erotic tone mesmerized her. "Just as we placed ourselves in your keeping. You belong to us." Her eyelids drifted closed, her body melting between them. "And we belong to you. We have the deepest love that can be shared, sweetheart. It's soul bound."

Soul bound.

Would she have allowed it if she had known it was possible?

Her breath caught at the feel of the buttons of her blouse being undone, leaving the silent question unanswered.

"We were dying without you, siren," Sebastian whispered, his hands spreading the edges of her blouse apart with a slow, seductive move. As it caught at her shoulders Shane eased it over her shoulders, down her arms and away.

They were doing it to her again. Completely mesmerizing her with the pleasure erupting through her senses. And was she strong enough to fight it?

"I'm crazy to let you do this to me," she moaned, but she didn't fight when Shane pressed her arms to her sides and Sebastian released the catch of her bra. "I should kick you both out now."

"Hmm, foreplay." The voice with the Texas accent was filled with amusement. "You're makin' me hard, darlin'."

Anything she would have come back with dissolved in her brain as Sebastian's lips wrapped around the stiff point of a nipple and sucked it into his mouth. Firm, hungry draws of his mouth had her arms wrapping around his neck and desperate mewls spilling from her lips.

"Oh God, the two of you are crazy. And it's contagious," she whimpered.

Behind her, Shane released the zipper to her skirt, allowing the material to fall to the floor. Sliding his palm between her thighs, he cupped the sensitive mound there, his fingers sliding over the silk and lace of her panties.

Sebastian's teeth grazed her nipple, his mouth suckling at her more firmly, filling her with so much pleasure that she didn't want to deny it.

How had she lived eight years without this? Without them?

"You're a stubborn woman, Alyssa," Shane whispered behind her a second before he nipped at the rounded curve of her shoulder.

They were just figuring out she could be stubborn? Weren't they paying any attention at all, outside sex, in Barcelona?

"If I were stubborn you'd not be in my room tonight," she gasped when Sebastian applied just enough pressure on the tight point he held captive in his mouth.

God, that was good. The gentle nips to the over sensitive tip, that edge of pleasure and pain spiking with such intensity she moaned at the sensation.

"If you weren't stubborn you'd accept you still belong to us," Shane growled.

"Been there, done that," she whimpered as his fingers applied a subtle pressure over her clit, barely there, causing the bundle of nerves to send a riot of sharp sensations racing through her sex.

The pressure eased around her nipple, but rather than moving to the next Sebastian eased back from her, his dark gaze moving along her nakedness, the black of his eyes flaring in lust.

"Been there, done that?" he repeated softly, his gaze narrowing, the features of his face tightening into a hard, dominant expression. "Not revisiting, baby?"

"I'll think about it later." Maybe.

They needed to just shut up and finish what they were starting, because she'd be damned if she'd give them the parts of her soul that she had managed to drag out of hell with her.

Her arms she curled around Sebastian's neck as his head lowered, his lips taking hers with dominant force. The deep, hungry kisses and sensual press of his tongue against hers built her pleasure, prepared her for the ultimate high.

As his lips made love to hers, his tongue teasing her, drawing her to taste even as he tasted, Alyssa let herself become lost in the sensations wrapping around her. So lost that when he lifted her and carried her to the bed, she was only barely aware of it.

Laying her back against the pillows, he lifted his lips from hers, the sensual, erotic spell he was weaving around her not dimming in the least.

"My sweet 'Lyssa." One hand slid to the side of her neck, his fingers curving around it, tilting her head farther back as she felt Shane move beside her.

"There, sweet baby." A lingering kiss to her lips and Sebastian rose, straightening from her as Shane turned her, his kiss taking over where Sebastian's had left off.

Where Sebastian's kiss had been slow, achingly sweet, Shane's was raw need. A melding of lips, his tongue pushing between them, stroking over hers demandingly.

He was naked. She could feel his broad, warm chest against her breasts as he drew her to her knees, his hands pushing beneath her skirt, stroking up her thighs to the elastic band of the silky panties she wore.

"We don't need these," he groaned against her lips, tugging at the elastic. "And they're so pretty. You always wore the prettiest little underthings."

Easing her back until she reclined against the bed, he removed the panties. Slowly, staring down at her, his expression absorbed, filled with searing emotion, as though she meant something. Like when the sun rose again nothing would change and they would always be there.

She wouldn't let herself believe. . . . She would just let herself enjoy. There was no tomorrow; there was only now.

"Come here, darlin'." Lifting her to him once she was naked, wearing nothing but the soft light from the lamp beside the bed, she felt Sebastian returning behind her.

Calloused hands caressed her back, stomach, her thighs. Fingertips rubbed, stroked, as she found herself drowning in pleasure. Her body became hyper-sensitive, the lightest brush of air against it another caress that burned through her senses.

Restrained now, her back against Shane's hard body, she arched into Sebastian's touch. It was like stepping back to that summer so long ago when they had completely filled her senses. A time when she had breathed for this magic and luxuriated in their single-minded determination to own her, heart and soul, with the pleasure they wrapped around her. When they had given her the world in the weeks they spent teaching her to belong completely to them.

They had branded her senses, marked her body as their own in a way she'd known, even then, that she would never be free of. She feared she had never wanted to be free.

A low, tortured moan parted her lips as Sebastian's kisses moved from them, to her neck, to the bend of her shoulder. There he began spreading a path of burning anticipation, moving steadily to the peaks of her swollen breasts.

Her nipples ached. She needed to feel his kiss, to feel him drawing them into the moist, suckling heat of his mouth again.

"Give me your hands, love." Shane captured her wrists as she tried to bury her fingers in Sebastian's hair. "No need to hold on to anything. I have you. I won't let you go, 'Lyssa."

Pulling her arms back to allow her fingers to grip his neck instead, he cupped the swollen globe of one breast and captured the tightly puckered nipple with his thumb and forefinger. Plumping it further with a firm, knowing grip, he worked the tip to a level of pleasure bordering pain.

Anticipation thrummed through her senses, building with such aching need that she could barely process the onslaught of sensation.

"It's been too long, sweets," Shane crooned as she felt Sebastian shifting on the couch, his lips brushing over the inner curve of a breast. "Far too long since we've felt you burning for us together. Burn for us now, baby."

Burn for them. God, she'd been burning for eight years and now they were stoking those fires, urging them to consume her.

"Open your eyes, 'Lyssa," Shane urged her, his tone demanding and filled with lust. "Watch him suck those pretty nipples."

Her lashes fluttered open, her gaze immediately captured by the sight of the reddened tip being covered by Sebastian's hungry lips.

He consumed her. The rush of pleasure overwhelmed her senses and her resistance. Sebastian's dark gaze locked with hers, his cheeks flexed, his hot mouth drawing on her as his tongue flicked over the peak, rubbed it, and sent forks of sharp, clenching pleasure racing to her womb.

It was so good. So good and she needed so much more.

"Don't tease me," she demanded, her tone sharp, the desperation building inside her at a speed she hadn't expected.

It had never been like this. Like a clawing, searing fever overtaking her senses, possessing them with a single, driving need. To be taken. To have every part of her body, all the dark hunger rising inside her, sated by the two men determined to see her consumed by the heat overwhelming her.

"How we missed this," Shane whispered at her ear, holding her to him as Alyssa fought to get closer to the chaotic pleasure Sebastian was inflicting on her swollen nipples. "How we missed feeling you burn."

Sebastian's lips moved to her other breast, drawing the neglected nipple into his mouth, increasing the lightning-hot strikes of sensation as he grew hungrier, his lust rising as his gaze remained on hers. She swore she could feel him clear to depths of her soul, pulling parts of her free that she hadn't known existed.

"I need you." Dazed, becoming mesmerized by the pleasure, she felt the words whisper unbidden from her lips. "I've needed you so bad. So long."

The sudden press of his teeth around the peak he was suckling sent static surges of sizzling sensation to her womb, then to the violently sensitized bud of her clit.

Alyssa shuddered, her thighs tightening, the agonized need for relief, for release, growing by the second. She was mesmerized by the pleasure, the hunger, the unbridled need beginning to whip through her, chaos building into a storm far quicker, stronger, than it had been when they'd touched her like this years before.

"Don't let me be dreaming again!" she cried out, her fingers curling, nails biting into her palms as Shane continued to hold her wrists. "Don't leave me alone in the dark again."

Please, God, not again. She couldn't bear it.

"You're not alone, baby." Shane nipped her ear as though chastising her for the fear. "Feel how good it's going to be. Better than before. Like magic and fireworks melting us together."

Magic and fireworks.

She fought to breathe. The flexing, drawing heat around her nipple echoed in painful need at her clit, the swollen bud throbbing, pulsing for release.

Every inch of her body was hyper-sensitized, every brush of sensation a whisper of air, another caress that only built an over-awareness of pleasure in each cell of her body.

Releasing her nipple with a groan, Sebastian's lips began to move lower. Stoking over her midriff, his tongue taking small tastes of her flesh as he kissed his way down her body. He pressed her thighs apart and moved to kneel next to the couch. His head tilted, lips moving inexorably closer to the saturated, swollen folds between her thighs.

"We dreamed of this, 'Lyssa. Of licking, tasting all that sweet flesh, and feeling you unravel for us," Shane groaned at her ear as the feel of his erection throbbed against her thigh.

"Shane, please . . ." Breathless, she felt the fear of losing herself, of losing her defenses, suddenly rising inside her.

How would she survive it when they left? When the world or

some other threat drew them away from her? How would she manage to force herself to breathe without knowing when they'd return?

" 'Please' what, baby?" Shane crooned as he eased her back to the pillows and stretched out beside her.

Sebastian eased between her legs. Broad shoulders spread her thighs, making a place for himself, his hands slipping beneath her rear to lift her to his hungry lips.

Staring down her body at him, Alyssa watched, burning need rushing through her as he licked his lips, then his tongue extended and pierced the swollen, slick folds of her sex.

"Oh yes. 'Bastian. Yes. Oh God, please . . ." Strangled, breathless, what should have been a cry was little more than a ragged whimper.

She couldn't take her eyes from him. He licked, flickering strokes racing over the sensitive folds, parting them, then drawing the slick essence of her response from her core.

"Sweet heaven, you make us crazy. You always have." Shane's voice was guttural now, low and rough, dark with his building hunger.

Alyssa struggled to process the pleasure, certain it was stronger, more intense, now than it had been before.

That the feel of Sebastian's tongue thrusting inside her sex, easing back to lick to her clit, stroking over and around the swollen bundle of nerves intoxicated her senses. When his fingers slipped into the narrow cleft of her rear, finding and caressing the hidden entrance, the spiking pleasure hit her harder, stronger, stealing the last of her defenses against them.

As he caressed the highly sensitive area with his fingers, his tongue tortured her clit, stroking and pushing her to an edge of pleasure she knew would destroy her senses.

She knew what was coming, knew what Sebastian was preparing her for. The knowledge had excitement running rampant across her senses. Eager, fiery flashes of sensation began pulsing through her, striking with excessive pleasure with each touch.

Sebastian's fingers rubbed over the tiny opening as she arched to him. Drawing back, his lips delivered a series of devastating kisses at her clitoris, only to ease the pressure as the blinding pulses of impending ecstasy tightened inside her. When his fingers returned to caress that hidden entrance again, they were slick, the thick lubrication he'd placed on them easing his way as he prepared her.

"I can barely wait to be inside you again. To feel you, so tight and hot around my cock," Shane whispered.

Sebastian pierced her anal entrance with one finger as Shane spoke at her ear, sliding inside her as his tongue continued to torture her clit.

Shane's lips covered her nipple, sucking it inside the heat of his mouth.

Sebastian worked two fingers slowly, gently, inside her rear, stretching her with wicked heat as she writhed beneath the pleasure. She was desperate for more, unable to resist the storm rising inside her or the knowledge that parts of her would never be the same.

Each slow, piercing thrust inside her anus increased the hot, overwhelming pleasure while the suckling pressure at her clit stole her breath.

"That's it, baby," Shane encouraged each desperate cry parting her lips. "That's it; let him have you. Let him open you for me. Get you ready. I'm going to fuck you so deep you'll wonder how you survived without us, without being locked between us."

But she hadn't survived. Not intact.

Applying another heavy layer of lubricant, Sebastian's fingers slid inside her again, stretching her further, dragging a ragged plea from her lips.

When she was certain she couldn't handle the steadily rising sensitivity and burning pleasure another moment, Sebastian eased back, his lips no longer torturing her, his fingers no longer stretching her rear channel.

" 'Bastian, don't stop!" Her cry slipped helplessly from her lips.

"Come here, baby." Moving, lifting her, Sebastian stretched out on the bed beside her and drew her over him. Her gaze was caught by the engorged stalk of his erection. His cock, flushed, the heavy veins throbbing beneath the tightly stretched flesh and glistening with moisture, rose from between Sebastian's thighs as he guided her over him.

Straddling his hips, Alyssa felt the wide crown parting the saturated folds of her pussy. She braced her hands against his chest, her senses reeling with pleasure.

Sebastian's hips shifted, the engorged head pressing into the clenched entrance of her pussy as Alyssa felt more of the slick wetness easing from her and spilling to the blunt force penetrating her.

"Ah hell, baby, I won't last long," Sebastian groaned as he began thrusting into the tight, clenched inner muscles. "It's been too damned long. And I've been so fucking hungry for the feel of you."

As he worked inside her, the slow, burrowing strokes stretching her, the pleasure-pain streaking through her nerve endings, she felt Shane behind her. Gentle, firm pressure pierced her rear. More of the lubricant eased his way while snug, nerve-laden muscles flexed around his fingers.

The overload of sensations was rising. Too fast. Too hot.

"You better last long enough for her to finish," Shane warned as Sebastian worked more of his cock inside her, the intensity of the pleasure stealing her breath and her last hold on reality as her pussy clenched in tight, involuntary spasms around his cock, drawing him deeper.

"That's it, baby," Sebastian groaned, his hands tightening on her hips, hard thighs bunching before he gave one hard, fiery thrust, burying his erection to the hilt inside her. "Take me, 'Lyssa. Every fucking inch."

A hard, heavy groan filled the air, meeting Alyssa's cry of piercing pleasure.

Shane moved behind her, his hand caressing the curves of her ass. Beneath her, Sebastian stilled, the wedge of his cock parting her, throbbing inside her, and intensifying the agonizing demand raging through her senses.

"There, baby," Shane whispered, the blunt crest of his erection tucking between her rear cheeks and pressing against that tighter entrance. "Breathe in. Give yourself to us. Give yourself to me."

A steadily widening pressure heated every nerve ending, stretching and burning as the sensations began building. As the small entrance parted, flaring over the width of the blunt crest stretching it, Alyssa felt the sharp ecstasy and sweet burning pain building at that forbidden entrance. He penetrated the ultra-tight flesh in a possession so intimate, so overwhelmingly dominating, that the last of her defenses against them evaporated.

"Shane! . . ." She held on to Sebastian, quivering, perspiration gathering on her flesh, waves of brilliant, blinding sensation began lashing at her vulnerable senses.

"I have you, baby," Sebastian answered her cry, his hand clenched at her hip, his arm secured over her shoulders to hold her against him. "You don't have to worry about it, 'Lyssa. I have you; I won't let you go."

He had her. She didn't have to hold on to her defenses; he would make sure she was safe. . . . He and Shane would keep the storm from destroying her completely.

Pushing into her, advancing by increments, Shane worked his cock inside her slowly. Stretching her open clenched, her pussy around Sebastian's erection tightening further. The slow, steady possession seared her, built the demand for more until she was crying out beneath them.

Beneath her, Sebastian's hips flexed, not exactly a thrust, more of a shift that had her back arching as she bucked against that lash of additional, brutal pleasure.

That one involuntary movement drove the flesh invading her anal passage that last inch needed, forcing the engorged head past the ultra-tight ring of muscles holding it back.

Alyssa cried out hoarsely as Shane's hips thrust forward then, burying his cock to the hilt inside her.

"So fucking hot and tight," Sebastian groaned. "Sweet 'Lyssa, you destroy me." The ragged whisper was followed by a slow, sensual roll of his hips and more sensation exploding through her.

She shook her head, desperate to fight whatever they were releasing inside her soul as they penetrated her body.

Shane's lips pressed to her shoulder, his breathing, like Sebastian's, hard as their bodies embraced hers.

As she lay against Sebastian's chest, her fingers laced with his now, her forehead pressed against his chest, the flames piercing her senses began to overwhelm her.

"Easy now, sweetheart," Shane groaned behind her, hips flexing. "Oh hell, 'Lyssa, I've got to move now. Sweet baby, that's it; just let us have you. We've got you, baby. We've got you. . . ."

Shane could feel Alyssa's flesh milking his cock with rippling, clenching shudders he knew from experience would be gripping her pussy as well.

Desperate little mewls escaped her throat; she writhed between them, clenching on each thrust filling her sleek little body.

She was a creature of pleasure, lost in the power of the need gripping all of them, burning so hot and pure he swore she was melting his soul with her surrender.

She was close. So fucking close. The tight, milking ripples of her inner flesh were becoming snugger, hotter, and tighter as he groaned with every fierce thrust inside her hot little rear.

Taking Alyssa to the point where she opened herself so completely to them had never been quickly accomplished, or easy. What it was, was a high so addictive he'd craved it every second for the past eight years. The withdrawal had been agonizing and never-ending. And this time, only death would drag them away from her.

Sebastian could feel Shane's movements behind Alyssa, his heavy thrusts tightening the spasms rippling through her pussy. The fist-tight grip increased to such brutal pleasure, he could feel himself losing control.

His balls were tight, drawn to the base of his cock, his testicles aching with the need to spill his cum inside her.

Holding her hips against the desperate, instinctive movements she made to fuck them back, Sebastian forced her tight against him. His rocking thrusts inside her pussy matched Shane's retreat from her rear as they began thrusting harder inside her.

Fucking her was like being in the middle of a storm that swirled with ever-increasing torrents of some sensation that went so far beyond pleasure. She was better than any drug. Hotter than any liquor. She was the pinnacle of sweet, carnal delight.

Holding her to him, forcing her swollen clit into position where every thrust ensured that little bud experienced maximum sensation, he felt the edge of rapture looming, pulling them all to that violent, consuming end that remade them each time Alyssa pulled them over it.

Rolling his hips against her, Sebastian's thrusts steadily increased, synchronized perfectly with Shane's. A natural, primal rhythm that needed no thought, asked for no restraint. Just her pleasure. Just her fucking pleasure wrapping around his soul—

Oh fuck— She was coming. Sweet perfect heaven, so tight

around his cock Sebastian swore he saw stars. The fierce grip of her pussy milked his cock with deep, contracting shudders, destroying his ability to delay his release.

"Oh yes, love," Sebastian groaned. "That's it, sweet 'Lyssa. God, I love fucking you. . . . Buried so tight–fucking destroy me."

There was no warning, no way to anticipate the sudden, explosive orgasm that locked her pussy around his cock, snug muscles rippling around him, her hot juices spilling over the engorged crown and sending his senses into white-hot rapture.

Sebastian was only distantly aware of Shane's suddenly tortured groan. Through the thin walls separating the two channels he was aware of the pulse and throb of Shane's erection as he spilled himself into the gripping depths of Alyssa's rear.

Alyssa's pussy flexed around his cock again, rippling, clenching, breaking the last hold he had over his senses. The quick, agonizingly ecstatic release slammed through him, sending his semen jetting to the suckling depths of the sweet pussy rippling around the pulsing shaft.

Each blinding ejaculation shooting from his cock sent jolts of sizzling rapture streaking from his balls, up his spine, and into the base of his skull, where the jolts detonated in pure rapture.

Then, sweet mercy, there it was, his addiction . . . that high rushed over him, burning through his senses and slamming to the depths of his being. His head fell back, his hips jerking hard against her, that feeling rushing through him, surging through his entire body in a slow, rapturous wave of pure white sensation.

Alyssa knew there was no place left to hide.

Brilliant, blinding sensation ripped down the walls, tore aside her defenses, and left her bared. Pleasure raced through all the hidden places, pulling free the emotions she'd fought to hide, intensifying each detonation of ecstasy flooding her senses in brilliant, arcing waves.

She was the center of the storm. Held in place, secure, given the freedom to fly.

This was what she felt lost without. This completion. This . . . In the arms of the lovers she couldn't deny, couldn't forget. Lost within a pleasure she knew would eventually destroy her and one she knew she couldn't resist as long as they were near.

She couldn't hide herself.

She couldn't hide the ecstasy that slammed through her in surging waves, or the climatic rush of euphoria whipping through her.

It went so far beyond pleasure that it was frightening. It was unlike any orgasm she'd ever read of, ever overheard other women speaking of.

This was why she felt as though she were slowly dying without them. This . . . pleasure? Addiction? She'd never understood it, never made sense of it, and in that moment she didn't care if she never understood it. As long as she had it. As long as she had Shane and Sebastian.

## 20

She'd waited for them.

The knowledge that she'd deliberately placed her life on hold waiting for them wasn't some sudden revelation. The signs had been there all along. The awareness of it had always been there.

Facing it, acknowledging it, was something else entirely.

She had known she was waiting. She had known, in that part of herself she'd locked down so tight, that they would have never willingly left her. She had *known*. And she'd been unable to face it, because facing it would have made being away from them unbearable.

As being away from her had destroyed both Shane and Sebastian.

That sense of them she had in Barcelona hadn't been a fantasy. The awareness of their love for her hadn't been a figment of her imagination. It had been real.

And it left her facing the knowledge that the risk of it happening again would always be there unless she managed to tame the untameable, and train the untrainable. God, talk about needing a miracle.

As she sat at her desk and went through mail, those emotions pulled and tugged at one another, demanding satisfaction, acceptance, and she was damned if she knew how to fix either problem.

She couldn't satisfy her need for answers, and she hadn't yet been able to accept that they hadn't trusted her enough to allow her to face that fight with them.

She understood their need to protect her; what she didn't understand was the unspoken idea that if they had revealed the truth to her she would have somehow endangered herself or their attempt to learn the identity of the blackmailer.

That one pissed her off and kept her in a state of near anger where her lovers were concerned.

"They're going to drive me crazy," she muttered under her breath. "I can feel the nervous breakdown getting closer."

With a shake of her head she put aside the stack of mail to answer and turned to her laptop. The buzz of a text message coming from her phone had a grimace pulling at her lips.

She had inherited her lack of interest in text messages from her mother no doubt.

Picking up the device, she stared at the screen for a moment. Just to make certain she was reading it correctly.

*You were warned!*

She stared at the message, the "unknown" listing of the number, and felt outrage explode inside her.

Like hell! She'd be damned if she was going to deal with this now. Shane and Sebastian were making her crazy enough. They did *not* need any help.

Jumping from her chair, she rushed to the door and jerked it open. A sudden blast behind her catapulted her into the hall and threw her into the wall across from her office with enough force to steal her breath and leave her crumpling to the floor.

Fighting to inhale as sirens began blaring around her, the sounds blasting through her ears, Alyssa struggled to draw air into her lungs. The force of the blow combined with the smoke rolling from her office made breathing a bit more difficult. She was going to kill whoever did this. Dammit, Dr. Brennan was going to bring that Amazon, Nurse Shaw, back and make her life hell. She couldn't handle it.

She wasn't going to handle it.

Emergency lights cast a red glow around her, making it harder to see through the heavy smoke, disorienting her before she placed her forehead against the floor, drawing in what little fresh air could be found.

Oh God, she hurt now.

Hell, the other bruises hadn't healed yet.

A painful, furious groan escaped her as her fist clenched, her teeth grinding in fury.

She was going to kill someone. . . . She swore she was.

"Alyssa!"

"Alyssa, where are you!"

"Dammit, 'Lyssa, where are you?"

She lifted her hand, almost laughing at the thought that there wasn't a chance in hell they could see her.

"'Lyssa, answer me!" Shane said. And he sounded really put out.

Spanish curses were ripping through the air and when Sebastian was cursing in Spanish, it was a sure indication he was seriously losing all that patience he swore he had. Not that she saw a lot of proof of it.

'Bastian was cursing harder than he had the day they learned she had a penchant for climbing.

She tried to call back to him, only to begin coughing violently in reaction to the smoke she drew into her lungs.

Oh, just let her get her hands on whoever did this. Coughing up smoke hurt, dammit.

"Alyssa!" Hard hands grasped her shoulders, pulling her up into a broad chest and quickly moving from the oxygen-deprived area and into the back courtyard.

As she drew in fresh air, another coughing fit wracked her chest from the abrasive smoke still lingering in her lungs. Spanish curses were still filling the air, which only pissed her off because she couldn't have a little hissy fit herself for the wracking spasms ripping her lungs apart.

"Here." A plastic oxygen mask was pushed over her face, pure oxygen spilling to her lungs as she breathed in, tears pouring from her eyes from the stinging effects of the smoky hallway.

"What happened?" Batting the mask away a second later, she lifted her head from where it had dropped to the hard shoulder it was resting against.

Sebastian's shoulder. He'd taken a seat on one of the large, comfortable iron chairs spread out around the shaded courtyard outside the offices at the back of the house.

"We're not sure yet." Shane tried to push the mask over her face again.

"Get that away from me." Pushing it aside again, she stared up at his face, watching as he checked the area, eyes narrowed, taking notice of each and every person gathered outside with them.

"My office was blown up." She turned to Sebastian. "A text came into my phone—"

"We got the text." He nodded, watching her closely.

"Pissed me off," she sighed. "I jumped up and headed for the door. The next thing I knew I was being thrown into the wall like some kind of damned doll. That was not fun, 'Bastian."

Her fingers were clenched into the material of the fine cotton shirt he wore. She turned her head to glare at him. "And I swear to God, if anyone calls Dr. Brennan I'll shoot them myself. You hear me?"

"No, I agree, that wouldn't be fun, baby. And I hear you loud and clear." Sebastian tightened his arms around her, his gaze tracking everyone in the yard, wondering who was stupid enough to plant an explosive device in her office. It had to have been someone in the house, because they'd just checked her office before they left her suite a few hours before.

"Alyssa?" John Raeg—pronounced "rage," as he was always quick to correct anyone who pronounced it otherwise—her father's chief of staff, moved across the stone terrace quickly, a heavy scowl on his craggy features, his cell phone to his ear. "Are you okay?"

She nodded, feeling Sebastian's hand as it continued to rub her back as a shudder raced up her spine. "I'm fine, Raeg."

Turning, he was speaking into the phone as he moved back toward the house, the sound of sirens rushing steadily closer.

"What the hell was that, 'Bastian?" she demanded as Shane eased away from them, moving slowly toward the edge of the courtyard.

"We'll know what it was soon," he promised.

"Someone put an explosive in my office. Are they fucking crazed?" An amazed laugh escaped her. She couldn't believe it. Someone had put an explosive in her office, for what? Because Sebastian and Shane intended to share her bed?

"We don't know that yet, sweets," he assured her, his voice low. "Let's wait and see what we find before we jump to conclusions."

Shane had completely disappeared now. Looking around, she didn't catch sight of him, but paramedics were rushing into the courtyard, along with Detective Allen. The suspicion on his face wasn't subtle. It locked on her, his gaze narrowing as he moved directly toward her.

"Ms. Stanhope," he greeted, pushing the lightweight jacket he wore back as he propped his fists at his hips. "Sure you don't know who's trying to hurt you?" he asked, a reminder of the same question he'd asked when he'd interviewed her after the attempted hit-and-run.

"Only one person would have wanted to hurt me, Carl," she sighed as his gaze sharpened on her. "And he's dead. Last I heard, ghosts have a hard time with some of the things going on around me."

"Ghosts might." He nodded slowly. "But some people get fixated on stuff. Maybe someone they were close to? Someone that loved them?"

"Then your guess is as good as mine." She laughed bitterly. "If you find anyone willing to admit to loving that bastard, even his parents, then please let me know. I'll say a prayer for them."

Shooting the detective a look, Sebastian gave a little shake of his head. He'd talk to Carl himself. He wanted Alyssa out of sight and safe. Now.

"Here's Landra and her bodyguards, Alyssa. I want you to go upstairs with them while I find Shane and see what's going on. Can you walk?" Sebastian's hand ran comfortingly up her back.

"I can walk." Pushing at his hands, she rose from his lap, though he could have sworn she swayed just a bit as she stood.

"Mr. De Loren." The lead security personnel nodded as Landra stopped in front of Alyssa, her voice low as she talked to the younger girl. "Mr. Collier said to follow your directions until we heard from him. What do you need?"

Sebastian nodded to where Landra actually managed to draw a low, shaky laugh from Alyssa. "Get them to one of the more secure suites upstairs until we have this taken care of. I don't want anyone but myself, Shane, the senator, or your boss in those rooms," he ordered them, his voice tight.

"Yes, sir," the agent responded soberly. "We'll make sure they stay safe."

Sebastian met Landra's gaze, then and nodded to the bodyguards, indicating she should take Alyssa and go with them.

"Come on, dear, let's get out of here so the boys can take care of this," Landra urged her, one arm wrapped around Alyssa's waist.

"They'll work so much better without us breathing down their necks."

Whatever Alyssa said, Landra gave a little laugh, filled with amusement. "Yeah, well, we like to let them believe they do, sweetie. It makes them happy; then we're happy."

Evidently Alyssa thought little of not being able to breathe down their necks.

"Sebastian." The detective stared around the courtyard, watching, taking everything in. "We have a problem here?"

A member of the Sinclair Men's Club and a personal friend of Ian's, the detective knew his main concern was protecting the club and its members.

"We have a problem here," Sebastian affirmed. "But it's not a club problem."

Carl snorted. "Doesn't mean much, according to Ian," he murmured. "We talking here or at your office?"

"Here. After they've all left." Sebastian nodded to the staff milling around. "The senator and Jeb will want to be there, so let's just do this once."

"I hear ya," Carl agreed. "I'll check things out inside then. We'll talk before I leave."

Sebastian nodded, catching sight of Shane as he eased from the doors leading into the back office and moved easily to where Sebastian stood.

"Anything?" Sebastian asked him.

"Low-grade explosive. I'll have to wait on analysis before I know the intent behind it. My opinion, though, if it wasn't meant to kill her, then it was meant to put her in a wheelchair. The text triggered it, but she didn't wait when she got the damned thing. She was at the door when it went off or she would have been wearing the chair leg like a stake."

"God, Shane," he bit out, the image far more graphic than he wanted to deal with.

Crossing his arms over his chest, Shane stared around the area again. "I'll contact Falcone, tell him to put a rush on it. We need him here as soon as possible."

Falcone and his partner, Gia Bennet, were currently wrapping up a lead on a suspected tie between Harvey Stanhope and Gregory Santiago. The private security investigator and his partner made up one of the teams Shane was considering for the international security firm he and Sebastian were putting together.

"Whoever it is, isn't wasting time. They have access to the house and the club, and they mean to destroy her, one way or the other. Send the names of the staff here to Khalid; let him run them against membership, see what we come up with."

By the sound of his voice, like Sebastian he wasn't expecting any matches.

"Someone's very, very stupid," Shane said, his lips barely moving, ensuring no one could follow the conversation. "If they knew what they were doing, they wouldn't have come after 'Lyssa like this."

If they knew what they were doing, then they would have checked out those surrounding Alyssa. They would have checked his and Shane's backgrounds and at least suspected there was more to them than meets the eye. Because damned sure, they weren't aware that Alyssa's lovers were far more deadly than they appeared. And the two showing up in the next twenty-four hours were guaranteed to fuck someone's shit up. And they wouldn't even know it until it was far, far too late.

## 21

Sebastian was waiting for her alone as she entered her room after showering. Thankfully, her living suite hadn't been affected, even by the smoke. The renovations made to it two years before had given her complete separation from the office and secured the other rooms from intrusion.

Probably to talk to those contacts he had at the CIA.

The CIA. She was still astounded. Why hadn't she suspected in Barcelona?

"What do you need, Sebastian?" she asked, her insides still shaking from the earlier attempt to decimate her body parts by whoever planted that explosive.

"To check on you, love," he answered from where he sat on the padded bench at the end of her bed. "You've not exactly had a chance to catch your breath lately, have you?"

"Oh, it's just been fun and games," she assured him. "Fun and games."

Yeah, right. How long had it been since she'd had the freedom for any kind of fun, let alone games? Oh yeah, right. Eight years. And they'd all paid for that one hadn't they?

"When do you get to have fun and games then, sweets?" he asked softly then.

Eight years ago, she repeated silently. Eight long, pain-filled years ago.

"When I have time." She watched as he began to unbutton his shirt, her insides melting at the thought of the pleasure to come.

The snow-white dress shirt made his dark Spanish flesh seem all the more appealing. His dark eyes watched her with wicked lust and a deepening emotion that made her chest ache.

"And do you have time very often?" He approached her slowly, the lean, powerful muscles of his chest coming into view as the last button slipped free.

Pulling the material from his shoulders, he dropped it negligently to the back of a nearby chair.

Alyssa's insides were shaking. No matter how hard she tried, she couldn't seem to draw enough air into her lungs now. Her lips parted; her knees grew weak. She tried to tell herself the reaction was a result of too many long, sleepless nights. That excuse was laughable.

She knew better. It wasn't the weariness; it was Sebastian, Shane, both. Whichever touched her, however they touched her. Whether they were together or apart, their effect on her was the same.

"You didn't answer me." Stopping in front of her, he lifted one hand, his fingers curving around the back of her neck. "Do you have time for fun and games very often?"

"I make time." She was such a liar. Evidently she'd learned more in observing the political bullshit on a daily basis than she'd meant to. The small spurt of amusement she felt at the thought almost had the corners of her lips tugging into a smile.

Who could suspect that the sweetly honest young woman he'd known in Spain could actually force such lies past her pretty lips? Not that she could do so without giving herself away, but he was surprised she kept trying.

"And you're making time for me now," he said, hiding the knowing amusement that filled him. "I feel very honored that you've fit me into your busy schedule."

"You should, all things considered." Her breathing was so hard, her heart racing so fast, that Sebastian wondered if they would both expire from lack of oxygen before the night was over.

Her gray eyes darkened as he rubbed at the back of her neck with the tips of his fingers, his head lowering to brush a whisper of a kiss at her shoulder.

Poor little sweet. Their return to her life hadn't exactly been peaceful, had it?

"And I assure you, love, I do consider all things," he said, the feel of her fingers moving timidly against his chest making it difficult to ensure he paid attention to each nuance of the woman he and Shane had despaired of ever touching again.

Now, watching her gray eyes darken to thunderclouds, Sebastian knew his control was just as weak around her at this moment as it was at any other time.

Already sensation was raking across his body just as he felt her shudder against him and knew the sharpness of her response after so long apart had caught her off guard. She couldn't hide her pleasure any more than she could hide her hunger for his touch, for the ecstasy she'd found in his and Shane's arms so long ago.

Hiding his smile, Sebastian let his fingers trail down her arm, experiencing the incredible warmth and silkiness of her skin.

Lifting his hand to the thin straps holding the bodice of her nightgown over the creamy curves of her breasts, he let his fingers play over the fragile material.

"I love the feel of you." Lowering his head, he let his lips play at the curve of her neck and shoulder. "The taste of skin as it heats with pleasure has filled my fantasies for many long, cold nights."

Her hands slid to his biceps, her fingers tightening over the bunched muscles as those destructive kisses moved lower.

"What about Shane?" A hint of nerves had her voice trembling. It had been so long for her, he knew. So very long since she'd had the touch she ached for. The touch her body had been branded with. The few nights they'd had weren't enough for any of them.

Sebastian chuckled at the question. "That isn't how this works, sweets. You know that. We don't need each other's permission to have you alone. Just as we each can't deny the other the pleasure of touching you, or having you at any time. You reserve that control alone."

It had been rarely, though, that they had taken her alone in the past.

"A seduction isn't required," she breathed out with a hint of desperation in her tone. Had she truly forgotten or so feared the pleasure they'd once shared? The bond it seemed to strengthen between them?

"Pleasure is required, sweet 'Lyssa." A little nip to her ear followed by a gentle kiss had her nails pricking at his upper arms.

Sebastian tightened his grip at the nape of her neck, lifted his head, then paused, waited for her gaze to find his. As he watched the helpless longing burning in her eyes, his head lowered and his lips settled over hers.

He'd meant to kiss her slow and easy, to build the fire burning between them. The second his lips touched hers all thoughts of slow and easy evaporated.

They could have lost her today. If the trigger on that explosive had been set right, if she had been a heartbeat slower, they would have lost her.

Smooth, experienced seduction became a ravenous hunger tearing aside his control.

Never had his sexual hungers taken control of him in such a way, though he remembered it had been close several times in the past when it came to this woman.

She met the hunger tearing through him with her own. Lips parting beneath the onslaught, desperate hands lifting to his neck before burrowing into his hair to hold him to her. She consumed his kiss, lips and tongue moving against his, her feminine mewls of rising need burning through any thought he might have harbored of drawing back, of easing the needs he was unleashing on her.

She was all that warmed his heart. Over the years only thoughts of Alyssa had kept him sane. Had kept him from drowning in the dark abyss he sometimes felt himself sinking into.

Sweet Alyssa. He would never sate this hunger for her, this need for her alone that captivated him.

As he devoured the sweetness of her kiss, Sebastian fought to remove the gown without tearing the delicate fabric. To carefully push the slender straps over her arms to allow it to fall, forgotten, to the floor at her feet.

And Alyssa, never one to simply take her due, had followed suit. Those nimble, graceful fingers released his slacks, allowing her to push the material over his hips and reveal the agonizing engorged erection the material had kept restrained.

Kicking off his shoes, Sebastian finished divesting himself of the pants as he tore his lips from the addictive sweetness of her kiss.

As much as he loved her hungry kisses, there were other places on her very lovely body that he longed to taste. He was addicted to her taste, her touch, to touching her.

"'Bastian, oh God, 'Bastian, I need you." It wasn't a whimper of sensual need. It was a demand. A feminine warning that her own hungers threatened to override any shyness or sexual uncertainties she might harbor.

Her touch wasn't one of experienced desires, rather that of a woman tormented by her need as well as the desperate longing to touch her lover.

Sebastian let his lips move along her neck, her collarbone, then to the rapid rise and fall of her breasts. Sweet, cherry red nipples hardened by passion and tempting him to taste, to take his fill of the swollen sweetness drew him with an irresistable force.

Greedy hunger rushed through his senses. He'd been too long denied her, ached for her for too many years.

Without preliminaries his head dipped, his lips covered a pebble-hard tip, and he gloried in her sharp cry of pleasure. The need to experience every facet of this longed-for treat drew a matching groan from his chest.

God help him. Never had a woman shredded his experienced control as this one delicate, far too tempting woman could.

She was his weakness, his most coveted dream, and a hunger he'd never been able to rid himself of. She was the only thing he couldn't deny himself.

✦✦✦✦

Sensation exploded through Alyssa's body as Sebastian's lips covered her nipple and drew the painfully sensitive flesh into the heat of his mouth.

Flash points of burning exquisite pleasure ricocheted from the tiny bundle of nerves to the flexing, empty depths of her vagina. Slick heat spilled between her thighs and the bare folds sheltering her sex became swollen and oversensitive while the engorged bud of her clit throbbed in heady demand.

The heavy draw of his mouth and flicking licks of his tongue against the tight point of her nipple sent fiery flashes of sensation to contract around her clit and pleasure burning through her with such consummate need it was like the most incredible high. Her favorite drug.

Burying her fingers in his hair and fighting to keep her knees from giving out, Alyssa forced her eyes to open. Savagely honed features were softened by lust and filled with decadent, wicked need. He looked like a fallen angel. Fierce and far too strong, his touch mesmerizing and impossible for her to deny.

When his hunger shifted to the opposite nipple, Alyssa whimpered.

Sebastian's fingers brushed against the slick, saturated folds between her thighs. Sharp pleasure lanced through her, sending a hard, convulsive spasm shuddering through her body.

Her knees gave out at the same second Sebastian's lips abandoned her breast and he lifted her to him, before turning and settling her rear on the chest of drawers just behind her.

"There's a bed," she gasped as he pushed her thighs farther apart and lifted his head to stare back at her, his eyes as black as sin and gleaming with hunger.

"This is closer." The rough cadence of his voice sent chills of pleasure racing up her spine as she swallowed against the emotions tightening her throat.

"Lay back, pretty siren," he crooned, sliding the fragile lace of her panties from her body. Tossing the scrap of material aside, his gaze centered between her thighs. "Let's see how crazy I can make us both."

He followed the statement with his tongue pushing into the narrow slit and disintegrated Alyssa's senses.

A low, pleading whimper escaped her lips as he slid his tongue to the throbbing flesh of her clit. Then he licked lower once again to find the snug entrance of her core and flicked against it teasingly before delivering a heated kiss to the sensitive lips flaring open at his touch.

He was diabolical. Wicked and carnal.

He slid his tongue into the narrow valley once again and the hungry licks moved back to her clit, circled it, then drew it between his lips to suckle it for just a few, torturous seconds before drawing back.

Each ravenous stroke of his tongue, each flexing draw of his mouth, rocked her senses and dragged desperate cries from her lips.

Oh God, it was so good.

Dancing like living flames over flesh too long denied, his tongue stroked the pleasure she'd been denied for so long, consumed the taste of her, and burned against flesh too long ignored. Thorough, destructive, each greedy lick, each suckling kiss, pulled her deeper into the flames twisting through her senses. Heightened sensation tormented the steadily building desperation to reach the center of the vortex tightening inside her.

"Damn you, Sebastian," she gasped as his lips released her clit yet again, his tongue then licking around the tortured nubbin of flesh. "Stop teasing me."

His answer was a heated breath of air over the painfully swollen bud and a long, far too gentle lick over and around it.

"'Bastian, please." She was willing to beg. For a minute anyway. "Please, you're killing me."

His hands tightened along the outside of her thighs as the tension in his body increased along with the hungry kisses he was torturing her sex with.

Staring down her body, her eyes connected with his. Lust-filled, a gleam of desperate hunger and rapidly faltering control reflected in his gaze as well as his expression.

"Please, 'Bastian," she whispered, trying to lift to him only to have his hold on her tighten as those destructive, heated licks moved lower once again.

Alyssa gasped a second later as he penetrated the clenched entrance of her pussy with a hard, ravenous stroke of exquisite pleasure. Her vision blurred, her body pulsed as her orgasm threatened to explode through her, only to have him pull back at the last second.

"No." Her vision cleared, but the imperative need only grew. "Don't torture me, Sebastian. Please. Damn you, let me come."

Something snapped in his gaze, a sudden knowledge or understanding Alyssa knew she didn't want him to have. But before she could figure out what she'd revealed his head lowered again, his lips surrounding her clit while two broad fingers began penetrating the snug, clenched depths of her pussy. Stretching her, owning her.

Each impalement of his fingers working inside her forced a ragged cry past her lips as the tightening pressure of his mouth around her clit sent her senses into a catastrophic meltdown.

Ecstasy exploded inside her, flinging her into a rapturous kaleidoscope of sensation and blazing heat. Pulses of white-hot electricity sizzled up her spine before meeting the pleasure exploding through the rest of her body.

She couldn't cry out. The rocketing orgasm stole her strength and her breath as her body and senses fought to adapt to a release she hadn't known in far too long.

Just when she felt the quicksilver ride through the clashing ecstasy begin to ease, her eyes flared open and the flames began consuming her again.

Eyes wide, her gaze locked on the penetration of her body, Alyssa could only whimper as the crescendo began rising again.

Glistening with her juices, the bare folds of her sex were parted, gripping the thick shaft working between them. Each forceful stroke stretched her inner flesh with the ecstatic pain she craved.

"Fuck, 'Lyssa." The rough, guttural groan dragged her gaze back to his. "Ah hell, baby, it's like taking you the first time. So fucking tight and hot."

The explicit words had her pussy clenching further around the invading shaft, rippling in demand with each thrust inside her.

Alyssa could barely process any form of reality. She hadn't remembered the true scope of pleasure she felt at his touch, hadn't remembered how he and Shane had so completely owned her senses, whether separate or apart.

Each heavy stroke impaling her responsive sheath, stretching it, blazed a path of intimate destruction. Each stroke inside her body eroded her control further, sent pleasure whipping harder, stronger, through her senses. Fiery lashes of arcing electricity stole reason and reality and when the second catastrophic explosion rushed through her, Alyssa could only whimper with the exquisite pleasure.

Ecstasy whipped through her, around her, and in a heartbeat, of time she felt Sebastian. Felt his heart beating in time to hers, his soul, just as tattered as her own, reaching out to her.

As the final shudders of her release rippled through her body, she closed her eyes and let her senses relish the pleasure and the bond she could feel only growing stronger.

Long moments later when Sebastian lifted her, carrying her to the bed, she didn't allow herself to slip from the cocoon she'd let herself slide into. His gentle cleaning the proof of her pleasure from her was a familiar ritual and one she realized she would have missed if it was neglected.

Moving into the bed beside her when he finished, Sebastian wrapped one arm around her and dragged her against him, her back to his chest, her head tucked at his shoulder, his hard, warm body wrapped around her. She was surrounded by warmth, by a sense of complete security she'd only felt with him and Shane.

A hint of a smile tugged at her lips, bittersweet and aching with loss. What was she supposed to do now? she asked herself. How was she supposed to rebalance her life after learning the sacrifices Shane and Sebastian had made for her? They'd fought for her. They had worked to destroy the hold a blackmailer had over them while she'd fought to just survive.

Her sacrifice hadn't compared to theirs and still she'd wondered if she would survive several times. They had taken care of what stood between them and her; then they'd come to Alexandria for her. And now, once again, they had to step up and protect her from something else, someone else determined that Alyssa not have the men who had claimed her heart so long ago.

Wrapped around her, Sebastian's arms holding her to his chest as they lay on their sides, Alyssa could feel Sebastian, warm and relaxed against her, his heartbeat steady, his breath feathering the top of her head.

"I always liked this with you," he said, amusement touching his voice. "Having you all soft and warm in my arms. Cuddling you was always good, 'Lyssa."

She hadn't had much cuddling in her life; it had made cuddling with them so much nicer.

"Do you remember the night we took the yacht out? We made love to you on the deck until the sun came up, then fell asleep there. Shane and I got our asses burned and you were safe and shaded between us?"

She smiled. Then, before she could stop, a laugh escaped her. "You two looked so funny," she said, still smiling at the memory, one she hadn't allowed free since she'd returned from Madrid.

"Hell, we couldn't sit for a week," he reminded her.

"And I rubbed cool aloe onto your poor burned butts three times a day." Turning to her back, she stared up at him, that memory so vivid the pleasure and happiness that filled her then invading her now. "I took care of both of you. Very gently, I might add."

He propped his head in his hand, his eyes gleaming at her through the darkness as one arm lay over her midriff. "Hmm, I remember you running around there naked, making us overexert ourselves while we were so wounded."

"But 'Bastian," she whispered up at him, barely holding her laughter back. "It was your butts that were burned, not your—"

His fingers were laid over her lips before the word could slip free, causing her soft laughter to spill around them.

"You were very naughty," he reminded her.

Sebastian hadn't seen her smile, hadn't heard her laughter, nearly enough since returning to her And he'd missed them, desperately. Now he wanted only to hold her, to fill her with the memories that had kept him sane as he waited to claim her.

"I was just trying to make you feel better," she pouted, the innocence in her voice, on her face, not wholly feigned. "The two of you just had such dirty minds all the time." She rolled her eyes.

God how she missed just laying in the dark and talking, laughing with him and Shane. Separate or apart.

Sebastian ran his fingers along her ribs, drawing an involuntary giggle from her as the tickling touch brought an instant reaction.

"That was just wrong," she accused, shaking her finger up at him. "I did nothing to deserve that."

"Of course you did," he retorted softly, lowering his lips to brush against hers. "Laughing at our weakness. We were in pain."

"'Bastian, you and Shane stayed aroused," she reminded him, her tone assuring him it still amazed her. "If your pants were off then you were hard."

"I thought that was how it was supposed to be." He smirked. "Would you have had it any differently?"

As she cast him a look from the corners of her eyes a little smile barely tempted her lips. "Well, probably not," she admitted. "I was afraid the two of you were going to strain something, though, as often as you made use of those hard-ons you were sporting. Hell, I thought I was going to strain something."

"Ah now, that we would have never allowed." Not even in a million years. "Straining you was something we would have never done, sweets. We needed you far too desperately."

Tucking her closer to him, he let his lips whisper over her shoulder, feeling her fingers stroking absently at his arm as she lay comfortably against him now.

"When I woke that morning, and you and Shane were gone, I knew something was wrong," she whispered. "I felt you leave the bed, but I was so tired, I fell back asleep. About two hours later, I woke again. I swore I heard you and Shane fighting and I couldn't imagine why."

Sebastian closed his eyes, remembering that meeting with

Fernando, the black rage that had filled him, and the overwhelming grief.

He tightened his arms around her. "Our sweet 'Lyssa, we conquered the evil dragon and came for the innocent princess. Did we not?"

"You did." A smile tugged at her lips again before easing away.

"Smile for me, 'Lyssa," he whispered against her ear. "Give me just a moment to bring you joy once again, to warm you as Shane and I used to."

"You two were crazy," she said softly, staring up at him, her hand lifting to cup his cheek. "The two of you are still crazy."

"We are?" His brow arched. "I remember stepping into our bedroom to see you perched rather unsteadily on the back of a chair, preparing to crash to the floor. You terrified me."

"I knew what I was doing," she assured him archly, her nose lifting. "I rarely fall."

He snorted at that. "You lie."

"I don't— 'Bastian, no. . . ." She giggled as his fingers ran up her ribs again, tickling the little spurts of laughter from her smiling lips, and the warmth of her happiness wrapped around him.

God, he needed this. Needed to hear this, to hold her, to feel her against him, to hear her pleasure and her joy.

They both needed it. Needed to feel her, to remember that time with her, to reaffirm what they had fought for all these years. And in the darkness, with him wrapped around her, her laughter drifted around him like silken threads, warming him in her pleasure. In the heart and soul of the woman he'd never been able to forget.

His sweets. His 'Lyssa.

## 22

Alyssa heard Shane enter the living area of the suite the next night. Sebastian had warned her he would be spending the night consulting with Khalid over the file they were still trying to decrypt at the Sinclair Club offices, which meant Shane had finally come in from dealing with the various investigators who had arrived concerning the explosion.

It was nearly midnight and the work that day on her office repairs had gone much slower than she'd liked.

Moving from the bed, not bothering with the slippers next to her bed, or her robe, and opening the door, she leaned against the frame, crossing one ankle behind the other as she stared at him.

He'd showered, and he looked tired. It still amused her that he and Sebastian were making use of the suite her father had given them upstairs rather than just using hers.

"Sebastian's at the club?" she asked, watching him closely.

"Khalid needed help tracking that program Ian found on the computers," he snorted. "It's driving them crazy."

She nodded slowly, swallowed with a tight movement, and remained quiet.

"Everything okay?" he asked.

She frowned back at him. There were days men were just too damned complicated. She'd always known that.

"Do they know anything about the explosive yet?" She asked, rather than giving in to her frustration.

"That could take a day or so." He grimaced. "The FBI has the investigation from this point, though Langley sent over one of their explosives experts to go over it as well."

Langley. The CIA.

"Were you and Sebastian working with the CIA while I was in Madrid?" she asked, frowning. They hadn't seemed ultra-secretive or James Bond–ish at the time.

"We were recruited in college." He shrugged, watching her closer. "Sebastian and I both attended college here in the states. Our recruiter and trainer was someone well known to us, and our families, which made it easier to cover training missions during holidays."

"Not quite the party boys everyone thought you were, huh?" she reflected.

She'd already known that, though. Not that she'd ever suspected they were some kind of agents, but she'd known they weren't the playboys they were rumored to be.

"We didn't party much after meeting you anyway," he said somberly, his blue eyes trained on her, his expression intent. "We were at a crossroads of a sort at the time." He shrugged. "We could have taken positions as information assets only and gone on with our lives, or slipped into covert status. After we lost you, we took the covert assignments."

"Why would you do something so dangerous?" she asked, terrified now of the danger they must have been in. "You were essentially spies for a foreign government. If authorities had known—"

"There were those in the government that knew." His lips quirked humorlessly. "Spain and the U.S. aren't exactly enemies. Sebastian and I were specifically targeted because of the De Loren name and the position our family held politically, both in Spain and here in the states. We had a certain level of protection. It also afforded us certain privileges and help in identifying the person responsible for those pictures and the blackmail."

But she hadn't known. She hadn't been able to worry about them, hadn't been there if they were hurt. She hadn't had enough memories to sustain her if the worse had happened.

"Are you still with them then?" she asked, wondering if that danger would continue to haunt them.

His lips kicked into a small grin. "One of Summer's demands the night we slipped into your room, after Harvey's attack." He grinned, then shrugged. "We were getting out anyway after eliminating the threat of those pictures against you. But she demanded we clear the CIA junk out of our lives before coming to you. She made sense. We couldn't have concentrated on completing those last assignments if we'd have stayed. She knew that."

"Why did the two of you do that, Shane?" she whispered then; the thought of the danger they had both no doubt faced would give her nightmares, she was certain. "Why risk your lives in such a way?"

"Seemed like a good idea at the time." His lips quirked ruefully. "It *was* a good idea at the time. But the time for it passed. We're just disowned, disavowed misfits now." He gave a hard shake of his head. "Making Fernando do that to ensure no one has such a hold on our families again wasn't easy. He's still furious that Father went along with it."

Sexual tension filled the room, racing around them, heating the air and settling over her flesh, sensitizing it and making it ache for his touch. The conversation wasn't in the least sexual, but the hunger was still there.

"I never understood what it was about the two of you," she said nervously as he stopped in front of her, one hand reaching up to brush her hair back from her cheek. "Why I couldn't ache for just one of you."

"You completed us," he whispered, his lips lowering to her ear, brushing against it, and sending tingles of heat to race across her flesh. "So sweet, and giving . . ." His lips moved along her neck. "So perfect that neither of us were willing to walk away."

One hand cupped the back of her neck, the other settling at her hip as his tongue flicked against the sensitive area just below her ear. "We missed you, baby. We missed you bad."

The words whispered over her lips just before his kiss exploded through her senses. With one arm wrapped around her back Shane pulled her to him with a sudden, unexpected movement as his lips claimed hers, pulling her into a storm rioting with carnal hunger so quickly there was no time to assimilate it.

His tongue swept past her lips, claiming her, branding her senses, and unleashing her from any control she might have had over herself.

She'd missed this with the same agonizing regret that she'd missed Sebastian's seduction of her senses. Missed the completion they'd given her each time they touched her.

Shane's hands slid down her back, rasping the silk of her gown over her skin, the warmth of his palm creating a friction that sent pleasure lancing through her. Reaching her hips, he bunched the material, pulling it up her body before breaking his possession of her senses and stripping her of the material in one smooth, unexpected move.

"Shane . . ." Breathless, surprised, she stared up at him as his gaze moved down her naked body.

"God, look at you," he whispered, catching her wrists and pulling them over her head, his expression tightening with the sexual need running rampant through both of them now. "So fucking pretty."

With his free hand he cupped the curve of a breast, his thumb rolling over the pebble hardness of her nipple, the friction sending arcs of sensation scattering through her senses.

"Shane . . ." As she arched into the caress her head fell back to the door, her breathing rough and uneven, then laced with a low, desperate moan as his lips covered the tight peak.

He didn't tease her gently. His mouth was ravenous, sucking the tip with hungry need as his tongue lashed at it, building on each sensation until she was mindless with the pleasure and the need for release.

"That's it; burn for me, 'Lyssa," he groaned as his lips lifted from her breast, his hand releasing her wrists to join the other in sliding to the curves of her ass.

Gripping the flesh, he lifted her to him, bringing a startled gasp from her lips. He moved only as far as it took to sit back on the sofa positioned near the door.

"No bed, huh?" she gasped, gripping his shoulders when he released her to divest himself of his pants.

"They're overrated." Gripping her hips, he moved her over the engorged length of his erection, groaning when the slick folds of her sex grazed the wide, blunt crest.

"I can't wait, 'Lyssa," he groaned heavily. "Foreplay next time."

"Next time," she agreed, feeling more of the slick moisture spilling from her as heavy pressure began parting the entrance.

That pressure increased, parting the clenched flesh, easing inside her with slow, rocking thrusts that devastated her senses.

"Ah, baby," Shane groaned as the inner muscles tightened around him and she rocked into each thrust, taking him deeper.

His fingers bunched in the hair at the back of her head, holding her still, her face lifted to his as he let his forehead rest against hers.

Powerful muscles tightened between her thighs, his hips tensed. Tightening her hold on his shoulders, Alyssa stared up at him as a grimace of pleasure contorted his face.

Iron-hard and throbbing, only the crown of his cock penetrated her, holding her suspended within the pleasure gathering inside her.

"What are you waiting for?" She was trembling in anticipation, moisture gathering, slick and hot and spilling along her inner flesh. "Fuck me already."

His hips jerked, a hard thrust that buried his cock deeper, parting the hyper-sensitive flesh with a sudden, shocking rush of pleasure-pain. That border where the body's ability to discern the difference and respond to both drew a low, desperate cry from her lips.

"So sweet." His voice was hard, tight from the effort it took to hold back. "I want to just feel you for a minute. So hot and slick. Stroking my cock as you tighten on me."

The muscles of her vagina flexed, rippling around him in a surge of exquisite sensation.

"Your minute's up," she whimpered. "God, Shane, I can't stand—"

His hips drove up, fully impaling her, his cock burying to the hilt as his lips slammed over hers, taking her sudden, shocking cry of pleasure.

Shocking, brilliant surges of sensation began racing through her body, burning through her senses as he began moving beneath her. Each thrust, each hard, burning impalement, stoked the gathering inferno building inside her.

She felt stretched to the limit, her inner flesh struggling to accept the width and length of him even as her senses gloried in each stroke of agonizing pleasure. Holding her to him, his lips covering hers and taking the desperate cries escaping her, he pushed her toward the gathering chaos building through her.

She felt too far away, unable to reach the brilliant arcs of ecstasy waiting to pierce her senses. They gathered , building, drawing her inexorably toward that chaos, but not fast enough. It was growing, brighter. Her pussy tightened around the shaft hammering at her senses, stroking through flesh growing more sensitive by the second, with each thrust, until she was crying beneath his kisses. She was desperate, mindless with the furious, white-hot need whipping through her. The sound of flesh meeting, perspiration slickening their bodies, her moisture growing slicker, hotter.

Shane's hands tightened at her rear, parted the rounded globes, allowing his fingers to find the little entrance of her rear, slick with the moisture spilling from her vagina. Stroking it, pressing against it. Tearing his lips from hers, he laid them against her ear, his fingers still pressing against that entrance, stealing her breath with the additional sensation gathering around her.

"I'll have Sebastian fuck that pretty pussy," he groaned, his breathing hard, rough. "I want inside this hot little ass, Alyssa. I want to hear your cries as I stretch you, watch you take me there again, feel you accepting me. . . ."

She could feel it, that storm beginning to wrap around her, to pierce her flesh, to burn inside her.

"Shane!" Crying his name, she shook in his hold, tremors beginning to overtake her, racing through her as the white-hot ecstasy took hold.

Shane's fingers pierced that entrance, stretching it, stroking, moving against it as the explosion ruptured her senses and imploded in white-hot, cataclysmic waves of pleasure so intense, so ecstatic, she was certain she couldn't survive it. Certain at one point that she died in his arms for a heartbeat of time.

Between her thighs Shane's thrusts became quicker, harder, shuttling through the tightening clench of inner flesh until he buried deep, a harsh, broken sound of pleasure rasping from his throat as she felt the first, hard pulses of his release. Jetting inside her, each hard surge of his seed another caress, another blinding sensation that extended the rapture holding her for precious, brilliant seconds.

It was the same with Shane as it was with Sebastian. Each time they touched her, took her, filled her with such impossibly ecstatic pulses of pleasure, they bound her more firmly to them. Each time they touched her, they locked her emotions tighter against any chance of another man possessing them.

They completed her.

And if they were taken from her again Alyssa feared there would be no surviving the loss or the grief that would destroy her.

And she had a very bad feeling that whoever was determined to get to her, to ensure she was forever taken from their lives, was going to be far harder to stop than any of them imagined.

## 23

"I simply cannot believe I wasn't invited, personally to this little soiree." The Georgia accent coming from the foyer as Alyssa stepped into the family room the next day had her pausing, a sense of fear instantly rising inside her.

No. She didn't need this. This was a disaster.

The complications in her life were going to give her a frickin' migraine. What in the hell had she done to piss off the Fates? Whatever offenses she'd committed, they were getting her back in spades now.

"There could be a reason, Summer," another, familiar feminine tone pointed out, the lack of accent as identifiable as the lyrical drawl had been. "You're not exactly relaxing company to have around."

Alyssa winced. Please, please, don't do this to me.

"Me? Not relaxin'?" Pure disbelief filled the tone. "Y'all are gonna break my heart."

"No, we're going to break your jaw if you don't keep that accent under control," the other woman snorted. "I swear to God, every time you go back to Georgia you come back sounding like someone shoved a wad of tobacco in your mouth. Stop already."

"Sugah, one of these days, I'm takin' ya back home with me. Let you see how the other half lives." The threat in Summer's voice wasn't pleasant. And Alyssa doubted Gia had any idea the retribution Summer would collect for the insult.

"I doubt it." Gia sounded horrified. "Go back with you? I'd kill your brothers in two hours flat. Your parents wouldn't make it five minutes."

"I declare, you're always killin' my family members, Gia. I'm gettin' rather tired of it. My family don't need killin'." No doubt Summer had her hands on her hips, her chin pushed out furiously, and those violet eyes glittering like amythests in her stunning face.

"Oh my God, listen to how you butcher the English language. Stop before I die."

"Ladies, don't force me to send you both home." There was the faintest hint of Spain in the dark, warning tone. "If you can't get along on this trip then you're going to regret it."

"Do I get time-out?" Summer drawled, all amused flirtatiousness now. "Really? Haven't you learned better by now, Falcon?"

"Falcone," Gia corrected, her tone heavy with irritation.

"I've learned the two of you are giving me a headache," he grunted. "Now shut the fuck up."

"He's bein' mean to me again. . . ." Summer thought everyone was being mean to her at one time or another.

"Not yet," he assured her. "But I'm getting there."

Stepping quietly through the family room, she moved to the doorway and stepped into the foyer slowly. She really didn't want this aggravation right now.

Esteban Santiago de la Cortez Falcone. Shane and Sebastian had just called him Falcone. Quiet, intense, thick black hair, and pale, pale blue eyes set among Mediterranean features that seemed carved from granite. He set a duffel bag on the marble floor, his gaze centering on the two women.

Gia carried a bulging backpack on one shoulder while Summer no doubt would have her luggage arriving later.

That was just a Summer thing.

"Can I help the three of you?" Alyssa asked them quietly, promising herself that she was not going to lose her temper.

They had known she was there. All three of them, despite the fact that their backs were turned to her.

Falcone was much harder than he'd been eight years before if his eyes and his expression was any indication. The look in his gaze reminded her of what she saw in the mirror each morning. Haunting grief, shadowed fury. She knew those emotions well.

Gia Bennett still looked like a damned teenager until Alyssa caught her gaze as well. Not as shadowed as Falcone's, but Gia had learned well how to hide whatever she felt. Otherise, she hadn't appeared to have aged much, with her long nut-brown hair pulled into a ponytail, tattered jeans and multi-colored sneakers, and a T-shirt proclaiming: *Yes, I do bite!* She could have just stepped from her apartment in Barcelona, ready for a day of shopping.

"Alyssa, you invited these two?" Summer batted thick, coal black lashes as she held her hand out to Falcone and Gia, palm up. "And didn't invite me? You're breakin' my heart again, sugah."

Again?

God, she didn't need this. She was already furious with Summer. She didn't need her friend here driving her insane and trying to talk her out of being mad at her.

"I didn't invite anyone," Alyssa assured her. "Especially you. So what the hell are you doing here?"

Neither Summer's smile nor her expression indicated the fact that she could no doubt tell Alyssa wasn't pleased to see her there. "I saw Gia and Falcone at the airport in D.C., actually, and just invited myself along." Summer's gaze narrowed on her. "And here I thought we were friends." Pretty, intense violet eyes, though warm and watching Alyssa fondly, flashed with her own displeasure. "I was headin' here anyway, though, so no biggie. Shame on you, not lettin' a friend know you're in all this kind of danger. I had to find out from Falcone. You know how much I love just shootin' people, and you didn't offer me the chance? For shame."

Pursing her lips in a pretense of thoughtfulness, Alyssa gave Summer a mocking look. "And you're not getting the chance now."

Summer merely rolled her eyes. "Not an acceptable apology, but you can try again whenever you pull that stick outta your ass and give me a hug. It's been forever."

"It's been six months," Alyssa reminded her.

"Well, like I said, forevah." Summer didn't give her a chance to refuse a hug. She moved far too quickly for the four-inch heels she was wearing with the white and floral print sundress with its fragile straps and snug bodice.

"I missed you, sugah," Summer whispered as she embraced her. "And you shoulda called me."

"I'll remember that," Alyssa assured her, and they both knew she was lying. "And you have some explanations to make when all this is over." She stepped back as Summer released her. "Now, all of you go home until you're invited to return."

Hurt flashed in Summer's eyes, followed by narrow-eyed displeasure.

"Alyssa." Falcone drew her attention. His expression had hardened, his gaze turning to ice. "Gia and Summer are both part of my team. They go no place unless I give them the order to do so. And I'm not giving it. But you can discuss it with Shane and Sebastian if you wish."

Discuss it with Shane and Sebastian, if she wished?

Alyssa shot Summer an accusing look.

"What sort of team, Falcone?" she asked sweetly, giving him a smile that she made certain was all teeth. "Or is that information privileged? Top secret perhaps?"

"That smile isn't a good thing, Falcone," Summer sighed. "She's not above throwin' us out."

"*You* were already told to leave," Alyssa reminded her calmly. "The rest of you can join her. Maybe you'll get lucky and she'll give you a ride back to wherever on her daddy's private plane."

"Now, Alyssa, sugah." Summer propped a hand on her shapely hip. "You know we're not going anywhere. So you can just stop with all the angry orders." Direct violet eyes met Alyssa's as Summer batted her lashes in an attempt to be charming.

Alyssa wasn't charmed.

She could see the stubbornness in that gaze as well, and she knew how irritating Summer could get when she was in one of those stubborn moods.

"And I don't care much for her daddy's plane. I prefer my own. Not that I'll be using it to leave this job. Now, where are Shane and Sebastian?" Falcone was running out of patience and wasn't that just too damned bad, Alyssa thought.

At that moment Raeg stepped from the family room on the other side of the foyer.

"Probably hiding," Raeg drawled with chilling disapproval as he turned to Alyssa. "Thank you, dear, for informing me that Miss Peach here was arriving."

"Raeg, what part of 'I wasn't invited' didn't y'all eavesdrop on? And I declare I've never heard of a Bartlett peach in the whole of my life. Why, y'all are just getting your fruits all kinds of confused, aren't you, darlin'? Rather like you do your women," Summer drawled with such southern ice that Alyssa was a bit surprised.

Raeg appeared pissed. Not just angry but also personally pissed.

"Or like you confuse your employers?" he snapped. "Who is it today? DHS? FBI? CIA? Or some other alphabet agency willing to overlook your lack of loyalty?"

Summer turned her startling eyes on Raeg with a pout. "Friends help busybodies, ya know? Employers give severance pay for the aggravation of having to kill. Multiple employers mean multiple benefits." Her smile was all innocent charm.

Falcone appeared bored by the theatrics, while Gia's smile was filled with amusement. Alyssa had just had enough.

"Raeg, have security escort them from the property while I track down Shane and Sebastian and let them know how much I appreciate warnings and so forth."

"Are y'all sellin' tickets to that little shindig, sugah? I'm buyin' if you are." Summer laughed.

"No, Summer, you are leaving. Now," Alyssa stated. "But don't worry, you and I will talk when everything here is settled. You can bet on it."

Refusing to argue further, Alyssa strode quickly through the foyer to the doorway at the end of the entryway. Striding quickly to her father's office, she decided it was time to inform her lovers of exactly what she thought of this latest development.

※ ✦✦✦ ※

"Summer and Alyssa were occasionally lovers . . . though very discreetly."

Alyssa pushed into the office just in time to hear her father inform her lovers of a small tidbit of information they really hadn't needed. Information she was certain no one but she and Summer were aware of. God, how much worse could this day get, anyway?

"Really, Father?" she demanded, outraged. "Why don't I just go find the widow and see what interesting little details of your private life she's unaware of?"

This was completely outrageous and the looks of surprise on Shane's and Sebastian's faces were offensive. Since when was this any of Shane's and Sebastian's business?

Propping one hand on her hip, she glared at her parent, unable to believe he'd tell such a private part of her life.

Hell, she hadn't even been aware her father had known such a private thing.

"So tell me," she demanded. "Do I get a list of every lover they've had in the past eight years? I believe that would only be fair at this point."

"Alyssa." Her father stared at her, a frown brewing between his brows. "I taught you to knock before entering a room."

Oh, she just bet he wished she would knock. Of all the scenarios she could have envisioned walking in on, this wasn't one of them. And since when did her life before they came to D.C. become any of their business?

"Is that really the best you can do?" she questioned him, disgusted by the attempt to distract her. A rather feeble one at that.

"It's not what you think," her father growled, throwing Shane and Sebastian a desperate look.

As though that were going to do any good. They couldn't exactly make her forget what she'd overheard, now could they?

"Oh, Daddy." She shook her head mockingly. "They can't help you. How many other secrets did I reveal while I was out of my mind with fever and pain?" She turned to her lovers. "I guess Summer neglected to give you that little tidbit of information when you showed up here?"

Because Alyssa sure as hell hadn't told her father about that element sometimes added to her and Summer's friendship. He could have only learned it while she was half out of her mind and pumped up on painkillers after having that knife shoved into her side. Or Summer told him. She hoped not, she'd have to kill her friend then.

"None. Hell, damn it, Alyssa, I was just trying to help," her father protested.

"You want to help?" she asked with mocking sweetness. "I just sent Summer, along with Falcone and Gia, packing. Please inform me before you invite any more of my so-called acquaintances to help protect me. I really don't need the aggravation and I sure as hell don't want to deal with it."

"The hell you did!" Shane was staring at her with an expression akin to horror.

"Yes, I damn well did!" she snapped. "I refuse to have security that I know will help the two of you lie to me for whatever reason. And while you're at it—"

"No, Alyssa." Sebastian shook his head as though dazed. "You and Summer? Good God. Were you crazy?"

Crazy?

No, she'd been out of her mind with grief and drowning in the tears she couldn't shed. If it hadn't been for Summer, she might have lain in that bed and drifted away after losing not just Shane and Sebastian but the baby she'd carried as well.

"What do you think, Sebastian?" She smiled sweetly. "Did you believe I'd be too fucking dead inside to need to be touched? To need a lover? Remember that little bit of recklessness I warned you I was known for." Her lips curled mockingly. "There's further proof of it."

"But Summer?" he asked again, clearly trying to deny it. "Alyssa, that is—"

"A friend I'm quite fond of," she broke in before he could say anything ignorant. "Should I protest your friendship with Courtney Sinclair? After all, you were her first lover, weren't you?"

A grimace pulled at his expression before he pushed the fingers of both hands through his hair.

"Courtney has a big mouth," Sebastian muttered.

Courtney was simply unable to lie to her friends, and she considered Alyssa a friend now.

"So does my father."

"We need to keep Falcone from leaving," Shane broke in. "If he makes it out the gates he won't come back."

"My friend." Falcone stepped into the room, his voice mocking. "Falcone wouldn't miss this for all the gold in the family vault." Smiling, he turned to Alyssa, arching his brow mockingly. "You and Summer? I must say, I always knew Summer had the potential—"

"Esteban!" The senator came to his feet quickly. "That is my daughter and I know you weren't getting ready to dirty her with any filth from your mouth. Her or my goddaughter."

Falcone lifted a brow, a grin quirking his lips.

"No, he isn't," Shane stated, his tone as dangerous as it was hard.

They were about to make her completely insane.

"Posturing!" she snapped. "Damn stupid male posturing. I'm so tired of the bullshit playing out around me that it's all I can do to keep from shooting all of you."

Turning, she stomped from the office; any attempt at a reasonable conversation was just a waste of time at this point.

She couldn't deal with this, not now, not with so many emotions ripping her apart and pushing her past her ability to keep them leashed. And if they escaped the hold she had on them . . . Her breathing hitched, throat tightening and that band around her heart constricted further. She was drowning. Drowning in all the tears she'd been unable to shed and the pain that had never found a way to escape.

And she had no idea how much longer she could continue treading the treacherous depths of those emotions.

The door slammed behind her. Instantly Falcone dropped the air of mocking amusement.

"There," he announced, his gaze going around the room. "I managed to ensure her exit. Perhaps this will allow you to come to grips with what appears to be a shocking bit of information." He inclined his head with such superiority Sebastian entertained throwing something at him. Something heavy.

Or shooting him.

"Who said we were having a problem with it?" Shane was definitely having a problem with it, Sebastian knew. Just as he was. They were in shock. Never had they imagined Alyssa could tolerate Summer long enough to become her lover for five minutes. Let alone off and on for years. It was inconceivable.

"You knew about it?" Shane crossed his arms over his chest as Sebastian wondered how the bastard was aware of the relationship the two women shared when he and Sebastian had been unaware of it.

Falcone stepped farther into the room. "Summer might have mentioned it to me," he said coolly. "Though I'd prefer not to deal with her temper should she learn I admitted it. She can get rather irate."

That helpless little southern belle act never failed to fool whomever she was turning it on. Innocence and flighty feminine naïveté seemed to personify her personality. Until it was too damned late to stop the knee to the groin or the knife she laid to a man's throat.

Summer did seem to love her knives. Especially when she was drawing blood with them.

"Now that we have that out of the way," Falcone stated dryly, "shall we discuss the matter of Ms. Stanhope's security or do we have other matters to discuss first?"

"Yeah," Shane growled. "Call her Ms. Stanhope again and I'll cut your fucking tongue out. We clear there?"

Falcone inclined his head mockingly. "Certainly. Shall we then discuss our target's security? I need a bit of sleep and I'd like to get the particulars out of the way first." He focused on Shane. "Or should we discuss other transgressions I may commit instead? I am of course at your disposal."

Mocking fucker.

Shane glared at him.

Sebastian just sighed.

The senator glanced over at them. "I don't remember him being so confrontational."

"Blame Summer," Falcone growled. "I always blame Summer. And I'm usually right."

They all sighed at that. No doubt any fractures in Falcone's legendary patience had to do with Summer.

"If she's around . . . ," Shane muttered.

"It's usually her fault," Sebastian finished for him.

The office door slammed open and Raeg stalked into the room, his expression furious. He moved straight to the bar and took the drink Falcone was pouring before swallowing it in one shot.

"Summer?" Falcone asked blandly.

"Summer."

"At least she's not boring, and she does keep us entertained when she's here," the senator pointed out. The observation wasn't appreciated.

Three sets of eyes turned on the senator; none of them were laughing.

No, boring she was not. For Falcone and Raeg, she was a guaranteed nightmare though.

+++++

Alyssa wanted to slam her door. She wanted to push it into the frame with every ounce of strength she possessed. She wanted to hear the violence of wood cracking against wood and have the satisfaction of hearing it echo around her. Instead, she closed it with the utmost control and patience. Just to prove she could do it.

"Your momma would just shake her head at us." The lyrical Southern belle accent had her turning quickly to the bedroom doorway. "Then she'd ask me what I'd done to just upset everyone so. You know Raeg is just foamin' at the mouth. He and Raeg are gonna be so ill now, aren't they?"

Alone, Raeg and Falcone dealt fine with her for some reason. Together, the sexual tension was so thick Alyssa doubted Summer could cut it with one of her knives.

Summer stood nervously at the entrance, her gaze filled with a quiet sobriety Alyssa found disconcerting. But then Summer had a way of making most people nervous, despite all that southern charm.

She was the queen of double-talk and bullshit when she wanted to be, Alyssa acknowledged, and Summer could see through it like others could see through glass. It was almost impossible to lie to her.

"Summer, this isn't your battle. Go home." She knew her friend wasn't going to listen, though. Summer never listened unless it suited her best interests at the time.

"You're wrong, ya know." Summer propped one delicate hand on her hip as she frowned back at Alyssa. "I told you to contact Shane and Sebastian before Harvey ever attacked ya," she reminded her. "Harvey was a crazy bastard. You wouldn't call, though. You should have known this was going to come back to haunt ya. I even warned ya."

"Father should have never let you stay—"

"Alyssa, your daddy was like a zombie, tryin' to keep you alive and take care of your momma's funeral arrangements while tryin' to distract reporters." Summer moved into the living area before going to the couch and curling into the corner of it. "Who better would he trust to take care of you than the friend his wife made certain was trained to do just that?"

Alyssa glanced upward as though searching the heavens. "Really, Mother?" she muttered. "You definitely had a bad-decision day there, didn't you?"

"Your momma didn't have bad-decision days, Alyssa," Summer assured her. "She was the queen of manipulators. Damn, I wish she'd been my momma."

No doubt Margot had wished that herself often. She and Summer would have been lethal in D.C. They would have started World War III before Davis Allen Hampstead even had a chance to get into the Oval Office.

"You have no business trying to help track down a would-be killer that's probably long gone anyway." The subject of mothers aside, Alyssa felt like shaking some sense into her friend. She rather doubted it would work, though. There would have to be the potential for common sense present first.

"But I know how." Summer grinned. "Come on, sugah, you knew I wasn't the helpless little belle I pretended to be. You were so busy hidin' from life, though, that you overlooked that as well."

"You make me crazy," Alyssa hissed. Summer made her feel like she was in high school again. And not in a good way. "I didn't overlook anything. You and Mother simply made certain I was never aware of it. Thank you for that. While you're at it, thanks for *telling me* Shane and Sebastian showed up when I was unconscious two years ago. I appreciate the hell out of all that."

In that instant Alyssa realized she was worrying the gems that hung on the gold chain like a talisman again. Jerking her hand down, she ignored Summer's smirk.

"You love lyin' to yourself, I have to say." The smug little laugh that came with the accusation set Alyssa's teeth on edge. "You knew the second you realized you were wearin' that necklace that they'd been here." Summer gave a little flip of her fingers and a roll of her eyes. "Like I said, you just ignore what you don't want to see at the time."

Crossing her arms over her breasts, she glared at her friend before muttering, "God help me."

"He's tryin', sugah," Summer expressed regretfully. "But you are just such a stubborn bitch you keep ignorin' all His hard work where you're concerned."

"Oh, so you're God now?" Alyssa questioned her mockingly.

Summer's smile was so sugary sweet Alyssa felt the need for a dentist.

"Really, Alyssa, don't you recognize His favorite angel? Why, just shame on you all day."

"You are outrageous," Alyssa accused her with a glower. "Well, try this one. Dad just informed Shane and Sebastian that we've been lovers. And Falcone overheard it."

Summer dropped her head to the back of the couch, her eyes closing momentarily before she turned her head and glared at Alyssa. "Why the hell did you tell Goddaddy, Alyssa?" She pouted. "That's wrong. And he didn't have to know."

"Me?" Pointing to herself, Alyssa stared back at her in astonishment. "I didn't tell a damned thing. So how did he know?"

Something flickered in Summer's eyes then. A glint of evasive knowledge Alyssa was all too familiar with.

"You told Margot!" Disbelief vied with pure outrage. "Why would you do something so ridiculous?" Throwing her hands up in complete surrender, Alyssa turned and stalked to the window. "Just how often did you and my mother conspire against me anyway?"

Summer made her crazy. There was no other word for it. She was like a tidal wave. A tornado or something. She swept in, upended everything, then swept back out again.

"Your momma guessed, Alyssa." Summer's voice was soft, saddened. "She wasn't stupid where you were concerned. And she didn't care. She was so worried about you."

"And of course you set her mind at ease," Alyssa snorted, wondering why she hadn't guessed that one. "What else did she know that I'm unaware of?"

Turning back to the other woman, she caught the odd expression on her friend's face before it cleared. Just for a second, she glimpsed a loneliness, a hurt, that filled her with a surge of guilt.

"Why now"—holding a hand to her side gracefully, palm up, Summer gave her another of those innocent expressions—"I just aint sure, sweetie. You know how Margot was. Eyes in the back of her head."

Eyes in the back of her head.

Alyssa had to force back a sudden smile because Summer wasn't exaggerating. Margot had known things she should have never known. She could look at her daughter and like a sixth sense, knew things she should have never known.

"She always knew what you were up to, too" she told Summer softly.

Summer rolled her eyes, but a flash of grief in her eyes was all Alyssa needed to see.

"She loved you, Summer," Alyssa assured her, not in the least jealous of the fact that her mother may well have loved Summer as much as she loved her own daughter. "She loved both of us."

Summer looked away for a long second. "If she loved either of us enough, then she wouldn't have done something so damned stupid!" she snapped, then inhaled slowly and shook her head. "Look, I'm really tired, and that damned Raeg just wears me down with all his glares. I'm gonna go to my room. My luggage should be here in a little bit."

Rising to her feet, Summer shot her a little wink. "Tell those bad boys of yours I said night-night."

"Summer." Alyssa moved to the other woman quickly, touching her arm lightly. "Are you okay?"

"Sweetie, I'm always fine," Summer drawled, flashing her a trademark Summer smile.

"I'm your friend too, Summer," Alyssa assured her. "It goes both ways."

For a second, just a second, the loneliness she sensed in her friend shadowed her eyes.

"Sweetie, I'm good as a tick on a hound, I promise," Summer said, giving her a quick hug and a bright smile. "We'll talk after we make sure you're nice and safe. A long girls' night. I promise." Stepping to the door, Summer glanced back again. "Jet lag has me, darlin'. See you after a quick nap. 'Kay?"

"Definitely," Alyssa assured her, for the first time feeling a drift in her friendship with the other woman.

Summer had been her lifeline more than once, and Alyssa realized that in the past two years Summer had told her next to nothing about her own life. Or the hurt lurking in her eyes.

## 24

Summer wasn't going to leave. She would gung-ho right into whatever danger could be found at any given moment. That was just Summer. The fact that Margot Hampstead had ensured Summer had the skills to do it just pissed Alyssa off. Margot had made certain Summer was CIA trained and well able to protect Alyssa if necessary. What Margot hadn't taken into consideration was Summer's personality.

She was crazy. A cyclone. A tidal wave. And a CIA trained one at that.

She drove everyone she came in contact with insane. Alyssa included herself in that category as well. It was one of the reasons Margot had always kept Summer's visits rather brief. After a month or so, she and Alyssa began squabbling, Margot would say with a resigned little sigh.

It wasn't squabbling. They were known to actually fight.

A smile tugged at her lips. They were still prone to fight.

Today had been rather mild, actually. That hadn't even been a good argument, she thought, amused by the confrontation as she usually was once Summer was out of sight.

It usually took Summer being out of sight, though, for Alyssa to see the humor in it.

There were other things she saw as well, though. Memories that she'd forgotten over the years that drifted through her mind.

Alyssa hadn't expected her mother's reaction when she met Summer. It had been the accent, Alyssa remembered. Margot had been waiting when Alyssa had arrived home with Summer after school. When Alyssa introduced them and Summer had hesitantly greeted her, very properly polite, Margot's eyes had widened, slid slowly to Alyssa, then a little grin had tugged at her lips before she'd nodded to Alyssa.

She'd approved.

It was the one and only time Margot had approved of a friend.

Even Gia hadn't gotten the Margot nod. Gia's family connections were impressive and Gia was just as polite as Summer. But like every other friend Alyssa had ever had, except Summer, Margot had simply overlooked her.

God, she wished Summer would just go home. She and Gia both. They had no business here. They had no business trying to protect her. Hell, she didn't even want Shane and Sebastian putting themselves in the line of fire. She didn't want anyone she loved dying for her.

Especially Shane and Sebastian.

She loved them with every part of her heart and soul. Every last shred that was slowly beginning to heal with their return.

Wrapping her arms around herself, she walked back to the window and sat down with a sigh, staring out to the slowly fading evening.

Where the hell was all this coming from? An attempted hit-and-run. An exploding chair? Really? Two days after Shane and Sebastian had killed Gregory, Harvey had tried to kill her. He'd been furious. It couldn't be coincidence that he'd been so enraged over Shane and Sebastian. Especially at that time.

"You mean I don't know about Shane Connor and Sebastian

De Loren?" Harvey had asked softly, the malice in his gaze growing brighter. "But I do know about them, Alyssa. I know about how you fucked both of them. Do you know how long I've waited to throw that in your goody-two-shoes face?"

She had assumed he hadn't known about her time in Barcelona for long. Why had she assumed that?

He had waited so long to throw that in her face, he'd said.

Pulling her lower lip between her teeth, she worried at it. Why had he waited to throw that in her face? How long had he waited?

Those questions had bothered her since she'd awakened after Harvey's attack. He'd been angry at her. Furious with her. And her affair with Shane and Sebastian. He'd mentioned that specifically.

Something hadn't been working out for him, so he was going to cash in on her insurance policy, he'd said.

The sitting room door opened, drawing her attention as she saw the image of Shane and Sebastian stepping into the room was reflected in the glass.

The door closed softly behind them.

"What's going on?" The sense of answers hidden by her own inability to remember whatever it was teasing her mind had confusion massing inside her. "What did I do to make someone hate me enough to kill our baby? And now, to attempt to kill me as well? What did I do . . . ?"

The pain in her eyes was killing him. That soul-deep burning agony that filled her gaze would destroy him, because he had no idea how to ease it.

Drawing her into his arms, Sebastian held her head to his heart, his gaze connecting with the fury in his cousin's. Because they had no answers for her. No way to ease the fear reflecting in her eyes. Or the pain.

"Make it go away," she whispered, her nails digging into the material of Sebastian's shirt.

Pulling her head back, she stared up at him, the plea in her expression breaking his heart. "Please, make it go away. Just for a little while."

Just for a little while.

Swinging her into his arms, he moved to the bedroom, aware of Shane closing and locking the door behind them as he placed her back on her feet.

"Alyssa . . ."

"I need you, both of you, 'Bastian. Please, take me away from this, just for now."

"My sweet Alyssa." As he lowered his head his lips sought hers. He needed for her pleasure to replace the pain in her eyes with ecstasy until he could figure out how to fix it.

She was his life. The fact that he shared her with Shane didn't dilute his love for her. The fact that she loved them both, fulfilled their needs with such generosity, only increased his love for her.

She answered the hunger inside him with a desperation of her own. Equal parts sensual need and emotional chaos. Gripping the hair at the back of her head, he pulled her head back farther, his lips claiming hers, reaffirming the claim he'd put on her soul eight years before.

She belonged to him. To him and to the cousin whose loyalty had been forged in blood so very long ago.

She was theirs.

+++++

Shane watched with narrowed eyes, cock throbbing as Sebastian gave in to the driving hunger that only built inside them as her pain laid waste to their control.

Sebastian had always given in first when she roused such powerful emotions inside them. Then they ended up trying to fuck her and themselves to death.

She simply filled their lives, then and now.

Rather than joining Sebastian in pleasuring her, he waited, watched. Knowing the pleasure that came from simply watching her give in to the sensual hunger inside her.

She was so damned pretty.

As Sebastian's lips moved from her lips to the smooth perfection of her graceful neck, he pulled the blouse from her jeans. He'd already unbuttoned it. When he pushed the material from her shoulders Shane moved behind her, pulled her arms from around Sebastian's neck, then smoothed the shirt from her.

The little moan that slipped from her lips had his cock jerking. Releasing the catch of her lacy bra, he drew it from her as well, allowing Sebastian to capture the curve of her breast in his palm, his thumb finding and rasping over the hard point of her nipple, his lips moving back to hers. Eyes closed, her body conforming to Sebastian's, Alyssa slipped deeper into the sensual storm Shane could feel brewing among the three of them.

It took only moments to undress her. To reveal the silken, creamy flesh they had spent hours kissing and caressing in Barcelona. Stepping back as Sebastian lifted her in his arms and laid her back on the bed, Shane watched in satisfaction as she looked back at them, pure, brilliant sensuality gleaming in her darkened gaze.

Shane watched, moving to the other side of the bed as Sebastian moved beside her, his head lowering to the hard peaks of her cherry red nipples. Her lips parted, eyes closing as her breath panted from between her lips along with the soft mewls of need.

He loved seeing her like this. Loved watching her pleasure, seeing her sink into the needs he and Sebastian stoked inside her.

Pleasure was suffusing her expression now. Reaching to the pillow beneath her head, her fingers fisted into it, holding tight as

Sebastian's lips moved from her nipples and began kissing, licking his way to the soft mount of her pussy as he spread her thighs.

Her juices glistened on the swollen folds, a sweet, tempting sight his cousin wasn't about to deny himself. Parting her legs further, Sebastian's tongue slid into those sweet folds for a slow, luxuriant taste as Alyssa's eyes drifted open and her gaze focused on him.

A soft kiss to her clit had her breath catching.

A moan whispered from her lips as he worked his tongue along the narrow slit, licking and tasting as her breathing became hard and heavy.

Lifting his head, his eyes black with lust, Sebastian gave an impatient groan before forcing himself from her.

"Don't stop." Demand gleamed in her gaze as Sebastian moved to the side of the bed and began undressing.

It was the perfect opportunity for Shane to steal a taste for himself and allow his senses to become intoxicated by her hunger for them.

"Bastard." Sebastian grunted as Shane moved between her thighs, taking full advantage of his cousin's move.

Pleasuring her was his favorite thing to do, Shane thought, his lips lowering to the swollen folds, his tongue moving between them with a long, slow lick.

God, he loved the taste of her. Clean, a hint of sweetness and pure silky heat.

She was perfect for them. They'd known that even eight years before. She reached for them even when they exhausted her; no matter how hard they'd taken her, how many times, her hunger had matched theirs.

And it matched theirs now.

Her hips lifted to the slow kisses and hungry tastes. Shane could feel the pleasure surrounding them, filling them, and it was rising, growing hotter and more intense. Those whipping, heated

sensations binding them together, creating a firestorm of sensuality they were all helpless to deny.

One none of them wanted to deny.

✦✦✦

Alyssa was dazed with the pleasure surging over and through her
body as Shane took her to the brink of orgasm before pulling back
and rising between her thighs. At the same time, Sebastian eased
onto the bed, kneeling beside her.

"Come on, baby." Sebastian lifted her from the pillows. "Let's
play a little bit."

As he eased her to her knees until she faced him, Sebastian's
wicked grin had anticipation clenching her vagina. Behind her,
Shane pressed her shoulders down as his lips lowered to smooth
over one rounded globe of her rear.

Alyssa shivered, a whimper falling from her lips as Sebastian
pressed the engorged crest of his erection to her lips, parting them
and pressing inside. Behind her, Shane's fingers smoothed down
the cleft of her ass, pausing at her rear entrance.

She knew their hungers, remembered well every touch she'd
shared with them in Madrid. They could be fast and hard, sending
a firestorm of hunger to unravel inside her. Or they could "play,"
and they were at their most destructive then. Because she could
never anticipate what was coming. They were diabolical, wicked,
and completely carnal. And she reveled in every second of it. In
every touch and in every caress.

Wrapping her lips around the engorged crest pressing into her
mouth, she licked over it, loved it as Sebastian's groan of pleasure
only spurred the hunger.

She'd done without for so long. She deserved this. She deserved
to be pleasured. She deserved to take her fill of them. For once,
for just this moment in time, she deserved the chance to give

herself over to her lovers without fear of the outside world, or her own emotions lashing at her.

"That's it, baby," Sebastian encouraged her as her lips tightened around his throbbing cock head and sucked it deeper.

Her tongue played over the iron-hard flesh, loving the taste of male heat and arousal stroking over it. The feel of satin flesh and hard power held so intimately had more of her juices spilling, slickening the bare folds of her pussy.

She was already so wet, so slick and ready for them, that waiting was torture. Yet she wanted every second, every moment, of the pleasure to last forever.

"Alyssa." Sebastian's throttled groan as her fingers surrounded the tight sac of his testicles sent a surge of power rushing through her.

Sucking the head to the back of her throat, she licked and caressed the sensitive underside, moaning at the dark magic surrounding her.

Slick, cool lubrication eased over her rear. Shane's fingers pressed against the entrance there before two began easing inside the sensation-rich depths. The immediate pleasure-pain biting into her senses had her locking her mouth tighter around Sebastian's cock. Suckling it with hungry need as those wicked fingers pressed into the tight ring of muscles guarding the inner depths.

Sebastian's hands speared into her hair, tightening on the long strands as she worked her mouth on his cock, worked her tongue against it, and moaned at the steadily building pleasure.

Behind her, Shane's breathing was becoming harder, quicker. As with her, the pleasure wrapping around him was affecting his control. Hers was pretty much shot, though, she admitted.

"Don't you even think about coming," Shane growled at Sebastian when a particularly deep groan left his lips.

"Fuck, Shane." Sebastian's voice was a stroke of pure, dark hunger racing over her senses. "Her fucking mouth is killing me here."

As she drew deeper, harder, on the shaft spearing between her lips, the waves of sensual, sexual intensity tore through Alyssa's body like liquid heat.

"You heard me. Now move, dammit; it's my turn." Shifting behind her, he watched as Shane pulled back, a harsh groan leaving his throat as her mouth tightened on him, causing his face to contort with pleasure as he pulled free.

"She's ready for you," Shane promised as they switched places.

"I'm going to be a while," Sebastian warned him, the dark, sexual drawl sending sharp forks of sensation to race through her body, tightening it as anticipation surged through her.

She remembered nights like this in Spain. Nights that they couldn't seem to get enough of her, riding her for hours as her body became one endless orgasm.

"Yeah, right," Shane groaned. "You won't last five minutes."

Sebastian's hand smoothed over her rear, his fingers finding the entrance he was searching for as Alyssa grew tired of waiting.

Wrapping her fingers around the hard shaft, she curled her tongue over the crest of Shane's cock, riding a sensual high so intense it was mesmerizing.

Parting her lips further, she took the engorged head into her mouth as Sebastian's dark voice crooned Spanish endearments while his cock pressed against the snug opening to her rear and slowly began parting the sensitive, ultra-tight entrance.

✦✦✦

Shane's senses, hyper-aware and trained on the incredible pleasure surrounding the head of his cock, were threatening to slip the control he was only barely maintaining.

Lips and tongue and sweet, suckling heat were killing him. Sucking him to the back of her throat, she moaned then, the sound vibrating around his flesh and causing his face to contort with the extreme sensations wrapping around his dick.

His gaze was locked on the heavy intrusion sinking inside her tight little ass. The stretch of the snug flesh as Sebastian's cock began entering her. The parting flesh gripping the erection working inside her, flaring around it, sucking the intruder inside her.

The smooth, hot grip of her anus was a unique, heated pleasure made richer by her trust, her instinctive knowledge that nothing meant more to them than her complete pleasure, Shane thought.

As her mouth worked over the crown of his cock, his balls tightening with the need for release, he watched as Sebastian moved deeper inside her; the sight of her taking the intrusion as her mouth worked around the heavy thrust of Shane's cock head was killing him. Hell, he might not make it five minutes himself.

That thought splintered in his head as Sebastian thrust to the hilt in Alyssa's rear channel and her mouth tightened impossibly around the head of Shane's dick. Beneath the engorged crest her tongue tucked against the nerve-laden center where it just rubbed. Rasping over the area, sending brilliant flashes of sensation to tighten around the throbbing crest before shooting to his balls and wrapping around them with fiery fingers of sensation.

Sweat beaded on his flesh. His breath panted from his chest as his fingers tightened in her hair. His hips rocked against the suckling torture, a desperate groan trapped in his throat. Shane could feel his release pulsing looser. Fuck, he'd be lucky if he held on as long as Sebastian did.

He thrust inside the snug depths of her body in heavy strokes, pounding inside her as mewls echoed from her throat. Each cry, each little swallowing motion, frayed his control further.

"Ah hell. Fuck. She's coming. . . ." Sebastian's groan of tortured pleasure came at the same second Alyssa's body tightened and shudders began racing down her spine. Her mouth was working over his cock head in carnal demand now, nearly triggering his own release before he could pull free of her.

Behind her, Sebastian's deep, guttural groan of release had another of those muted, mesmerized little moans leaving Alyssa's lips just before she collapsed to the bed.

+ + + + +

The orgasm took her by surprise, flashing through her senses and laying waste to her ability to actually think. Of course, she'd never wanted to think whenever they took her. She had only wanted to wrap herself in their gentleness, their dominant hungers, and her own emerging desires. She'd never wanted anything but to claim them as they claimed her.

As she lifted her head as she felt Sebastian ease from her, her gaze met Shane's, his blue eyes burning with lust and that something more that always mesmerized her. Her gaze flicked to his erection then, the straining flesh, dark and throbbing, demanding relief.

Glistening with moisture from her mouth as well as the pre-cum beaded on it, the engorged head throbbed with the need for release. Heavy veins, dark and pulsing, lined the thick shaft while his testicles were drawn tight to the base.

"My turn," he told her as her gaze lifted to his once again. "Stay right there, baby. Just like that."

Kneeling, her hips lifted, completely open to him, and without defenses. She didn't need defenses here, she told herself as he moved behind her, her eyes drifting closed. A moan escaped her. Shane moved behind her, one hand gripping her hip as the head of his cock pressed against the clenched entrance of her pussy.

Oversensitized flesh clenched at the feel of the broad crest, sending pulses of lashing sensation to her clit. Her womb clenched, stealing her breath.

"Shane!" she cried out, his name a trembling sound of need, hope, and fear, and the realization of the last two emotions dragged a whimpering sigh from her lips.

"I have you, baby," he promised, pressing inside her, stretching the snug entrance with the slow, steady penetration of his cock.

Alyssa's shoulders collapsed against the bed, her knees trembling, and another cry slipped past her lips as the pleasure began consuming her once again.

"That's it." His voice was strained, hoarse. "Let it have you, darlin'. Just let it have you."

He thrust inside her again, pulled back, entered again. Each impalement sent brutal flashes of rising ecstasy to sear her senses. Each thrust pushed him deeper inside the clenching, sensitive depths of her pussy and pushed her deeper into the chaos rising through her senses.

Pleasure shuddered through her, tore down her spine, clenched the flesh surrounding his shuttling shaft, and spilled more of the slick juices along her channel. The next heavy thrust sent his cock to the hilt, the swift stretch and pleasure-pain burn jerking her hips against him and dragging a startled cry of intense ecstasy from her lips.

Sensation rocked her senses, burned through them as he began moving. Pulling free of her, burying again in one hard, heavy thrust before repeating it again. Her hips jerked, rolled, and pushed back into each impalement as the quickening flashes of impending release began striking at her senses.

"Shane, oh God, it's so good," she tried to scream, but the sound was muffled, weakened by the need to breathe instead.

"I've got you, 'Lyssa." Shane came over her, driving inside her as his lips feathered against her ear. "I've got you, baby, and when I don't, Sebastian will."

His thrusts turned harder, the pleasure becoming a whirlwind inside her, his whispered promises trying to take hold in a heart so tattered that promises and vows given no longer found hold.

Yet that promise, Shane's promise, she found herself holding on to desperately as she was driven closer to the brink of ecstasy. Flaming sensations she couldn't get enough of began whipping around her, through her, dragging her into the surging, chaotic storm of rapture washing over her. And Alyssa jumped into those flames eagerly.

Behind her, Shane buried deep inside the convulsing depths of her core, a groan tearing from his chest as his release jetted inside her. Each fierce pulse of semen sent a shudder through his hard frame as Alyssa fought to remain as immersed in the aftereffects of her orgasm as possible.

"We have you, baby," Shane groaned, despite the fact that Sebastian wasn't with them. "And we won't let you go."

## 25

*"Wake up, Alyssa. Come on, baby. I need to talk to you."*

*Baby?*

*"Alyssa, wake up!"* Margot's voice was more imperative now, pulling at her. *"Wake up now, girl!"*

Alyssa jerked awake, sitting straight up in the bed and staring around the bedroom, certain the ghost of her mother would be floating next to her bed.

Her heart was racing, adrenaline surging through her body with a fight-or-flight instinct that had her throwing the blankets from the bed and moving for the bureau.

Shane and Sebastian weren't in the bed, and she knew when she'd drifted off to sleep they'd been there, one on each side of her, surrounding her with warmth.

Moving from the bed, she hurried to the bureau where she'd laid out clothes for the next day. Jeans, T-shirt, and sneakers. She dressed hurriedly, only distantly realizing she should have opted for the gown and robe next to the bed.

For some reason, the clothes seemed the better choice, though.

Looking around the bedroom, she moved back to the bed and her cell phone. Grabbing it, she quickly hit the activation button and waited for it to load.

No missed calls and no messages, not that she expected there to be. But as the screen loaded, a message displayed that her volume was muted. She never muted her phone unless she was going into a meeting. And she hadn't had any meetings in a while.

Only Shane or Sebastian could have muted the phone, and they would have only done so to ensure she stayed asleep.

Moving silently to her dresser, she opened the center drawer and drew out the small, holstered handgun Margot had insisted she learn how to use years before. Securing it between the band of her jeans and the small of her back, she stared around the room once again.

She was scared.

She would feel damned stupid if everyone was gathered downstairs for coffee and cake, but she was really scared.

Retrieving the cell phone from where she'd laid it while dressing, she hurriedly typed in a message to Shane's phone.

*Okay?*
*OK.* [The answer came back quickly.]

She was just beginning to relax when the next one lit up the screen.

*Keep doors locked, phone off. Stay in room.*

She stared at the message.
Oh God, what had happened?

*B there soon.* [Sebastian's text lit up the screen then.]

B there soon.
Dimming the light again, she pushed the phone into her back pants' pocket before rubbing at the chill racing up her arms.

What should she do?

Just wait there like Shane told her to do?

God, she hated waiting; she always had. It was torture.

Walking cautiously through the bedroom and into the sitting area, she strained to hear anything over the sound of her pulse racing in her ears. How did anyone control their nerves enough to be spies or agents anyway? She'd end up giving herself away from nerves alone.

Watching the shadows carefully, she worked her way through the room, heading for the door leading to the hall when a hard surge of panic stopped her in her tracks.

A second later a sound at the bedroom door had her heart racing so hard she wondered if she was going to be light-headed. She nearly jumped out of her skin at the low knock a minute later.

"Alyssa? It's Steven, from ground security. Shane sent me for you." Shane sent one of the security guards hired to patrol the grounds rather than one of the military trained security guards hired for inside? Or even Crane, her father's personal bodyguard?

He wouldn't do that. She barely knew Steven. Hell, she could barely remember what he even looked like.

The very sound of his voice sent terror racing through her though. It struck so swift, so hard, she had to cover her lips with her hand to hold it back.

Shane would have texted her if he'd sent anyone for her, as would Sebastian.

She was really going to have to talk to them about waking her when danger required them to leave her bed.

"Alyssa, I need you to open the door now," he ordered, his voice still low. "We have to go."

Pulling the phone from her jeans, she sent Shane another text.

*Did you send Steven for me?*

*No!* Shane texted immediately.

She heard Steven test the doorknob again. If he thought she was asleep he would definitely find a way in.

"Stupid fuckers," he cursed, not bothering to keep his voice lowered now. "Changing the fucking locks and not letting anyone know."

Hurriedly Alyssa headed to the connecting door to her office. Opening it silently, she slipped past it before easing the door just almost closed behind her.

Now what?

Once he realized she wasn't in her room would he check the office?

If Steven didn't have a damned good excuse for being here, then Shane and Sebastian would take him apart.

She could hear something from the other room. A scraping sound she couldn't identify. Had he already gotten into the room?

Where the hell were Shane and Sebastian?

"Fuck!" That curse came from inside her bedroom, only a few feet from the door, she was certain. "You fucking bitch."

"Dammit!" Steven cursed before the sound of him running from the room had her finally releasing the breath she hadn't realized she was holding.

Laying her head against the door frame, she nearly collapsed to the floor, her breathing harsh, jagged.

"Alyssa!" Shane's voice snapped through the silence and had her throwing open the door to rush to him.

He caught her in his arms, his warmth wrapping around her as she buried her face against his chest, emotion swamping her with such violence that she swore she nearly passed out.

"It was Steven Richards." Her fingers tightened in the dark cloth of Shane's shirt as she finally lifted her head to stare up at him. "One of the ground guards. Why would he be here if you didn't send him? He said you sent him."

Before he could answer the sound of several gunshots ricocheted through the house, seeming to echo through it as Alyssa felt her heart suddenly drop, freezing her with fear as she felt Shane push her behind him.

"Fuck. Fuck." Falcone's voice came clearly through the radio Shane wore at his belt. "Sebastian's down. Sebastian's down. . . ."

+ + + +

Sebastian was waiting for Steven Richards when he slipped into the dimly lit kitchen, heading for the back door and the car he'd left parked behind the manager's cottage. Falcone and Summer had found the vehicle no more than moments ago and disabled it. Once he'd known where the vehicle was hidden, Sebastian had known which way the son of a bitch would attempt to leave the house.

Alyssa's would-be assassin wasn't nearly as bright as Sebastian had given him credit for being, though. Khalid had cracked the program in a matter of days and contacted Sebastian with the programmer's ID no more than an hour before Alyssa texted.

"Going somewhere, Richards?" Sebastian asked softly from where he stood in the shadows at the other end of the kitchen. "Or should I say Barkley?" Training his weapon on the other man's head. "That's your real name, I believe. Kevin Barkley. We've been looking for you."

His identity had come through after Alyssa had gone to sleep, the picture and information sent by Khalid once he'd cracked the computer program and tracked it back to the programmer.

Turning to face him, Kevin smiled slowly, the cocky confidence in the move enough to piss Sebastian off that much more.

"Very good," Kevin drawled. "I knew when the self-destruct notice on my program didn't arrive this evening that you'd figure it out. You didn't do it, though, did you? Someone else did."

"Ah, that's a story for later," Sebastian assured him. He wasn't about to reveal who had cracked the program, just to make certain if Kevin got away there was nowhere else for him to strike.

"A story for later," Kevin grunted, his hazel eyes gleaming in the dim light spilling from the counter behind him.

"Why come after Alyssa?" Sebastian asked him softly. "You knew we'd come for her once we heard she was being threatened. Why take that risk?"

Kevin chuckled at the question. "Hell, Harvey was supposed to kill her two years ago when you found Gregory and the files. It was a sweet deal we had, ya know? Wait five or six years, cash it out, Harvey would kill his bitch wife, collect the insurance, and we'd all be set for life. That stupid-assed bastard never could do anything right. But I would have left her alone if you and Shane had stayed away from her. You and that fucking cousin of yours. When you decided you could come here and have her, I decided to take her. Permanently. That's what you deserved. First you killed Gregory; then that fucking bitch Margot killed Harvey. Fuckers. I didn't have a damned thing to show for six years of my life. Why should you get the girl?"

"So it was all for the money," Sebastian said softly. "How stupid are you, Kevin? Harvey and Gregory are dead. Did you really want to join them that bad?"

"How stupid am I ?" Kevin's smile disappeared. "You didn't even know who was after her, De Loren. You and Shane were stumbling around in the fucking dark. I could have taken her out at any time."

"So why choose Alyssa?" Sebastian asked, watching Kevin carefully. He was what Shane called a little punk. Cunning, but stupid. "You've lost your mind, Kevin. Do you really think you would have made it past me and Shane? Really? I would have thought you were smarter than that."

"Oh, I'm not finished, Sebastian," he sneered. "Not by a long shot."

"Then let's say I end it right here," Sebastian suggested.

"Oh, you don't have the guts." Kevin smiled as Sebastian narrowed his eyes on him. "But I do. . . ."

Sebastian expected it. He'd been waiting for it. He just hadn't expected the direction it would come from. Kevin was cunning; there had never been a doubt about that. That was why Sebastian was prepared to fire the moment the other man moved. What Sebastian didn't expect was the sheer tenacity that kept the other man in place after taking a fatal shot to his chest.

Even though Sebastian jumped as the other weapon fired, suspecting Kevin could manage to buy that single second to pull the trigger on the weapon that dropped from the sleeve of his jacket, he didn't expect the other man's aim to be quite so good.

The bullet ripped into Sebastian's chest, the impact throwing Sebastian back against the wall as agony tore through his senses.

Fuck. Alyssa was going to be upset.

As his legs slowly lost strength he felt himself slide down the wall until he was sitting on his ass, staring over at Kevin's fallen body rather ironically.

Didn't it just fucking figure?

As he sat there, feeling the blood oozing from the wound, the sound of the kitchen door slamming open was followed by the blinding overhead lights searing his eyeballs.

"Sebastian!" Summer's voice was too loud. She had to pipe it down just a little.

"Shush," he groaned. "Alyssa will hear—"

"Falcone, 'Bastian's down. He's down. We're in the kitchen. Call nine-one-one now."

Okay, she piped it down. She actually sounded rather calm, for Summer, as she knelt beside him and slowly eased him to the floor.

He forced his eyes open in time to see her strip her T-shirt off, then had to grin at the sight of the snug Lycra T-shirt she wore beneath it.

Balling the material up, she pressed it to the wound, attempting to slow the bleeding. She wasn't going to help it much. He'd felt that bullet go in and he knew the damage it had caused.

That hole was a bitch.

"Summer." He caught her wrist as he stared up at her imperatively. "Help Shane. . . . Alyssa will be upset—"

"You stupid fucker. I hate your sorry ass!" Summer snapped, ice filling her voice as her violet eyes burned with fury. "It won't matter who helps Shane. She loses either of you and she won't make it. Don't you dare—"

" 'Bastian!" Alyssa's scream of rage, of pain, had his eyes closing briefly. "Oh God. 'Bastian. What did you do? What did you do?"

He opened his eyes just in time to see her execute a perfect slide that would have done any base-stealing ballplayer proud.

"No. Oh God, what have you done?"

"Look at her," he marveled, staring up at her. "So fucking pretty, grown men weep of love for her."

She was the prettiest thing he'd ever seen in his life.

"What did you do?" She touched his face, her cool palms against his cheeks so soft. "What did you do, 'Bastian?"

"Made sure you were safe." He couldn't take his eyes off her. "I think I miscalculated his speed, though." He frowned a bit at the thought.

This was bad and he knew it. He could feel it. If he lost it all in this moment then he wanted her to be the last thing he saw when he took his final breath.

"How could you do this?" She stared down at him, her gaze filled with shock and denial. "How could you do this to me? How will I ever be safe without both of you? Haven't I suffered enough?

Lost enough?" Pure rage filled her voice as he stared up at her, feeling just a bit of trepidation. "Don't you dare die on me!"

Damn, she was madder than he expected.

"Umm, 'Lyssa." Damn, his fucking chest hurt. Bad. And she wasn't showing the love like she should be, he decided.

"If you die"—her eyes narrowed, thunderclouds gathering in them—"then I choose Shane's third myself."

He could still be shocked, even with death knocking at his door, Sebastian found.

"Huh?"

"You heard me. I will choose our third myself. Not Shane. And I promise you, I'll do it before I put your ass six feet under."

"I want first option, sugah," Summer spoke up, causing Sebastian to glare at her furiously. "We'd make a helluva threesome, ya know."

"Shall I call second option?" Falcone drawled. "I state club rules, Shane, just to make it official."

Like hell.

Shane would never allow it.

Still, Sebastian's gaze sliced to his cousin, the bastard. He merely shrugged rather fatalistically.

"Club rules." He grimaced. "Who can argue with them? Besides, she'll be grieving. You know I can't bear to see her cry."

By God, he could.

Never would Sebastian even consider sharing Alyssa with anyone but his cousin and yet Shane would consider such a thing?

He was lying there dying and they were already vying for his place in her bed, pushing him into the grave and he had yet to take his last breath?

"I'm finished grieving, Sebastian!" she snapped as his gaze slid back to her. "I'm finished waiting for the two of you. If you can't love me enough to live then why shouldn't I give someone else the love I've saved for you?"

"Uh-oh, she said the *l* word," Summer drawled. "We're all in trouble now."

"Don't you dare die on me, Sebastian De Loren." Her eyes were so bright.

God no, were those tears?

"Leave me and I'll let Falcone and Summer take turns as Shane's third. So help me I will."

Sirens were blaring, lights striking Sebastian's vision, and a cacophony of voices assaulting his ears. Female cries, male demands. The hell if he knew what was going on. What he did know was that if there was a drop of blood left in his body for him to hold on to, then he'd live. He'd be damned if Falcone or that Georgia-talking southern belle was taking his place in Alyssa's bed.

Not if he had anything to do with it.

## 26

It was the second most horrifying event of Alyssa's life. The sight of Sebastian sprawled on the kitchen floor as Summer tried to keep the blood from flowing from his chest completely terrified her.

God, how she loved him. Him and Shane both. Why had she tried to deny it? Why had she tried to hold back something that was already so much a part of her? What had she thought she was protecting? Her heart? Her soul? They already belonged to these men. So much so that she had shut down every part of her that belonged to them to ensure she was able to wait for them.

"'Lyssa?" Sebastian whispered her name as she hurried into the seat next to the gurney the EMTs secured in the back of the ambulance.

He wasn't going anywhere without her.

"Yes, 'Bastian." She caught his hand as he lifted it to her weakly.

"I love you, baby." He stared up at her, the blue of his eyes barely discernible they were so black. "I always loved you."

"I know that," she told him, trying to smile. "I always knew that, 'Bastian. If I hadn't known, I wouldn't have been here, waiting for you."

His gaze was almost feverish, pain and the loss of blood finally affecting his incredible strength.

"I was there when you left," he told her then. "I watched you board the plane. The way you kept looking back, the hope and pain on your face, destroying me. I stayed drunk for weeks. Shane and I both did. We couldn't have let you go, couldn't have protected you, otherwise."

She leaned closer to him, determined to keep the EMTs from hearing her, just as determined to tell him what she remembered.

"After I lost the baby, I dreamed of you and Shane," she told him softly. "It was very dark, but I could hear you. Both of you. You were talking to each other. Assuring yourselves that I would wait for you. That I loved you enough to know you would never willingly let me go. Just as you felt me in your heart, I would feel you in mine."

Surprise widened his eyes, tightened his fingers around hers.

"The loss of our baby would have been too much for me if I hadn't made myself believe that dream was a bond to you and Shane."

"You'd been gone for over two months," he said faintly. "The nightmare . . ." He swallowed tightly. "Both of us heard you crying. Screaming for us."

Tears fell from her eyes now. "Don't make me live without you. Please, 'Bastian. Don't make me do that."

"Hold on to me," he sighed, his voice so weak, faint. "Don't let me go, 'Lyssa."

"Never, my 'Bastian," she swore. "I'll never let you go."

+ + + +

She wasn't a crier. Alyssa often thought it was the only trait she shared with her mother. Margot, to her knowledge, had only cried once in Alyssa's life. The night she'd sat beside Alyssa's bed just after Harvey's attempt to kill her.

*"I didn't protect you as I should have,"* Margot whispered as Alyssa fought to keep her eyes open. *"Now, I'll protect you the only way I know how."*

*"He knows," Alyssa whispered, so weak. She had never been so weak.*

*"What does he know?" her mother questioned then. "What, Alyssa?"*

*"Spain . . . he knows."*

*"Don't worry, darling." A tear slipped from Margot's eye as she touched Alyssa's cheek gently. "He'll not tell a soul. I'll make sure of it."*

Her mother had given her life to protect Alyssa, and now, Sebastian may well do the same.

As the ambulance raced into the emergency entrance, Sebastian's eyes drifted closed, but his grip on her hand remained until the EMTs rushed him from the emergency vehicle.

Following, she found Shane waiting as she went to step from the ambulance, his hands gripping her hips and lifting her out, placing her gently on her feet before they rushed into the emergency entrance behind the EMTs.

Alyssa was only barely aware of the crowd that followed them. And it wasn't a small crowd.

"Shane, your grandfather's en route." The Texas drawl in the male voice barely registered with Alyssa as she watched Sebastian disappear through a restricted-access entrance. "Father's already been in contact with the hospital administrator and Mother's prepping to assist the surgeon. He'll pull through this, Shane."

"Of course he will." Shane's arm tightened around her, though, holding her to his chest. "He's too damned stubborn not to."

It was then Alyssa lifted her gaze to stare at the man beside him. Several years older, he could have actually been Sebastian's twin, they looked so much alike. She would have suspected he was the mysterious Lucien if it hadn't been for the Texas accent.

"Alyssa, this is my brother, Murphy Connor," Shane introduced them. "Behind him, my father, Gavin, and my sister, Lark. Our mother, Francesca, is with Sebastian in surgery."

"Francesca." Alyssa nodded. "I met her a few years ago. Hello, Gavin." She smiled back at the black-haired giant she'd met just after her marriage along with Shane's mother. "It's good to see you again."

"You as well, my dear," Gavin assured her, that Texas drawl so similar to Shane's. "Take her to meet Sebastian's parents, Shane—"

"We've met, about five years ago." Alyssa eased from Shane's hold as Sebastian's parents moved closer. "Tabitha. Alberto."

"My dear." Tabitha had been crying. Her eyes were red, her cheeks wet, as she embraced Alyssa gently. "You are as pretty as always. Sebastian chose well, did he not, Alberto?" Stepping back, she made room for Alberto, who embraced Alyssa with gentle warmth.

"He chose very well." Alberto smiled before glancing to Shane. "As did you, Nephew."

"They chose very well," Shane's father agreed from his side.

"Alyssa." A familiar voice drew her gaze as another of Sebastian's family members stepped to the group.

"Lucien." Surprise filled her voice as the tall, black-haired older version of Shane strode toward her. "I wondered if you were here as well."

Wrapping his arms around her in a firm embrace, Lucien De Loren patted her shoulder gently before easing back. "Ah, as always, my dear, you are a gentle light within the darkness," he complimented her.

"And you're still a poet in denial," she responded, her voice husky as she stared at Shane's and Sebastian's families fondly. "It's good to see you again." Her lips trembled. "I only wish—"

"As do we, darling," Tabitha assured her as Alyssa drew in a deep breath as emotion threatened to swamp her. "I know my 'Bastian, though. He'll be grumbling like the horrible patient he is and informing us all it is time for him to go home before we know it. He's strong, that son of mine."

Alyssa looked around curiously. "Is Sebastian's grandfather here?"

"He'll be here soon," Alberto sighed. "Knowing Sebastian has been wounded, we cannot keep him away. Be warned, though, he is difficult."

Alberto sighed. "The jet returned to Barcelona to pick him and 'Bastian's sister, Angel up. They will be here sometime tomorrow, the pilot assured us. He'll drive us all crazy. Sebastian especially."

Alyssa nodded, glancing toward the doors Sebastian had disappeared through as she heard her father and Landra greet the family members.

Shane's mother, a premier trauma surgeon, was with Sebastian, Alyssa reminded herself. She didn't know why the family had shown up, but she was thankful they had.

She'd met them all at one time or another. None of them had mentioned knowing about her, but she'd sensed they had. Their quiet warmth, the familiarity in their gazes, had been unmistakable.

She glanced toward the doors again. What she wouldn't give to be able to turn back time to keep this from happening.

"This wasn't your fault, Alyssa." Her father moved to her then, reaching out to touch the side of her head in a soft caress. "You couldn't have stopped it."

"I can't bear this." She shook her head, the guilt tearing at her. "I can't bear for him to be gone because of me."

"Alyssa, this is not your fault," he repeated firmly. "Stop taking the guilt of every action on your own shoulders."

Alyssa shook her head, feeling Shane's arm tighten around her, his warmth sinking inside her.

She'd already lost so much, had to wait so long. She was tired of waiting, tired of holding herself back to ensure the men she loved had the time they needed to return to her. She'd followed her heart, followed a dream, and she'd waited.

"I'm okay, Dad," she said, swallowing tightly, feeling as though she were smothering amid so many concerned family members.

"Shane, Alyssa looks about ready to fall down. Let's find a seat, get some coffee." Gavin grimaced wryly. "Perhaps not good coffee, but coffee all the same."

Someone had taken the time to ensure it was good coffee. Several fresh pots along with sugar and a variety of creamers had been placed in the private waiting room they were shown to by a young nurse.

The coffee was kept fresh, sandwiches and snacks brought, but there was no word from surgery. An hour passed, then four. And Alyssa knew it was taking too long. There was no news, not even a hint of how Sebastian was doing.

She couldn't stand the wait. She could feel her stomach clenching, nerves crashing through her system until she felt as though she were shaking apart from the inside out. It wasn't tears threatening to spill, but every drop of coffee she'd consumed while waiting.

Rising to her feet, Alyssa moved to the bank of windows that looked out to the parking lot. There Falcone, Raeg, and Summer were talking. Summer, with her usual flare for drama, was using her hands to emphasize a point. She probably drove Falcone crazy on a daily basis, and poor Raeg, she gave him hell every time they were in the same room.

There was definitely a lot of history between the southern belle and her father's chief of staff. One of these days she was going to have to ask Summer about it.

Turning away from the windows, her head lowered, Alyssa wrapped her arms over her breasts, frowning as distant memories teased her mind but refused to come into focus. Summer beside her bed. Summer was crying, but Alyssa was as well. Not the quiet, gut-wrenching sobs coming from her friend, but silent, miserable tears. Why was she crying with Summer? She couldn't remember a time she'd ever done so.

There was her father; he wasn't crying, but he was telling her something she couldn't quite understand. Distant memories of Margot sitting next to her, and those really confused her, continued to tease at her mind until she thought she'd go insane.

There were simply too many people around her. She couldn't seem to think for the quiet background conversations and the anticipation each time a nurse was glimpsed moving up the hall.

Glancing around, Alyssa found Shane with Lucien and Murphy, deep in conversation. Lark sat alone close to the entrance to the room texting on her phone. Moving to her, she asked the younger girl to let Shane know she was heading to the chapel. She needed to think, to recover the memories she'd pushed back as she'd pushed her emotions back.

At Lark's silent nod Alyssa left the waiting room and moved down the hall, pushing the door open to the Chapel. Candles lit the interior, the quiet, solitary atmosphere more peaceful than she'd expected.

Moving into one of the pews, Alyssa let that peacefulness wrap around her, over her. Wiping a hand over her face and breathing in deeply at the ache tightening her chest and the constriction at her throat.

Tears were for grieving, she reminded herself, and there was so much she'd never allowed herself to grieve over.

*"Now, I need you to make me a promise." Margot leaned close, the tears on her face dried now, though her eyes still glistened with moisture. "Promise me you won't cry over me, Alyssa. Remember, tears are for grieving only. There's no reason you should ever grieve for me. I don't deserve your tears."*

*"I always loved you," Alyssa had to force herself to speak, it was so hard. The fever clouded her mind so much, made everything seem like a dream. "You were always my momma, Margot. No matter your faults."*

*Margot seemed to freeze for a moment before she lowered her head slowly and wiped at her eyes.*

*"I don't deserve it," she finally muttered.*

"You made me strong," Alyssa sighed. "Taught me how to be patient. I've had to be patient. . . ." She had to wait for Shane and Sebastian, as much as she'd hated it.

Margot's head lifted as she leaned forward slowly and kissed Alyssa's brow. "I have always loved you, squirt," she whispered. "You were so tiny, so fragile, I never knew what to do with you. But I have always loved you."

Margot didn't look at her again. Straightening, she left the bedroom as Alyssa tried to call her back, tried to make her return so she could explain why there would be a reason to grieve.

"Don't go . . . ," she whispered as the fever dragged her under once again. "Don't go. . . ."

✦✦✦

"Come on, Alyssa, don't go like this." Gia stood at the door as the driver carried Alyssa's luggage to the car.

The other girl, suntanned and dressed in cutoffs and a bikini top, leaned against the door frame, arms folded, a frown on her face. "At least tell me what's wrong."

"Nothing's wrong, Gia." Alyssa looked around, making certain she hadn't forgotten anything.

Then again, the apartment had been mostly cleaned out sometime yesterday while she slept, waiting for Shane and Sebastian. Everything was gone, even the little white test stick she'd left in the bathroom for them. Even the pictures of them were gone. Every last one. There wasn't even a memory for her to take with her.

"Something's wrong. First those hunks that sneak in here completely disappear; now you're leaving and you weren't even going to tell me good-bye. That's not like you."

"I would have stopped by your apartment," Alyssa lied, wondering when Shane and Sebastian would finally stop her, keep her from leaving. They weren't going to let her leave. She knew they wouldn't.

"Yeah, I hear you." Gia was still frowning at her as Alyssa moved to the doorway.

"It's been a great summer, Gia," she said softly, painfully. "I'll see you back in D.C."

Stepping past her, Alyssa had almost turned down the hall when Gia's door opened. She barely glimpsed the young man who stepped into the hall. She'd paid him such little attention. And she hadn't wanted to remember leaving the apartment she'd shared with Shane and Sebastian.

But she remembered him now.

Gia's apartment. He'd come from Gia's apartment. Steven Richards had been there. She'd seen him only a few times, though, perhaps twice the whole summer. She'd never seen him while Shane and Sebastian had been at the apartment, though.

Gia would have known he was at the estate. She would have known he was there because he was her brother.

"Brothers." Gia grimaced as she and Alyssa walked from the beach toward the brooding young man standing next to Gia's scooter, his back to them. "They're a curse."

Alyssa had laughed and turned for the beachside apartment building while Gia had strode across the sand to her brother.

Her eyes jerked open as she flinched at the realization and the memories as they slowly emerged. She had to find Shane.

"Going somewhere?" Gia asked as Alyssa moved to rise from the bench and rush back to the waiting room.

Alyssa jerked around instead, staring into Gia's somber face and glimpsing the handgun she held, pointing at Alyssa.

"Gia . . ."

"I knew you'd remember who Kevin was eventually," she sighed, her smile a little shaky. "He was my older brother, ya know? Illegitimate little bastard, my father used to call him. But I loved him." Her voice trembled as she spoke quietly. "And Sebastian killed him."

"He intended to kill me, Gia. He wouldn't have stopped. You know that." Alyssa glanced to the weapon before looking up at Gia then, her gaze holding the other woman's. "He wouldn't have stopped."

"But he would have." Certainty marked Gia's expression. "I would have gotten him to listen to reason, Alyssa. He loved me. He would have listened if I'd had just a little more time."

"You know better than that, Gia." Alyssa could feel her nerves stretching to the limit as she watched Gia's gaze begin to glitter with anger.

"If they hadn't killed Gregory. Or if they had just let the money go," Gia ground out furiously. "He would have let it go, Alyssa. It was Harvey's idea, but Kevin did all the work. The cameras, the overseas accounts, everything. Harvey just married you and lived off his daddy's money. Kevin didn't have that option."

"He would have killed me, Gia. That was what he intended to do tonight." Alyssa had a feeling there was very little that would sway Gia Bennett from whatever course she'd set for herself. Alyssa just had a very bad feeling that course was not in her own best interests.

"I would have made him listen." Sorrow filled Gia's voice, her gaze. "He used to be so kind and caring." Her eyes filled with tears. "Until he met Harvey. That was why our father sent him to Spain that summer. To separate them. Harvey made him . . ." Gia frowned. "He made him mean, Alyssa."

"Gia, he tried to kill me. Not just once, but twice." If the other girl couldn't see him for what he was, then there was little hope for her. "Sebastian is now fighting for his life, because of your brother. Do you expect me to feel sorry for him?"

Gia simply stared at her with tear-filled eyes and a miserable expression.

Unfortunately, Alyssa didn't know her nearly as well as she knew Summer. She had no idea how to handle Gia while she had a weapon trained on her. Hell, she wouldn't have any idea how to handle Summer if she had a weapon trained on her, either.

"Gia, you need to talk to Falcone," she finally told the other woman softly. "He'll tell you what needs to be done."

A short, bitter laugh left Gia's lips. "You think Falcone is such a nice guy, do you, Alyssa?"

"I think he cares for you and Summer," she answered quietly, trying to remain calm. "And I don't think he'd turn his back on you."

Gia turned her gaze just enough that she wasn't staring into Alyssa's eyes but kept her in her periphery. The thoughtful expression on her face would have given Alyssa hope if it weren't for the anger that flashed in the other woman's gaze.

"He would easily walk away from me because of this," Gia murmured, still looking away from her.

"What do you intend to do, Gia, that would cause Falcone to turn away from you?" Alyssa asked her carefully.

Gia's gaze moved back to hers, her eyes flat and hard.

"We need to leave here." Gia wasn't even breathing hard. She was calm, cool. "I don't want to spill blood in God's house, Alyssa. That would only compound my sin."

Alyssa was anything but cool and she knew it. She wasn't scared; she was pissed.

"Do you think I'm just going to walk out of here with you and let you kill me for your brother, Gia?" Incredulity raced through her. "Do I actually give the impression of stupidity?"

A grin quirked at Gia's lips. "You managed to snag both Shane Connor and Sebastian De Loren and hold them for eight years that the three of you were apart. I think you're anything but stupid. But you aren't always wise, are you, Alyssa?"

"What about you, Gia? You think this is wise?" Her brow arched curiously. "Walk away now. You've broken no laws; you've done nothing that Falcone even needs to know about. It doesn't have to end badly."

"You talk as though you have the upper hand," Gia murmured, giving the gun a little wave. "I don't believe that's the case."

"I believe it is." Allowing a smug, confident expression to fill her face, Alyssa glanced over Gia's shoulder.

Gia stilled completely, her eyes narrowing on Alyssa.

"Just lay the gun down," Alyssa suggested softly. "It can be over just that easy."

"I'm not stupid, either." Gia smiled slowly.

"There the two of you are." Summer headed toward them, frustration filling her expression. "Gia, Falcone needs you."

Alyssa watched Gia's eyes. Resignation filled her gaze, somber grief and acceptance.

"Don't do it," Alyssa whispered. "Don't do it, Gia."

"I hate that bitch!" Gia turned, swinging the gun around.

"No!" Alyssa yelled as she moved, pulling her feet to the bench and launching herself over the back of it at the other woman.

Alyssa caught Gia in midturn, but the force of her collision against the other woman's shoulder sent the bench tilting back, rocking, then finally crashing to the one behind them.

Instinct had her reaching for the gun, grabbing Gia's wrists, and trying to use the force to knock the gun from her hands.

She could hear Summer, but she was damned if she could make out a word of it.

"You bitch!" Gia cursed, and with a hard buck of her upper body nearly managed to pitch Alyssa off her.

Being short sucked.

Gia was taller, stronger, her bones a bit larger. She was built like Margot, while Alyssa knew her shorter, more delicate build was nothing to brag about in a fight.

Even her martial arts instructor had shaken his head at her more than once.

But she'd learned.

Swinging her elbow around, she caught Gia in the side of the head as her nails dug into the other woman's wrist.

"Bitch!" Gia grunted again, managing to put her elbow in Alyssa's side before Alyssa threw her head forward, slamming it into the other woman's and hearing a satisfied cry of surprise and pain.

Alyssa quickly followed it up with her knee to Gia's abdomen as they rolled again. Her hands nearly slipped from the wrists she was fighting to keep down, and the gun out of her direction.

Dammit. What made her think she could take on an Amazon anyway? This was ridiculous.

"I'll kill you," Gia grunted again as Alyssa managed to slam her knee into the other woman's ribs. "You bitch!"

Hell, Gia needed to learn a few more insults. That one was getting old.

As they rolled again Gia managed a surprisingly hard blow to Alyssa's face, bringing a grunt and silent curse at the thought of the bruise she would have for it.

As hard as she tried, as much effort as she put into it, size did matter, and Gia had quite a bit on her. Not to mention Gia's advanced training. Before she could outmaneuver her, Gia had her on her back, lifting her arms, tearing her wrists, and the gun, from Alyssa's hold.

"Dead." Gia's face contorted with rage as she tore her wrists from Alyssa's hold. At the same time, her weight was lifted, shock on her face as the gun was torn from her grip and Shane tossed her to the floor like a sack of potatoes. Falcone held the gun, staring at it a second before his gaze moved to Gia where she lay on the carpet, staring up at the ceiling as she fought to catch her breath.

Reaching down, Shane quickly pulled Alyssa to her feet, his expression savage, his eyes so blue they were scary.

"'Bastian?" she whispered, fear seizing her, nearly stealing her breath.

"He's in recovery," he growled, his gaze on Gia as she continued to lie on the floor. "He's going to make it."

Bending, bracing her hands on her knees, Alyssa drew in a hard breath, fighting the weakness threatening to overcome her.

"What's going on, Gia?" Falcone asked her, his tone like chipped ice, sharp, incredibly cold.

Gia turned her face to the side, staring away from them.

"I trusted you." Falcone's voice was low, and as cold as it was, the betrayal in his gaze was just as hot. "You could have come to me, Gia."

Gia shook her head.

"Why didn't you come to me?" his voice rose, cracking like a whip in the stillness in the room.

"Why would I?" she sneered, her gaze moving to Summer, hatred spilling from it, spitting back at the other woman. "You keep your nose so far up that little cunt's ass you don't know if you're coming or going."

Alyssa watched Summer, saw the backward step she made, the shock on her face as she stared at the woman she had believed was her friend.

"Summer?" Falcone snapped. "What does she have to do with this?"

"Everything and nothing." Gia laughed even as tears ran from the corners of her eyes. "She's one of those little bitches you love yet you hate. Like a two-year-old without the ability to grow up? So everyone fawns over her. How pretty she is. How sweet she is. And that stupid accent of hers. She sounds like she has a mouth full of fucking chewing tobacco all the time!" she screamed the last words.

"This has nothing to do with Summer!" Falcone yelled back at her.

"She's why I couldn't come to you." Gia came to her feet in a surge of fury and honed instincts.

And in her hand she carried a smaller, though just as deadly, weapon she'd pulled from her ankle.

Falcone simply stared at it as Gia pointed it at his chest.

"Kevin Barkley is your brother, and you again helped him attempt to kill Alyssa," Falcone stated softly. "I received the proof of your relationship not twenty minutes ago. You've had plenty of time to come to me rather than turning this on Alyssa or Summer. You want to blame others for your own mistakes," he stated icily. "All you had to do was come to me."

"And betray my brother," she sneered. "The funny part is, I would have," she whispered. "I was going to. When I heard you tell her to shadow me. To watch me, Falcone? You didn't trust me, but you trusted her?"

"I was worried," he breathed out, incredulous disbelief filling the sound. "I was worried about you. She was to watch after you, not watch you," he explained, disgust filling his expression. "Such guilt, Gia. You carry such guilt you must suspect everything and everyone. I should have known months ago what you were doing. I should have known when Summer nearly died in Russia."

Gia slid a slow, mocking look to where Summer stood still and silent. "Yes, you should have," she said softly. "I would have let her die." She gave Alyssa a look filled with malicious cruelty. "Like I let Kevin poison that fucking brat of yours. I knew what he was doing and I didn't stop him. I didn't even try because I knew if you had that kid there would have been no keeping Sebastian and Shane away from you. And Harvey would have gone ballistic. Kevin wouldn't have survived that."

Alyssa lost the strength in her legs, agony piercing her with such force she nearly cried out.

Her gaze moved back to Falcone. "Good-bye, Falcone. It's been fun."

There was no stopping her. The gun came up so quickly, her finger tightening on the trigger. The shot that exploded through the Chapel threw Gia back, shock widening her eyes as her gaze locked to Summer.

Summer was crying. She still held her weapon in her hand, but tears ran down her cheeks as she slowly lowered her arm and dropped the gun to the floor.

"Like I didn't know how you hated me anyway," she said softly, but the sound of her voice was that of betrayal. "But that's for killing that sweet little baby. For breaking all our hearts, Gia."

"Get them out of here, Shane, now," Falcone ordered him. "I'll handle this."

"Falcone—"

"Go!" he snapped. "Get them out of here. Security will be here in seconds."

Grabbing Alyssa's arm and striding to Summer, Shane gripped hers as Falcone scooped her weapon from the floor. Shane was rushing them through a side door as security rushed into the Chapel entrance.

It was over, but the pain and betrayal left behind wouldn't be easily forgotten, Alyssa knew. It would be impossible to forget. Especially for Summer and Falcone.

## 27

Alyssa approached Sebastian's bed slowly, quietly.

His thick, dark blond hair was disheveled, mussed around his pale face. His chest and shoulders were bare but for the large white bandage over the right side where the bullet had gone in.

"He's going to be okay?" She looked at where Francesca Connor stood at the bottom of his bed, checking his file.

Deep black hair shot with just a bit of silver was gathered in a low ponytail and trailed to between her shoulders. She was tall, five seven at least, and slender. The trauma surgeon didn't look like a surgeon. She looked like a model.

"He's going to be fine," Francesca promised gently. "If he rests, doesn't overdo things." She shrugged. "Sebastian isn't a good patient, though."

"Well, he is now." Turning a fierce gaze on him as she moved to his bedside Alyssa decided then and there he would definitely make certain he took care of himself.

He opened one eye. "I hear you've been in trouble." His voice was scratchy, weaker than she was used to you. "Mom told me all about it."

She breathed out wearily. "I think we need a vacation when you get out of here, 'Bastian. Sun. Sand."

"Barcelona," he and Shane both said softly.

"Barcelona," she agreed, smiling, feeling that anticipation, the warmth and freedom she hadn't known in eight years. Then she narrowed her eyes on him. "When you've healed. Completely."

"Days," he assured her.

"Six weeks," his aunt injected, her voice firm. "No less. More if he doesn't behave himself and rest."

"He'll behave himself." Touching his arm to feel his warmth, to know he was still there with her, Alyssa let her hand move to his, felt his fingers link with hers, and felt the prickle of tears as emotion swamped her, love filling her until she had no idea what to do with the overload.

"I love you," she whispered, glancing at where Shane stood beside her then. "I love both of you."

"Hey, you know how to use the *l* word," Sebastian joked weakly. "Knew you had it in you."

But his eyes were drifting closed, weakness overtaking him as he slipped back into sleep.

Leaning to him, Alyssa let her lips touch his and felt the faintest response.

"Love you, 'Lyssa," he sighed. "Love you."

He was going to be okay.

Beside her, Shane slipped his arm around her waist, holding her close as both of them watched over Sebastian.

They were hers. Her Goof and her Cowboy. They were hers now.

"I love you both," she whispered. "So much."

"Forever," Shane vowed. "We'll love you forever, Alyssa."

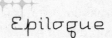

# Epilogue

**FOUR MONTHS LATER**
**BARCELONA, SPAIN**
**DE LOREN HACIENDA**

Shane and Sebastian stepped warily into their grandfather's office, remembering well the last time they were called in for a meeting in such a way.

They paused just inside the door, allowing it to close softly as they faced Fernando and Sebastian's parents, as well as Lucien. Standing off to the side like a recalcitrant teenager, arms crossed over her checkered blouse she wore with jeans and boots, Alyssa shot them a look of silent amusement.

Sebastian restrained the groan that threatened to break free. This was becoming a weekly thing. Fernando demanding their presence to demand they do they something about yet another of their wife's shenanigan's as Fernando called them.

Sebastian rubbed at the back of his neck, aware of Shane breathing out a hard breath. They stepped forward together, uncertain of what she could have done. For the first time in the weeks they had been at the hacienda, their grandfather's expression was bland rather than a mix of amusement and bemusement. He rarely knew what to do with her, or what to say to her.

"What did you do this time?" he muttered as he neared his wife.

She gave a little roll of her eyes. "He's blowing it completely out of proportion you know."

Hell.

Fernando's expression lapsed into one of complete amazement. He looked from Alyssa then back to them then to Lucien.

Narrowing his eyes on his brother, Sebastian watched as Lucien lowered his head, pinching at the bridge of his nose and giving it a little shake.

"I promised them I wouldn't do it again, for a while," she muttered, crossing her arms over her breasts. "They wouldn't even listen to me. Just called you like Summer's parents used to call Momma." Exasperation filled her voice. "Completely uncalled for if you want my opinion."

"Sebastian. Shane." Fernando stared back at them broodingly as someone smothered a chuckle, probably his father, Sebastian thought. He was completely smitten by his daughter-in-law. As far as he and Tabitha were concerned, Alyssa could do no wrong.

"Yes Grandfather?" Shane asked broodingly. "What did she do this time?"

"This is really unnecessary, Grandfather." She turned to the old man with a winsome smile, her expression filled with such sincerity. "I did promise after all."

The old man stared back at her, his expression softening as he stared at that smile. Sebastian couldn't blame him. That same smile had the power to blow their minds as well.

"Grandfather." It rarely worked on Lucien though. He adored his 'little sister', as he called her, but that smile rarely affected him.

Alyssa glared at him. "Tattletale," she muttered.

"I was viewing security tapes from several weeks ago, Sebastian," Lucien informed him then. "I was given quite a show."

"Look." Alyssa stepped forward, her hands on her hips, her expression less than pleased. "I said it won't happen again."

"I will make certain of that," Lucien drawled.

"It can't happen again," she bit out.

"Alyssa," Lucien growled. "Your safety."

"I just learned I'm pregnant, Lucien. I would never risk my baby."

The room went silent.

"That was a month ago," she informed him archly. "I always make certain I'm not pregnant before doing something . . ." she smiled, pausing. ". . . the males of this family would disapprove of."

Still, no one spoke.

Fernando sat down slowly, still staring at her in shock, while Sebastian felt a surge of such emotion explode inside him that it nearly brought him to his knees.

"A great-grandchild," Fernando said softly. "I have a chance to see my first great-grandchild."

"Good God, he'd let her hang glide if she wanted to," Lucien growled. "Father. Mother. Stop staring at her like that."

"But Lucien, a grandchild," her mother exclaimed with a little hitch of her breath. "My first grandchild."

Alyssa was staring at him and Shane worriedly.

"I wasn't pregnant then," she assured them. "It was just a little ride."

"On Diablo," Lucien snapped.

"And he loved me." Excitement filled her voice. "He was a sweet-heart, I swear he was. And he runs like the wind, Sebastian."

He blinked at her.

Diablo was huge, midnight black, and completely unridable. Or so Lucien bitched often.

"That fucking horse is in love with her," Lucien growled. "And that's besides the point."

She was pregnant.

Nothing else mattered.

Because as she said, she would never risk their child. For the next nine months or so, they would have a wife that walked as though on eggshells.

And they would have a child.

She flashed them a smile of such joy that Sebastian felt his heart melt all over again. She was his beloved, she was their beloved.

He took a step toward her.

"You're certain?" he whispered.

"Have you been home yet?" The little seaside home his grandfather had given them.

Sebastian shook his head.

That smile that tilted his lips . . . If she hadn't held his heart before, she held it now.

"Test strip is in the bathroom."

Before he could move, Shane did. He swept her up in his arms as she gave a joyous little laugh.

"Coming?" she asked as Shane walked past him, heading for the door.

"She has you two wrapped around her little finger tighter than a Christmas puppy," Lucien informed him broodingly.

"Fall in love, brother," Sebastian suggested softly. "And then tell me that."

Turning, he followed his cousin and their wife. And the child they had created together.

It would never matter which of them fathered the babe, he or she would always belong to both of them.

Just as the mother belonged to both of them.


## WASHINGTON D.C.

*We're pregnant!*

*OMG. I'm god-mommy!*

*Of course you are. Come see me Summer. I miss you.*

*Very soon sugar. I promise* ☺

*Better be soon. Love ya*

*Love ya :P*

A tear dropped on the phone's screen before Summer tossed it to the mattress and returned to staring at the wall, slowly dampening the pillow beneath her cheek with her tears.

It was so much easier to fool Alyssa by text than it was by voice. Thank God her friend hadn't actually called. Had she done so then Summer would have never hid the tears, the pain she couldn't stop.

*"You look like a fucking Barbie doll, bitch," Gia muttered as Summer arrived at Falcone's home for a pre-assignment briefing.*

*"Why sugah, that was the point behind it all," Summer laughed, believing the other woman was teasing.*

*The pretty sundress bared her shoulders and the upper mounds of her tanned breasts. It hugged her body like a lover from breast to scant inches below indecent along her thighs. She looked good. She knew she did.*

*Left loose but for the small amount pinned back from her face, her hair hung down her back in rich, black curls, falling to her waist with a healthy, silken sheen.*

*"Take the tobacco out of your mouth," Gia sounded irritated, but she would always flash Summer a smile to show she was teasing. That was her way. Or so Summer thought.*

*Her brothers hadn't liked Gia. Especially her older brother, Caleb. She and Caleb had gotten into a horrible fight when he called Gia a trashy little tramp.*

*Margot never said anything nasty about Gia, but she rarely gave any notice to Gia when she was around either.*

*"You should cut that stringy hair," Gia snarled as she watched Falcone help Summer braid the long strands. "It's a fuckinig hazard . . ."*

*"I would spank you, little one," Falcone laughed, tying off the braid. "Your hair is lovely."*

*"I would have let her die . . ." Hatred filled Gia's voice.*

*"She always sounds like her mouth is filled with chewing tobacco . . ."*

How stupid she had been. So stupid. She should have known how Gia was lying to them all these years. It was her fault Alyssa had lost her lovers, her fault that sweet little baby had died. Oh God, how had Alyssa ever forgiven her?

Perhaps she hadn't really forgiven her. Alyssa was so sweet she would never deliberately hurt anyone. Especially someone with the history they shared.

They had saved each other so many times. Now, there was no one there to save Summer, though. No one to take away the agony resonating inside her. And it hurt. Oh God, it hurt so bad she couldn't stand it.

The tears fell harder again, and though she didn't sob, still, the ones she tried to contain had her breathing with harsh, ragged sounds. It was just hard enough, just enough to cover the sound of the intruder sneaking into the room.

"My God! What have you done to yourself?" Falcone's enraged exclamation had her coming up in the bed, her weapon clearing the pillows before she could halt the action.

Before she could actually aim the gun at him, she dropped it to the bed instead and just stared back at him, her shoulders jerking with a contained sob as she met his gaze.

She knew what he saw.

Tears poured from her eyes as she looked around at the long strands of her hair thrown haphazardly on the comforter. The scissors lay somewhere on the floor where she'd thrown them.

"Summer. All your beautiful hair," he whispered, sounding grief-stricken. "Baby, what have you done to yourself?"

The long midnight black curls were gone. Her hair was a slick, black cap that ended at her nape in a shaggy cut that testified to the haphazard snips she'd made with the scissors.

"Leave, Falcone." There wasn't a hint of the accent everyone found so distasteful.

She'd taken voice classes at Margot's insistence. She'd learned how to not sound as though her mouth was full of chewing tobacco. But Margot had heard it the first time and declared she wasn't Summer without her unique drawl. But only Margot had liked it.

Rising from the bed and quickly drying her tears she turned back, hating that look of icy emotionlessness on his face. She'd always hated it. She would flirt, joke, become completely outrageous until it cracked.

His pale blue eyes moved over her nearly naked body, taking in the black boy shorts and black sports bra she wore. The only tattoo she had was thankfully covered. God wouldn't it be a mess if he saw it. He would be so regretful of course, but probably so amused.

"You have let her destroy you," he said coolly. "I did not think anyone could do that to you."

She snorted at the statement. "She didn't break me, Falcone," she assured him. "She merely drove home the fact that a few changes needed to be made, nothing more."

She hadn't broke her, but Gia had broken her heart. She'd damaged a part of her that Summer had no idea how to heal.

He didn't say anything for long moments. Those icy blue eyes kept moving over her, becoming colder by the minute.

"Get dressed and get your gear," he snapped. "We have an assignment."

"I'm not ready . . ."

"Then fucking get ready." He was in her face so fast she didn't have time to jump back. And he was furious. Madder than she'd ever seen him. "Get dressed and get your gear now! You will get ready to go out on assignment and you will get your head out of your ass immediately. Because if you don't, I will call Caleb and answer every question he's ever asked me. Do you hear me?"

Her eyes widened. "Caleb would kill you."

His smile was filled with anticipation. "Let him try. You want to risk it?"

No, she didn't. She knew her brother, and she knew Falcone. They would kill each other if Caleb ever learned some of the assignments Falcone had taken her on.

"Bastard," she hissed.

"Oh, baby, you haven't seen the bastard in me yet," he assured her. "But you're getting ready to. I promise you, you're getting ready to."